and Other Stories

Yevgeny Zamyatin

Translated by Galya and Hugh Aplin

ALMA CLASSICS

ALMA CLASSICS
an imprint of

ALMA BOOKS LTD
Thornton House
Thornton Road
Wimbledon Village
London SW19 4NG
United Kingdom
www.almaclassics.com

This collection first published by Alma Classics in 2024
For publication details of the individual stories, see the Introduction

Translation © Galya and Hugh Aplin, 2024
Introduction © Hugh Aplin, 2024

Cover design: David Wardle

Printed and bound by CPI Group (UK) Ltd, Croydon, CR0 4YY

ISBN: 978-1-84749-929-5

Contents

Introduction

Both within and beyond the borders of his native Russia, Yevgeny
Zamyatin is best known today for his brilliant novel *We* – and
rightly so. It was a different matter, however, during his lifetime:
though potentially familiar to Western readers in translation, the
novel, written in 1920–21, was not published in Russian in full
until long after Zamyatin's death in Parisian exile in 1937, and
only decades later did it appear in Russia itself. And yet he was
nonetheless a highly significant and influential figure in Russian
letters in the 1920s. In part this was due to his work as a literary
critic, theorist and teacher, activities to which he devoted himself
after the revolutions of 1917, having abandoned his earlier career
as a naval engineer. But it is also true that he had made his name
as a writer even before the outbreak of the First World War,
a period of his career represented by two of the stories in this
volume. Notable, too, is that, considering the relatively short span
of his literary career, his writing went through a quite significant
evolution – unsurprising, perhaps, for a man who wrote a good
deal on what he saw as the dangers of entropy. Irrespective of the
status of *We*, then, his oeuvre as a whole is undoubtedly worthy of
greater recognition today, not just for the context it affords readers of the novel, but also for the light it can shed more generally
on Russian literature, culture and society of its time – as well as,
most importantly, for its own intrinsic merit.

Yevgeny Ivanovich Zamyatin was born in 1884, the son of
a priest, in the small provincial town of Lebedyan, located in
Tambov Province, 300 kilometres south of Moscow. There he lived
until 1896, when he moved to the neighbouring provincial capital
of Voronezh to complete his schooling. In 1902 he travelled further
afield, both geographically and culturally, to the imperial capital,
St Petersburg, to study naval engineering at the Polytechnical

Institute. Here he soon began to engage in political activities and joined the party of the Social Democrats, which would see him begin his association – one that was to colour his life right up until his death – with the Bolsheviks. He inevitably found himself caught up in the events of the first Russian Revolution of 1905, and it was only in 1913 that a cycle of arrest, exile and illegal return to the capital was ended by the amnesty that marked the Romanov dynasty's tricentenary on the Russian throne.

By this time, he had already graduated – in 1908 – and begun working in shipbuilding and associated teaching, but had also taken up the pen in earnest. A couple of early stories made no great impact, but that was not the case at all when 'Provincial Life' came out in 1913 in the fifth issue of the Petersburg journal *Testaments* (*Zavety*). Written two years earlier in Lakhta, not far from the capital, the story's origins were, however, far away. In his article 'Backstage' (1930) Zamyatin recalls returning north by rail from a visit to Lebedyan: "At some small station not far from Moscow I woke up and raised the blind. Right in front of the window – as though inserted into a frame – the physiognomy of the station gendarme drifted slowly by: a forehead pulled down low over little bearlike eyes, terrible four-cornered jaws. I had time to read the name of the station: Barybino. There Anfim Baryba and the tale 'Provincial Life' were born." Equally important in the genesis of the work was the author's intimate knowledge of Lebedyan – its topography, its mores, its language, all of which find their reflection in the narrative. The monastery, the tavern, the pond and so on – all were to be found in real-life Lebedyan.

Readers can judge the characters and events of the narrative for themselves, but in presenting an example of the harshly realistic, even sordid, depictions of Russian life that were many and varied in Russian literature of this period, Zamyatin was drawing pictures familiar from his schooldays and later periods in exile. Of the odious Chebotarikha, for example, he recalls: "I saw her a number of times in my childhood, she was firmly fixed inside me, and maybe to rid myself of her I had to expel her from myself into a tale. I did not know her life, all her adventures were my invention, but she really did have a tannery, and her appearance in 'Provincial Life' is a true portrait. I left her real name almost unchanged in the tale: no matter how I tried, I could not call her anything else…"

The language Zamyatin used in the tale is far from the cultured, literary Russian of St Petersburg. Another major writer of the period, Boris Pilnyak, suggested that Zamyatin had written his story with a dictionary at his elbow, peppering the entire work with obscure lexis from every corner of the Russian Empire. What is certainly true of this example of a *skaz* narrative – one in which both the characters and the narrator deploy non-literary language – is that it puts into practice some of the advice Zamyatin would subsequently offer to students of writing in the lecture 'On Language' from around 1920. First and foremost, he advocated use of the language of the setting: "All the author's remarks, all the descriptions of the setting and characters, all the landscapes should be rendered in the language of the milieu depicted." Vocabulary unfamiliar to readers from another sphere of life is therefore justified, as long as meanings can either be inferred or else suggested by near-synonyms. The emphasis throughout, not just in dialogue, should be on the spoken language – hence the absence in Zamyatin of long, complex sentences, full of subordinate clauses, like those found in the work of contemporaries such as Ivan Bunin. And the resultant dynamism can even be further developed when depicting scenes of stress and emotion or thought processes by omitting words, as people realistically do, intensifying the prose's sense of urgency through fragmentation. If, as his prose evolved over the following decades, some elements of his theoretical approach became less marked, one piece of advice from this source can be seen as a constant: "The art of artistic economy is one of the essential demands on a master of prose fiction: the fewer words you say and the more you manage to say with those words, the greater will be the effect, all other conditions being equal – the greater will be the artistic 'efficiency'."

'Provincial Life' provoked a huge number of reviews with titles such as 'A Coming Force' and 'A New Talent'. Sufficient to quote one critic's conclusion on the tale: "A remarkable work of contemporary literature, and in its depth, significance and artistic merits it can find no rivals." Reviewers differed in their interpretation of Zamyatin's treatment of the life and inhabitants of the Russian provinces, some seeing nothing but savagery and darkness, others good-natured affection for the grotesques he was depicting – but the overall positive evaluation of the writer's talent was not to be doubted.

'At the End of the Earth', Zamyatin's next major work, written in 1914 and published in the third issue of *Testaments* that same year, was not destined to share this critical success – nor, indeed, to be read at all at the time. Because of the perceived anti-military nature of the tale's content, the relevant issue of the journal was confiscated by the censors; Zamyatin was taken to court and found himself in exile once again.

The vivid portrayal of the life of an artillery battery, stationed near Vladivostok in the Russian Far East, shares a number of the qualities of 'Provincial Life' and much of its predecessor's exploration of moral turpitude. On this occasion, however, Zamyatin had no lived personal experience on which to draw, other than a military prototype, observed in childhood, for the culinary obsessive side of General Azancheyev. Yet what the author deemed "a strange thing" is described once again in 'Backstage': "...two or three times I happened to come across former officers from the Far East who assured me that they knew the living people depicted in the tale, and that their real names were such-and-such and such-and-such, and that the events took place in such-and-such and such-and-such. And yet I have never travelled farther than the Urals, all these 'living people' (apart from 1/10th of Azancheyev) lived only in my own fantasy, and of the entire tale, only the one chapter about 'the Lanzepuppes' Club' was based on a story I heard from someone." His assurances that he had never been in the army drew the response: "All right! Keep pulling the wool over our eyes!" All this led Zamyatin to the conclusion that a rich imagination combined with a convincing narrative could work wonders: "'Pulling the wool over people's eyes', constructing even without personal experience an unfamiliar way of life and the living people in it, turns out to be possible. The flora and fauna of the writing desk are much richer than people think, and this is still very little studied." The distance from the earthbound 'Provincial Life' to the futuristic We is immense, but the reactions to 'At the End of the Earth' encountered by Zamyatin demonstrated the imaginative power that enabled him to cover that ground.

Before then, though, the world and the writer had to get through the First World War. The most striking period of the war for Zamyatin was the year and a half spent in Britain, mostly around the docks of England's north-east, where he was engaged in the construction of icebreakers for the Russian government. Many of the impressions he formed about the English character, the country's society and its way of life found their expression in the tales 'The Islanders' and 'A Fisher of Men'. These two works mark something of a change in the writer's style, their prose being even more dynamic than that of his already fast-paced tales, and their imagery even more daring. His return to Russia in the new circumstances of September 1917 meant he could finally have 'At the End of the Earth' available to readers, and it was from this point on that he devoted himself fully to literature. He began to produce a lot more work himself, taught a class on literary prose in the Petrograd House of the Arts, participated in the work of the World Literature publishing house, wrote critical articles for periodicals and so on. Of particular note was his association with the other talented young authors of the Serapion Brothers grouping, but all this activity as a whole put Zamyatin at the very heart of the new literary life of the new post-revolutionary Russia.

His most significant work of this period was, of course, the dystopian science-fiction novel We, which he completed in 1921. But as it remained unpublished in Russia until long after its author's death, it was through his other writings of the period, such as the two short stories in this collection – 'The Cave', first published in *Notes of Dreamers* (*Zapiski mechtatelei*), No. 5, 1922, and 'Mamai', first published in *House of the Arts* (*Dom isskusstv*), No. 1, 1921 – that contemporary Russian readers knew of his response to life under the Bolsheviks. Both stories reflect aspects of the terrible conditions endured by the citizens of Petrograd in the years of the civil war and owe much to Zamyatin's own experience. Extracts from 'Backstage' once again detail the snippets of life that provided inspiration for these little literary gems: "The night watch in winter, in the courtyard, 1919. My comrade on watch – a frozen, famished professor – was complaining about the lack of firewood: 'If I could only steal some firewood! But the whole trouble is that I can't: I might die, but I won't steal.' Next day I sat down to write the short story 'The Cave'." Another acquaintance from Zamyatin's days as a student became "the founder of a sect of book lovers. In the first, hungry years of the revolution he often dropped in to see me and always had a basket full of books – they were bought with the last of what he had, with money from the trousers he'd sold to a Tatar. And wearing make-up to the point of being unrecognizable, he came on stage again in the role of 'the Mamai of 1917' in the short story 'Mamai'." Thus events, characters and imagery, too, came from the real life of Petrograd: "In a brief story the image may become integral, spread throughout the whole thing from beginning to end. The six-storey, fiery-eyed building on a dark, desolate 1919 street, echoing with gunshots, presented itself to me as a ship in the ocean. I believed in this completely – and the integral image of the ship determined the entire system of images in the story 'Mamai'. And it's the same thing in the story 'The Cave'." A fine sense of what Zamyatin sought to add to the literature of St Petersburg, so important in the nineteenth-century tradition, comes from an article in part reviewing Alexei Tolstoy's *The Road to Calvary*: "...it is, of course, impossible to tell the whole of Petersburg if the narrator has in his hands a collection only of realistic colours, without any admixture of Gogol,

Hoffmann. Sharpness is needed, hyperbole, the grotesque, a kind of new reality is needed, the seemingly incredible reality which is revealed to the person looking at a scrap of human skin through a microscope." The little men at the mercy of the metropolis are common to both Zamyatin and his great predecessor, Nikolai Gogol, another who oscillated between depictions of the city and the provinces, the mundane and the fantastic.

To say that Zamyatin lived through turbulent times – the end of empire, revolution, civil war, the birth of a new social order – would be an understatement, and their reflection in his work was bound to make for some harrowing reading. The publication of *We* abroad – in English, Czech and French – at intervals during the 1920s made his life in Russia no easier, especially as the artistic freedoms and experimentation of the immediate post-revolutionary years gave way to increasing demands for orthodoxy and regimentation. Arrest, imprisonment, the threat of expulsion from the country continued to be his lot, just as they had been under the tsarist regime. The light-hearted, ironic satire of the story 'X' – published in *New Russia* (*Novaya Rossiya*), No. 2, 1926 – comes perhaps as something of a surprise, then, in the middle of such a difficult decade. Here we return to the world of Lebedyan, where the prototype of the poet-telegraphist was a postal clerk "who declared he had eight pounds of poems at home" ('Backstage'); added to the mix of provincial types now, though, are the new Bolshevik officials with their novel acronyms, a new set of official figures to be feared. And the narrative here is undeniably different in style, liberally sprinkled with knowing literary and theatrical references. After the sparse, tight prose of the Petrograd tales, this shaggy-dog story allows the reader to better appreciate Zamyatin's mastery of humour, so easy to overlook amidst the horrors of so much of his writing.

The final story in this collection, 'Flood', was published in Book IV of *Land and Factory* (*Zemlia i fabrika*) in 1929, the year when Zamyatin was preparing a multi-volume edition of his works, including the plays he had been producing for most of the previous decade. However, the publication was truncated as a campaign of attacks upon the author intensified, leading to his announcement of his withdrawal from the Union of Writers in that same year. This in effect marked the end of his active involvement in Soviet literature. There is nothing remarkable, then, about the absence of humour in 'Flood', and it is tempting to see the resolution of the heroine's suffering as something of a parallel to the writer's impending release from his own cycle of torment. Zamyatin's comment on the story in the context of work on the collected edition is particularly interesting: "Incidentally – this was an opportunity to look back at the entire path I had trodden over fifteen years, to compare how I used to write and how I write now. All the complications I went through, as it turns out, were in order to arrive at simplicity (the short story 'The Yawl', the tale 'Flood'). Simplicity of form is legitimate for our epoch, but the right to simplicity must be earned." Gone here are the portrait galleries and dialectisms of the early tales; gone, too, is the dramatic imagery of six-storey ships and mammoths from the civil war era; instead there is a quite simple narrative of personal anguish and family relations, with simple leitmotivs – "Sofya is also a bird, Ganka is also a cat". And as Zamyatin comments further in 'Backstage': "…here the integral image of flood runs through the story on two planes; the real Petersburg flood is reflected in the spiritual flood, and into their common channel flow all the basic images of the story." For all its references to the Petersburg tradition in literature, the fundamental, universal human emotions examined by 'Flood' make it perhaps the most easily relatable work in this collection.

In June 1931 Zamyatin wrote his famous letter to Stalin, requesting permission to leave the country. In November that permission was granted, and the writer left for Riga, then Berlin, and finally, in February 1932, Paris. He continued his writing in France, becoming particularly active in the production of film scripts, and was even accepted into the newly formed Union of Soviet Writers in

1934. Retaining his Soviet citizenship, he was able to be a member of the Soviet delegation to an antifascist writers' congress in 1935. His was one of a number of tragic cases of Russian artists driven to live abroad who never really came to terms with their absence from their homeland. He died in March 1937 of a heart attack and was buried by a small but very distinguished group of writers, demonstrating how the respected position he had held in Russia in the early 1920s was still very much his fifteen years later in Paris. Wider and deeper familiarity with his work can surely only enhance that position today.

– Hugh Aplin, 2024

X
and Other Stories

Provincial Life

THE FOUR-CORNERED LAD

His father's forever nagging: "Learn all you can, or else you'll be like me, stitching boots." But how's he supposed to learn, when he's first in the register, and so as soon as there's a lesson, the first thing they do is drawl out:

"Baryba, Anfim. If you please."

And Anfim Baryba stands sweating, pulling a forehead that's low enough as it is right down to his eyebrows.

"Not the foggiest again? Dear, dear, dear, and a fully grown fellow too, aren't you, ripe for marriage. Sit down, lad."

Baryba sits down. And sits there good and proper – for a couple of years per class. And so it was that, dawdling along, unhurried, Baryba got to the final one.

At that time he was about fifteen, or even a bit older. His whiskers were already sprouting like good winter crops, and he'd run down to the Streltsy* pond with the other boys to watch the women bathing. And in the night-time afterwards he might as well not have gone to bed: he kept on having such hot dreams, and they set off such a song and dance that...

Baryba would get up in the morning grumpy and loaf around all day. He'd tootle off to the monastery wood until night-time. School? It could just go to hell!

In the evening his father would start giving him a belting. "Ran away again, did you, you disobedient skiver?" But he was completely out of hand and didn't give two hoots: he'd grit his teeth and not one squeak. Only all the corners of his weird face would stick out even more spikily.

3

Right enough: corners. Not for nothing did the kids at the District School give him the nickname Flat-Iron. Heavy iron jaws, a great wide, four-cornered mouth and a narrow forehead: a flat-iron all right, with the pointed end at the top. And Baryba's all broad, bulky and lumbering somehow, all made of rigid straight lines and corners. But one thing's fitted on to another in such a way that it's as if from all the ungainly parts some sort of order does emerge: it may be uncouth, it may be ugly, but it's order all the same.

Kids were a bit scared of Baryba: a beast, he could beat you into the ground with his heavy hand. They'd tease him from around a corner, from a *verst** away. But at the same time, when Baryba was hungry, they'd feed him rolls, and then they'd make fun of him to their hearts' content.

"Hey, Baryba, crunch these up into bits for half a roll."

And they slip him some stones, choosing ones that are good and hard.

"That's not enough," Baryba grumbles sulkily. "A whole roll."

"Greedy devil!" – but they'll come up with a whole roll. And to the amusement of the kids Baryba will start crunching the stones, grinding them down with his iron nutcrackers – just keep on adding more! It's amusing stuff for the kids, weird and wonderful.

Jokes are all very well, but when exams came around even the jokers had to sit down with their books, regardless of green May outside.

On the 18th, Empress Alexandra's Day,* it was the first of the leaving exams, on Scripture. And in the evening once, his father put aside his shoe-thread and boot, took off his glasses and said:

"You remember this, Anfimka, you mark my words. If you don't pass this time either, I'll be turning you out of the house."

Things couldn't have been better, so it seemed: three days to prepare. But as ill luck would have it, the kids began playing pitch-and-toss – and oh, what a tempting game that is! For two days Anfimka was out of luck and lost all his capital: seven ten-kopek coins and a new belt with a buckle. He could have topped himself! But on the third day, praise the Lord, he got all of it back and won more than fifty kopeks in cash on top.

On the 18th, of course, Baryba was called out first. Not a peep from the other schoolkids – they're waiting: he'll be all at sea now, poor bloke.

Baryba drew out his question and stared at the white sheet of paper. The whiteness and his fear made him feel slightly sick. All his words slipped away somewhere at a stroke: not one left.

Some prompters at the front desks whispered:

"The Typhus and Euphrates... The Garden lived in by... Mesopotamia. Meso-po-ta... The deaf devil!"

Baryba began speaking; he started cracking out words, one after another, like stones – leaden, sparse.

"Adam and Eve. Between the Tigris and... what's it... Euphrates. Paradise was a huge garden. In which there were mesopotamuses. And other animals..."

The priest nodded, seemingly very kindly. Baryba took heart.

"And who are these mesopotamuses? Eh, Anfim? Do explain to us, Anfimushka."

"Mesopotamuses... They're these... prehistoric wild animals. Really fierce. And so they're in paradise. Living side by side..."

The priest was snorting with laughter and hiding his mouth with his upturned beard; the kids fell about on their desks.

* * *

Baryba didn't go home. He knew very well – his father was an upright man, as good as his word. What he'd said, he'd do. And might give him a good walloping with his belt as well.

2
WITH THE DOGS

Once upon a time there lived the Balkashins, reputable merchants, and they had been boiling malt at their mill for a long time, but suddenly in a year of cholera they all somehow went and died.

They say their heirs live somewhere far away in a big town, only they never come. The vacant house stays grieving and empty. The wooden tower's leaning over, the windows are boarded over crosswise, weeds have taken root in the yard. People chuck blind puppies and kittens over the fence into the Balkashins' yard, and stray dogs crawl under the fence from the street in search of prey.

And it was here that Baryba made his home. He took a fancy to the old cowshed, as, luckily, the doors weren't locked and there was a manger in the shed, knocked together from planks: a regular bed. It's paradise for Baryba now: you don't have to learn anything; you can do whatever pops into your head, swim until your teeth start chattering, wander around the merchant quarter after the organ-grinder all day if you want, spend days and nights in the monastery wood.

Everything would have been fine, but soon there was nothing to eat. Was a lousy rouble or so ever going to last that long?

Baryba started going to the market to find pickings. With ungainly animal artfulness, long-armed, hiding inside himself and looking out from under his brows, he prowled between the white, upward-pointing wagon shafts, the horses chewing oats, the tirelessly tongue-wagging women: as soon as some Matryona was off her guard – in a flash Baryba had snaffled his dinner.

If he had no luck at the market, Baryba ran off to the Streltsy quarter. In places walking, in places crawling, he scours the backyards, behind the barns, the vegetable gardens. The pungent smell of wormwood tickles his nostrils, but God forbid he should sneeze: the mistress, there she is – there, weeding a bed, with her red headscarf bobbing in the greenery. Baryba will gather potatoes, carrots, and bake them at home – in the Balkashins' yard – then, burning himself, he eats them with no salt – and it seems like he's full. Better one small fish, of course, than an empty dish.

If some day he has no success, no luck, Baryba sits hungry and looks at the dogs with envious, wolfish eyes: they're scrunching a bone, playing happily with a bone. Baryba looks on...

* * *

Days, weeks, months. Oh, how sick and tired he is of living with the hungry dogs in the Balkashins' yard! He's grown weak, grown rough, Baryba, got hairy, blackened; thinness has made the corners of his jaws and cheekbones protrude even more rigidly, and his face has become even heavier, more four-cornered.

He'd love to run away from this dog's life. To have people, something like other people do: to have some nice hot tea, to sleep under a blanket.

There were days when Baryba spent the whole day lying in his shed, face down in the straw. There were days when Baryba spent the whole day going round and round the Balkashins' yard looking for people, something human.

In the neighbouring yard, the Chebotaryovs', there were people about from first thing in the morning: tanners in leather aprons, carters with wagonloads of hides. They'll see someone's eye going back and forth in a hole in the fence and they'll prod with a whip handle:

"Hey, who's there!"

"Maybe there's still a house-sprite left in the Balkashins' yard?"

With wolfish leaps Baryba heads for his shed, into the straw and there he lies. Ooh, if he could only get his hands on those carters: he'd really show them, he'd really give them...

From midday in the Chebotaryovs' yard there's the clatter of knives from the kitchen, there's the smell of roasted livestock. So that Baryba's all a-shake by the chink, by his chink in the fence, and he won't unglue himself from it till they've finished having their dinner there.

When they've finished having dinner it's as if he feels a bit better too. They finish, and out into the yard creeps Chebotarikha herself: she's red, been sitting down too long, can't walk for overfeeding.

"Ooh..." Iron on iron, Baryba starts grinding his teeth.

On holidays, above the Balkashins' yard, at the top of the side street, the Church of the Intercession rang its bells – and the ringing made Baryba even more vicious. Ringing and ringing, a buzzing in his ears, chiming...

7

"Now that's where I should go, isn't it – to the monastery, to Yevsei!" It dawned on Baryba with the ringing.

When still a little boy, after a beating, Baryba had gone running to Yevsei. And Yevsei always used to give him tea with the monastery's altar bread. He gives him a drink and he himself keeps on talking – anything at all, as long as it cheers him up:

"Oh dear, my boy! The other day the hegumen* grabbed me by my holy hair, and even so I... Oh dear, boy... And you're blubbing?"

Baryba ran to the monastery and arrived feeling cheerful: he'd left the Balkashins' dogs behind now.

"Is Father Yevsei in?"

The novice covered his mouth with his hand and started cackling:

"Out there! You won't even find him with hunting dogs now: Father Yevsei's hit the bottle and spent all week in Streltsy on a bender."

Yevsei's not there. The end – there's nowhere else to go. Back to the Balkashins' yard again.

3
THE CHICKS

After the night service or after mass, the Intercession priest would catch up with Chebotarikha, shake his head and say:

"This is indecent, good lady. You need to walk, take a promenage.* Or else, if you don't look out, the flesh will conquer completely."

But Chebotarikha would spread out like dough on her wagonette and, pursing her lips, say:

"That's just not possible, Father – my heart's beating unceasantly."

And Chebotarikha drives on through the dust, plastering herself over the wagonette – it's a single unit with her, cumbersome, running, sprung. Otherwise – on her legs alone, without wheels – nobody ever saw Chebotarikha outdoors. Their, the Chebotaryovs', bathhouse (her husband had left her the tannery and the public bathhouse) couldn't have been closer, but even so she drove there in the wagonette on Fridays – the women's day.

And that's why the wagonette itself and the piebald gelding and the coachman Urvanka are highly thought of by Chebotarikha. And especially Urvanka: curly-haired, ever so strong, the devil, and all black – perhaps he was a Gypsy. Kind of smoky, squat, wiry, all like a knot from good rope. Word had it that he was, so they said, not only Chebotarikha's coachman. And they said on the quiet – they were too scared to say it too loud – if he, Urvanka, gets his hands on you, he'll give you such a licking, lad, that... Beating someone half to death is Urvanka's number-one pleasure: because he's been badly beaten himself, having been a horse thief.

But Urvanka did have love too: he loved horses and chickens. Horses he'd sometimes be brushing and brushing, combing their manes with his copper comb, or else he'd start talking with them in some language or other. Perhaps he really was a heathen?

And Urvanka loved chickens because in the spring they were chicks – yellow, nice and round and soft. Sometimes he's chasing after them all over the yard: ducky, ducky, ducky! He'll get underneath the water cart, crawl under the porch on all fours – and when he's caught it, he'll sit it on his hand and – his number-one pleasure – warm the chick up with his breath. And so that no one could see his mug at the time. God knows what it was like. Without having had a look, you couldn't possibly imagine: that Urvanka and a chick. Strange!

It turned out, to Baryba's misfortune, that he too came to love Urvanka's chicks: very tasty, and he got into the habit of pinching them. A second one missing, a third, Urvanka spotted. But where the chicks had got to – he hadn't the faintest idea. Was there maybe a ferret about?

After noontime once, Urvanka was lying next to the shed in a cart. The scorcher's making him feel drowsy. The chicks, even they've hidden themselves away next to the shed, sat down in the shade by the wall, shut the inner lid over their eyes, and off they're nodding.

9

And the poor things can't see that the plank behind them has been ripped off and reaching through the hole, reaching towards them is a hand. Snap – and a chick's begun squealing and going numb in Baryba's fist.

Urvanka leapt up and started yelling. In a trice he'd jumped over the fence.

"Catch him, catch him, catch the thief!"

Wild, animal flight. Baryba reached his manger and backed into it, got under the straw, but even there Urvanka found him. Pulled him out, set him on his feet.

"Right, just you wait! For my chicks I'm gonna give you…"

And he dragged him by the scruff of the neck to Chebotarikha: let *her* come up with a punishment for the thief.

4
HE DID SHOW MERCY

Chebotarikha had turned out the cook – fat-faced Anisya. Why? So she couldn't make a play for Urvanka, that's why. Had turned her out, and now she was tearing her hair out. There were no cooks in all the merchants' quarter. She'd had to take on Polka – a feeble slip of a girl.

And now they were ringing for the evening service at the Church of the Intercession, and this Polka was sweeping the floor in the hall after sprinkling it with used tea leaves as Chebotarikha had taught her. Chebotarikha herself was sitting there, too, on a cretonne-covered sofa, and dying of boredom, gazing at a glass jar flytrap: there was *kvas** in the flytrap, and the flies were drowning themselves in the *kvas* out of boredom. Chebotarikha was yawning and making the sign of the cross over her mouth. "Oh Lord our Father, have mercy…"

And He did show mercy: some sort of stomping and hubbub in the lobby – and Urvanka shoved Baryba in. Baryba was so nonplussed, seeing Chebotarikha herself, that he even stopped trying to tear himself free, and it was only his eyes darting back and forth into every corner like mice.

Chebotarikha heard about the little chicks and began boiling over, splashing out spittle.

"Raised a hand against the little chicks, God's lickle ay-gels? Oh, the villain, oh, the wretch! Polyushka, bring the besom. Bring it, bring it, I don't want to hear another word!"

Urvanka bared his teeth, gave Baryba a whack from behind with his knee – and in a trice he's on the floor. He tried to start biting, twisting like a snake – but what could he do against that devil Urvanka? He laid him out, straddled him, in a trice tore Baryba's holey trousers off and was only waiting for the word from Chebotarikha to begin the payback.

But Chebotarikha couldn't get so much as a word out for laughing – such a fit of laughter had come over her. It was all she could do to open her eyes: what have they gone quiet for down there on the floor?

She did open them, the laughter retreated, and she leant closer to Baryba's tensed, animally strong body.

"Go away now, Urvan. Get off, I tell you, get off! Let me question him properly…" Chebotarikha didn't look at Urvanka; she turned her eyes towards the corner.

Urvanka got off slowly, turned around on the threshold and slammed the door with all his might.

Baryba jumped up and made a quick dart for his trousers: Heavens, there was nothing of the trousers but rags! Right, run without a backward glance…

But Chebotarikha held him tight by the arm:

"Whose little boy would you be, then?"

She kept on sticking her lower lip out, said "lickle" instead of "little", kept putting on airs and graces, but there was something else Baryba sensed.

"I'm the co-cobbler's…" and at once he remembered the whole of his life and started to whine and howl. "My father turned me out over an exa-am, I've been li-iving… in the Bal… In the Balkashi-i…"

Chebotarikha threw up her hands and sang out sweetly and sadly:

"Oh, my little orphan, oh, you ill-fortunate thing! Out of the house, his own son, eh? A father, he calls himself…"

She was singing and dragging Baryba away somewhere by the arm, and Baryba went, miserable and obedient.

"…And there's no one to teach you goodness. But the enemy – there he is: steal, steal the little chick – isn't that right?"

A bedroom. A huge bedstead with a mountainous feather mattress. An icon lamp. The icons' metal mountings are a-twinkle.

She shoved Baryba onto some kind of rug:

"On your knees, get down on your knees. Pray, Anfimushka, pray. The Lord is merciful – He will forgive. And I will forgive…"

And she herself sank down somewhere behind him and began heatedly whispering a prayer. Stunned, Baryba knelt without stirring.

"I should get up and go. Get up…" he thought.

"What is it you're doing, eh? How were you taught to cross yourself?" Chebotarikha seized Baryba's hand. "Now, it's done like this: to your forehead, to your stomach…" She plastered herself over him from behind, breathing on his neck.

Suddenly, to his own surprise, Baryba turned round and, locking his jaws, thrust his hands deep into something soft, like dough.

"Oh, you so-and-so, ah? What are you doing, is that it, eh? Well, so be it, then – for you, for an orphan, I'll sin."

Baryba drowned in sweet, hot dough.

Polka made him up a bed of felt on a chest in the hallway for the night.

Baryba shook his head: well, wonders never cease. He went to sleep full up and contented.

5
LIFE

No, it's not at all like how it was in the Balkashins' yard here – this is life. Living with all needs provided for, in comfort, on soft mattresses, in hot rooms, heated with thatching straw. He wandered about all day in sweet idleness. Snoozing in the dusk on the stove-bench beside Vaska, who'd be purring for all he was worth. Eating till fit to burst. What a life!

Eating till he was hot and sweaty. Eating from morning till evening, giving his whole self up to food. That's the way of things at Chebotarikha's.

In the morning – tea with baked milk and rye buns made with buttermilk. Chebotarikha in a white (though not *very* white) bed-jacket, her head covered with a kerchief.

"And why are you always wearing a kerchief?" asks Baryba.

"The way you've been taught! Really, can a *woman* possibly go about bareheaded? I don't think I'm a single girl, am I, so it's a sin, isn't it? I'd been covered with my bridal crown, hadn't I, when living with my husband. It's the uncovered ones who just shack up, the good-for-nothings…"

Or else they'd have some other conversation that was beneficial for the food: about dreams, the dream book, Martin Zadek,* about omens and various love spells.

This and that – and lo and behold, it's already gone eleven. Time for a midday snack. Jellied meat, cabbage soup, catfish, or else salted carp, fried intestines with buckwheat porridge, tripe with horseradish, preserved watermelons and apples, and all sorts of other things too.

At midday you mustn't sleep or bathe in the river: there he is, the midday demon, and he's sure to get hold of you. But you do feel like sleeping, of course: what's forbidden's tempting and makes you yawn.

Bored stiff, Baryba will go to Polka in the kitchen: she's a complete idiot, but at least she's a living person. There he'll hunt out the tomcat, Polka's favourite, and set about cramming him into a boot. There's screeching and uproar in the kitchen. Polka wanders about like one possessed.

"Anfim Yegorych, Anfim Yegorych, do let Vasenka go, for Christ's sake!"

Anfimka grins and shoves the cat in even farther. And now Polka's begging Vasenka:

"Vasenka, don't cry now, it'll be all right, little one, it'll be all right! Just a moment, he'll let you go in just a moment."

The cat's crying in a heart-rending voice. Polka's eyes are round, her plait's tumbled forward and she's tugging at Baryba's sleeve with her weak hand.

"Go away, or I'll be giving *you* a whack on the head with the boot!"

Baryba will launch the boot, along with the cat, into the corner and, content, he roars, as if rumbling over potholes in a cart.

* * *

They would eat dinner early, before nine o'clock. Polka would bring the food, and Chebotarikha sends her off to bed to get her out of her sight. Then she takes a decanter from the cabinet.

"Have a drink, Anfimushka, have another glass."

They drink in silence. The lamp makes a thin little squeaking noise and smokes. For a long time, no one notices.

"It's smoking. Should I say?" thinks Baryba.

But he can't turn his sinking thoughts, can't get them out.

Chebotarikha pours some more for him and for herself. Under the dying light of the lamp, the whole of her face fades into one dim blur. And her greedy mouth alone is visible and crying out – a wet, red hole. Her entire face is her mouth alone. And ever closer to Baryba is the smell of her sweaty, sticky body.

For a long time, slowly, the lamp is dying in anguish. The black snow of soot is hanging in the dining room. It stinks.

And in the bedroom there's the icon lamp, the flickering of the icons' foil mountings. The bed is ready and on the rug beside it Chebotarikha is bowing in prayer.

And Baryba knows: the more she bows, the more ardently she prays for the forgiveness of her sins, the longer will she torment him in the night.

"Oh, to hide away somewhere, to creep into some crack or other like a cockroach…" he thinks.

But there's nowhere to go: the doors are locked, the window is sealed by darkness.

* * *

Baryba's job, there's no denying, isn't an easy one. But on the other hand, Chebotarikha dotes on him more and more from one day to the next. He's gained such power that all Chebotarikha can think about now is what else she can do to gratify Anfimushka.

"Anfimushka, have another plateful…"

"Oh dear, there's such a nip in the air today! Let me tie your scarf for you, eh?"

"Anfimushka, have you got a tummy ache again? What a nuisance! Here, here's some vodka with mustard and salt, drink that – it's the number-one remedy."

Smart boots with shiny tops, a silver watch on a neck-chain, new rubber overshoes – and Baryba walks around the Chebotaryovs' yard like some kind of swell, giving out orders.

"Hey, you, loafer, cartman, where have you dropped the hides off? Where were you told?"

And before you know it, he's fined him two silver kopeks, and the peasant's crumpling his holey old hat in his hands and bowing.

There's only one person Baryba steers well clear of, and that's Urvanka. It even happens occasionally that he'll have a go at Chebotarikha herself. He puts up with her, puts up with a lot, but now and again has the joy of such a hard night… Next morning everything's foggy – oh, to escape to the world's end. Baryba will shut himself in the hall and he roams around, roams around as if in a cage.

Chebotarikha will turn meek, grow quiet. She calls Polka.

"Polyushka, go and see how he's getting on. And tell him it's time for dinner."

Polka runs back, giggling:

"He's not coming. He's ever so cross and… and he's going to and fro across the floor so!"

And Chebotarikha delays dinner for one hour, for two.

And if she's delaying dinner, if she's disrupting the sacred dinner time, then that means…

6

IN CHURILOV'S TAVERN

Baryba put on weight by being in the position of steward and by eating good food.

When his old acquaintance, Chernobylnikov the postman, met him on Dvoryanskaya Street he just spread his hands:

"Unrecognizable. Fancy that, a real merchant!"

Chernobylnikov was envious of Baryba: the lad was getting on well. One way or another, Baryba clearly ought to celebrate and treat his friends in the tavern: what would it cost him, the moneybags?

He cajoled the lad, talked him into it.

Towards seven o'clock, as agreed, Baryba arrived at Churilov's tavern. Well, and what a merry place it is, oh Lord! Noise, hulla-baloo, lights. White waiters rushing about, drunken voices flying around like spokes in a wheel.

Baryba's head started to spin, and, taken aback, he couldn't find Chernobylnikov at all.

But Chernobylnikov's already shouting from some way off:

"Hey there, merchant, over here!"

Chernobylnikov's postman's buttons are gleaming. And next to him is some other chap. He's sitting there, small, sharp-nosed, and it's as if he isn't sitting on a chair but bouncing on a perch, like a sparrow.

Chernobylnikov nodded at the sparrow:

"This is Timosha, a tailor. He's a talkative one."

Timosha smiled and lit a warm icon lamp on his sharp face:

"A tailor, yes. I do alterations to brains."

Baryba's jaw dropped; he wanted to ask a question, but he got a nudge in the shoulder from behind him. A waiter holding a tray at arm's length, right beside his head, was already putting beer down on the table. There were voices making a racket and getting confused, but there was one above them all – a red-haired townsman, a swindling horse-dealer, was yelling:

"Mitka, hey, Mitka, misery guts, are you gonna bring it or not?"
And he started singing again:

Along you, street so wide and sweeping,
One final time I walk…*

When Timosha learnt Baryba was from the District School he
was pleased:

"So it was that priest, then, that did the dirty on you? Well, of
course, I know him, I do. I've done work for him. But he dislikes
me, and how!"

"What does he dislike you for?"

"For various conversations we've had. The other day I says to
him: 'How are our saints gonna be,' I says, 'in the other world, in
heaven? Merciful Timofei, my angel and protector, if he sees me
roasting in hell, will he be having another heavenly apple? There's
all-merciful for you, there's a holy soul! And he can't not see me,
not know – he has to, according to the catechism.' Well, and the
priest shut up, didn't know what to say."

"Clever!" Baryba rumbled and bellowed with laughter.

"'You'd be better off,' the priest says to me, 'doing good works
instead of prattling on like this.' And I says to him: 'Why should
I do good works? It's better if I'm wicked. Wicked is of more use
to my nearest and dearest because, according to the Gospel, in
the other world the Lord God will reward them a hundredfold
with good for my wickedness.' Oh, what an earful the priest
gave me!"

"That showed him, the priest, that showed him!" Baryba crowed.
He might have taken a liking to Timosha straight away for that,
for giving the priest such a clever ticking-off – might have done,
but Baryba was difficult, hard to stir, and he wasn't one to be
turned to liking.

At the table where the red-haired townsman was sitting, there
was the clinking of glasses. A fearsome fist, covered in red hair,
came crashing down onto the table. The townsman screamed:

"Come on, say it! Come on, say it again! Come on then, come on!"

His neighbours leapt up, crowded round, craned their necks: oh, how they do love a dust-up here, it's meat and drink to them!

Some long-necked beanpole wriggled his way out of the scuffle, came over to the table and said hello to Chernobylnikov. Under his arm he held a cap with a cockade.

"It's astonishing... And even now they're all piling in like sheep," he said in a goose's thin voice and stuck his lips out scornfully.

He sat down. Took no notice of Baryba and Timosha. Talked to Chernobylnikov: a postman's an official of sorts, after all.

Without a moment's hesitation, Timosha explained to Baryba quite audibly:

"He's the Treasurer's son-in-law. The Treasurer married him to his last daughter, who was on the shelf, and fixed him up with a job as a clerk in the Treasury – well, and so he acts all high and mighty."

The Treasurer's son-in-law pretended not to be listening and said to Chernobylnikov even more loudly:

"And then after the inspection he was recommended for Provincial Secretary..."*

Chernobylnikov drawled out respectfully:

"Pro-o-vincial?"

Timosha could stand it no longer and butted in on the conversation:

"Postman, Chernobylnikov, do you remember how the other day the District Chief of Police shoved him out of the Nobles' Club with his you know what?"

"Please... Mo-ost humbly, please!" said the Treasurer's son-in-law furiously.

But Timosha finished the story:

"'...You won't dare go!' – 'Yes I will!' Well, one thing led to another, and they had a bet on it. He got himself inside the Nobles' Club. And as it happened, the Treasurer was playing billiards with the police chief. And our young buck went up to his father-in-law and whispered in his ear, as if he'd come on some official business. And he stayed standing there. And the police chief started aiming his cue, all the while moving back, moving back, and as if by chance he shoved him out with his you know what. Oh Lord, what a laugh it was!"

Baryba and Chernobylnikov were splitting their sides laughing. The Treasurer's son-in-law got up and left, paying them no heed.

"Well, we'll make friends again," said Timosha. "And he used to be a decent lad, you know. But now: a cockade on his cap, and under the cap – crap."

7

THE ORANGE TREE

Polka, the barefoot idiot, has only the one window in the kitchen, and even in that one the glass is covered in bloom and all different colours from age. And on the windowsill Polka has a tin.

A long time ago now – about six months it would be – Polka planted an orange pip in the tin. And now, lo and behold, a whole little tree's already grown up: one, two, three, four leaves, teeny-weeny and glossy.

Polka will potter around a bit in the kitchen, clatter about a bit with the pots, then go back over to the little tree and sniff the leaves.

"It's a miracle. It was a pip, and now..."

She took care of it, tended it. Someone said it was good for growth, they said, so she started watering it with soup, if there was any left after dinner.

One time, Baryba came back from the tavern late, got up in the morning really, really cross, gulped down some tea and went straight into the kitchen to let off steam. Polka never called him anything but "master" now: very flattering.

And it was at her window that Polka was busy, by her dear little tree.

"Where's the cat?"

Polka carried on busying herself, without turning round. Timidly she replied:

"He's gone, master. Must be somewhere in the yard, where else?"

"What are you cooking up there?"

She fell quiet, got nervous, said nothing. There was a saucer of soup in her hand.

"So-oup? You're watering the grass with it? Is that what you're given soup for, you blithering idiot? Give it here right now!"

"But I mean, it's an arange, master..."

Polka started quivering with fear: oh dear, what was going to happen now?

"I'll show you an arange! Watering it with soup, eh, idiot?"

Baryba grabbed the tin with the orange. Polka started bawling. Why waste loads of time here with her, the idiot? He tugged the little tree out, roots and all; out of the window it went, and he put the tin back in its place. Easy as that.

Polka was bawling at the top of her voice, there were the dirty stripes of tear-tracks on her face, and she was keening like a grown woman:

"Oh, dearest, my arange, how on earth am I going to live without you-ou..."

Baryba cheerfully gave her a couple of kicks from behind, and she rolled out of the door, across the yard and straight into the cellar.

He'd cracked some stone here with Polka, with that orange, and at once he was feeling better. Baryba was grinning, getting drunk on it.

Through the window he'd seen Polka go down into the cellar. A kind of millstone started turning slowly in his head – and suddenly his heart began to pound.

He went out into the yard, looked all around him and plunged into the cellar. He shut the door tight behind him...

After the sunshine, straight into the darkness – he was completely blinded. He stumbled and fumbled his way along the damp walls.

"Polka, where are you? Where've you hidden yourself away, you idiot?"

Polka could be heard snivelling and whimpering somewhere, but where… It was musty, tomb-like, damp. He ran his hands over potatoes and barrels and knocked a round wooden board off some sort of jug.

Here she is, Polka: she's sitting on the heap of potatoes, smearing her tears around. There's a tiny little hole of some sort up above, and a single sly, squinting little ray of light has got through and cut out a piece of Polka's plait with its rag ribbon, her fingers and a dirty cheek.

"Enough, enough, stop bawling, dry up!"

Baryba leant on her lightly and she toppled over. She moved obediently and was all like a rag doll. But she began whimpering even more frequently.

Baryba's mouth went dry, and his tongue was barely working. He babbled something or other just to occupy her mind, to distract her from what he was doing:

"How d'you like that, what a thing, an arange! And you go bawling? In place of the arange, why don't we buy you an eranium… an eranium, it's… what's it… fragrant…"

Polka was all atremble and whimpering, and there was a particular sweetness for Baryba in that.

"Right, ri-ight! You can bawl now, go on, bawl all you can," Baryba kept saying.

*　*　*

He sent Polka packing. He himself stayed on, stretched out on the heap of potatoes, resting.

Suddenly Baryba started grinning from ear to ear, contented. He said out loud to Chebotarikha:

"Well, you old mattress, swallow that, aha?"

And stuck two fingers up in the darkness.

He came out of the cellar and screwed up his eyes: the sunshine. He looked in the direction of the shed: busy doing something there with his back to him was Urvanka.

8

TIMOSHA

They were sitting in the tavern having tea. Timosha kept looking hard at Baryba.

"You're kind of uncomfortable, I see. You must have been beaten, that's what."

"Of course I was," Baryba laughed. It was even flattering: he used to be beaten, but now, go on, try it.

"That's why you've turned out like this, my son. Your soul, your conscience, is exactly the size of a chicken's…"

And he started on his favourite topics, talking about God – He doesn't exist, he says, but it still turns out you have to live in God's way – and about faith, and about books. Baryba wasn't used to grinding so much with his millstone, and Timosha's queer words tired him out. But he listened and dragged along behind Timosha like a heavy cart. Who was he to listen to, if not Timosha? He was a clever fellow.

And Timosha had already got to his most important point:

"So one day it'll appear He does exist. But you turn things around again and weigh them up – and again there's nothing there. Nothing: no God, no land, no water – only the swell beneath the heavens. Just semblance alone."

Timosha turned his head around like a sparrow; there was something oppressing him.

"Semblance alone. What a place to get to! No, but living eye to eye with this nothing alone, feeding on air. Now that, lad…"

And he saw that Baryba had already got lost, fallen behind, stumbled.

Timosha gave up the struggle:

"Oh, what's the point! This means nothing to you – you live through your belly… For you, God's edible."

They left the tavern. It's a June night, not a hot one; there's the scent of lime trees; the crickets are trilling in the grass. But Timosha's dressed up in an awful wadded coat – isn't he odd, eh?

"Timosha, why do you wrap yourself up like a ridiculous old woman?"

"Leave it alone! Don't even ask. Tu-ber-cu-leo-sis, lad. That's what the orderly at the hospital said. Getting cold – God forbid!"

"How about that – so that's why he's so weedy," thought Baryba, and he suddenly had a powerful sort of sense of the weight of his strong, animal body. He walked, heavy and contented: it was nice treading on the earth, trampling the earth, crushing it – like that! Take that!

In Timosha's tiny room with its tattered wallpaper there were three kiddies sitting at an unpainted table, freckled and sharp-nosed.

"Where's your mother?" Timosha cried. "Out again?"

"She's gone to the sheriff's – there was someone here," said the little girl shyly.

And she started putting her half-boots on in the corner: she felt awkward with bare feet now some strange man was here.

Timosha frowned.

"Let's have the millet porridge, Fenka. And bring the bottle from the lobby."

"Mamasha said no to the bottle."

"I'll give you Mamasha. Hurry up, hurry up! Sit down, Baryba." They sat down at the table. Squeaking thinly up above was a lamp with a tin shade, covered in dead flies.

Fenka was about to begin pouring the runny millet porridge from the bowl into a wooden dish for the kiddies.

Timosha shouted at her:

"What's this? Squeamish about your own father, are you? Still your mother teaching you? Well, I'll teach her, so I will, when she comes back! Knocking about somewhere…"

The kids started eating from the common bowl, none too eagerly, dejectedly. Timosha had a wry giggle and said to Baryba:

"There – I'm tempting the Lord God. They say at the hospital it's catching, the consumption. Well, so I'll see whether it's catching for the kiddies or not. Will His hand, the Lord God's, be raised against innocent kiddies – will it be raised, or not?"

There was a gentle, fearful knocking at the window.

Timosha hurriedly threw the frame open and sang out venomously:

"Aha, so you're here?"

And then to Baryba:

"Well, lad, gather up your belongings. There's nothing more for you to see here. Things here will be getting serious."

9
ELIJAH'S DAY

The evening before Elijah's Day* is special, and the ringing of the church bells is unique and special: there's a table in the cathedral, there's a table in the monastery, the cooks in all the houses are baking pies for the next day, and in the sky the Prophet Elijah's preparing thunderclaps. And what's the sky like before Elijah's Day? It's clear and quiet, as it is in a hut given a clean-up for a feast day. Everyone's hurrying to their churches: God forbid they should be late for Elijah's anthem, or tears will be falling all year like the rain ordained for Elijah's Day from time immemorial.

Well, there'll be somebody who's late, but not Chebotarikha: she's the number-one woman for praying in the Church of the Intercession. Good and early, well ahead of time, Urvanka's got the horses in harness.

He's got them in harness and is going across the yard – right past the cellar. Lo and behold, the door's open. Urvanka had a grumble:

"Look at that, the devils, they've left the door wide open. There's people going to pray to God, while they... I'll be damned. The brazen lot!"

And he added salt with a stronger word. He was about to shut the door, but no. He stood for a moment and gave a smirk.

He came and reported to Chebotarikha: everything's ready, he says.

"But may I ask you to go out through the back door..." And Urvanka knotted a smile on his smoked face: come on, figure out what it means.

"You're up to something, Urvanka!" said Chebotarikha. She sailed off, though, swishing her brown silk flowered dress.

Puffing, she went down the steps. Walked past the cellar.

"You might have realized you should shut the door. I have to tell them and show them everything..." Chebotarikha's a dignified, house-proud woman, and will such a one pass calmly by an open door? Even if there's no need, she's going to close it.

"What, are you telling me to shut them in there?"

"Who's this 'them'?"

"What do you mean, 'who'? What about Anfim Yegorych and Polka? I guess they ought to go to the night service before Elijah's Day too?"

"You're talking nonsense, you scoundrel, you! Never in my life will I believe that Anfimka and her—"

"May Elijah strike me down with thunder tomorrow if I'm talking nonsense."

"Go on then, cross yourself!"

Urvanka crossed himself. It must be true, then.

Chebotarikha turned pale and began shaking like leavened dough that's risen to the very edges of the dough trough. Urvanka thought: "Now she's going to start howling." No, she evidently remembered she was wearing a silk dress. She thrust her lip out solemnly and, as if nothing in particular had happened, said:

"Urvanka, shut the door. It's time, time we went to church."

"Yes, ma'am."

He clicked the bolt shut, untied the horses, and Chebotarikha's famous wagonette set the dust flying along the road.

* * *

Chebotarikha stood, as always, at the front by the right-hand choir-place. She folded her hands on her stomach and fixed her eyes on one spot, on the deacon's right boot. A bit of paper of some sort had got stuck to the boot; the deacon was standing on the ambo in front of Chebotarikha and the bit of paper gave her not a moment's peace.

"'For the sick and the suffering'..."* she thought: "And for me, then, the suffering me. Oh Lord, what a scoundrel he is, that Anfimka!"

She'd bow to the ground, and the bit of paper on the boot – there it was, forever flickering before her eyes.

The deacon left, and it was even worse: she couldn't get that damned Anfimka out of her head. And there she'd been, pampering him, eh?

Only during the "Alleluia" did Chebotarikha get a bit distracted and forget about Baryba a little. No, how do you like that: the deacon's Olgunya, the educated one, she just stands there! There's her education – she wants everything her way, to be different to everyone else. No-o, I'll have to have a word with the deacon about her...

The sexton in his retired soldier's tunic was snuffing the candles in the church. The deacon brought some bread out on a plate for Chebotarikha: she was an exemplary parishioner, God-fearing, and she paid well.

Chebotarikha pulled him towards her by the sleeve and spent a long time whispering in his ear about Olgunya and shaking her head.

* * *

Urvanka leant on the door and drew the bolt back. Baryba leapt out like a scalded cat.

"Go and have some tea," said Urvanka with a smirk.

"Can it be that he hasn't said?" thought Baryba.

Chebotarikha sat po-faced in her silk dress, as stiff as bast, breaking the bread the deacon had presented her with into little pieces and swallowing them like pills, ever so noisily: who on earth chews blessed bread?

"Well, I wish she'd hurry up and say something," thought Baryba as he waited, and his heart fluttered and ached.

"Should I maybe order some baked milk to be brought to go with the tea?" Chebotarikha looked at him seemingly even with affection.

"Is she making fun of me?" he thought. "Or perhaps she really doesn't know?"

"Now, who knows where she is, that Polka? She's starting to get huffy, that awful girl. You need to keep an eye on her, Anfimushka."

That's how Chebotarikha spoke – simply, as if nothing were wrong – swallowing the bread down bit by bit; then she swept up the blessed crumbs from the table and tipped them into her mouth.

"She doesn't know, does she, as God's my witness." Baryba was suddenly convinced. He cheered up, smiled his four-cornered smile, roared with laughter and recounted how that blithering idiot Polka had been watering her arange tree with soup.

The sun was setting, bronze and fierce: Elijah would be giving them a storm tomorrow. The white cups and plates on the table were turning scarlet. Chebotarikha sat solemn and silent and didn't smile even once.

* * *

Baryba was cheerful as he bowed in prayer beside Chebotarikha in the bedroom and thanked some unknown saints: it was over, it had passed, Urvanka hadn't told her!

The icon lamp went out. The night before Elijah's Day is stifling, hard to bear. In the darkness of the bedroom there's the greedy, gaping, drinking mouth and the rapid breathing of a wild animal at bay.

Baryba's heart stopped beating; green circles started shifting about in front of his eyes; strands of his hair stuck together on his forehead.

"What's the matter with you? Have you gone barmy?" he said, working himself free of her body.

But she clung all over him like a spider.

"No-o, darling, no-o, dear! You can't escape, no!"

And she tormented him with wicked caresses, invisible and incomprehensible in the darkness, and she herself sobbed: she wet the whole of Baryba's face with tears.

* * *

Until morning. In a sleep of stone Baryba heard the bell for Elijah's Day mass. In his sleep he heard some kind of singing, turned his petrified thoughts over and strained to understand.

But he only woke up when the singing had ended. He leapt up at once, wide awake. "That was priests holding prayers in the hall!" he thought.

He got dressed, his eyes still sleepy, his head not his own.

The priests had already gone. Chebotarikha was sitting alone in the hall on the cretonne sofa. Again she was in the silk dress, as stiff as bast, with her best lace pinned to her hair.

"Slept through Elijah's service of prayer, eh? Anfim Yegorych?"

Perhaps because it was true – he had overslept and it was already around midday – or perhaps because the hall smelt of incense, Baryba felt awkward somehow, out of sorts, not himself.

"Sit down, Anfim Yegorych, sit down. Let's have a chat."

She was silent for a while. Then she closed her eyes and made a face as though it wasn't actually a face but a yeast-dough-pastry pie. Her head to one side, and in a sweet voice:

"So, then, our sins are grievous. And praying won't see them forgiven. And in the next world, He, the Father, will remember everything, He, the Father, will smoke out all the folly in a sulphurous Hyena."*

Baryba was silent. "And where's all this leading?" he thought. Suddenly Chebotarikha stretched her eyes wide open and, spluttering saliva, shouted:

"Why do you stay silent, you scoundrel, you, as if your mouth's full of water? Do you think I know nothing about your fooling around with Polka? Do you think nothing of deflowering the girl, you lecherous scoundrel, you?"

Baryba, dumbstruck, shifted his jaws in silence and thought:

"They slaughtered a sucking-pig yesterday, didn't they – I dare say that was for today's dinner."

Baryba's silence had Chebotarikha boiling right over. She began stamping her feet as she sat.

"Out, out of my house! Snake in the grass! I warmed him on my breast, the louse, and this is what he gives me! That's me for Polka, is it, eh?"

Not understanding, powerless to stir his soused thoughts, Baryba sat in silence like a dead man. He gazed at Chebotarikha.

"Look at that, the way she's spluttering and spluttering, eh?" he thought.

He pulled himself together when Urvanka came into the hall and said to him with a cheery smile:

"Well, that's it, son, that's it. Off you go, now. There's nothing of yours here, son."

And he slammed Baryba's cap onto his head from behind.

*   *   *

The sun was baking hot before the Elijah's Day storm. They were waiting – the sparrows, the trees, the stones. They were parched, languishing.

Baryba staggered about the town like a mad thing, sitting down on all the benches along Dvoryanskaya Street.

"What's next now, eh? What now? Where do I go?"

He shook his head but was still quite unable to shake off the Balkashins' yard, the manger, the hungry dogs fighting over a bone.

Then he wandered down some backstreets, over green grass. A water cart was driving past; the iron tyre had slipped off one of the wheels and was jangling. Baryba sensed he really did feel thirsty. He asked, and drank his fill.

A storm cloud had already come down from the north, from the monastery, and broken the sky into two halves: light blue and cheerful, dark blue and frightful. The dark blue kept on growing, swelling.

Somehow, unaware of what he was doing, Baryba found himself in a porch. In the entrance to Churilov's tavern. It was pouring with rain; crowded together in the entrance were some women with their skirts pulled up over their heads; Elijah was rumbling. Well, what did it matter – go ahead, thunder, pour!

It turned out quite naturally somehow that Baryba went to spend the night at Timosha's. And Timosha wasn't even one tiny little bit surprised, as if Baryba came to spend the night with him every day.

10
DUSK IN THE CELL

Four o'clock in the summer is the deadest time in our parts. No good people will even so much as poke their nose outside: the scorching heat's unbearable. The shutters are all closed, and you sleep sweetly with a full belly after dinner. Only little grey swirls of dust dance like noonday demons along the empty streets. The postman will go up to some gate or other and he knocks and knocks. No, don't be angry: they're not going to open it.

At this time, unattached and idle, Baryba's plodding along. As though he doesn't know himself where to. But his feet are carrying him to the monastery. Wherever else? From Timosha to Yevsei in the monastery, from Yevsei to Timosha.

The crenellated wall, overgrown with moss. A sentry box like a kennel by the iron-bound gates. And out of the box, making faces and carrying a tin mug, comes Arsentyushka the simpleton – he's got St Vitus's dance – the gatekeeper and persistent collector of donations.

"Would you believe it, badgering me, the pest!"

Baryba handed him two silver kopeks and walked over the burning-hot paving, past the graves of the eminent men of the town behind their gilded railings. Eminent people liked being buried here: it's flattering for any man to lie in a monastery and for the heavenly host to be praying for him day and night.

Baryba knocked at Yevsei's cell. No one answered. He opened the door.

At the table, without their under-cassocks, in nothing but white long johns and shirts, sat two men: Yevsei and Innokenty.

Yevsei hissed at Baryba furiously: sh-sh-sh! And returned to staring, unblinking, swollen, glassy-eyed, at his glass of tea. And Innokenty – a milksop, a woman with whiskers – was frozen over his own glass.

Baryba stopped by the doorpost, looked and looked: what was wrong with them? Gone half-witted, had they?

Standing by the other doorpost was Savka, a novice: lank, greasy straight hair and big red lobster-like hands.

Savka turned away and gave a respectful snort:

"Khm! The thing is, any minute now a fly may settle in Father Yevsei's glass. Can't you see?"

Not understanding a thing, Baryba gawked.

"Isn't it clear? This is their most favoured game right now. They'll bet five kopeks, ten kopeks – and then they wait and wait. The first Father a fly ends up in the glass of – so he's the one who's won."

Savka's keen to have a natter with a man from the outside world. He talks, all the while shielding his mouth with his huge red hand out of respect.

"Look, look, Father Yevsei…"

Yevsei, purple and swollen, had bent towards his glass, his mouth grinning ever more broadly – and suddenly he banged down his hand and slapped his knee:

"Ye-es! There she is, the sweetheart! The five kopeks are mine!" And he fished the fly out of his glass with a finger. "Well, lad, you almost did me a bad turn there. You almost frightened the dear old fly, you know."

He went up closer to Baryba, stared at him with his glassy eyes and started babbling:

"We didn't even expect to be seeing you, lad. Heard you'd become a completely bad egg. Thought the woman was going to ride you to death. I mean, that Chebotarikha, she's a woman who, my word, can't get enough!"

He sat Baryba down to have tea, and he himself drained the glass from which he'd fished the dear old fly. And what sort of meeting is it without moonshine? Yevsei put a half-bottle out on the table too.

Savka brought a second samovar. On the table there were copper coins, a psalter, pretzels, glasses with chipped stems.

After the vodka Innokenty got upset about something – his eyes were sleepy and he kept putting his head on the table, propping it up with his fist. He suddenly started plaintively singing 'O gladsome light'.* Yevsei and Savka joined in. Savka sang bass, turning aside to clear his throat and covering his mouth with a big red hand. Baryba thought: "Oh, it's all the same!" and he too began howling along woefully.

Suddenly Yevsei broke off and yelled:

"Sto-op! Stop, I tell you!"

But Savka carried on singing. Yevsei threw himself at him, grabbed him by the throat and pressed him up against the back of his chair, crazy, a savage. He was going to strangle him.

Innokenty got up, stooping, and with the little steps of an old woman he went up behind Yevsei and tickled his armpits.

Yevsei began chuckling, gurgling, waving his arms about like a drunken windmill, and he let go of Savka. Then he sat down on the floor and started singing:

> On the mountain stands a cripple,
> Used his thing to kill some people...*

They all joined in heartily singing 'O gladsome light', as before.

* * *

Everything grew dark, merged and started swaying in the drunken cell. They didn't light a light. Innokenty whined and, mumbling, kept pestering them all – an old woman with whiskers and a grey beard. He'd got it into his head that he'd choked on something. He kept on and on about it being stuck there in his throat. He poked and poked about with his finger, but it didn't help.

"Come on, will you have a go, Savushka, my dear, with your finger? Maybe you can feel something."

Savushka reached in, wiping his finger afterwards on the skirt of his inner robe.

"There's nothing there, Your Reverence. It's the drunken demon tempting you."

Yevsei curled up on the bed and lay there for a long time, without so much as a peep. Then he suddenly leapt up and gave his shaggy locks a shake.

"I reckon, boys, it's time we hopped over to Streltsy now. To celebrate meeting. Baryba, lad, what about you? We could do with getting hold of some lolly from somewhere, though. Maybe from the cellarer? What about it, Savka, eh?"

Invisible by the door, Savka laughed like a horse. Baryba thought: "Well, I suppose it'll take my mind off things. Be good to forget about everything."

"If you pay it back tomorrow... I've got a little bit of money, the last of it," he said to Yevsei.

Yevsei promptly perked up, shook his head like a cheerful dog, his glassy eyes agoggle.

"Before the True Christ, I'll pay it back tomorrow – I mean, I've got it, only it's well hidden away."

The four of them walked past the graves. A half-dead moon twinkled from behind a cloud. Innokenty caught his inner robe on some railings, panicked, started crossing himself and turned back. Three of them clambered through the wall over some bricks specially knocked out to allow passage.

II
THE BROKAR POT*

And here's a heavily hot, somnolent afternoon again. The white paving on the monastery path. The avenue of lime trees, the buzzing of bees.

In front is Yevsei in a black cowl with his unruly hair greased down: it's his turn to celebrate vespers today. And behind is Baryba. He's walking along, on the point of once again opening up his four-cornered smile, like a gate.

"You look really odd in that cowl, Yevsei, and unfitting. You should wear a peasant's tall cap or a Cossack hat – that'd be a lot more fitting."

"The thing is, I wanted to go to military school, lad, but got on the booze by mistake. And that's how I ended up in a monastery."

Oh, Yevsei! What a red-faced, purple-nosed Cossack captain you'd have made. Or a parish clerk, a drunkard, a good mate of the peasants. But look at you now, by God's will...

"Yevsei, the way you danced to that dance tune in Streltsy yesterday, eh?

> Took the monastery's vow.
> Bought up samovars – and how!"

Yevsei started grinning, was about to start twitching his shoulders. But no, there was no way he could do it, not in this woman's costume. This is how it had been yesterday: he'd been wearing a rope as a belt around his shirt, like a peasant, just below his armpits, thick white linen trousers with blue stripes, his red spade beard, his eyes on the point of popping out, a real village wood demon, and a nimble dancer. The Streltsy girls had roared with laughter to their hearts' content.

They arrived. Baryba stood for a minute by the old church doors. Yevsei came out and beckoned with his finger.

"Well, come on, lad, come on. There's no one here. The sexton – even he's gone off somewhere."

The low, old, wise church – in the name of the ancient Elijah. It had seen much in its time: it had defended itself against the Tatars, and the boyar Feodor Romanov – in monastic life Filaret* – had held a service in it, they said, when passing. Old lime trees look in through the barred windows.

Even here, Yevsei, the Cossack captain in a cowl, is muttering, making a noise, won't stop. The old, thin, big-eyed saints on the walls cower away from the loud, bearded, arm-waving Yevsei.

Yevsei knelt down and fumbled about under the altar.

"Here it is," he said, and brought out into the light a dusty pot for Brokar pomade. He opened it and, licking his fingers, riffled through some twenty-five-rouble notes.

Baryba started turning his flat-iron over uneasily. "Look at that, the devil! A dozen, or maybe even more. And what use are they to him?"

Yevsei set one note aside.

"And the rest of them – either I'll leave them for my soul to be remembered in prayers, or else, you know, someday I'll take them all and give them to the Streltsy girls for them to have a drink."

The white paving of the monastery path. The bees are humming in the old lime trees. The heavy heat makes a hungover head spin. "And what use are they to him?" thinks Baryba.

12
THE OLD MONK

Beside the Elijah church, on a stone bench, warm from the sunshine, sits an old, old monk. His cassock has faded and turned green, there's a greenish tinge to his grey beard, and his hands and face are covered in moss. He's been lying somewhere, like treasure, under an old oak tree; he's been dug up, brought here and sat down in the sun to get warm.

"How old are you, then, Granddad?" asks Baryba.

"Oh, I've forgotten, my dear. But I remember that Tikhon of yours, of Zadonsk.* He conducted a good, devout service, the father."

Baryba keeps hovering around the green monk, trying to get in with him. Oh, and not without reason!

"Let's go inside the church, Granddad – I'll help you with the sweeping."

And they move about beneath the cool, dark vaults. The monk lovingly tidies his old church and whispers with the saints. He'll light a candle and stand feasting his eyes, glimmering in front of it.

"If I blow, the candle'll go out and so will the monk," thinks Baryba.

He follows the monk around: he'll hand him one thing, hold another. The monk takes a liking to Baryba. People today have no respect – they've all forgotten the old man and there's no one to exchange a word with. But this one…

"I dare say it's scary alone at night in the church, isn't it, Granddad?"

"Oh, good Lord, what do you mean – with my very own church, scary?"

"Granddad, can I spend the night here with you?"

The monk speaks sternly from his deep hollow:

"For forty years I've been spending the night with it one to one. And no one else besides is allowed to spend the night in it. You never know what might go on in the church at night…"

Take care of it, take care, zealous one! It's true, who knows what might go on in the old night-time church?

"All right, I'll wait," thinks Baryba, and follows him around.

During the night service on the eve of Tikhon of Zadonsk's holiday, the old monk got so tired. The people were countless. And afterwards he and Baryba were tidying and tidying, and they had a real job finishing.

The monk examined all the doors, checked all the rusty locks and sat down for a short moment to have a rest. Sat down – and went out, the ancient, fell asleep. Baryba waited, gave a cough. He went up and touched the monk's sleeve – he's asleep. He's quickly off into the altar-space and come on – get fumbling underneath the altar. He fumbled and fumbled and found it.

The old monk's sound asleep – he's already learning to sleep a deathly sleep. The old monk heard nothing.

13
APROSYA'S HUT

Dvoryanskaya Street's coming to an end, the last run-down stalls and lamp-posts. And then it's the Streltsy pond, old willow bushes growing thickly all around, the slimy, moss-covered jetty, women bending down and banging their battledores, ducklings diving.

Neighbouring the pond, right next to it on the Streltsy side, is Aprosya's hut. It's not so bad, warm and dry. A thatched roof, cut like a peasant's hair, windows made of fragments of glass, covered in bloom. And what more do Aprosya and her boy need, the two of them? She's leased out her two-person plot of land, and then, who knows, her husband may send a little present for the holiday – three roubles, a fiver. And a letter.

And again a loving low bow to my dearest wife Aprosinya Petrovna... And I inform you too that we have again been given a rise of three roubles a year. And Ilyusha and I have again decided to stay on as re-enlisted men...*

Aprosya pined to begin with, of course – she was young – but then her husband, as a re-enlisted soldier, faded away and was forgotten. She pictured him as if he were a stamp on a letter, or a seal: *his* stamp, like, *his* seal. But nothing more. And so Aprosya did without, became weather-beaten, dug in her kitchen garden, made clothes for her boy, did other people's bits of washing.

And it was from her, from this Aprosya, that Baryba rented a room. He liked it at once: homely, clean. They agreed on four and a half roubles.

Aprosya was pleased: a respectable tenant, not some ne'er-do-well, and he evidently had money. And not particularly standoffish or proud: sometimes he'd have a talk. She now had two to look after: her boy and Baryba. All day on her feet – weather-beaten, demure, golden-yellow, strong-breasted: a pleasure to look at.

It was quiet, bright, clean. Baryba was having a rest from his old life. He slept without dreams, he had money: what else did he need besides? He ate without hurrying, solidly, a lot at a time.

"Well, all right, I must suit him, then," thought Aprosya.

Baryba bought a lot of books. Just popular ones, cheap stuff, but really entertaining. *Tyapka, the Brigand of Lebedyan*, *The Criminal Monk and His Treasures*, *The Spanish Queen's Coachman*.* Baryba lay around, cracking sunflower seeds and reading. He wasn't drawn anywhere: he felt sort of awkward before Chernobylnikov the postman and the Treasurer's son-in-law: they'd probably found everything out by now. And he didn't even want to look at women; the dregs still hadn't settled after Chebotarikha.

He went walking in the fields – they were reaping there. The gold cloth of the evening in the sky, the gold of the rye obediently falling, the sweat-soaked red shirts, the ringing of the scythes. And now they've stopped and gone to jugs of *kvas*; they drink and there are drops on their moustaches. Oh, how they've enjoyed their work!

It seemed to Baryba he'd like to do that. His strong hands were itching, his chewing muscles were clenching... But what about the Treasurer's son-in-law? What if he saw?

"I ask you, what an idea, becoming a peasant! Maybe take hides to Chebotarikha's tannery too? The very thing..." Baryba grumbled at himself angrily.

Whichever way you look at it, he needs to think of something: you can't survive like this on Yevsei's money, doing nothing – it's not thousands and thousands.

Baryba racked and racked his brains and dashed off an application to the Treasury: perhaps they'd take him on as a clerk, an assistant to the Treasurer's son-in-law. Then he'd have a cap with a cockade – just look at me then!

By evening it was unbearably stuffy. All the same, Baryba struggled into his velvet waistcoat (a remnant of his comfortable life with Chebotarikha), a cotton collar and his "Sunday best" trousers, and went out onto Dvoryanskaya Street: where was the Treasurer's son-in-law to be found, if not there?

He's here, of course. The long-legged, skinny loafer's walking around giving everyone sour looks and swinging his walking stick. He just longs to say: "Who are you? Well, I'm an official, you see – a cap with a cockade."

He slipped Baryba a sour smile:

"Oh, it's you! An application? Hm-m."

He perked up, hitched up his trousers, adjusted his collar. Felt himself to be the affable boss.

"Well, all right, I'll pass it on. I'll do what I can. But of course, of course, old acquaintances."

Baryba walked home and thought:

"Ooh, I'd like to smash your ugly, sour mug in. What can you say, though – behaves in an educated way. And what about the collar? Real linen, no less, and apparently a new one every time."

14
THE MERRY WINE WAS LEAKING OUT

Mitrofan the cellarer sniffed and wormed everything out, the dog, regarding Yevsei's outing to Streltsy. It's possible, of course, that Yevsei himself spread the word, bragging. But the cellarer knew everything, down to the last detail: how Yevsei had cavorted, wearing just his shirt, belted under the armpits, and that song, 'Took the monastery's vow', and the merry ride in a cab around Streltsy. The cellarer told the hegumen, of course. The hegumen summoned Yevsei and gave him such a wigging that Yevsei flew out as if from the top shelf in the bathhouse.

Yevsei was ordered to work for the baker as penance. He didn't conduct any services. The baker's cellar is as hot as hell. The chief devil – red, hairy Silanty – yells at the kneaders while himself whisking thirty-pound loaves into the oven on a peel. The kneaders, wearing just their white shirts and with their hair tied up with string, turn the dough, grunting, and work themselves into the ground.

But on the other hand, Yevsei slept as he hadn't done in ages. And his glassy eyes seemed to get a bit better. There was no time even to think about a half-bottle.

This was all very well, but the penance came to an end. The old life kicked off again. Yevsei began conducting services, chanting prayers. Again Savka, the novice, thrusts himself upon him with his great lobster-like hands, and Innokenty, the woman with whiskers, whines.

Savka told a story about Innokenty:

"The other day, Father Innokenty went to the bathhouse. There was a deacon there, a merry one, one of the exiles. As soon as he saw Father Innokenty in his natural state, he shouts: 'Good Lord, but that's a woman – look, look, her breasts are sagging, she must be a mum.'"

Innokenty wrapped his cassock tighter around him.

"He's shameless, that deacon of yours. That's why such a thing occurs to him."

It was this deacon that did for Yevsei. The deacon had come from the outside world, so, understandably, he was bored, and that's why he'd roam around from one cell to another. One day he wandered into Yevsei's. Yevsei and Innokenty were sitting over their glasses, going mad playing "the fly" again – who'd be first to get a fly in their glass. The deacon saw this and died laughing, tumbling onto Yevsei's bed with his legs dangling, well I'll be (his legs are short, tiny, his eyes like cherries).

The deacon was in the mood for merriment – and off he went, off he went. He poured out all his anecdotes from the seminary, and was he a dab hand at it. Discreetly at first. But then off he went about a priest, one who'd sent penitents away to finish off their sinning: he'd fixed a penance of fifteen bows to be done in two goes – well, and the calculation had been impossible, it had always come out as a fraction. And about a nun who'd been chased and caught in a wood by a whole group of five tramps, and afterwards she'd say: "That was good, all I wanted and without sinning too."

Well, in a word, he had everyone rolling around. Yevsei choked with laughter and banged his fist on the table.

"Good stuff, deacon! You've really given us a good time. I'll clearly have to stand you a drink. Will you wait, Fathers, eh? I'll just be a second."

"Where's the wind taking you?" asked the deacon.

"To get some money. I've got it tucked away, brother, imperishable. Here, nearby. Be back in the blink of an eye…"

And indeed – the deacon hadn't even had time to finish a new story, and there Yevsei was. He came in and leant against the doorpost.

"Come on, moneybags, come on, show us!" the deacon cried merrily and went over to Yevsei. Went over – and went numb: it was Yevsei, yet not Yevsei. He'd sagged, gone limp, completely drained somehow: something sharp had made a hole in his side and all the merry wine had leaked out, leaving an empty wineskin.

"What is it you're so quiet about? Has something happened?"

"Stolen," said Yevsei in a quiet voice not his own, and he threw the last two banknotes down onto the table: the thief had left them for the fun of it...

Even before this, to tell the truth, Yevsei had been soft in the head, but now he lost the last of his marbles. He spent the remaining twenty-five-rouble notes on drink. He wandered around the town drunk, scrounging five-kopek coins for a hair of the dog. A policeman took him in to the station for merry behaviour in the street – he smashed the policeman's nose in completely and bolted to the monastery.

In the morning, his friends and acquaintances came to see him: Savka the novice, Father Innokenty and the little deacon. They started remonstrating with him: pull yourself together, what are you doing, if the hegumen turns you out of the monastery, going to go begging, are you?

Yevsei lay on his back and stayed silent. Then he suddenly started snivelling, had the slobber running all down his beard:

"What am I to do, brothers? It's not the money – I'm not sorry about the money. It's just that before, if I wanted, I could leave the monastery that same day. But now, like it or not... I used to be a free man, but now..."

"And who could it have been that swindled you?" said the deacon, bending down to Yevsei.

"I didn't know, but I do now. Not one of us – an outsider. And he seemed to be all right, the lad, but then... Him, there's no one else. No one, apart from him, knew where my money was."

Savka laughed like a horse, as if to say: ah, I know!

In the evening, by the light of a candle, at an empty table – there was no desire even to get the samovar going – they tried to thrash out what to do. They came up with nothing.

15
AT IVANIKHA'S

In the morning after mass Innokenty dropped in. He brought a communion roll for good health. He began whispering:

"I know now, Father Yevsei. It's come to me. Let's go to Ivanikha's, quickly. Ooh, she's well known, she'll put a spell on the thief – he'll show up in a trice."

A dewy, pink morning; the day's going to be a hot one. The sparrows are having a holiday.

"Why've you got me up at this unearthly hour?" grumbled Yevsei. Innokenty was taking his little steps, like a woman's, holding on to his cassock over his stomach.

"No other way, Father Yevsei. Or don't you know – a spell only takes effect on an empty stomach?"

"You always seem to be talking nonsense, Innokenty. We're just going to no purpose. And it's shameful for clerics."

Ivanikha's a really tall old woman, a beanpole, big-boned, with thick eyebrows, eyebrows like an owl's. She didn't greet the monks especially warmly.

"What do you want? Here for some love spell, are you? Or with a prayer service? Well, I don't need your prayers."

And she made herself busy, clattering about with the pots at the back of the stove.

"No, no, we've come to you about… Father Yevsei's been robbed. Can you put a spell on the thief? We've heard…"

Father Innokenty was a bit scared of Ivanikha. He'd have liked to cross himself, but probably shouldn't in front of her: this here was an evil spirit – frighten it off and the whole thing would come to nothing. As a woman does her winter fur jacket, so Innokenty wrapped his cassock around his chest.

42

Ivanikha threw a glance down on him, lashed him with her owl's eyes:

"So what have *you* got to do with it? *He's* been robbed – he and I need to be left alone."

"Well, Mother, I suppose, I…"

He gathered up the skirts of his cassock and, bent over, minced off with his little steps like a woman's.

"What's the name?" Ivanikha asked Yevsei.

"Yevsei."

"I know it's Yevsei. Not you, but the one you suspect – what's *his* name?"

"Anfimka, Anfim."

"How do you want the spell cast? On the wind? Or else on an apron's good, too, if it's spread out over birch branches. Or maybe on water. And then he gets invited, the little darling, and given tea that's been made with that same water."

"That's good, give him tea, eh? That'd be clever, Mother, eh?"

Yevsei brightened up, began nattering, had started believing: the old woman Ivanikha was really very impressive and stern.

Ivanikha scooped up some water with a hollowed-out wooden dipper, opened the door into the lobby, stood Yevsei on the other side of the threshold and took up her own place on the threshold. She thrust the dipper into Yevsei's hands.

"Hold this and listen. And look out, not a word to anyone, or else everything will turn back on you yourself."

She started slowly, persuasively reciting the following, and fixed her owl's eyes firmly on the water in the dipper:

"On the sea – on Kiyan, on the island of Buyan, stands a huge iron chest. In that chest lies a huge Damascus steel knife. Run, knife, to Anfim the thief – stab him in the very heart so that he, the thief, returns what was stolen from God's servant Yevsei and conceals not a single thing. And if he does conceal anything, let him, the thief, be run through by my word, as by the Damascus steel knife, let him, the thief, be damned to the underworld, to the mountains of Ararat, to boiling pitch, to burning cinders, to marsh mire, to a homeless home, to a bathhouse pitcher. If he does conceal anything, let him, the thief, be pinned with an aspen stake to a doorpost, withered worse than grass, chilled worse than ice, and may it be for him to meet with a violent end as well.

"That's enough now," said Ivanikha. "Give him the water to drink, the little darling, give him the water."

Yevsei poured the water carefully into a bottle, gave Ivanikha a silver rouble and set off, contented:

"I'll give you some tea, dearie. I'll loosen your tongue!"

16
NOTHING WILL GET THROUGH

In the night, out of the blue, Baryba was struck by a fever. He shook, curled up, and unnatural dreams wound around him.

In the morning, he sat at the table in a kind of fog and propped his thirty-pound head up on his hands.

There was a knock at the door.

"Aprosya?"

But he couldn't turn his head, it was so heavy. There was a cough from a bass voice by the door.

"Savka, is that you?"

The man himself: lank hair, big red lobster-like hands.

"You're invited – you must come. He really misses you, does Father Yevsei."

Then he went up closer and guffawed:

"He wants to give you tea that's had a spell put on it. But don't you drink it, not on your life."

"What spell?"

"Well, that's obvious, what spell: to catch a thief."

"Aha!" Baryba twigged.

He found it very funny. The idiot, Yevsei! His head was in a fog and pounding; there was something amusing wriggling around.

In Yevsei's cell there's a purple haze and cigarette fumes: the merry deacon's filled it with smoke.

"Ah, dear guests!"

And, waggling his bottom, the deacon offered Baryba his arm, crooked at the elbow.

There was no vodka on the table: they'd deliberately decided not to drink so as to keep their heads clear and catch Baryba out.

"How is it you've got so thin, Yevsei? Has someone put a love spell on you?" Baryba smirked.

"You'd get thin too. Haven't you heard anything?"

"Had your lolly nicked? Of course I've heard."

Merry, waspish, the deacon bounced up:

"And how did you find out, Anfim Barybych?"

"Well – Savka said. That's how I found out."

"You're an idiot, Savka," said Yevsei, turning round despondently.

They sat down to have tea. One glass, half filled, was standing on the tray separately, to one side. Innokenty hurriedly filled the glass with boiling water and handed it to Baryba.

Everyone stared and waited: well, any minute now…

Baryba stirred it and took a leisurely sip. They were silent, watching. Baryba grew amused, unbearably so, and he started chuckling – rumbling over stones. Savka laughed like a horse behind him, and the deacon let out a thin peal of laughter.

"What is it?" Yevsei looked; his eyes were fish-like, popping out.

Baryba was rumbling, rolling downhill, and couldn't stop now – there was a pounding and a green fog in his head. A giggly mood was gripping him, pushing him to say: I'm your man. It was me that stole it.

Baryba finished his drink but remained silent and smiled four-corneredly, like a beast. Yevsei couldn't sit still.

"Well, tell us, then, Baryba. Why not?"

"Tell you what?"

"You know very well what."

"Shark, shark, why the fumbling in the dark? Tell you about the money, eh? Well, I'm telling you: Savka told me. And that's all I know."

Baryba spoke in a deliberate voice, as if to say: I'm lying, but just try catching me.

The deacon bounced up to Baryba and slapped him on the shoulder:

"No, brother, there's no magic potion going to get through to you. You're strong, cast-iron."

Yevsei began shaking his long locks:

"Oh, it's hopeless! Run and get some wine, Savka."

They drank. There was a fog and a pounding in their heads. The smoke from the baccy was green. The deacon did a sailor's dance.

* * *

Baryba went back home in the dusk. And right by Aprosya's gate he suddenly felt his knees buckling; his eyes had clouded over. He leant against the doorpost, got scared: he'd never experienced such a thing.

Aprosya opened the door and looked at her lodger:

"You're a terrible sight – what is it? Unwell, are you?"

As though in a dream, he found himself on his bed. A lamp, Aprosya by the bedhead. On his forehead a wet cloth soaked in vinegar.

"My poor dear thing," said Aprosya cosily and pitifully, rather through her nose.

Aprosya ran to the neighbours and got hold of some medicinal powder for Baryba. In the night, his head would get hazy then clear again, and Baryba would see Aprosya dozing on a chair by his bedhead.

On the third day, towards morning, it had passed. Baryba lay under a white sheet with grey, autumnal shadows on his face.

He'd become transparent, somehow, become human. "And it's true," he thought, "I'm a stranger to her, aren't I, yet she sat through the night, didn't sleep..."

"Thank you, Aprosya."

"It's nothing, my poor, dear little thing. You must be ill, after all."

And she leant towards him. She was wearing only a stripy coarse cotton skirt and a linen chemise, and there was a glimpse, right in front of Baryba's eyes, of two sharp, pricking points on her breast under the thin linen.

Baryba closed his eyes – and opened them again. In through the windows looks a burning summer's day. The Streltsy pond is sparkling out there somewhere, people are bathing, there's a white body...

An even hotter pounding began in his head. Baryba started restlessly moving his heavy jaws and drew Aprosya towards him.

"What's this?" she said in surprise. "But might it not be bad for you? We-ell, hang on, it's time to change your cloth."

She calmly changed the cloth and carefully, like a good house-wife, lay down on the bed next to Baryba.

* * *

And that became the way of things. Aprosya, the Streltsy soldier's wife, is bustling about, keeping house, clattering her pots the whole day. There's her boy, and now there's Baryba too – look after him as well. He may have got over his illness quick, but all the same, coping alone isn't easy.

Anfim Yegorych will get back from somewhere in the evening and look in on Aprosya:

"Come later on this evening."

"Come, you say? All right. You've put me off my stroke now. And there was something I had to do – it's gone right out of my head. Yes, that's it, get all the eggs out from under the hens: that darned ferret'll suck them dry again."

She'd run to the hen house. Then get the samovar going. Alone in his room, Baryba had tea and leafed through some book or other. "And he keeps reading, and he keeps reading – it won't be long before he ruins his eyes like this." She'd put her boy to bed. Sit down on the bench and buzz away with her spindle, spinning grey woollen thread for winter stockings. A fat, black cockroach would fall with a plop from above, from the ceiling. "Well, it must

47

be late, it's time." She'd scratch her head with the blunt end of the spindle, yawn, make the sign of the cross at her mouth. Diligently, spitting on the brush, she'd clean Anfim Yegorych's boots, get undressed, folding everything neatly on the bench in the corner, and take the boots to Baryba.

Baryba was waiting. Aprosya put the boots down by the bed and got in.

She'd leave half an hour later. Have a bit of a yawn. Make ten bows, say Our Father and fall fast asleep: she'd done a hard day's work, and there was still so much to do.

17
SEMYON SEMYONYCH BLINKIN

Baryba said to Timosha once:

"What sort of tailor are you, then? You don't even have any sewing here at home."

But why he didn't was very simple. This is what Timosha's like, isn't it: for a time he's all right, he's all right, and then he'll go on one hell of a bender. Well, and then that's the end of a customer's trousers: he'll be sure to drink them away. People knew this way of his and were wary of giving him anything to take home. And so he'd go to other houses to do his sewing. He made clothes for a lot of merchants and for people of quality too – he was good at tailoring, the scoundrel. Among other things, he was well in, it could be said, with the lawyer Semyon Semyonych Blinkin. This is what Blinkin called him:

"My court tailor."

Timosha rarely had his boots on: they were mostly in pawn. And he would go to Blinkin's in old rubber overshoes with white canvas shoes wrapped in paper under his arm. In the entrance hall he'd be sure to kick off his overshoes, put the white shoes on – and he's ready. And he and Blinkin would have unusual conversations: about God and the saints, about how everything in the world is semblance alone, and how you ought to live. Timosha thought of

48

Blinkin as a clever man. And that's what he was, Blinkin, Semyon Semyonych.

Blinkin – that's not his real name, by the way, but just a nick-name, apparently: it's what he was teased with on the street. And you only had to look at him and you'd say straight away: Blinkin – that's him.

Semyon Semyonych's face was gaunt, dark, kind of like on an icon. Huge great eyes, black as black. And perhaps either kind of astonished, or perhaps unashamed – but very much too big. The eyes were the only thing on his face. And he was constantly blinking them. Blink, blink – as if he was ashamed of his eyes.

But that's nothing, the eyes. It was the whole of him, Semyon Semyonych, that was somehow kind of winking. When he sets off down the street and begins limping on his left leg – well, he really is, the whole of him, winking his entire being.

And how the merchants loved him for his cunning!

"Semyon Semyonych Blinkin? Oh, he's a dab hand, a viper! That one, brother, will go far. He'll worm his way in and out of anything. Look, just look, the way he winks, eh?"

It became the way of things that he conducted all the merchants' dark cases: cases to do with debt or – best of all – insolvency. And one way or another he'd manage to weary the court to death and emerge successful. And in return he was paid well.

* * *

And it was to Blinkin that Timosha brought Baryba. It was high time too.

That autumn was a kind of wet one: the snow fell, and the snow melted away. And melting away with the snow went Baryba's Yevsei money. A reply came from the Treasury: they refused him, the devils, who knows why – what the hell more did they want? Well, so there was a need to find himself any sort of work that was available. People do, after all, want to eat.

Semyon Semyonych took Timosha aside and asked about Baryba:

"Who would this be, then?"

"This is – well, kind of my assistant: I sew and talk, and he listens. Without an assistant you're not going to talk, are you? Not to yourself."

Semyon Semyonych began rattling, laughing. "Well, that means he's in a good mood: things are going to go well," thought Timosha.

"And what did you do before?" Blinkin asked Baryba.

Baryba hesitated.

"He was the esteemed entertainer of a certain widow." Timosha helped him out, poking his needle into his sewing.

Blinkin began rattling again: there's a job, to be sure.

But Timosha continued unperturbed:

"Nothing so special. It's a matter of trade. Everything we do now, by virtue of the times, is a matter of trade – that's the only way we can live. A merchant sells herring, a girl sells her belly. Each to his own. And what makes a belly, say, worse than a herring, or a herring worse than a conscience? They're all goods."

Blinkin grew very cheerful, winked, rattled, slapped Timosha on the shoulder. Then he suddenly grew serious, became like an icon, stern, about to swallow you with his eyes.

"So, then, you want to earn some money?" he asked Baryba. "There's work to be done. I need witnesses. You look impressive – you'd appear to do."

18
AS A WITNESS

And so it was that Baryba started acting as a witness for Blinkin. Not a complicated business. The evening before, Blinkin would prime Baryba: mind you don't forget this – Vasily Kuryakov, the merchant's son, this fat fellow, he was only the first to raise his hand. But the first one to strike was the lower-class townsman, the red-haired one, yes, yes, red-haired. And you, you'll say, were by the garden fence and saw everything with your own eyes.

And in the morning, Baryba was standing at the magistrate's, sleek, respectable, occasionally smirking: this was all really very strange. He told his story accurately, as Blinkin had coached him. Vasily Kuryakov, the merchant's son, prevailed; the lower-class townsman was put in the slammer. And Baryba got a three-rouble note or a fiver.

Semyon Semyonych had nothing but praise for Baryba.

"You're really solid, brother, and determined, tough, too. You can't be put off your stride. I'll soon start using you for criminal cases."

And he started taking Baryba with him to the neighbouring town where there was a courthouse. He bought Baryba a long-skirted frock coat, like a merchant wears. In this frock coat Baryba spent hours knocking about in the corridors of the courthouse, yawning and idly awaiting his turn. He gave evidence in a calm and businesslike way, and never got muddled. The prosecuting or defence counsel might try to get him flustered, but no chance: he'd dig his heels in and couldn't be budged.

There was one particular will on which Baryba earned well. The merchant Igumnov had died. He was a reputable man, a family man; there was a wife, a girl. He was in the fish trade, and everyone in the town knew him because we're very strict about observing fasts. This Igumnov's hands were all absolutely covered in warts. They said it was because of the fish: he'd pricked himself, they said, on fishes' fins.

Igumnov had lived, thank God, like everyone else. But in his old age something had happened to him: there's no fool like an old fool. His daughter's teacher – well, simply, the governess – had wound him round her finger. He'd turned his wife and the girl out of the house. Horses, wine, guests, lashings of drink.

Only on the point of dying had the old man come to his senses. He'd summoned his wife and daughter, asked for forgiveness and written a will in their favour. But his first will had remained with Madame, with this governess, and in that will everything had been left to her. Well, and so a case started. Now, of course, Semyon Semyonych had his arm twisted:

"Semyon Semyonych, my dear man. It's essential to prove he wasn't in his right mind when writing the second will. To produce witnesses. Money will be no object."

Semyon Semyonych and Baryba mulled it over. Baryba dug deep in his memory and remembered: he'd seen the late Igumnov once – he'd run out of the bathhouse in the winter and rolled around in the snow. The most ordinary thing for us to do. But it was presented in such a manner that he'd been running around the streets in winter the worse for wear. And they found some more witnesses: well, a lot of people really had seen it.

And when Baryba was giving this evidence in court, he set everything out so accurately and weightily, as if he were laying a stone foundation, that he even believed it himself. And he didn't bat an eyelid when Igumnov's widow, looking like a nun in a black headscarf, gave him a hard stare. And after the proceedings, Madame made eyes at him:

"You really are my benefactor."

She let him kiss her hand and said: "Come and see me sometime." Baryba was delighted.

19
THE TIMES

"No, no, it won't come to us," said Timosha mournfully. "No chance of that. We're living like we're in Kitezh-grad* at the bottom of a lake: not a single thing can be heard here, the water above us is cloudy and sleepy. But at the surface everything's ablaze, they're sounding the alarm."

Well, let them. This is what they'd say on that account here:

"Just let them go mad out there in their Babylons. For us it's all about having a peaceful life."

And indeed: if you read the newspapers, people are going mad. Think how many centuries we've lived through, fearing God, revering the tsar. But now it's as if the dogs have broken loose, so help me. And just where have such warriors sprung up from, from among the fat and slimy?

Well, we here have no time to spend on these various trifles: as long as we can feed the kids – after all, everyone has no end of kids. Out of boredom, is it? Who knows why, but people here are dreadfully fruitful. And for that reason, domesticated, devout, steady. Gates with iron locks, guard dogs running around in yards on chains attached to ropes. Before letting an outsider into the house, they'll ask three or four times from behind the door who they are and what they want. Everyone's windows have lots of geraniums and rubber plants standing in them. That way you can be more certain no one's going to look in from outside. People here like warmth: they overheat their stoves, go around in winter wearing quilted waistcoats and skirts, cotton-padded trousers – you won't find trousers like that anywhere else. And so that's how they live, in a fair to middling way, stewing like manure in the warmth. And it's for the best: look what chubby little kids they rear.

Timosha and Baryba came to see Blinkin. Blinkin's sitting with a newspaper.

"So, a minister's been bumped off* – had you heard or not?"

Timosha smiles – he's lit the cheerful icon lamp:

"We had – how could we have failed to? We're walking through the market, and I hear them talking: 'I even feel really sorry for him: I dare say he got twenty thousand or so a year, after all. Really sorry.'"

Blinkin positively shook with laughter:

"There they are, everyone here, our folk: twenty thousand or so... really sorry... Oh, I'm going to die laughing!"

They were quiet for a while, rustling the newspapers.

"And our Anyutka, the archpriest's girl, was arrested in Piter* too – see where education got her," Baryba remembered.

Blinkin immediately picked up on this and set about needling them – he knew what Timosha's understanding of women was: having anything to do with them in any serious matter was as good as stirring fruit jelly into cabbage soup.

"A woman as a guest is more or less all right – you can let her in. But into yourself – no, no." Timosha wags his dry finger. "Let her into yourself and you're done for. A woman, brother, she takes root like burdock. And they can't be got rid of, no way. And so you'll end up completely overgrown with burdock."

"Burdock." Baryba laughs and rattles.

And Blinkin bangs his fist and yells in an unnatural voice:

"You give it them, Timosha, give it them! Come on, prophesy some more, O King of the Jews!"

"What's he putting on an act for, what's he yelling for?" thought Baryba.

It's true, Semyon Semyonych enjoyed putting on a bit of an act. That's the sort of ungenuine man he was, a bluffer, always winking, looking out, harbouring a hidden grudge. And his eyes – either shameless or else anguished.

"Bring us some beer, beer, beer!" Semyon Semyonych yelled.

Clear-eyed Dashutka brought it on a tray – a fresh girl, like grass just after it's rained.

"Is she new?" said Timosha, without looking at Blinkin.

Blinkin changed them practically every month. Blonde, dark, skinny, buxom. And Blinkin was equally affectionate with all of them:

"Well, they're all the same. And you won't find the right one anyway."

Over the beer – what do you know? – Timosha started on about his favourite subject, to do with God, and began pressing Blinkin with tricky questions: if God can do anything and doesn't want to change our lives – then where's love? And how is it that the righteous are going to stay in heaven? And where's God going to put the minister's murderers?

Blinkin doesn't like talking about God. He's insolent, a sneerer, but now he'll quickly darken, like the Devil faced by incense.

"Don't you dare talk to me about God, don't you dare about God."

And he says it in a quiet sort of way, but it's horrible, listening. Timosha's pleased and laughs.

20

A MERRY EVENING SERVICE

During Lent, everybody goes around seething with anger and wrangling because of the lousy food: carp and *kvas*, *kvas* and potatoes. But when Easter arrives, everyone will at once get kinder: because of the fatty cuts, the fruit liqueurs, the flavoured vodkas, the ringing of bells. They'll get kinder: instead of one kopek they'll give a beggar two; they'll send a slice of the master's Easter cake to the cook in the kitchen; if Mishutka's spilt the liqueur onto a clean tablecloth, they won't give him a flogging on account of the holiday.

Understandably, things would come Chernobylnikov's way, too, when he was going from house to house handing out coloured postcards and offering the householders best wishes for the holiday. In some places they'd give him twenty-five kopeks, and in some even half a rouble. Chernobylnikov collected it up and took his friends to Churilov's tavern: Timosha, Baryba and the Treasurer's son-in-law.

As the spring's approached, Timosha's faded: he's going around looking pitiful; like a little sparrow in autumn, he staggers in the wind – and yet swaggers and puts on a brave face too, if you please.

"You ought to get some treatment, Timosha, honest to God," Chernobylnikov lamented. "Look at you now."

"Why get treatment? I'm going to die in any case. And as far as I'm concerned, it's a curious thing, dying. Of course it is: I've been moping around all my life in the trading quarter, been nowhere, and now – travel to unknown countries on a free ticket. That's pleasing, I'd say."

Timosha keeps right on laughing.

"You shouldn't be drinking like this, at least – I mean, it's bad for you."

No, you can say what you like. Following his old custom, he drinks beer with vodka, and doesn't lag behind. And he's always coughing into a red calico handkerchief: he's got himself a great big handkerchief – the size of a sack.

"This," he says, "is so as not to hawk on the floor in some public place."

The bells rang for the evening service. Old Churilov switched the silver coins from his right hand to his left and crossed himself, devoutly, gravely, like.

"Hey, Mitka, take the money!" cried Chernobylnikov.

The four of them left together. The spring sunshine's making merry, the bells are doing a dance. They're somehow reluctant to disperse, to break up the party.

"Oh, I love the Easter evening service," said Timosha, narrowing his eyes. "It's more a dance than a service. Let's all go together, eh?"

Baryba suggested going to the monastery, seeing as it was nearby.

"And after the service I'll take you to see a monk I know for tea – he's this odd fish."

The Treasurer's son-in-law took out his watch:

"I can't possibly, I promised to go to dinner, and it's not the thing to be late for the Treasurer."

"Oh dear, there's an injury: it's not the thing!" Timosha started laughing and coughing, and reached for his handkerchief: it's not there. "Wait, lads, I dropped my handkerchief upstairs. I'll run back quick."

He flapped his arms and took off, the little sparrow. The merry bells are ringing, people are dressed up and going to the merry Easter evening service.

"Hang on, there's some shouting upstairs… what's going on?" said Baryba, pricking up his big cauliflower ears.

The Treasurer's son-in-law pulled a face:

"Another fight, I expect. People don't know how to behave in a public place."

Cr-rash! A windowpane had been smashed up above and, with a jangling, down came the shards. And at once it went quiet.

"Oho," said Chernobylnikov, cocking an ear, "no, there's something here…"

And suddenly, head over heels, out tumbled Timosha, red, dishevelled, panting.

"Up there... they gave... the order. And everyone's... put their hands up and stood still..."

Cr-rack, cr-rack! came crackling from up above.

The Treasurer's son-in-law craned his long neck and stood for a second looking up with one eye, like a turkey at a vulture. Then he cried out in a shrill, piteous voice: "They're shoo-ooting!" And he took to his heels.

But from the staircase came the clattering of great boots and roaring, and everyone came pouring down from upstairs.

"Ee-ee-ee! Sto-op him..."

And again: *cr-rack, cr-rack.*

For a second: in the doorway, ahead of everyone – a red, eyeless face.

"He must have closed his eyes in fright," flashed the thought.

But he's already in the side street opposite, the eyeless one, already vanished. And out after him from upstairs poured everyone, as if drunk – wild, rowdy, fast-running.

"Sto-op him! Don't let him go! There, there he is!"

Downstairs by the porch they grabbed someone, fell on him, pinned him, thumped him – and all the same roared: "Sto-op him" – it's perfectly simple: they needed to pour everything out through their throats.

Lowering his head like a ram, Baryba fought his way forward. This had to be done for some reason – he sensed with all his being it had to; he clenched his iron jaws, and something ancient, bestial, long wished-for, predatory stirred. To be with everyone, to yell like everyone, to thump whoever everyone else was thumping.

On the ground, inside the circle, lay a little boy – black-haired, with his eyes shut. The collar of his shirt was ripped down the side; on his neck there was a black mole.

Old Churilov was standing in the middle of the circle and kicking the little boy in the ribs. His beard, so dignified, was all tangled now, his mouth twisted – where had all the prayerfulness gone?

"They've taken it! Oh, the devils! One's run off, run off with a hundred roubles! Oh, the devils!"

57

And he kicked him again. There were sweaty fists reaching towards the prostrate boy from behind Churilov's back, but they didn't dare: it was Churilov who'd been robbed, so he was in charge here and it was for him to do the beating.

Suddenly Timosha emerged from somewhere, right in front of old Churilov's nose; he leapt up, red and angry, and started haranguing him, bombarding him, waving his arms about:

"What are you doing, you old fart, you vicious heathen bastard? Do you want to kill the lad over a hundred roubles? Maybe you already have. Look, he's not breathing. Devils, animals, is a human being not worth so much as a hundred roubles, then?"

Old Churilov was taken aback at first, but then let fly:

"What, are you in it with them? Sticking up for them! You watch out, brother. You have some nice conversations in the tavern, too, people have heard. Grab him, Christian men!"

They were on the point of coming closer, but hesitated: after all, Timosha was supposed to be one of them, whereas these others weren't our folk. So the old man had probably got it wrong...

The red-faced, red-haired townsman, the horse trader, had struggled into cotton cuffs on account of the holiday. The cuffs had slid down in the mêlée; ginger hairs were sticking out between the sleeve and the white cloth, and his enormous hands were even more frightening.

The hands reached out towards Timosha and gently shoved him out of the circle. The red-haired townsman said:

"On your way, on your way, while you're still in one piece. We can manage without you and your sticking up for them."

And he started searching the black-haired boy in a businesslike way, turning him over like a carcass.

* * *

Going to the monastery was out of the question – did they feel like it now? Baryba sat at Timosha's the entire evening. Chernobylnikov came along a bit later. And he recounted:

"So, I'm walking along Dvoryanskaya Street… I hear them sitting on the bench by the gates telling tales: 'And helping them,' one says, 'was our Timosha the tailor – there's a lost soul.'"

"Idiots," said Timosha. "Gossipmongers. And Churilov, the evil devil, he got what he deserves. Will he be any the worse for losing the hundred? And maybe they hadn't eaten for two days?"

He paused, then added:

"Well, might it actually even come to us? And if it did, honest to God, I'd jump right into the whirlpool. If they bump me off – well, so be it, there's only a smidgeon of my life left anyway."

21
THE POLICE CHIEF'S TROUBLES

Well, as if there wasn't enough to worry about already. Hands up – we're at it too, this is happening here! And now Ivan Arefyich, the police chief, has no end of trouble.

A whole load of people, a military court, had come from the provincial capital – and all because of some little rascal of a boy. The President, a colonel, thin, with a short tuft of grey hair, suffered with his stomach. The grief Ivan Arefyich came to know with him! He can't eat this, he can't eat that – well, an utter disaster.

The first time the uninvited guests came, Ivan Arefyich organized a superb lunch: bottles on the table, unsealed cartons, hams, meat pie. But the colonel went all green with rage. He'd poke here and there with his fork and sniff:

"Seems very fatty."

And he'd get the hump and not eat. The police chief's wife, Marya Petrovna, was quite worn out with suffering:

"Oh, for mercy's sake, Colonel, whyever aren't you eating?" she said, while thinking: "My Ivan Arefyich will really catch it now, I expect."

The nice public prosecutor, on the other hand, was supportive. A plump little fellow, bald and pink, like a little piglet. He probably goes to the bathhouse a couple of times a week. And he's always in fits of laughter, chuckling away, and helps himself to two portions of everything.

"Come on, some more meat pie – goodness me. You know, it's only in such mouldy places as your trading quarter that people in Rus* nowadays know how to bake pies in the genuine, old-fashioned way…"

But in the evening in the police chief's study there are candles alight on the desk (never in your life have they been lit before) and documents laid out. Ivan Arefyich puffs on his Cannon cigarette* and waves the smoke away: God forbid the smoke should reach the colonel.

The colonel read through the documents and pulled a sour face: "Why on earth are we going to be messing about with this one boy? When you can't get a single word out of him. It's a terrible shame. It's what you're the Chief of Police for, to know how to detect."

* * *

Ivan Arefyich sat on the bed, pulling off his boots, and kept going on at his wife:

"I just can't get my head round it, Masha. Give them more, one's not enough. Where am I going to get him if he's run away? Yes, and don't forget this either: for twelve o'clock tomorrow, make the colonel some good oat porridge with milk, and get him a bottle of Narzan.* Oh, I'm scared of him and the harm he might do me, the bad-tempered thing!"

Marya Petrovna wrote it down:

"Oat porridge… Narzan… And what you should do, Ivan Arefyich, is you should get some advice from Blinkin. He's an old fox, he can get hold of anything you like – honest to God, give it a try."

Ivan Arefyich made a mental note of this and slept a little more peacefully.

* * *

On the square in front of the police station, in front of the peeling yellow walls is the market. Shafts up in the air and tied together, horses with bags of oats strapped to their faces, squeaky piglets, tubs of sour cabbage, carts loaded with hay. People are slapping hands, haggling, touting for custom in ringing tones; waggons are creaking; the sheriff's coachman in a jerkin is trying out an accordion.

But in the police chief's study an interrogation's under way. The colonel's in misery, paying careful attention to himself, to his insides: there's a muffled rumbling in his stomach. "Oh Lord, there's been nothing for a whole week, but now again, seemingly..."

In came old Churilov, dignified, long-skirted, his hair white as snow. He crossed himself:

"What happened? Well, it was like this, to give everything in order..."

He gave his account and wiped himself with a calico handkerchief. Stood and thought for a while: "It'd be good to put in a complaint against that cocky devil Timoshka – the authorities seem to be kind enough."

"There's this too, Your Honours, there's a tailor here, Timoshka – a lost soul, a cocky devil. He started standing up for this boy – the one that was shooting. And I says to him: 'You're one of them,' I says, 'are you?' And in front of them all, in front of the people, he..."

The old man was dismissed. The prosecutor rubbed his soft, sweaty little hands, undid the bottom button of his tunic and said quietly to the colonel:

"Hm. This Timosha... What do you think?"

Outside the window there was haggling, shouting, creaking. The colonel could bear it no longer:

"Ivan Arefyich, do close the window! I've got a splitting headache. What a way to go about things – a market right in front of the study!"

On tiptoe, Ivan Arefyich closed the window and called:

"Next!"

Languidly, with false modesty, the Treasurer's son-in-law gave his account. The prosecutor asked:

"Right, so he went back to the tavern, and then ran out again? Aha? Well, and the handkerchief? I think you mentioned something about a handkerchief. Did he go back for the handkerchief?"

The Treasurer's son-in-law remembered Timoshka's spit-spattered red handkerchief, pulled a sour face and said in irritation through his nose:

"What handkerchief? I don't remember any handkerchief."

It even felt somehow unseemly for him simply to be recalling that handkerchief.

Baryba followed the prosecutor's questions with his customary instinct. And when it came to the handkerchief he said with certainty:

"No, there was no handkerchief. He simply said: 'I've got something to do upstairs.'"

When Baryba had been dismissed, the prosecutor took a mouthful of cold tea and said to the colonel:

"Would you have me write a directive for the detention of this Timosha? It seems to me, all these testimonies... I know you're sometimes overly cautious, but here..."

There were cramps and something rising in the colonel's intestines, and he was thinking:

"The devil knows! That fat idiot, the police chief's wife – what is this provincial way of making everything fatty..."

"As I was saying, Colonel—"

"Oh, leave me alone, for God's sake! Write whatever you like. I've got a dreadful stomach-ache."

22
SIX TWENTY-FIVERS

When Timosha was arrested, no one was even surprised.

"He's been heading that way for ages."

"He was a dab hand at letting his tongue run away with him. He shows no respect! He'd talk about God in just the same way he did about Averyan the shopkeeper."

"And poked his nose in everywhere he shouldn't, judged everyone. I ask you, a real case of Maremyana the aged nun,* worried sick about everyone."

And Blinkin said:

"Heads like his don't last long here. Baryba and I, now – we'll survive."

He slapped Baryba on the back and looked at him with his big, icon's eyes – was it with contempt or with affection? Just try working it out – he's a bluffer.

In the evening that same day, Ivan Arefyich, the police chief, invited Semyon Semyonych to come and see him for a cup of tea. And begged him in God's name:

"Set that... what's-his-name of yours... on the right track. That's it, that Baryba. So that he gives more specific evidence somehow at the trial. I mean, I know you've got him expert at it, and well, it's no big deal, no big deal, we're all friends: honest to God, they've completely screwed my neck off, these people from the provincial capital, and if I could be rid of them, I'd be off the hook. But that colonel with his fads: he doesn't like this, doesn't like that..."

After some haggling, they agreed on six twenty-fivers.

"Well, why too little? It's not too little. And for that... what's his name?... for that Baryba some sort of job can be arranged. What could be better? As a clerk, say, a police constable..."

And the following day, over some Kronberg beer,* Blinkin used all sorts of approaches in approaching Baryba, buttering him up. Baryba continued to hum and ha.

"But we were sort of friends – it's really kind of odd, awkward."

"Oh, my dear man, is it for you and me to feel embarrassed and to ponder things? We'll get completely bogged down, you know, go under. What does it say in some fairy tale: to look back is to die of fright? Then better not look back. And it's still a long way to trial, too, you know. If you get a bad taste in your mouth, there'll be time for you to say no."

"That's right," thought Baryba, "to hell with him, there's the consumption anyway... and if I could wangle a nice job out of it too... What, am I to go on for ever living hand to mouth?"

And out loud Baryba said:

"Just for you, maybe, Semyon Semyonych. If it wasn't for you – not for anything."

"If it wasn't for me... I know, my dove, that you wouldn't have turned out such a treasure without me. You'd have been neither this, nor that. Whereas now..."

He paused, then suddenly leant towards Baryba's ear and whispered:

"Do you dream about devils? They're in my dreams every night, every night – do you understand?"

23
A PESKY LITTLE ANT

He agreed and went to see the police chief, and the police chief gave him a whole pile of money and made such big promises... At this point Baryba should have been happy. But there was something nagging at him, bothering him. Some kind of little mosquito, a little ant had got into his insides and it's crawling around in there, crawling around, and there's no chance of catching it, of squashing it.

Baryba was going to bed and thinking:

"Tomorrow evening. So there's still a whole day before the trial. If I want, I'll go and say no. I'm my own master."

He was asleep, yet wasn't. And it was as if he was keeping on thinking through some unthought-through idea in his sleep:

"And there's only a smidgeon of life left in him."

And again he dreamt of the District School, the exams, the priest shoving his beard into his mouth.

"I'll fail again, a second time," thought Baryba.

And he was thinking it through:

"He was brainy, though, Timosha, if truth be told.

"...Why 'was'? What's this 'was'?"

He opened his eyes wide in the darkness and could sleep no longer. The pesky little ant was crawling around, tormenting him.

"Why 'was'?"

24
FAREWELL

When it was already late, at about midday, Baryba woke up in his little room in Streltsy: everything all around was bright and clear, and everything that needed to be done at the trial was revealed as so simple. As if there'd been nothing of what had been tormenting him in the night, nothing of the sort.

Aprosya brought the samovar and white bread and stood by the threshold. Her sleeves were rolled up, and she put the palm of her left hand under the elbow of her right arm and her simple head on her right hand. And she was ready to listen to Anfim Yegorych, to listen, to stand like that, horrified, sighing sympathetically, shaking her head tender-heartedly.

Baryba finished drinking his tea. Aprosya handed Anfim Yegorych his frock coat and said:

"You're quite cheerful today, Anfim Yegorych. Are you about to get some money?"

"I am," said Baryba.

At the trial Timosha was all right, putting on a brave face, turning his little head to and fro, and his neck was long and thin, so thin – it was terrible to see.

But the black-haired little boy was ever so odd somehow: the whole of him had sagged, as though all his bones had suddenly become soft and melted. He was positively toppling sideways. The guard was forever straightening him up and leaning him against the wall.

Baryba spoke confidently and clearly, but he hurried: after all, it would be good to get away from here, anywhere, quickly. When he'd finished, the prosecutor asked:

"Why did you say nothing before? So much valuable material."

The court was already set to rise when Timosha suddenly leapt up and said:

"Yes. So, farewell, then, everyone."

No one answered.

25
IN THE MORNING ON MARKET DAY

In the morning on a cheerful market day, in front of the jail, in front of the official buildings, there's the squealing of piglets, dust, sunshine; there's the smell coming from carts of apples and horses; confused, encrusted with the hubbub of the market, there's the ringing of bells – there's a religious procession somewhere, they're praying for rain.

The police chief, Ivan Arefyich, in a tunic that's gone green, with a Cannon cigarette, contented, came out onto the porch and said, gazing sternly at the crowd:

"The criminals have paid the lawful penalty. I am forewarning you…"

In the crowd, which was quiet, there was a sudden rustling and swaying, as if a wind had sprung up in a wood.

Someone threw off their hat and crossed themselves. And in the ranks at the back, farthest away from the police chief, a voice said:

"Gallows-birds, the devils!"

"Who are you talking about there – who is it, eh?"

Ivan Arefyich turned abruptly and left. And at once in front of the porch it was as if they'd woken up. Everyone started hollering at once; arms were raised; everyone wanted to be the one to be heard. The red-haired townsman was waving his arms about as if swimming.

"They're lying, they haven't hanged them," he said earnestly. "It's something unthinkable. How can you hang a living person? Are they really going to let it happen, the living person? They'll fight tooth and nail... And for a living person to allow it to be put on their neck – is that really something thinkable?"

"This is what it is: it's education, books," said an old man from among the traders. "Timoshka was far too clever, he'd forgotten God, that's what..."

The red-haired townsman looked down malevolently at the old man and saw that he had hairs growing out of his ears, long grey ones.

"You should shut up – you've got one foot in the grave yourself," said the red-haired man. "Look, you've already got hairs growing out of your ears."

The old man turned angrily and, forcing his way out of the crowd, muttered:

"All sorts have appeared... The old way of life in the trading quarter's over – they've stirred things up, they have."

26
BRIGHT BUTTONS

A white tunic, never washed as yet, little silver suns of buttons, gold braid on the shoulders.

"Holy Mother! Can it really be true? The Balkashins' yard and all that – and now here am I, Baryba, walking along in epaulettes?"

He had a feel: there they were. Well, so it must be true.

Out from the notary's, out of the porch with its sign, came Chernobylnikov the postman with his bag. He stopped and stared. Fooling about, saluted:

"Mister Constable."

But Baryba's pride stopped him in his tracks. He carelessly threw his hand up to the peak of his cap.

"Have you been in post long?"

"Oh, three days or so. The tunic was only finished today. It's quite a to-do now, having a uniform made."

"Gra-and! A higher-up, then? Well, I'll take my leave."

They said goodbye. Baryba went on his way: he had to report to the police chief today. He walked along and glowed, satisfied with himself, with the May sunshine and with his epaulettes. And he smiled his four-cornered smile.

By the jail Baryba stopped and asked the police watchman:

"Is Ivan Arefyich in?"

"No, sir, he's gone out to a murder."

And the watchman, from whom the Baryba who had thieved at the markets had once hidden – the watchman politely saluted.

Baryba was even glad the police chief had gone out to a murder: he could walk around some more in the sunshine in his new tunic for everyone to salute. "Oh, it's good to be alive in the world! And what an idiot – very nearly said no." His iron jaws clenched – he'd have liked to crack some of those very hardest stones now, like he used to once at the District School.

"Oho! That's what! This is when I should go and see my father. The old fool – turned me out – let him take a look at me now."

Past Churilov's tavern, past the empty market stalls, down a footpath of rotted boards, and then, without a footpath at all, down a side street through grass.

By a door upholstered with tattered oilcloth – oh dear, an old acquaintance! – he paused for a moment. He all but loved his father. Hey, why not, he could have kissed the whole trading quarter now: how could he not kiss them when for the first time he's wearing a tunic with epaulettes and bright buttons.

Baryba knocked. Out came his father. Oh brother, how he'd aged! Grey stubble on his cheeks – he lowered his glasses onto his nose and gazed for a long time. Had he recognized him or hadn't he? Who knows, but he stays silent.

"What do you want?" he barked.

Gosh, isn't he cross? Well, he clearly hadn't recognized him.

"Well, don't you recognize me, old man? You threw me out, remember? Now, though – you see. I was appointed three days ago."

The old man blew his nose, wiped his fingers on his apron and said calmly:

"I heard about you, I heard – of course I did. Good people talk."

He looked calmly again over the top of his glasses.

"About Yevsei, the monk. And about the tailor too."

The grey stubble on his chin suddenly started jumping.

"And about the tailor, of course, of course."

And suddenly the old man started shaking all over, shrieking and spluttering:

"Get out of my house, get out, you good-for-nothing! I t-told you not to dare to come near my door. Get out, out!"

Flabbergasted, Baryba stared with bulging eyes and stood for a long time, quite unable to understand. When he'd got the picture, he turned in silence and started back.

* * *

It was already getting gloomy outside. There was an evening breeze coming from the window.

At a table in Churilov's tavern, with his legs set wide apart and his hands in his pockets, sat Baryba, who'd already had quite a skinful. He was muttering under his breath:

"Well, I don't give a damn. He's gone gaga. Don't give a damn."

But there were already dregs of some sort deep down – something had muddied things. There was no cheerful day in May.

Settled at a table in the corner opposite Baryba were three cloth salesmen: one, leaning forward, was telling some story, two were listening. And suddenly all three collapsed, roaring with laughter. It must have been something really very droll.

"Ah, so is that it? Ah, so is that the way you are? Then I'll sh-show 'em, I'll show 'em all," muttered Baryba under his breath.

His eyelids were swollen, his angry, four-cornered mouth was snarling, his iron, chewing jaw muscles tensed.

The salesmen collapsed merrily again.

Baryba suddenly took a hand from his pocket and banged his knife on his plate – with drunken, stumbling blows.

A waiter came running – Mitka, misery guts – and bent down, smirking with one cheek – the one turned towards the salesmen – and expressing respect to Mister Constable with the other. The salesmen poked out their noses and listened.

"L-listen. T-tell them I do not p-permit them to laugh. I do not… It is now str-strictly forbidden to laugh here… No, ha-ang on, I'll do it myself!"

Huge, four-cornered, oppressive, he stood up, swaying, and started to move, rumbling, towards the salesmen. As if it wasn't even a person walking, but an old carved figure of a woman, risen from a burial mound, a grotesque Russian stone-carved figure of a woman.

1912

At the End of the Earth

I

GOD'S YAWN

There is in every man something that is him, the whole of him all at once, by which you can distinguish him from a thousand others. And that something in Andrei Ivanych is his forehead: the expanse and sweep of the steppe. And next to it – his nose: a little Russian snub nose, tow-coloured whiskers, infantry epaulettes. When the Lord God was creating him, He made a broad sweep: the forehead. And then he yawned, got a bit bored for some reason – and finished off any old how, haphazardly: that'll do. And so Andrei Ivanych embarked on life with God's yawn.

Andrei Ivanych took it into his head last summer to study for the Military Academy. This was no joke: he spent seventy roubles on books alone. He pored over the books all summer, and in August chanced to get into a concert by Hofmann.* My God, what power! How could he possibly pursue the Academy: it was clear – Andrei Ivanych was to be a Hofmann. Not without good cause did everyone in the regiment say that listening to the way Andrei Ivanych played Chopin's funeral march,* you couldn't help but cry.

All the Academy books went under the sofa; Andrei Ivanych got himself a teacher and sat down at the piano: in the spring he'd be going to the Conservatoire.

But the teacher was a blonde lady, and she had some special kind of perfume. The way it turned out, music wasn't what Andrei Ivanych was doing with her the whole winter at all. And the Conservatoire bit the dust.

Well, so is Andrei Ivanych now to go sour as a subaltern in some place like Tambov? Why, now you're just being mischievous:

others, maybe, but Andrei Ivanych isn't going to give in. The main thing is to start everything from scratch, send everything from the old life to the devil and head off to somewhere at the world's end. And then: the truest love, writing a book of some sort and conquering the whole world...

And that's how Andrei Ivanych found himself serving at the world's end, at the end of the earth. He's lying on the divan now and cursing. What is this, honest to God? Three days since he arrived, and for a third day you can't breathe freely for the fog. And what a fog, really: it's enough to give you the creeps. Dense, shaggy, like intoxicated slumber, there's a blur in your head from it – you'll dream of some weird monster, and you're frightened of falling asleep, you mustn't: the monster will have your head in a whirl.

Wanting some human voice, any voice at all, to fell the apparition, Andrei Ivanych called his orderly:

"Hey, Neprotoshnov, come here a minute!"

The orderly flew in like one possessed and stuck to the doorpost.

"It's dreary here, Neprotoshnov: what a fog, eh?"

"W-wouldn't know, Y'r 'onour..."

"Good Lord," he thought, "what fishlike eyes. But there's something that ought to get him to..."

"Well, Neprotoshnov, home in a year's time, eh?"

"Yissir, Y'r 'onour."

"Do you have a wife?"

"Yissir, Y'r 'onour."

"I expect you miss her? You miss her, I'm saying, eh?"

Something inside Neprotoshnov flickered dimly.

"As she is my life's competition,* my wife, then I..." and Neprotoshnov died away, checked himself, stood up even straighter.

"What is it: stopped loving her, have you? Well?"

"W-wouldn't know, Y'r 'onour."

"Oh, damn it all... I mean, he probably used to be the best in his village on the accordion, but now he's got eyes like a fish. No," he thought, "I'm going to have to get rid of him..."

"All right. Go to your room, Neprotoshnov."

Andrei Ivanych fell back onto his pillow. The shaggy, cotton-wool fog was creeping in through the window: well, you just can't breathe freely.

He stuck it out – and, albeit accompanied by snoring, did manage to breathe freely. Andrei Ivanych heard himself snoring and wanted to leap up: "Good Heavens, what am I doing – asleep in broad daylight!"

But the fog had entangled him in its web – and he could move neither arms nor legs.

2

A RAPHAEL OF THE POTATO

"His Ex'lency the commandant's not at home."

"You find out properly, old fellow. Say it's Lieutenant Polovets. Polovets, Andrei Ivanych."

"Polove-ets?"

The general's orderly had not a face, but a polished copper samovar: so round was it, so shiny. And the samovar had been lifeless, but now it suddenly began to bubble and come to the boil:

"Polove-ets? Oh, good Heavens, I forgot, he *is* at home. Polove-ets – why, of course: he's at home, this way! Only he's a bit busy."

The orderly opened the door out of the lobby to the left. Andrei Ivanych stooped and went through. "No," he thought, "maybe I'm in the wrong place?"

Utter pandemonium, smoke, commotion, something sizzling, the smell of fried onions...

"Who's the-ere? Closer, closer, can't he-ear!"

Andrei Ivanych stepped closer:

"I have the honour of reporting for duty to Your Excellency..."

The devil take it, is this really him, the general? A cook's apron and a pregnant belly propped up on pudgy little legs. The bare, pop-eyed head of a frog. And all spreading, splayed out, a huge

73

frog – maybe underneath the clothes his belly's even mottled with white and green splodges.

"Reporting for duty? Hm, good thing, good thing... I don't have enough officers. Soaks, now – as many of *them* as you like," the general growled.

And he busied himself again with what he'd been doing: cutting grainy white potatoes into wonderfully thin slices. He finished his slicing, wiped his hands on his apron, jumped sideways towards Andrei Ivanych, stared, looked him over and, from somewhere deep down, like a merman from a whirlpool, shouted angrily:

"Well, what the devil brought you here? Been reading a lot of Mayne Reids,* eh? You should have stayed in Russia, my little pigeon, under Mama's skirts, what could be better? Well then, well – why? You'll only end up making trouble for me here!"

Andrei Ivanych quite lost his nerve: the general had laid into him so immediately:

"Your Excellency, I... In Tambov I... Whereas here, I'm thinking, the sea... There's the Chinese here—"

"He-ere! They come here thinking that here they'll find..."

But the general didn't finish what he was saying: something on the cooker began sizzling a dying sizzle, steam began billowing, there was the smell of burning. In an instant the general had leapt over there and showered someone, beaten them into the ground, with ripe curses.

Only now did Andrei Ivanych notice a little Chinese cook in a blue *changshan*:* he stood before the general like some timid little animal on its hind legs.

"Take that!" and a ringing blow smacked into the little cook's ear.

But he was all right: he merely wiped his slanting eyes with his little fists, in an odd sort of way, quickly, like a rabbit.

The general was puffing, and his belly was slopping around under his apron.

"Oof! They've worn me out, through and through. They know nothing, they don't have a clue: just turn around, and the things they'll cook up... And I absolutely hate it when they make a botch job of dinner, willy-nilly, without any kind of feeling. Food, my duck, is a gift from God... What was it, now, they used to teach us: we eat not to live, but live to...* Or what was it?"

Andrei Ivanych stared in wide-eyed silence. The general had picked up a napkin and was lovingly, carefully, wiping the thin slices of potato.

"Potatoes, yes. Chuck them in the frying pan, you say, and fry them any old how? Yes... But anyone who's been given talent by God understands that it can't be in butter, not under any circumstances... In butter? God forbid! In deep oil – without fail, for certain, remember it, write it down, brother, once and for all: in deep oil – d'you hear?"

The general had picked up a lemon and was squeezing the juice out onto the slices of potato. Andrei Ivanych plucked up his courage and asked:

"And why the lemon, Your Excellency?"

The general was evidently transfixed by such ignorance. He's recoiled and he's yelling from somewhere deep down – the merman from the bottom of the whirlpool:

"What do you mean, why? Without it the result will be rubbish, a profanation! But if you sprinkle them, but if you wipe them quite dry, but if you fry them in deep oil... Potatoes *à la lyonnaise** – heard of it? Well, how could you have! A treasure, a pearl, a Raphael!* And what's it made from? From plain potatoes, from something worthless. That, my dear man, is what art means, creative work, yes..."

"Potatoes, Raphael, what nonsense! Is he joking?" wondered Andrei Ivanych, looking at him.

No, he isn't joking. And even under the ash of his face – it can still be seen now – there is something human, distant, flickering and dying away.

"Well, so be it, of the potato – a Raphael of the potato, if nothing else..." he thought.

Andrei Ivanych bowed to the general and the general shouted:

"Larka, take him to my wife. Goodbye, little pigeon, goodbye…"

Sometimes in a wood there are clearings where there's been illegal felling: three pointless trees are left, and they only make things even worse, emptier. And the general's reception hall is the same: chairs few and far between, and like an eyesore on the wall – a regimental group photo. And somehow out of place, pointless, perched in the middle of the hall on a bent-wood sofa is the general's wife.

Sitting with the general's wife was Captain Nechesa. Andrei Ivanych already knew Nechesa: he remembered his dishevelled beard, covered in crumbs, from the day before. Andrei Ivanych went up to the general's wife and kissed her outstretched hand.

The general's wife switched a glass containing something red from her left hand back to her right and said to the lieutenant in a monotone, while gazing right past him:

"Sit down, I haven't seen you… in a long time."

"What does that mean – haven't seen you in a long time?" he thought.

And at once she had Andrei Ivanych all muddled, and his entire prepared speech slipped his mind.

Captain Nechesa, ending some conversation, barked hoarsely:

"And so, ma'am, do permit me to ask you to do me the honour of being the godmother…"

The general's wife took a sip of her drink, and her eyes were far away – she hadn't heard. Apropos of nothing, on some topic of her own, she said:

"Lieutenant Molochko has got warts appearing on his hands. And were it only on his hands – but it's all over his body… Dreadfully unpleasant – warts."

As she said "warts", something behind Andrei Ivanych's back sniffed and snorted. He turned round and saw behind him, in the crack of the door, someone's eye and freckled nose.

Captain Nechesa was repeating fawningly:

"…Do do me the honour of being the godmother!"

Now the general's wife must have heard. She's broken into cheerless, cracked laughter – and keeps on laughing, keeps on laughing, just won't stop. Turning to Andrei Ivanych, it was all she could do to say:

"The ninth... Captain Nechesa's wife's been delivered of her ninth. Won't you join me – as godfather?"

Captain Nechesa began crumpling his beard:

"Forgive me, dear lady, for the love of Christ. There's already a godfather, you know. My lodger, Lieutenant Tikhmen, he's long been promised..."

But again the general's wife had heard nothing, again she was gazing right past him, sipping from her glass...

Andrei Ivanych and Captain Nechesa left together. The slush squelched under their feet, the fog settled in drops on the roofs and thence fell onto their caps, their epaulettes, down their necks.

"Why is she so sort of... strange, I suppose?" asked Andrei Ivanych.

"The general's wife? Lord, she used to be a good woman. I mean, I've been here twenty years, I know everyone like the back of this hand... Well, there was this business – about seven years back now, a long time ago – she had a baby, her first and last, it was born and then died. She got lost in her thoughts then – and that's how she's stayed, lost in thought. But when she starts talking – the things she sometimes comes out with, honest to God... Like that – about Molochko, about the warts: you don't know whether to laugh or cry!"

"I don't understand a thing."

"Live here a while and you will."

3
PETYASHKA GETS CHRISTENED

Well, all right. So Captain Nechesa's wife's had her ninth. So there's a christening – you might think: what's so special about that? But for the gentlemen officers it's the only topic of conversation. Out of boredom, is it, out of emptiness, out of being idle? It's a fact, after all: they set up some post that nobody needed, put in a load of cannons, herded people to the end of the earth: sit here. And here they sit. And just as in the night, in the sleepless emptiness, every mouse's rustling and every fallen twig grows, alarms, fills everything – so it is here: every trifle rises up beyond measure, and the incredible is made credible.

Well, let's suppose Captain Nechesa's wife's ninth baby isn't quite such a simple matter: whose is it? Just try getting to the bottom of that. The captain's wife has a baby every year. And one little one's the image of Ivanenko; another's for all the world like the adjutant; a third's Lieutenant Molochko to the life, his pink calf's face all over... But whose, then, is the ninth?

And more than anyone it was that same Molochko who took the question on. Why is quite straightforward. Last year people had got him up as father to the captain's wife's baby, offered their congratulations and insisted he treat them: he, too, now wanted to drop someone in it.

"Good Lord, hang on, will you, gentlemen," Molochko cried, jumping up and down like a baby goat, like a happy little calf which had been sucking milk from someone's finger. "I mean – Tikhmen, their lodger... Surely the captain's wife hasn't failed to put him to use? That can't be so! And if that's the case, then..."

"Br-ravo, Molochko can be quick on the uptake too – bravo!"

And so they decided upon Tikhmen: he may not be the guilty party in either body or spirit, but it really is most gratifying to make fun of him, as Tikhmen is unendingly serious, long-nosed and, the devil take him, reads Schopenhauer or some fellow called Kant.*

And to catch Tikhmen unawares, so that he didn't run away, it was only half an hour before this christening that Molochko was sent to warn the captain's wife of an invasion by members of a foreign tribe. In the local language here, this was known as "inviting yourself".

The captain's wife was lying in bed, all nice and round and little: a nice, round little face, quick little round eyes, little round curls on her forehead, and nice and round are all the captain's wife's feminine charms. Only just now had the captain come out of the bedroom, having given his spouse a peck on the cheek. And some little glass had not yet fallen quiet, it was still ringing on a shelf from the captain's footsteps, when in went Lieutenant Molochko and, with a familiar "hello", pecked the captain's wife on the cheek in the same spot as the captain had.

The captain's wife disliked coincidences such as this intensely – there was something positively indecent about it. She rolled her little round eyes angrily:

"What are you all over me with kisses for, Molochishko? Can't you see I'm ill?"

"Oh, come on, now, come on – how chaste you've become!"

Molochko sat down beside the bed. "How should I broach things with Katyushka," he wondered, "so we're not inviting ourselves straight away?"

"D'you know what?" Molochko jumped up and down. "I was at the Shmits' and they're kissing all the time, can you imagine? Coming up to three years married – and to this day... I don't understand it!"

Madam Captain Nechesa grew stronger, began to turn pink, and her little eyes opened.

"Ooh, that Marusechka of Shmit's, she's such a princess on a pea,* so la-di-da... Doesn't want to have anything to do with anyone. I just hope God punishes her for her pride..."

They tore Marusya apart and threw away the pieces, and then there was no more to say. There was evidently nothing for it, he had to begin. Molochko cleared his throat.

"You see, Katyusha... Yes... Well, in short, we're all going to come to the christening – we want to invite ourselves. We've got to congratulate Tikhmen on being the father. It was me that thought of it – can you imagine?"

Molochko certainly hadn't expected Katyushka to agree just like that. She burst out laughing, went into fits of round laughter, kicked her legs about under the blanket, even holding on to her stomach: ouch, that hurts!

"Well, you are a storyteller, Molochishko: Tikhmen as the father, eh? Our long-nosed Tikhmen! Serves him right, he's far too fond of reading…"

And so – there was the christening. The general's wife smiled, gazed into the air up above, and her eyes were somewhere else. The garrison priest read in a sleepy voice from the Book of Needs.* The whole of the back of his cassock was covered in fluff.

The godfather, Lieutenant Tikhmen, gazed at these bits of fluff the whole time. Lanky, skinny, all flimsy somehow, he stood with the child in his arms and moved his long nose around with an air of surprise, thinking:

"Honest to God, I've got myself in a tangle here… If this thing in my arms starts bawling, what am I going to do?"

But "this thing in his arms" proved even worse: Lieutenant Tikhmen felt in horror that his arms had suddenly got wet, and something started dripping from the warm bundle onto the floor. At this point Tikhmen forgot about any kind of subordination, shoved his godchild any old how into the arms of the general's wife and stepped back. God knows where he would have retreated to if the group standing behind him with Molochko at its head hadn't put him back in place.

And now the time had come to dip the baby into the font. The sleepy priest turned to the general's wife to take the child, but she wouldn't let him. She's pressed it up against her and doesn't want to let go, crying:

"I'm not giving him up, so there – I'm not, I'm not, he's mine!"

The priest retreated timidly towards the door. Good Lord, what's going on? There was a kerfuffle, whispered conversations. If not for Molochko, then the christening might not have been completed. Molochko went up to the general's wife, took her firmly by the arm and whispered:

"Let go – what do you want this for? You'll have your own, you can imagine. If I say so… Don't you believe me? Me?"

The general's wife laughed blissfully and let go. Well, thank the Lord! One way or another the christening was completed, and the boy was named Petyashka.

And it was now that the gentlemen officers set about Lieutenant Tikhmen. All at once, on command, they all bowed low:

"We have the honour, dear Papa, of congratulating you on the newborn, Petyashka, and now you owe us a drink, if you please!"

Tikhmen started waving his arms around like a windmill:

"What do you mean – Papa? I don't want you saying any such thing! I can't bear it…"

"In the matter of children, my dear man, God alone decides freely, you know. It makes no difference whether you can bear it or not."

They pestered so, it was enough to make a man weep. There was nothing for it: that evening, Tikhmen entertained them at the mess. And it went on from there: every day at training someone would ask after the health of his little son, Petyashka. They harped on and drove Tikhmen crazy with this Petyashka thing.

4
THE LIGHT BLUE

Does a man need much? The sun's come through, the accursed fog's made itself scarce – and now Andrei Ivanych finds the whole world likeable. The company's standing waiting for his command, but he can't stop looking: he's afraid to move, lest the light-blue crystal chambers should come crashing down.

The ocean… there used to be Tambov, and now there's the Pacific Ocean. Down below, at his feet, its sleepily light-blue baccy is smoking; it's purring a somnolent, bewitching song. And the golden pillars of the sun that have been lying quietly on the light blue down below have now suddenly grown up, arisen and propped up walls that are unbearably dark blue. And floating smoothly past into the light blue, into the depths, is the Madonna's yarn, autumnal gossamer, and for a long time Andrei Ivanych follows it with his eyes. Someone behind him is shouting at a soldier:

"...Where are your three positions? Animal! Swallowed them, wiped them away?"

But Andrei Ivanych doesn't hear, doesn't want to; he doesn't turn around; he keeps on flying after the gossamer...

"Well, then, Tambovver? Like it, do you – can't stop looking?"

There was nothing for it – Andrei Ivanych tore himself away and turned around. Looking at him with a grin was Shmit – tall, a lot taller than Andrei Ivanych, and solid, as though too heavy even for the earth.

"Do I *like* it? That really is a very small word, Captain Shmit. After all, apart from Tambov's River Tsna, I haven't seen anything – and suddenly... You understand – it's overwhelming... and not even that: you completely turn to dust, you're flying with the wind, well, like... It's really joyous..."

"Is that right? Well, well!" And again, Shmit's grin – maybe kind and maybe not.

For Andrei Ivanych it was kind: the whole world was kind. And, unexpectedly even for himself, he shook Shmit gratefully by the hand.

Shmit lost his grin – and his face even seemed to Andrei Ivanych almost unpleasant: kind of uneven, made of something too hard, and it hadn't been possible to even it up properly – it was too hard. And the chin...

But Shmit was already smiling again:

"You're fed up, apparently, with your orderly? Nechesa was telling me."

"Yes, he's just too 'yes, sir'... I want to swap him for anyone at all, as long as..."

"What's stopping you? Swap with me. My Guslyaikin's a drunkard, let me be frank. But he's a cheerful sort in the extreme."

"Thank you, thank you ever so much! I simply don't know how I'm to..."

They said goodbye. Andrei Ivanych walked home, still completely full of the light blue. He'd have liked to walk alone and carry it carefully inside him – but Molochko tagged along.

"What's up, what's up?" he said, poking his little pink face with its silly eyes up close to Andrei Ivanych: he was eager to find out something new so that he could give an enthusiastic account of it to the general's wife, to Katyushka and in the mess that evening.

"Nothing in particular," said Andrei Ivanych. "Shmit's offered his orderly."

"Himself? Is that right? It's incredibly rare that Shmit's first to start a conversation, can you imagine? Have you been to the Shmits'? And the commandant's? Oh yes... the commandant's on leave. There's a good life – on permanent leave! I wish we were the same, can you imagine it?"

"I haven't had the time to go to the Shmits'," said Andrei Ivanych absent-mindedly, still thinking about the sleepy light blue. "I've been to the Nechesas' and the general's. The general's wife – suddenly, out of nowhere, she's going on about warts..."

Andrei Ivanych stopped himself, but by then it was too late. Molochko blushed the colour of poppies, puffed up like a turkey and said grandly:

"P-lease! Might I ask you... I'm proud to be honoured, one might say, with the trust of such a woman... Warts have absolutely nothing to do with anything... Ab-so-lutely!"

He went into a sulk and fell silent. Andrei Ivanych was glad.

Beside a rotting little wooden house Molochko stopped.

"Well, goodbye: this is me..."

But, having said goodbye, he turned around again and in one minute had managed to say of the general that he was the philanderer of all philanderers; had managed to point out the Shmits' little green house and tip the wink about something to do with Marusya Shmit; and had managed to talk a lot of nonsense about some incomprehensible Lanzepuppes' Club* and Lieutenant Tikhmen's Petyashka...

Andrei Ivanych was barely able to shake it all off. But shake it off he did, and he set off sleepy and enchanted once again, floating in the light blue; there was no earth beneath his feet, and it was unclear what the fences, trees and houses were standing on. And it was amazing that the houses were just the same as in Tambov, with doors, chimneys, windows...

At one window there was a glimpse of something, and someone began a cheerful staccato drumming on the window.

"Who's that at – me?" wondered Andrei Ivanych, stopping in front of the little green house. "No, not me," and he walked on.

Suddenly the window of the little green house flew open, and a cheerful voice called:

"Hey, new man, new man, come here!"

Puzzled, Andrei Ivanych went over and doffed his cap, wondering: "But how on earth – but who is this?"

"Listen, let's get acquainted – we're going to have to anyway, after all. I'm Marusya Shmit, have you heard of me? I was sitting by the window and I'm thinking – shall I knock? Oh, what a remarkable forehead you've got. My husband was telling me about you..."

Andrei Ivanych mumbled something, and his eyes drank it all in: the narrow, mischievous little face of perhaps a baby mouse or perhaps a sweet wild goat. Long, narrow eyes, a little slanting.

"What, surprised, are you? This isn't how it's done? Well, I don't care. I absolutely love playing pranks! At boarding school, I was on duty in the kitchen and made the headmistress a rissole out of crumpled paper... Dear me, the to-do! And for Shmit's portrait... Do you know Shmit? Good Lord, yes, he was telling me about you, wasn't he? Come and see us in the evening sometime, no need for formalities!"

"With pleasure... Do excuse me, I'm in such a mood somehow today that I can't speak..."

But Andrei Ivanych saw that she too had fallen silent and was looking somewhere past him. She was frowning a little. Beside her lips were hints of unchildish lines: they weren't there yet, but someday they'd appear.

"Gossamer," she said, gazing after the Madonna's golden yarn. She turned her eyes to Andrei Ivanych and asked:

"Have you ever thought about death? No, not about death even, but about the one very last little second of life, delicate, like gossamer. The very last: any moment it'll be cut short – and all will be quiet…"

For a long time, the eyes of both flew after the gossamer. It flew away into the light blue; there it had been – and was gone…

Marusya laughed. Perhaps she was embarrassed that she'd suddenly spoken of death like that? She slammed the window shut and vanished.

Andrei Ivanych went home. "Everything's fine," he thought, "everything's splendid… and to hell with it, Tambov, and may it go to blazes. They're all nice here. Better, I must get to know them better… They're all nice. And the general – well, he's all right…"

5
THROUGH GUSLYAIKIN

It was with pleasure that Andrei Ivanych got rid of his "yessir" stuffed dummy Neprotoshnov. Guslyaikin, received in exchange from Shmit, did indeed prove garrulous, like a woman, and – not at all like a woman – a soak. He was forever appearing with a battered phiz, adorned with bits of black plaster (this plaster was styled "placester" by Guslyaikin – from "to place": perfectly simple). But even like this, with black patches, and albeit a bit drunk, he was nevertheless more likeable in Andrei Ivanych's eyes than Neprotoshnov…

Guslyaikin evidently noticed his new master's favourable disposition and took him into his confidence – as a token of gratitude. As required by his womanly nature, Guslyaikin must have spent days and nights on end at keyholes and cracks in doors at the Shmits'. He immediately came out with such a thing about the Shmits' bedroom that Andrei Ivanych blushed and sternly cut Guslyaikin short. Guslyaikin was not a little surprised: "Good

Lord," he thought, "any lady, and any gentleman from round here, too, would be showering you with money for such stories, listening as if to a nightingale, yet this one... but he's probably just pretending..." and he started again.

No matter how Andrei Ivanych tried to be done with it, no matter how he reprimanded Guslyaikin, the latter stuck to his guns and planted some dark, hot, disjointed visions in Andrei Ivanych's head. First, here's Shmit carrying Marusya in his arms like a child and in the same way holding her in his arms during dinner, too, and hand-feeding her... Next, Shmit's stood Marusya in the corner for some reason – she stands there and is happy to do so. Then they've filled the stove with wood, they're stoking the stove together, in front of the stove there's a bearskin rug...

And when Andrei Ivanych finally got round to calling on the Shmits and was sitting in their dining room with the nice log walls of a peasant's hut, he was simply frightened to raise his eyes: what if she, what if Marusya, saw from his eyes what thoughts... Oh, that damned Guslyaikin!

But Shmit spoke in his even voice, as clear as ice:

"Hm... So, you say you liked the Raphael of the potato? Yes, he's a fine one, Sugar Honeyich! They wouldn't have shoved a general out to the end of the earth for good deeds. And now there's this: where's the soldiers' money disappearing to, and the money for the horses' fodder? I've already got a feeling, I've a fee-eeling—"

"Come on, Shmit, you're going too far," said Marusya affectionately.

Andrei Ivanych could stand it no longer: with a curiosity he himself found repugnant he raised his eyes. Shmit was sitting on the sofa; Marusya was standing behind him under a palm. Now she leant over towards Shmit and softly, once, drew a hand over Shmit's coarse hair. Once – but with such apparent tenderness, with such apparent tenderness...

Andrei Ivanych's heart positively missed a beat. "What's it got to do with me?" he thought. No, nothing. But his heart aches more and more. "If somebody ever did that to me – once, just once..."

Andrei Ivanych woke up when Shmit uttered his name.

"...Andrei Ivanych is our one and only innocent little lamb. Otherwise, everyone's much the same. Me? I was sent here for assault and battery. Molochko for public indecency. Nechesa for being useless. Kosinsky for cards... Beware, little lamb: you'll go down the drain here, drink yourself to death, shoot yourself."

Maybe because Marusya was standing under the palm or else because of Shmit's grin, it became unbearable, and Andrei Ivanych jumped up:

"That really is a bit much, you know – I've got enough about me for that, not to drink myself to death. And what's it got to do with you?"

"How... gr-rumpy you are," laughed Marusya. "You're joking, Shmit, aren't you? You are, aren't you?"

Again she leant towards Shmit from behind the sofa. "As long as she doesn't stroke him... Don't do it, don't," Andrei Ivanych prayed with bated breath... She appeared to have asked him a question – he replied off the top of his head:

"No, thank you..."

"What do you mean – thank you? Whatever are you thinking of, if you please? I mean, I'm asking if you've been to the Nechesas'?"

And only when Shmit wasn't there would Andrei Ivanych become Andrei Ivanych – there was no Guslyaikin, there was no need to be afraid she was going to stroke Shmit, everything was straightforward, everything was affectionate, everything was joyous.

When it's the two of them there's no need to think what to talk about: the talk comes on its own. The words positively dance, and they sparkle like spring rain. Such a torrent that Andrei Ivanych breaks off, doesn't finish what he's saying, but that doesn't matter: she ought to understand, she does understand, she can hear the most... Or maybe it just seems that way? Maybe Andrei Ivanych has just invented his Marusya for himself? Oh, it doesn't matter, as long as...

One evening sticks in the memory – it's stowed away in the treasure chest. One moment the weather was all fine, it was warm, the men were going about without their greatcoats, and this was in November. And then suddenly there was a blast of cold north wind, the blue turned pale, and by evening it was winter.

Andrei Ivanych and Marusya didn't light a light; they sat listening intently to the whispering of the twilight. In plump flakes, the snow was falling thick and fast, dark blue, quiet. Quietly it sang a lullaby – and oh, to float, float, rock in the waves of twilight, listen, and lull the sadness...

Andrei Ivanych deliberately moved away from Marusya to the far corner of the sofa: it was better this way, this way there'd be only the finest, the whitest thing – the snow.

"There: the tree's all white now," Marusya thought out loud, "and on the white tree there's a bird – it's been drowsing for an hour now, for two, and it doesn't want to fly away..."

Quiet snowy glistening outside the window. Quiet pain in his heart.

"It's winter at home now too, in the countryside," replied Andrei Ivanych. "The dogs have a special way of barking in winter, don't they, do you remember? Yes? It's soft and round. Round, yes... And in the twilight, the smoke from a straw fire above a white roof's so cosy. Everything's dark blue and quiet, and coming towards you there's a peasant woman with a yoke and buckets..."

Marusya's face with its closed eyes was so gentle, slightly pale bluish from the pale-blue snow outside the window, and she had such lips... So as not to see – and better not to see – Andrei Ivanych closed his eyes too.

But when they lit a lamp there was no longer a thing, not a thing of what had seemed to be seen without the lamp.

And all those words about the bird drowsing on the snowy tree, about the dark-blue evening, seemed so lacking in significance, not at all special, and even a little ridiculous.

But they stuck in the memory.

6
HORSE FODDER

The Russian stove has such a mouth, you know: it's insatiable. One bundle's been burnt, and another, and a tenth – and still it's not enough, and more gets crammed in. And that's how the general is at dinner: he's already had soup and a pile of Lithuanian meat dumplings, eaten buckwheat porridge with eggs and almond milk, put away about a dozen ravioli and seen off two portions of Cherkassk beef, braised in red wine. The bunny-like cook brings a new dish – some complicated kind of pâté, smelling of strong pepper and nutmeg: well, how can you not eat some pâté? The general's soul wants some pâté, but his belly's full, right up to here. The general's artful, though: he knows how to make the mortal body follow the spirit.

"Larka, bring me the vase!" the general croaked.

Larka the samovar ran off and instantly lugged in a large, long, narrow vase of decorated Chinese porcelain for the general. The general turned aside and relieved himself in the manner of Ancient Rome.

"Phew!" he sighed afterwards – and put a piece of pâté onto his plate.

It wasn't the general's wife acting as hostess: give her the role and she might do something untoward. Acting as hostess was Agniya, his sister-in-law, with her sharp, freckled nose. The general's wife had settled herself a little apart, eating almost nothing, her eyes somewhere else, forever sipping from her glass.

After eating, the general was in a good mood:

"Come on, Agniya, tell us, do you know: how might ladies learn a lot at university – well, do you know?"

Freckled, flat-chested, faded Agniya sensed some sort of mean trick coming and started fidgeting on her chair. No, she didn't know...

"De-eary me! How is it you don't know that? Ladies might learn a lot at university if they were under... Well, under what? Under what, eh? Get it?"

Agniya started quivering, turning scarlet, coughing. She simply didn't know what to do with herself: after all, she was a spinster – and suddenly such an... indecent thing... But the general was roaring with laughter: first of all down low, at the bottom of a bubbling marsh, and then up high, like a shrill little frog.

Agniya fell into a reverie and busied herself with the pâté, her eyes on her plate, dispatching tiny little pieces quick-quick into her mouth. But the general was slowly bending, bending towards Agniya; he froze – and then bawled at her in such a bass voice, it seemed to come from a whirlpool:

"B-boo-oo!"

Agniya screamed blue murder, started jumping about on her chair, blinking and wailing:

"May you... may you... may you..."

About twenty times there was this "may you" – and quietly at the very last: "...burn in hell... May you burn in hell, bu-urn in hell..." This was something oddly customary for Agniya: out of boredom the general was forever making her jump, from around corners – and so she was used to it.

The general enjoyed listening to Agniya's wails and turned red in the face, quite unable to draw breath and guffawing:

"Ho-ho-ho, there's a raving woman for you, she's possessed, there's a featherbrain, ho-ho-ho!"

But the general's wife sipped away without hearing, living not here but somewhere far off.

Larka ran in, breathless.

"Your Ex'lency, Captain Shmit's here wanting to see you."

"Shmit? What brings him here?... They don't even let you have a proper bite to eat, d-damn it! Ask him in."

Agniya the sister-in-law leapt up from the table and into the next room, and soon her freckled nose, once glimpsed by Andrei Ivanych, was already poking in through the gap in the door.

In came Shmit, tall and heavy. The floor began creaking beneath him.

"A-a-ah, Nikolai Pe-tro-vich, hello. Would you like to have something to eat, my dear fellow? Look, there's some e-excellent ravioli! I made it myself, my sweet: how could I possibly trust those lousy creatures? Ravioli's a sophisticated thing, made entirely of such delicacies: bone marrow, parmesan, young celery – no older than July's, not on a-any account... Please do, my little dove."

Shmit put a square patty onto a plate, swallowed it indifferently and began speaking. His voice is even, cut-glass, sharp, and a smirk, not to be seen on his lips, is audible...

"Your Excellency, Captain Nechesa's complaining that the horses aren't getting any oats – they're eating nothing but cut straw. This is completely unthinkable. Nechesa is, of course, too scared to come and tell you himself. I don't know what the problem is. Perhaps that favourite of yours, what's his name... Mundel-Mandel – oh, what's his name..."

The general's in the most delightful mood; he's screwed up his bulging eyes and purrs:

"Mendel-Mandel-Mundel-Mondel... Oh dear, Nikolai Petrovich, my little dove, this isn't what happiness is about. Why, what more do you want? I saw your Marusya the other day. Why, what a pussycat, why, what a darling – quite simply... wow! And you hooked her! Well, what the hell more do you want, eh? In your shoes I wouldn't give two hoots about Nechesa or anyone else..."

Shmit sat silent. His small, deep-set iron-grey eyes receded even deeper. His tight lips squeezed even tighter.

Only now did the general's wife hear Shmit, catch a little bit and ask in a cracked voice:

"Nechesa?"

And forgot and fell silent. Constantly going up and down in the crack in the door was the sharp, freckled nose.

Shmit repeated insistently and already with anger:

"Once again, I consider it my duty to report to Your Excellency that the horses' fodder money is disappearing somewhere. I don't want to start guessing who, whether it's Mundel or not..."

Suddenly the general's wife woke up again, heard "Mundel" and blurted out:

"The fodder money? That's not Mundel at all, but him," and she nodded towards the general. "He's short of money for his meals – he spends such an awful lot on food," and the general's wife laughed almost merrily.

Shmit fixed his steel-like gaze on the general:

"I've known that for a long time, if truth be told. And another thing too: money's disappearing, those three-rouble notes that the soldiers are sent from home. And you know, people might suspect me – I'm the paymaster. I can't permit that."

Shmit's lips are squeezed tight; his face as a whole is calm, like ice. But like strained blue ice in a snow-melt flood: it's going to crack any second – and the shattering, frenetic spring torrent will come bursting out with a crash.

But the general had already burst out. In his visceral bass he bellowed:

"Per-mit? Wha-at?" and immediately renounced it for a furious shriek: "Captain Shmit, on your feet, stand to attention – this is General Azancheyev talking to you!"

Shmit stood up, calm, white. The general leapt up too, made a clatter with his chair, and fell upon Shmit, showered him with curses and hit him hard on the head:

"W-whipper-snapper! You d-dare to not per-mit, eh? Me, Azancheyev? D'you kn-know, in twenty-four hours I'll have you…"

He was searching for the way to inflict the most painful wound on Shmit:

"It's not so long ago you were standing here and asking my permission, yes, per-mission to get married. And now you've set yourself up with a pretty young girl and think you're a b-big man and can do anything! W-whipper-snapper!"

"What… was… that?" One at a time, Shmit snapped back the piercing – three-line bullet* – words.

"…Set yourself up with a young girl, I'm saying, and that's what you think! You wait, my dear, she'll be passed around, just like the rest of them here. Otherwise, would you believe it – I this, I that!"

Shmit's hard, jutting chin was infinitesimally trembling. The floor creaked, Shmit took a step – and gave the general a sharp, precise slap in the face, as measured as Shmit himself.

And at this point everything got jumbled up, as happens when little lads ride down a hill on sleds and at the very bottom go crashing into one another: snow flies from a ploughed-up drift, the sledges are runners uppermost, and there's cheerful shrieking and the plaintive crying of one who's hurt.

Larka dashed forward and obligingly stood the chair up, and the general flopped down like a sack. The crack in the door opened wide and Agniya the sister-in-law jumped up in convulsions, wailing crazily: "May you, may you, may you burn in hell..." The general's wife held her glass in her hand and laughed a cracked, hollow laugh – the way a hoopoe laughs on a belltower in the night-time.

Without his voice, with his insides, the general croaked:

"Court martial... I'll have you jailed!"

Shmit rapped out in soldierly fashion:

"As you please, Your Excellency."

And left about turn.

Larka enjoyed dramatic scenes: he turned his head contentedly to and fro, puffed like a samovar and fanned the general with a napkin. Agniya groaned, and the general's wife drank in little sips from her glass.

7

LITTLE BITS OF HUMANS

Molochko stuck to Andrei Ivanych like a leech.

"No, *attendez*!* You've already been here a month, and not once have you dropped into the mess, can you imagine? That is swinish behaviour on your part. I expect you're ambling round to the Shmits' every day!"

Andrei Ivanych turned a barely discernible pink. "It's true, if I go to the Shmits' today, too, it really will be definitively clear, and that means owning up…" he thought. What was clear, and owning up to what – that Andrei Ivanych hadn't yet plucked up the courage to say even to himself.

"All right, to hell with you, I'll come," said Andrei Ivanych, waving him away.

There were some fifteen greatcoats hanging in the cloakroom. The paint wasn't yet completely dry: feet were sticking to the floor and there was the smell of turpentine. Molochko was blathering away about something incessantly in his ear, filling Andrei Ivanych's head with rubbish:

"Well then, how d'you like it here? There's a watchtower upstairs! Nice and new, eh? No, but can you imagine: I've heard there's this fire-resistant paint, what about that, eh? No, but did you read about how the French had a theatre full of people burn down, eh? A hundred people, what about that? I follow literature very closely…"

The tobacco users had filled the hall upstairs with so much tobacco smoke that you could cut it with a knife. And in the hubbub, in the ginger mist, there weren't people, but only little bits of humans: here someone's head, bald as a watermelon; there, down low, cut off by the cloud, Captain Nechesa's bandy legs; a little farther off, a bouquet of hairy fists hanging in the air.

The little bits of humans were floating, moving, existing self-sufficiently in the ginger mist – like fish in the glass tank of some crazed aquarium.

"Ah, Polovets – about time, brother, about time!"

"Where did you get to? Why haven't you been here?"

The little bits of humans clustered around Andrei Ivanych, squeezed in, started making a din. Molochko dived into the mist and disappeared. Captain Nechesa introduced him to some new people: Nesterov, Ivanenko, someone else. But everyone seemed the same to Andrei Ivanych: like fish in an aquarium.

Two green tables had been opened up. Candles smeared a lustreless light over people's faces. Andrei Ivanych pushed forward to see how they gambled here, at the end of the earth: was it just as fervently as in distant Tambov, or were they already bored, maybe, fed up?

Hanging above the table and shining dimly was the head, bald as a watermelon, and there were cards laid out in even rows. The watermelon was furrowing its brow, whispering something and prodding the cards with a finger.

"What's this?" asked Andrei Ivanych, turning to Captain Nechesa.

Nechesa sniffed a bit and said:

"Naval sloop veers uprun."*

"Uprun?"

"Why yes. What, from another planet, are you? It's that card trick."

"But why... But why on earth is no one playing cards? I thought..." Andrei Ivanych was already feeling shy; he could see people grinning all around.

Captain Nechesa barked out in a good-naturedly fierce way:

"We've tried, brother, we've tried, we have played... We stopped. Enough."

"But why?"

"Brother, we've got ever such a lot of, yes, geniuses in the field of cards. They really do play very well. Yes. It's no fun..."

Andrei Ivanych became embarrassed, as if he were to blame for the fact that they really did play very well.

At about nine o'clock the whole horde moved off to have dinner. And the tobacco smoke floated right behind them, from the cards room into the dining room, and again the self-sufficient little bits of humans began scurrying about in the ginger clouds: heads, hands, noses.

In the dining room they caught sight of the long, sad nose, quite unnaturally twisted to the left, of Lieutenant Tikhmen. They livened up.

"A-ah, Tikhmen! Well, how's your Petyashka?"

"Are his teeth coming through? It must be a lot of bother for you, eh?"

Captain Nechesa smiled blissfully and could no longer hear anything at all: he was pouring himself sweet-grass vodka. Tikhmen answered seriously and with concern:

"The little boy's quite unwell – I'm afraid it's going to be difficult with his teeth."

A volley of merry guffaws, well and truly from the belly.

Tikhmen cottoned on, flapped an arm wearily and sat down at the table next to Andrei Ivanych.

At the head of the table, acting as host, sat Shmit. Even sitting down, he was taller than anyone else.

Shmit rang a bell. Up ran a perky, sly-eyed soldier with a patch on his knee.

"I bet he's a thief…" Andrei Ivanych thought for some reason, looking at the patch.

A minute later, the soldier with the patch brought a huge green-glass Japanese tumbler on a tray. Everyone started yelling and roaring with laughter:

"A-ah, to christen Polovets! Let him have it, Shmit!"

"The sea monster, the winged centaur!"

"This, brother, is called the winged centaur: well then?"

Andrei Ivanych knocked back the brutal mixture of wormwood and quinine, stared like a stuck pig and gasped – he didn't draw breath, he couldn't. Someone put a chair underneath him, and the newly christened man was forgotten – or else it was him that was out cold…

Andrei Ivanych came to because of a rasping voice, repeating one and the same thing in an irksomely mournful way:

"It's no joke. If I knew… It's no joke… If I knew for certain… If I…"

Slowly, with difficulty, Andrei Ivanych realized it was Tikhmen. He asked:

"What? If you knew what?"

"…Knew for certain: is Petyashka mine or not?"

"He's drunk, yes," thought Andrei Ivanych. "But I'm not…"

But at this point Andrei Ivanych was put off by laughter and roaring. People were guffawing, collapsing onto the table, dying laughing. Someone was repeating the final phrase – the punchline – of a dirty joke.

Now Molochko started telling one: they must have already been telling them for quite some time. Molochko had gone red in the face and was blabbing like anything, and weighty Russian words were positively hanging in the air.

Suddenly, from the head of the table, Shmit cried abruptly and firmly:

"Shut up, you idiot, don't you dare say a thing more! I won't permit it."

Molochko jerked and leapt up from his chair – then immediately sat down. Uncertainly he said:

"Shut up yourself."

He fell silent. And everyone fell quiet. The little bits of humans swayed and flickered in the mist: red faces, noses, glazed eyes.

Somebody started singing, quietly, hoarsely, howling like a dog at the melancholy silver of the moon. People at one end of the table and at the other joined in, in a drawn-out drawl with their heads thrown back. And now everyone's howling dolefully, in unison, like wolves:

> There was a priest who had a dog,
> And how he loved it.
> The dog once went and ate a hog,
> Then the priest killed it.
> He dug a grave to take his dog,
> Set up a stone there.
> And upon the stone he wrote:
> There was a priest who had a dog,
> And how he loved it.
> The dog once went and ate a hog…*

97

The clock struck ten. The endless circle of words, as senseless as their lives, was bewitching; they kept howling and howling with their heads thrown back. They'd grown sad, remembered something. What was it?

B-boom: half past ten. And suddenly Andrei Ivanych sensed in horror that he, too, was dying to start singing, howling, like everyone else. In a moment he, Andrei Ivanych, would start singing, in a moment he'd start singing – and then…

"What's this," he thought, "have I gone… have we all gone mad?" His hair stood on end.

> …Then the priest killed it.
> He dug a grave to take his dog,
> And upon the stone he wrote:
> There was a priest who had a dog…

And Andrei Ivanych would have started singing, howling, but Tikhmen, who was sitting to his right, slowly slid down under the table, put his arms round Andrei Ivanych's legs and quietly – maybe Andrei Ivanych alone heard it – began a piteous whining:

"Oh, my Petyashka, oh, Petyashka…"

Andrei Ivanych leapt up and pulled his legs free in alarm. He ran to where Shmit was sitting. Shmit wasn't singing. His eyes were stern, sober. "There he is," he thought. "He alone can save me…"

"Shmit, see me out, I don't feel well – what are they singing for?"

Shmit grinned and stood up. The floor beneath him started creaking. They went outside.

Shmit said, "Dear oh dear!" and gripped Andrei Ivanych firmly by the hand.

"That's good, firmly," thought Andrei Ivanych. "That means he still doesn't…"

Ever more firmly, ever more painfully. "Should I cry out?" he wondered. "No…" His bones cracked; the pain was hellish. "But what if Shmit, too, if Shmit, too, is mad?" he thought. Andrei Ivanych didn't cry out, though; he controlled himself.

"So you're all right, then: you can bear things," Shmit said with a grin and looked Andrei Ivanych intently in the eyes, and the grin took in his enormous forehead and his little snub nose, bashfully nestling in the shelter of the forehead.

8

THE SONATA

After what had gone on the day before, he felt wretched and dull all day. And when the evening crept in through the window, the dullness utterly enveloped and overwhelmed him. He hadn't the strength to remain face to face with himself like this. Andrei Ivanych gave up the struggle and set off for the Shmits'.

"The Shmits have a piano, and I need to play, I really do. Otherwise, as it is, it won't be long before I completely forget how to..." thought Andrei Ivanych, trying to fool Andrei Ivanych.

Marusya said joylessly:

"Oh, did you know: Shmit's been locked up in the guardhouse for three days. What for? He didn't even tell me. He was just very surprised that it was such small beer – three days. 'And I was thinking,' he says... Do you know what it's for?"

"Something happened between him and the general, but what – I don't know..."

Andrei Ivanych immediately sat down at the piano. He leafed through his sheet music cheerfully, thinking: "Shmit's not here, Shmit's been locked up."

He chose Grieg's sonata.* Andrei Ivanych had fallen in love with it long before: from the very first, somehow, it had struck a chord with him. He started playing it now – and in a second, in the midst of the dullness there began to shine a sunny green island, and on it...

Andrei Ivanych pressed on the left pedal, and everything inside him started trembling. "Come on, please, softly, ever so softly..." he implored himself. "Softer still: morning – a golden gossamer... And now stronger, come on – at once sunshine, at once – my whole heart wide open. This is for you – here, everything wide open – see..."

She was sitting on a home-made ottoman, covered in Chinese silk, with her little fist propping up her narrow little face, which was sad about something. She was looking at the distant, oh-so-distant sun...

Now Andrei Ivanych was playing the mournful little four-flat part.

...Ever softer, ever slower, slower, my heart's stopping, it's impossible to breathe. Staccato – dry whispering – outstretched, beseeching arms, agonizingly parched lips, someone on their knees... "You can hear. There you are – there you are, I'm down on my knees. Tell me, perhaps you need something more? I mean, anything you..."

And suddenly – loudly and sharply. The mocking chromatic chords are ever quicker. It seems to Andrei Ivanych that he can sometimes be like this – he can be so divinely wrathful; he strikes, shaking, the three final blows – and silence.

He's finished – and there's nothing, neither wrath nor sunshine; he's simply Andrei Ivanych, and when he turned to Marusya he heard:

"Yes, that's good. Very..." She stood up straight. "You know, Shmit is cruel and strong. And yet, I mean, I'm happy submitting even to his cruelties. You understand: submitting in everything, completely."

The gossamer – and death. The sonata – and Shmit. There'd appear to be no connection, but if you looked into it...

Andrei Ivanych got up from the piano and started pacing round and round the sofa. Marusya said:

"What's the matter? Finish, go on... There's still the minuet, isn't there?"

"No, I'm not going to play any more – I'm tired," said Andrei Ivanych, and he kept on pacing, kept on pacing round the sofa.

"You're walking so far around the sofa, neglecting the sol-fa," said Marusya, suddenly fooling around, and once again she became a cheerful, fluffy little animal.

It was the Shmit thing that came out on top in Andrei Ivanych, and he laughed:

"You're a mischievous one, by the looks of it."

"Oh-oh-oh! What was I like as a girl, then – dear me, hang on to your hat! They were forever tying me to the sideboard on a string to stop me fooling around."

"And aren't you on a string now, then?" Andrei Ivanych teased.

"Hm... maybe I'm on a string now too, it's true. But the things I used to do then to fall over and break it – accidentally... I was so-o crafty! Or else, I remember, we had a garden, and in the garden there are some plum trees, and in the town there's cholera. I was strictly forbidden to eat unwashed plums. But washing them's boring and takes a long time. And so here's what I came up with: I'll put a plum in my mouth, lick it, lick it clean and eat it... it was clean now, after all, so why on earth not eat it?"

They were both laughing from deep down, like children do. "Come on, more, come on, laugh some more," Andrei Ivanych begged inside.

But Marusya had already stopped laughing, and again there was sadness on her lips:

"I don't laugh very often here, you know. It's boring here. And possibly even scary too."

Andrei Ivanych recalled what had gone on the day before, the faces howling at the moon, and how he himself – he'd start singing at any moment...

"Yes, maybe scary too," he said.

The orderly, Neprotoshnov, had come in unheard and stood rooted as one with the doorpost. They hadn't seen him. He coughed.

"Y'r 'onour. Madam..."

Andrei Ivanych glanced into his fishlike eyes with malicious envy, thinking: "He's here every day, always near..."

"Well, what is it?"

"Lieutenant Molochko's outside."

"Tell him to come in here," said Marusya, furrowing her brow in a discontented, funny way, and she turned towards Andrei Ivanych.

"She wanted it, then, she wanted us to be alone together…" thought Andrei Ivanych, and he greeted Molochko joyfully.

Molochko came in and started jumping up and down and chattering: it came pouring out like peas from a ripped sack… for Heaven's sake! Whether they listened or not, it didn't matter: just as long as he was talking and having a little chuckle at his own words himself.

"…And Tikhmen got down under the table yesterday, can you imagine? And he went on and on about his Petyashka…

"…And Captain Nechesa's got a problem: Private Arzhanoy's gone missing – what a louse, he runs off every winter…

"…And in Paris, can you imagine, there was a dinner, a hundred deputies, and then after the dinner they started counting, and five silver plates had gone missing. Surely not the deputies? I was thinking about it all the way here – I know I won't get to sleep tonight now…"

"Yes, it's evident you follow literature," said Andrei Ivanych with a smile.

"Yes, I told you, didn't I? Of course, of course. I follow literature very closely…"

Andrei Ivanych and Marusya exchanged a stealthy glance and barely concealed their laughter. And it was so good, so good: the two of them were like conspirators…

Andrei Ivanych loved Molochko now. "Come on, my dear fellow, more," he thought, "tell us some more…"

And Molochko told them how he had once been at a fire. A fireman had jumped down from the second floor and survived safe and sound – "Can you imagine?" And how an artillery NCO had made a young soldier stick his finger in a rifle: like that he could hold back the bullet, he'd said.

"And his finger got blown off, of course – can you imagine?"

Marusya had already laughed at everything, she'd used up all her laughter, and now she sat unsmiling. Andrei Ivanych got up to go home.

They were saying goodbye. "Should I kiss her hand or not?" he wondered. But Molochko leapt forward first, bent down and gave Marusya's hand a long, smacking kiss. Andrei Ivanych only shook it.

9
THE TWO TIKHMENS

Not without reason had Lieutenant Tikhmen been getting down under the table: his affairs were in an utterly dreadful way.

Tikhmen had this illness: thinking. And that's a very bad illness around these parts. Much better to be guzzling vodka in front of the mirror, better to be gambling on cards day and night – anything but that.

That's how good people explained it to Tikhmen. But he stuck to his guns. Well, and of course, his reading and thinking reached their conclusion: "Everything in the world is nothing but what the eyes see, my impression, the creation of my will." How about that, then: Captain Nechesa's an impression? Perhaps the general himself is too?

But that's the way Tikhmen is: what he's once got into his head – in that he will persist. And he continued in his disdain for the world, the female sex, child-rearing: Tikhmen never spoke of love in any other way. And children – to him they were always like a thorn in your side.

"For pity's sake, what are you going to try and explain to me? It's my view that all parents are numbskulls, pea-brained fish caught with a rod and line, yes. Children, so-called... For movement, for movement, I say – they're a barrow attached to your leg, it's all over... The end of flowering, sale for scrap – that's for the parents... You're laughing, though, gentlemen – well, to hell with you!"

But how can you refrain from laughing when Tikhmen's nose is so long and twisted to the left, and when he waves his arms about like a windmill? How can you refrain from laughing if Tikhmen is the great sceptic exclusively in his sober form, yet as soon as he's had a drink… And here, after all, in a remote spot, in a mousetrap, at the end of the – God forgive me – damned earth, how can you refrain from having a drink here?

And every time, after having a drink, the disdainful Tikhmen turns into an idealist: as in the ancient Eden, the tiger and the lamb get on very nicely in the soul of a Russian man.

After having a drink, Tikhmen is invariably daydreaming: a castle, a beautiful lady in a blue and silver dress, and before her – the knight Tikhmen with his visor down. The knight and the visor – all this is convenient because Tikhmen can hide his nose with the visor and leave just his lips exposed – in a word, can become handsome. And then, by the light of torches, the mystery of love is consummated, life flows so languidly, so quickly, and golden-haired children appear…

After sobering up, however, Tikhmen would curse himself for a numbskull and a pea-brained fish with no less fervour than he would his fellows, and was filled with still greater hatred for the substance that plays such jokes on people and that people frivolously style a turkey.*

A year before… yes, that's right: almost a year had now passed since the day when the ironic turkey had laughed at Tikhmen so meanly.

It was Yuletide – this place's mindless, slovenly, blind-drunk Yuletide. On the very first day Lieutenant Tikhmen got through his share of visits, got thoroughly plastered and returned home towards night-time a knight with his visor down.

Captain Nechesa was out and the captain's orderly, Lomailov, had put the children to bed long before. Alone and bored before the festively appetizing board was Captain Nechesa's wife: the first day, after all, is always festively boring.

It was with unwonted gallantry that the knight Tikhmen kissed the hand of the beautiful lady. And receiving a portion of goose from her little hands, said he:

"How glad I am it's night."

"And why is it that you're glad it's night?"

The sober Tikhmen, in the shape of a compliment, would have answered at the very most: "Because at night all cats are grey." But the knight Tikhmen said:

"Because the beauty that's concealed from us by daylight is revealed to us in the night-time."

This was to the taste of the captain's wife: she flashed all her countless dimples, gave the little round curls on her forehead a shake and launched her feminine charms upon Tikhmen.

They finished their meal and went into the captain's wife's boudoir, also her bedroom.

And again: the sober Tikhmen always avoided this haven of love like the plague – the two elephantine beds and, reposing side by side on a rack, the two Chinese gowns which the captain and his wife sported in the early morning and late evening. But the knight Tikhmen entered this castle willingly and joyfully after the beautiful lady.

Here the knight and his lady sat down to play "coachmen":* with a pencil stub they put circles representing towns on a sheet of paper and spent a long time driving each other about and trying to entrap one another.

Subsequently the knight was already guiding his lady's hand across the paper, to lighten her labour. And thus, imperceptibly, they drove all the way to the captain's wife's bed...

Had it not been for that accursed day, what would all the idiotic jokes about Petyashka have been to Tikhmen? Zero, two absolute hoots. But now... yes, the devil knows, maybe Petyashka really is...

"Oh, you numbskull, fool, pea-brained fish!"

Thus would Tikhmen take his head in his hands and chide himself... the sober one.

But the drunk one lamented the fact that he didn't know for sure whose Petyashka was. The drunk one's heart was simply breaking. And the main thing is, there's no knowing how to find out, is there? That's the truth, isn't it, eh?

But today Tikhmen had come back woozy after a dinner party at the general's and knew what to do, knew how to find out about Petyashka.

"What, then – won, have you? Well, I'm going to find out all the same…" Tikhmen teased the mysterious substance.

It was still early; the feast at the general's was still in full swing, Nechesa was still there, but Tikhmen deliberately, on purpose, to find out, had made his way quietly home – and was straight into the boudoir.

The captain's wife was still confined to bed: owing to her frequent labours, there was something wrong with her down there, and for a month now she'd been unable to summon up the strength to get properly well.

"Hello, Katyusha," said Tikhmen, kissing her little round hand.

"You seem polite, my dear, the way you were… back then. Don't forget there are children present."

Yes, everything here is as it was on that Yuletide evening too: the elephant beds, the robes on the rack. Only there are the children: eight of them, eight piggy-wiggies, each smaller than the other, and behind them, like Bruin on his hind legs, the orderly, Yashka Lomailov.

"Well, send the children away, I need to have a talk," Tikhmen said seriously.

The captain's wife winked at Yashka. Yashka and the eight kids vanished into thin air.

"Well, what is it, what the blazes do you want to talk about now?" the captain's wife asked angrily. But inside, curiosity had really flared up: "What's this? What can this stuffed dummy be on about?"

Tikhmen spent ages creaking and going all round the houses, forever quite lacking the courage to say what he really wanted.

"You see, Katyusha… Straight away it may even seem like, er… Well, in a word, all right, I want to know for sure: is Petyashka definitely mine – or not mine?"

Already round to begin with, at this point the captain's wife's little eyes grew even rounder and stared at Tikhmen in silence. Then she spluttered and started shaking her curls:

"There's a dolt, what a dolt – you've got me laughing, oh dear, honest to God! Well, and if I don't know – what then?"

"Is that true – you don't know?"

"There's an oddball! What, be hard for me to tell you, would it? I don't know – and that's the long and the short of it. Thinks he's an interrogator!"

"...She doesn't know either," he thought. "Now all's lost." Tikhmen set off crestfallen for his room.

In the corridor he bumped into Captain Nechesa: he too was walking along, seeing nothing.

"Oh, the devil take you! What's the matter with you, down in the mouth, eh?" the captain cursed.

Tikhmen glanced at Nechesa:

"And why are *you* down in the mouth?"

"Oh, brother! I've got a headache: Arzhanoy ran away, and though I didn't give a damn about that, he's now been found, and it turns out he's bumped off a Chinaman."

"Well, for me it's..." and without saying what, Tikhmen flapped an arm hopelessly.

10
O SOLDIER BOYS, BRAVO, MY LADS*

A true, good peasant is one who, if he's followed the plough for a bit and sniffed the earth, will never ever forget that earthy smell. That must have been the way of it with Arzhanoy. Let's say they send Arzhanoy for water on the company's Dobbin. He'll ride down the street with such a swagger, it really is quite something. Or if a spade gets thrust into Arzhanoy's paws: again, the clods simply fly, and the hole digs itself. And that's how it is with anything to do with husbandry. But when he was put into the ranks, he just gawped. He's a real headache for Captain Nechesa: Arzhanoy's a hefty right-flank man,* but he stands there gawping, do with him what you will…

"Arzhano-oy! What are you standing there like a stuffed dummy for, you oaf? What are you thinking about? What have you got in your head?"

And the devil knows what it is: quite likely, it can't be put into words. It's probably a dewy spring morning, there's steam rising from the ploughland, the ploughshare's greasy from the earth, gorged with earth, and there's a lark in the sky. And it's as if it's this bagatelle, the skylark, that's the key to the entire mechanism. And Arzhanoy keeps his head thrown back, keeps on gawping, as if to say: is that skylark up there, then?

"Arzhanoy, you slob, level up your bayonet with the middle line – can't you see?"

Arzhanoy looks at his bayonet – gosh, the way the sunlight's playing on it! – looks and thinks: "Now if, say, a ploughshare could be forged out of this bayonet – boy, what a ploughshare that'd be for breaking up new ground!"

And yet this would all be neither here nor there; this is all an in-house matter. But the way Arzhanoy had blotted his copy-book now – he'd bumped off a Chinaman – you can't just cover that up, you'll just have to go to the general with that, oh dear Lord…

Captain Nechesa shakes his shaggy head, and his little purple nose shakes too, lost in his beard, in his moustache.

"How could you, Arzhanoy, eh? Who was it put this into your head? Why?"

Arzhanoy had sprouted stubble while he'd been on the run, his cheekbones had become even more prominent, he'd become even more weather-beaten, had given himself up to the earth.

"It was like this, Y'r 'onour. These damned soldiers told me there are these Chinamen, they're going along the highway now, they said, like, with stags' antlers, and the price of these antlers is apparently five hundred… Well, I, like, runs off and lies in wait for a Chinaman…"

The captain started stamping his foot at Arzhanoy, barking furiously, and began laying into him good and proper. But Arzhanoy stands there grinning: he knows Captain Nechesa won't hurt a soldier, and the cursing's no big deal – harsh words won't break any bones.

And it was only when he heard he'd have to go before the general that Arzhanoy lost his nerve: at that point he even went quite white with terror.

Captain Nechesa saw this, turned off his fountain of invective, poured half a tumbler of vodka and angrily thrust it at Arzhanoy:

"Here, you so-and-so, drink this! And don't be afraid: we may be able to help you out somehow."

Arzhanoy's been taken away to the lock-up, and the captain's pacing uneasily around the room, thinking:

"A rascal like him goes horsing around, and it's you that has to sort out the mess, you have to find a way out. And what mood will we find the general in, too? He might even want a court martial..."

The captain paces around, not knowing what to do with himself. He's started on his favourite song, the only one the captain sings:

> O soldier boys, bravo, my lads,
> Where, then, are your wives?

One of Katyushka's admirers is sitting with her: gosh, how round her chuckling is, and resonant. There's no point going anywhere near Tikhmen just now; he's walking around as black as thunder, whereas at least you could have a game of suicide draughts with him before and forget about your troubles and sorrows while playing... Oh dear!

Giving up on things, the captain takes out his glasses in their black horn frames. The captain reads with the naked eye, and the glasses are put on in only two instances: the first is when Captain Nechesa is mending some part of his attire, and the second...

Captain Nechesa picks up his weapon – a cheap needle which Lomailov, his orderly, has set specially into a good walnut handle. Captain Nechesa strikes up his favourite – and only – song and wanders around beside the dining-room walls. At one time the walls had undoubtedly been papered with excellent pale-blue wallpaper. But now all that was left of the wallpaper was an unpleasant memory, and across that memory crawl ginger cockroaches with long antennae.

> Our wives are loaded rifles,
> That is where our wives are!
> O soldier boys, bravo, my…

"Aha, you devil, got you! Take that!"

Quivering on the cheap needle there's a ginger cockroach. It must be because of the glasses that the captain's face is owlish, ferocious, and as for shaggy – my goodness, it is… The captain gazes at the cockroach with bloodthirsty satisfaction, throws his catch down onto the floor and squashes it under his foot with enjoyment.

> Our sisters are sabre weapons sharp,
> That is where our sis…

"A-ah, you so-and-so, crawling into the sideboard? Be crawling now, will you? Will you?"

And to look at Captain Nechesa now – well, honest to God, it's even scary: oh, you animal, great big beast, won't you tell your name at least?* But anyone who's eaten a peck of salt with the captain is very well aware that the captain's ferocity is only for the cockroaches and beyond the cockroaches he won't extend it.

Take the captain's wife, for example: the captain's wife has children every year, and one looks like the adjutant, another like Molochko, a third like Ivanenko… But Captain Nechesa couldn't care less. Either it doesn't occur to him, or else he thinks: "So be it, they're all little babies, all God's angels," or else it simply can't be otherwise in these here parts, at the damned end of the earth, where any woman, even the most useless, knows her own considerable worth. But Captain Nechesa loves all eight of his children, and the ninth, Petyashka, into the bargain – loves them all equally and fusses over all of them.

So now, too, after wiping his cockroach-stained hands on his trousers, he goes into the nursery to quieten his anxiety over Arzhanoy. Eight tatty, cheerful, grimy little ragamuffins… And for a long time, until it gets quite dark, Captain Nechesa's playing hide-and-seek with the grimy kids.

The orderly, Yashka Lomailov, Bruin, sits on a chest in the entrance hall with a candle and puts a patch on the knee of Kostenka's trousers: the little lad's clothes are quite worn out. And from the captain's wife's boudoir, also the bedroom with the elephant beds, Katyushka's merry laughter can be heard. Oh, Heavens! Don't let there be a tenth, come summer!

II
A GREAT WOMAN

Shmit was detailed by written order to travel into town. Shmit was not a little surprised. It might have been a matter of taking delivery of new sighting devices, but all the same, it was generally small fry who'd be detailed for such things, second lieutenants. And now suddenly him, Captain Shmit. Well, so be it…

Off he went. Andrei Ivanych and Marusya were on the jetty. They saw Shmit off and went home together. The ice on the puddles crunched with a cold crackle beneath their feet. The earth – frozen, dingy, bare – lay like an unwashed corpse.

"Back home now it's soft, there's snow and snowdrifts," said Marusya.

Her chin sank still deeper into her soft fur, she became still more a fearful, fluffy, dear little animal.

Showing black to the right are ridges, bushy with forest, and below them a misty valley. And stirring in the mist, standing right by the road, like beggars, are seven tottering wooden crosses.

"The Seven Crosses – d'you know?" asked Marusya, nodding in that direction.

Andrei Ivanych shook his head: no. He was afraid to use his tongue in case this thing that was beating inside him now and was frightening to name should take off and fly away.

"Seven young officers – did for themselves... And not so very long ago, about eight or nine years. All in the same year, as if of an infection. The graveyard wasn't allowed for them, of course..."

"...Seven," he thought. "Did they do it separately or all at once? Yes, the mess, there was a priest who had a dog... Ugh, what nonsense! An infection. Maybe love?"

That was the road Andrei Ivanych dashed down, and out loud he said:

"Well, of course, love is a sickness, isn't it? Lunatics... I don't know why no one's tried treating it with hypnosis. It would probably be possible."

Andrei Ivanych sought her eyes to see whether she was hearing what he was saying, what he wanted to say. But her eyes were hidden.

"Yes, perhaps," Marusya replied to herself. "A sickness... Like sleepwalkers, like cataleptics. To bear any pain, suffering, to crucify oneself for... for... Oh, it's all good, it's all sweet!"

Now Andrei Ivanych could see her eyes. They were really shining, radiant. But who for, on whose account?

"...I'll tell her – I'll tell her everything today," thought Andrei Ivanych. He started to tremble with a delicate, very sharp tremor, and he heard it like the sound of a string somewhere at the far right end of the piano keyboard – it kept ringing and ringing.

Before entering the settlement they stopped and looked back one last time at the sky. Sunset was blazing in the ragged clouds: something alarming and red had surged up from below and frozen, hung there, bent over, growing...

The Shmits' sweet log dining room. The familiar smell – maybe hemp-nettle, maybe goatweed. But everything here had been simple, bucolic, calm before, and now it was moving, changing every second; all the time there was something cracking. And never before had Andrei Ivanych seen this trembling red tongue of the lamp.

Marusya was too cheerful. She was telling a story:

"Shmit was still a young cadet in a white canvas... Even then he was cruel, stubborn. I so wanted him to kiss me, but he... And I was swinging on a swing – it was hot. Well, I thought, just you wait! And I went crashing to the ground off the swing..."

There was a knock at the door. In ran the general's shiny samovar, Larka, and standing like a statue in the semi-darkness somewhere behind him was Neprotoshnov. Marusya nodded cheerfully to Larka, tore open the envelope he'd handed her and put it down on the table: first she had to finish what she'd been saying:

"...crashing to the ground – and I cry: ouch, I've hurt myself! At that point, of course, Shmit's heart could bear no more: 'Where,' he says, 'where?' I pointed to my shoulder: 'Here.' Well, of course, he... But I pointed to my lips as well: 'I've hurt myself here too,' I say. Well, and on the lips too... So that's how cunning we are, women, you know – if we want to be!"

She burst out laughing, turned pink, and was that same girl on the swing.

"Now, I'll tell her everything now..." thought Andrei Ivanych, gazing at her.

She took out the letter and read. The swing was sinking slowly downwards, ever downwards. But her smile still held out on her face like a frozen little autumn birdie on a leafless tree: it was already frosty, it was already time to fly away, but it was still sitting and chirping – seemingly the same as in the summer, but with quite a different result.

"Here... I don't even understand, I can't... Here... you..." and she ran out of breath. She proffered the letter to Andrei Ivanych:

Dear Madam, my sweet Marya Vladimirovna. On the fifteenth of November this year your dearest hubby committed an act of assault and battery upon me (the witnesses: my orderly, Larka, my wife and my sister-in-law Agniya; the last-named saw everything through the crack in the door). The price for such things is, of course, not the three days in the guardhouse which Captain Shmit has served, but something a little more serious: penal servitude – from twelve years upwards. The course of this matter hereafter, viz. its consignment to the discretion of a military court or to eternal oblivion, depends entirely upon you, dear madam, Marya Vladimirovna. If you wish to settle your hubby's account, then come to me tomorrow at twelve noon, before lunch. And if you don't wish to, then that, my sweet, is up to you. But if you were to come, I, an old man, would be oh so glad!

Your admirer, Azancheyev.

Marusya clung to Andrei Ivanych's eyes, begged him with her frozen, disbelieving smile to say it was untrue, that nothing was going to happen to Shmit…

"It's untrue, isn't it, isn't it – untrue?" It seems as if she's about to get down on her knees.

"It's true," was all Andrei Ivanych could say.

"Lord, no!" Marusya sobbed, just like a child. She put a finger in her mouth and bit as hard as she could…

She sat like that for a long time, then turned away. Andrei Ivanych heard some strange snatches of what was either laughter or else deathbed hiccups.

"For a minute… for God's sake… go out… into the hall, I need to be alone…"

Alone. She stood up, went over to the wall, leant her face against it so no one could see… Everything in her head had dislocated, tumbled down, downhill, uncontrollably. She had a vision – and where from? – of an icon lamp before a holy day, her mother prostrated before the icon, so odd, folded in two, and one of them, one of the children, lying ill.

"Well, and if I don't go?" she thought. "But he won't take pity on Shmit, will he… No, he won't!"

"Mama!" she cried softly.

No one replied.

"Sweet Mother of God, you've always loved me, haven't you, always… Don't forsake me, dear, I've got no one – no one, no one…"

When Andrei Ivanych went back into the cheerful log dining room, Marusya wasn't there. Marusya, the cheerful girl on the swing, had died. Andrei Ivanych saw a stern, doleful woman who had both given birth and buried: those deep lines around the corners of the lips – are they not signs of burial? And let life plough the furrows yet deeper – a Russian woman can bear anything, lift anything.

Marusya said calmly, but very, very quietly:

"Andrei Ivanych, please… Go and say to the orderly that, all right, I'll…"

"You'll? You'll go?"

"I have to, don't I – otherwise…"

Everything inside Andrei Ivanych started trembling, grew dim. He got down on his knees; his lips were shaking, he was searching for words…

"You… you… you are a great woman… How I loved you…"

He didn't dare say "love". Marusya looked down calmly from above. But her hands, her fingers were intertwined very tightly.

"I'm better alone. Tomorrow… no, come the day after tomorrow, when Shmit will be coming back. I can't meet him by myself…"

Neither moon nor stars, a heavy sky. Down the middle of the street, stumbling on the frozen mud, ran Andrei Ivanych.

"No, it can't be allowed…" he thought. "It's unthinkable, outrageous. Something has to be done, something has to be done… There was a priest who had a dog… Oh Lord, what's that got to do with it?"

As if delirious, he ran all the way to the general's house: blind, dark windows; everyone's asleep.

"Shall I ring?" he wondered. "They're all undressed. It's past midnight, isn't it. Absurd, ridiculous…"

He ran around it one more time: not a single light. If there were just one, just one, then he might yet… But as it is – maybe better wait till tomorrow?

Andrei Ivanych felt his back pocket:

"And I haven't got my revolver – what, am I going to do it with my bare hands? Ridiculous, it'll just be ridiculous! Oh dear..." he thought.

In the same way, like mad, headlong, he ran all the way home. He rang and waited. And at that point he suddenly pictured it clearly: Marusya and the general's pot belly, maybe even white with green splodges like a frog's. He gnashed his teeth: "Oh, I'm damned!"

But his orderly, Guslyaikin, grinning amiably, was already locking the door.

12
THE BENEFACTOR

The general had got up ever so early today: by nine o'clock he was already feeling hale and hearty, had knocked back his coffee and was sitting in his study. On Fridays the general administered justice and meted out punishment.

"Well, Larka, who's here? Give me a quick turnaround, I want you spinning like a top – well?"

The general flopped down into his chair: the chair even let out a groan and barely remained standing. He screwed his eyes up contentedly and let his fingers play on his belly:

"Will the little darling come or not?" he wondered. "Oh my, what a little birdie, nice and slim, nice and jolly... Oh my!"

The general was roused by the deep, watchdog's bark of Captain Nechesa:

"It's Arzhanoy, Your Excellency, who killed the Chinaman. He's here, may I report, I've brought him."

"Oh, she'll come, the little darling, yes, and she'll humour an old man – she'll come," mused the general with a smile like a pancake swimming in butter.

"What is it he's grinning for? What's he so happy about?" wondered Nechesa, goggle-eyed. He moved closer to the general.

"Shall I bring them in, Your Excellency? They're here."

"Bring them in, my dear, bring them in! Just be quick about it..."

They came into the study and stood by the two doorposts: Arzhanoy – steady, as always, though after being on the run he was stubbly and tousled – and the witness, Opyonkin – pock-marked, with a beard like shredded bast, a village gossip, by the look of it, a chatterbox and a loudmouth.

If horses had been dragged into the study from the stables now, they'd probably have backed off, reared up and snorted in fear in just the same way. And just as with Arzhanoy and Opyonkin, Captain Nechesa would have been unable to get a word out of them with red-hot pincers.

"Don't be afraid – what's wrong with you?" the captain cajoled Opyonkin. "This isn't your concern, is it: nothing's going to happen to you."

"My concern or not, if the general gets worked up..." thought Opyonkin, silently rearing up. However, bit by bit he got his bearings and opened his mouth. And once he had, there was no stopping him: he chatters away, loving the sound of his own voice.

"Well then, the Chinese, ord'n'rily, the Chinaman – a Chinaman, that's what 'e is. I come across 'im, y'might say, on the outskirts, 'e's walkin' along an' 'e's got a whoppin' great sack on 'is back. Well, of course, 'e says to me: ''Ello 'ello.' An' 'e started babblin' away in their lingo, an' off he went... Well, I says, waddya want, you nutter? Don't understand nuffin', I says. Why can't you, like, talk our lingo, like I do? S'easy, like, an' anyone can understand. But oh no – like 'ell, 'e's manglin' 'is words like an idiot—"

"Hey now, brother, you're way off! Better tell us about Arzhanoy: how did you come across him?"

"Arzhanoy? Well of course, oh Lord! The way 'e started tellin' me about 'is brother's wife, about the littl'uns... Each one smaller than the other, 'e says, they wanna eat an' they got their mouths, 'e says, wide open. They've opened their mouths wide, like... An' Arzhanoy 'ad me so tearful with those words, 'e 'ad me so tearful... I'm walkin' along the footway sobbin' me 'eart out, y'might say, an' there I changes me boots..."

At this point even the general woke up, stopped grinning about some matter of his own, and his froggy eyes popped out of his head:

"I changes me boots? Why on earth is that, then: I changes me boots?"

And how is it the gentlemen don't understand what's what? So now he's got Opyonkin confused, and that's the end of it. How can you possibly interrupt a man like that? So now Opyonkin's gone and forgotten everything, and there's nothing more.

Arzhanoy told his story in a steady manner in his bass voice. The main thing was – if they'd only let him go and dig them there antlers up. Or else some damned soldiers would find out... The antlers are worth five hundred, after all, oh Lord...

"Your Excellency, do allow me to go and get 'em. I mean, it's, like, it's what us peasants do, the money's needed so bad, there's the taxes again..."

The general was smiling again, bouncing around a little in his chair like this: up and down, up and down. He was tickling his tummy:

"Ah, the little darling, she's crying, I dare say, overflowing..." he thought. "Ah, sweet child, how could I comfort you? Or maybe take pity on you, eh?"

The general shook his head at Arzhanoy:

"Dear me, you lummox! All you want is the antlers. And don't you think anything of bumping a man off? You have to take pity on a man, my dear fellow, take pity, that's what."

"Your Excelle... But I mean, they're Chinamen. Are they really men? They're kinda like big partridges. Even God's not gonna make you answer for them. Your Excelle... let me have the antlers – I mean, the little kiddies, food and drink... their mouths wide open..."

The general started cackling, and his belly started shifting and flopping around:

"What, what? Like partridges, you say? Ha-ha-ha! Well, all right, here's what. This here son of a bitch... Ha-ha! So they're like partridges, you say? Give it him with the lash as an informal procedure, got it? And then to hell with him, let him go and get the antlers, and then he's under arrest for ten days, there…"

Arzhanoy plopped down at his feet, thinking: "So the antlers are mine, then?"

"Your Excelle… my protector, my benefactor!"

As he was leaving, Captain Nechesa thought:

"Ah, there's something behind this, he's being terribly kind somehow today!"

The general went out into the drawing room, screwing his eyes up and smiling. His wife was sitting by the window and warming a glass with something red in it in her hand.

"Whose voice was it I heard, Mother? Molochko, was it? Are you still keeping company?"

"Molochko seems to have started shirking," said the general's wife, looking absent-mindedly past him. "He's got warts growing on him, so unpleasant. You should take him in hand…"

Agniya came leaping up. She wriggled and bounced around beside the general:

"Molochko was talking about Tikhmen: the fellow's gone completely barmy, still trying to find out whether Petyashka, the captain's wife's ninth, is his or not…"

Agniya giggled into her dry little fist. The general nudged her merrily in the ribs:

"And you, Agniya, when are you going to have a baby, eh? Perhaps you ought to marry Larka: why go to waste like this?"

And Larka had arrived just at that moment and was standing in the doorway. Agniya caught sight of him and started jumping and wailing: "May you, may you, may you b-burn in hell…"

Larka sidled up to the general fondly:

"Your Excellency, there's someone waiting for you through there… They've come to you personally, they say."

The general started positively quivering. "Has she really actually come?" he wondered.

He minced off in a hurry. His belly hurried off in front – it looked as if the general was wheeling it in front of him on a barrow. His trousers were hitched up high and flapping above his boots.

Agniya instinctively sensed something going on and, saying "Back in a minute," she flitted away from the general's wife to her room.

The tiny room is a little shoebox, and yet there's cheerful wallpaper, with crimson bouquets, and the smell of some kind of pink, bubbly soap. And all the walls have portraits cut out of *The Field* and *Homeland** plastered all over them: Agniya would neatly cut out all the portraits of men and take them off to her room – generals, bishops and famous scholars too.

Yet neither the bouquets nor even the portraits are the main point. But rather the fact that under a large portrait of Alexander III* Agniya had hidden a hole, made with long labour and skill, through into the general's study. And now, with her ear glued to the hole, she could catch, like manna from heaven, everything going on at that moment in the study.

13
A HEAVY LOAD

Shmit came back from town ever so cheerful: Andrei Ivanych hadn't seen him like this in a long time. The three of them walked from the jetty: Shmit invited him to dinner. Andrei Ivanych went to try and refuse, but Shmit would have none of it.

"Dear me, there's slush ice moving down the gulf," said Shmit. "There's lumps of ice scraping by the launch, the engine's banging for all it's worth... Dear me, what a good thing it is, a struggle!"

He walked along, tall, too heavy for the earth, gulping down the frosty air.

"A struggle," thought Andrei Ivanych out loud. "It's exhausting, a struggle. What's the point?"

"A rest is even more exhausting," chuckled Shmit.

"No, he won't be getting tired any time soon," thought Andrei Ivanych, looking at Shmit. "He wouldn't have stopped to think about their being asleep, about not having a revolver... And none of this would have happened. Or maybe it didn't as it is?"

For the first time that day, Andrei Ivanych plucked up his courage and glanced at Marusya. Nothing... But just that immobility of her face and the firmly entwined fingers...

"She was there – it... happened," thought Andrei Ivanych, going quite cold.

"Well, what have you been doing, Marusya? What have you been dreaming about?" asked Shmit, leaning down towards Marusya. His harsh, forged chin disappeared. Shmit became all soft.

It can sometimes happen that stevedores strain and strain at a load, but it simply won't budge. They've sung 'The Little Oak Tree' and come out with some astounding couplet about the contractor* – come on, one more time! – they've exerted themselves: and it won't budge, as if bewitched.

In the same way Marusya, too, was now straining to smile: she's gathered all her strength in one place – her lips – and she can't, she just can't, they won't budge, and her whole face is trembling.

Watching without breathing, Andrei Ivanych could see it: "My God," he thought, "if Shmit just looks round at her now, if he just looks round..."

A second, just one endless little second – and Marusya had gained control and smiled. And only her voice was barely perceptibly trembling:

"Good Lord, the way you sometimes dream about pointless things, it's ridiculous! All night I was dreaming about having to divide seventy-eight by four. And then I've already seemingly done the division, I've got it, but when it comes to writing it down, I've forgotten the number again and it's gone. And again, seventy-eight divided by four – I don't know how to do it, I'm losing, but I know I need to. It's so horrible, so agonizing..."

"Agonizing" – that was a little window to that place, to the truth. And Marusya even felt happy to say the word, to imbue it with all her pain. And again, Andrei Ivanych caught all of it, once more he went cold and turned to ice.

Shmit was walking in front of the two of them with his confident, firm, heavy step. Without turning around, he said:

"Oh dear, Maruska, you sound like it's something serious! You need to be able to shrug off such trifles. And not only trifles, by the way, but everything…"

And at once Shmit suddenly became odious for Andrei Ivanych; for some reason the way Shmit had shaken his hand came to mind.

"You're… you're an egotist," said Andrei Ivanych angrily.

"An e-go-tist? Do you think, then, dear boy, there are altruists? Ha-ha-ha! It's just the same egotism, only in bad taste… They follow lepers around and do all sorts of disgusting things… for the sake of their own satisfaction…"

"The d-damned devil…" thought Andrei Ivanych. "And what about what she's done? Does he really… does he really not notice, not sense anything?"

But Shmit was laughing:

"E-go-tist… Do you know how young ladies write that word? Oh Lord, who was it that told me the story? There's a couple sitting on a bench and the girl traces 'i—t' in the sand with her parasol. 'Guess,' she says, 'what it is I've written about you.' Her admirer looks and, of course, reads 'idiot'. And it's a tragedy… But actually it was 'igotist'…"

Marusya needed to laugh. Again the bewitched load, and the stevedores exerted themselves for all they were worth… She bit her lips, and Andrei Ivanych turned pale.

Finally she laughed… thank God, she's laughed! But at that same second her laughter cracked open, the fragments started tumbling and rattling and her tears gushed out in three streams.

"Shmit, dear! I can't go on any more, I can't, forgive me, Shmit, I'll tell you everything… you'll understand, won't you, Shmit, you've got to understand! Or else what?"

She was throwing her little child's arms about, and the whole of her was reaching out to Shmit, but she didn't dare touch him: after all, she...

Shmit turned towards Andrei Ivanych, towards his contorted face, but saw no surprise in it. Shmit's eyes narrowed, became blade-like.

"You... you already know? Why do you know this before I do?"

Andrei Ivanych frowned, there was a lump blocking his throat. He waved a hand in annoyance:

"Oh, leave it, you and I can have it out later! Just look at her: you should be falling at her feet, you know."

Through gritted teeth Shmit squeezed out:

"The mus-si-cian! I know these mus-si..."

But behind him he heard a light rustling. He turned around, and as Marusya had been standing, so had she sat down onto the ground, with her legs folded beneath her and her eyes closed.

Shmit took her in his arms and carried her off.

14

A PATTERN OF SNOW

Every day, in the evening, Andrei Ivanych would go up to the Shmits' gate, take hold of the bell and go away again: damned as he was, he couldn't, he just couldn't, go in there and see Marusya. Of course he was damned: why hadn't he killed the general that night? Shmit would have.

But even so, still less could he sit in his hateful room and not know what was going on there.

"Good Lord," he thought, "if I could just somehow get a glimpse, if only a little one, of how she is, how she's getting on..."

And on the fifth day, towards evening, Andrei Ivanych managed to come up with something. He pulled on his overcoat, started to pick up his sword, then put it back in the corner.

"Where is it you're off to at this time of night?" asked Guslyaikin with, it seemed to Andrei Ivanych, a wink.

"I... I'll be some time – go to bed."

Outside, snow had fallen the day before. Not real snow, of course, not Russian snow, just a little on the surface.

"Snow – that's not good," he thought. "There's the crunching, and the moon makes it as bright as day… It doesn't matter. I have to…"

Andrei Ivanych couldn't stop his teeth chattering – was it from the cold? Of course not: the frost was nothing out of the ordinary.

The Shmits' windows were veiled with a brilliant pattern of frost. Andrei Ivanych stood up on tiptoe and began patiently warming the glass with his breath so as to get a glimpse – Lord, if only a little one, only a little one!

Now he could see: they were in their dining room. The door out of it wasn't shut properly, and in the drawing room there was a blue half-light and dimly sharp shadows from the palm – on the sofa and on the floor.

Andrei Ivanych shivered and gazed in through the thawed circle. His hands and feet were getting cold. Sometime later, maybe half an hour, maybe an hour, it occurred to him:

"Standing spying, spying like some Agniya or other! To what an extent, then, am I… I have to go away…"

He took a step back – and stopped: he didn't have the strength to go away any farther. Suddenly he saw: on the snowy screen of the window, two shadows had started swaying, a large one and one rather smaller. He forgot everything, flung himself towards the window and started shaking as if in a fever.

The thawed patches on the window were already obscured by a film of snow and nothing could be made out… "What's going on?…" he thought. "What are they doing in there? What are they doing?"

The small shadow had become smaller, had knelt down, or maybe fallen, or maybe… The large shadow bent down towards it…

Andrei Ivanych sank the whole of his being into the damned snowy veil, striving to tear it apart…

Cr-rack! The glass broke, there was the sting of pain on his forehead, something wet. Blood... Andrei Ivanych leapt back, gazed stupefied at the shards by his feet, stood and gazed as if transfixed: he didn't even think of running.

When he came to his senses, Shmit was already beside him.

"A-ah, so it's you, the mus-s-si-cian? Prying, were you, sir?"

Andrei Ivanych saw Shmit's sharp, wild eyes very close to him.

"Charming! You've ac-climatized quickly."

"Should I raise a hand? Strike him?" wondered Andrei Ivanych. "But it's true, isn't it, but it's true..." He groaned. And stood there. And was silent.

"On this occasion... Cl-lear off!"

Shmit slammed the gate behind him.

"...Straight away – at once! Get back and blow my brains out... Straight away!" thought Andrei Ivanych as he ran off home. His face was burning as if he'd been slapped.

Andrei Ivanych couldn't say now whether Guslyaikin had unlocked the door or not. He thought not, but he was already sitting at the table, nonetheless, and gazing at his revolver – so horribly shiny under the lamp.

"But after all, absolutely no one saw," he thought. "Though that isn't even the point either. The main thing is that Marusya will be left alone, won't she – alone with him. I mean, it's possible he beats her, and if I'm not here..."

He put the revolver away, hurriedly locked it up. He blew out the lamp and without undressing – as he was, wearing his boots – he flopped onto the bed and gritted his teeth: "Oh you damned... you damned coward."

...A slimy, mistily grey morning.

Guslyaikin was mercilessly shaking Andrei Ivanych awake:

"Y'r 'onour, they've brought the shopping from town."

"What, what's that? What shopping?"

"You ordered it yourself last week, you did, y'r'on. I mean, it's Christmas Day tomorrow, I think!"

His thoughts, healed by sleep, woke up and started aching.

Christmas... His favourite holiday. Bright lights, a ball, someone's lovely, perfumed handkerchief, stolen and kept under his pillow... It had all happened, it was all finished, and now...

This was how it was: he had sunk to the bottom, he was sitting at the bottom, and moving above his head was a troubled, heavy lake. And everything that could be heard from up there, from above, was muffled, obscure, clouded.

On the first day, Andrei Ivanych found it very strange to put on his tunic and go out paying visits. All the same, wound up by some kind of winding mechanism, he went. He gave his best wishes, kissed hands, even laughed. But he himself could hear his laughter...

Somewhere – maybe at the Nesterovs', maybe at Ivanenko's, maybe at the Kosinskys' – there was a dispute about a sucking-pig, how it should be served up. Should it be decorated with paper frills or not? A ham, of course, should be, anyone knows that, but what about a sucking-pig? And when the disputants asked Andrei Ivanych's opinion ("You've come from Russia only recently, after all – that's very important"), it was then that Andrei Ivanych burst out laughing and heard himself thinking: "Me, laughing? Me?"

At one house – the Nechesas', it would seem – visible through open doors from the dining room were two bulbous marital beds standing next to each other. Looking in that direction and knocking back maybe his fifth, maybe his tenth glass, Andrei Ivanych unexpectedly asked:

"What's going on now at the Shmits'?"

"You're an odd fish, I mean, you've got such a treasure – Guslyaikin. Ask him: he's in the Shmits' kitchen day and night," advised the captain's nice round wife.

The brandy, the vodka and the oppressive slab of the night made the troubled lake even deeper, even heavier.

After his visits, Andrei Ivanych sat at his table, gazed senselessly at the lamp, and didn't listen to what Guslyaikin, standing by the doorpost, was recounting. Then it came to mind: a treasure... Andrei Ivanych livened up and asked without looking:

"And have you been at Captain Shmit's recently?"

"I was there today. You bet. The doings there, the doings there, wow... It's a farce!"

Andrei Ivanych couldn't listen – but still more he couldn't not listen. He was completely ablaze with shame – and he listened. And he said:

"And then? Well, and what next?"

And when Guslyaikin had finished, Andrei Ivanych staggered over to him.

"How d-dare you tell me such... such things, how dare you?"

"But Y'r 'onour, I mean, you yourself..."

"...How dare you... about her, about h-her, you b-bastard!" Smack! Andrei Ivanych's hand just sank into a kind of jelly-like blancmange – so wishy-washy were Guslyaikin's cheeks. It was so disgusting: as though his whole hand was now soiled.

15
AN EVIL SPIRIT

The 25th of January is the feast day of Felicitas the Holy Martyr,* the name day of the general's wife, Felitsata Afrikanovna. And this is the way things are done at General Azancheyev's: a dinner on Felicitas's Day and a party in the evening. And not a simple dinner or a simple party either, but always with a ruse, some kind of tricky snag. The general might present all the officers' wives with a bunch of roses before dinner: "Here you are, my dear ladies – I grew them for you myself in the orangery and picked them myself too." The ladies, of course, are pleased and grateful: "Oh, how sweet of you, *merci*, what a scent..." They take one sniff, another, and then they all start sneezing: the roses have been given a good dusting of snuff! Or else at the last dinner – the previous year, then – the fun had been like this. Dinner was cooked by the general, splendidly, too, but particularly noteworthy was the bouillon. And indeed: amber in colour like champagne, islets of limpid fat on the surface, and a sprinkling of Chinese pasta

– there's dragons, and stars, and fish, and little men. After dinner, walking was more than the guests could manage: the general took his guests for a drive, promised to show them some sort of curiosity. And when they'd gone five *versts* or so, the general gave the command – stop! – and announced to all his loyal subjects:

"It wasn't fat on the bouillon, gentlemen, that was castor oil floating on the surface. And it never occurred to any one of you, ha-ha-ha!"

We-ell… The things that went on then!

There was no doubt that there'd be something of the sort this year too. Although the general had run away to town to escape Shmit, and although he was sitting there to this day, it wasn't possible that he wouldn't come back for St Felicitas's Day. Of course not – after all, Captain Nechesa, the senior man during the commanding officer's everlasting leave, had already had orders from the general to round up all the soldiers and start work on levelling a field. Exercises of various kinds and shooting practice were called off, of course: there's plenty of that nonsense every day, whereas the general's wife's name day is only once a year.

And the soldiers scattered all over the field behind the powder magazine – just like grey ants. Thank the Lord, too, it was foggy and there was a thaw, or else it would have been quite impossible to bite into the soil. True, it was pretty muddy, the clay got very messy, smearing and clinging, and all the soldiers looked like roughnecks. But, well, there's nothing that can be done about it: that's soldiering. And they dig and dig, shunt wheelbarrows about, swarm around, grey, docile, bent in two. Perhaps there were going to be races in the field or perhaps something else: until St Felicitas's Day not a single living soul knew the general's secret…

Sitting on a cut log off to one side with his back turned was Tikhmen: he was overseeing the work. He was sick of everything: of the besmeared louts of soldiers and their docile yessirring, of the fog – a creeping yellow snake – and, most of all, of him himself, Tikhmen.

Truly: some snotty little Petyashka – and suddenly everything's going to the devil. Everything used to be so clear: there had been "things in themselves", which had been of no concern whatsoever to Tikhmen, and there had been "reflections of things" in Tikhmen, obedient to, and dependent upon, Tikhmen. And now – if you please! It was just as though some kind of evil spirit had got into him, honest to God!

…A church, a ray of sunshine. One of the adults is leading Tikhmen away by the hand, but he's pulling back; he wants to listen some more to a raving woman calling out – it's interesting and scary: she's simultaneously calling in her own voice, a woman's, and in one not her own, a dog's.*

"Yes," he thought. "And isn't this all just dogs' stuff? Both this filth, this love, and that lousy whelp Petyashka?"

But the dog's voice – the evil spirit – inside Tikhmen is whining:

"Petyashka… Oh dear, how could I find out? For certain? Whose is Petyashka really?"

"Hello, Tikhmen. What are you dreaming about?"

The two Tikhmens – the real Tikhmen and the dog Tikhmen – gave a start, joined together as one, and that one leapt up.

Sitting in front of Tikhmen in a little box, the regimental cabriolet, was Captain Nechesa's wife. She had got out of bed for the first time today, and her first outing was to see the general's wife – or, strictly speaking, to see Agniya. She was burning to ferret out in detail what had happened and how between the general and that Marusya of Shmit's. "Oh, thank God," she thought, "the Lord's punished her for her pride, she's such a princess on a pea…"

The captain's wife had a bit of a gossip, flashed her dimples a bit and drove off. And at once the two Tikhmens settled down again on the log, started jostling and arguing.

The dog Tikhmen said:

"Captain Nechesa's at home by himself now, isn't he, yes…"

And with his inherent canine sense of smell he discovered a track, invisible to a man, and ran off, winding and prowling along it. He spent some time wandering in circles and suddenly – stop, found it, sniffed it out:

"A dullard, I'm a dullard! Why, of course: go and ask the captain himself. He must know whose Petyashka is. How could he not know?"

Tikhmen stood up and beckoned Arzhanoy over with a finger.

"Well, how are we getting on?"

A gawper in the ranks, here, working the land, Arzhanoy's a trump card and past master, and answers for everyone.

"Well, Y'r 'onour, almost everyone's finished their jobs by now. There's maybe about ten of them or so men left…"

"Ten of them or so men? Well, all right." Tikhmen gave up. "Finish off without me, I'm going. You keep an eye on things, Arzhanoy."

Tikhmen ran hurriedly into Nechesa's dining room. And so it is, thank God: the captain's at home.

In front of the captain stood a soldier. Captain Nechesa was very gravely pouring out some powder. He added a little more and weighed it up in his palm: that'll do.

"Here you are – take this for the good of your health. Oh, don't mention it, don't mention it!"

Nechesa imagined himself to be a really good healer. And a soldier would go to him more happily than to the medical orderly or the doctor: those two were far too clever.

There was just one difficulty: about five years before, one of Nechesa's patients had stolen *The School of Health*, and the captain had been left with only *The Home Veterinary Book*.* There was nothing for it: he had to function on the basis of the veterinary book. And honest to God, the results were no worse: well, what's the difference really? It's the same mechanism, whether it belongs to a man or a beast.

After he'd been practising medicine, the captain was regularly in a marvellous mood. He tickled Tikhmen's ribs:

"Well, what is it, brother Pushkin?"*

"The thing is, I was wanting to ask—"

"No, brother, you sit down first, have a drink, and then we'll see."

They sat down. Had a drink and a bite to eat. Tikhmen plucked up his courage again and started to approach the matter in a roundabout way: this and that, and how it was going to be hard to help Petyashka find his feet... But the captain promptly cut Tikhmen short:

"Over food? Talking about lofty matters? You've gone daft! You evidently don't understand the first thing about medicine. How can we possibly be having the kinds of conversation that make the blood go to our heads? We need to have it all going to our stomachs..."

Oh good Lord! What can you do? And at this point in flew all eight of the captain's ragamuffins, too, and with them Bruin on his hind legs – the orderly, Yashka Lomailov.

The little Nechesas were giggling and whispering to one another – there was some kind of conspiracy. Then, chuckling, the eldest little girl, Varyushka, went flying up to Tikhmen.

"Mister, hey mister, do you have any liver? Eh?"

"Li... liver," laughed the captain.

Tikhmen frowned.

"Well, yes, but what do you want it for?"

"Today for dinner we had fried liver, for dinner we had..."

"For dinner we had... for dinner we had..." the little witches started yelling, jumping and clapping, dashing around in a circle. The captain couldn't resist, and he leapt up and started spinning around with them – it didn't matter whose they were: the captain's, the adjutant's, Molochko's...

Then they all played hide-and-seek together. Then they made up medicines: the captain and the little witches were doctors, Yashka Lomailov was their assistant and Tikhmen was the patient... And then it was already time for bed.

And so Tikhmen was back to square one: again he'd found out nothing.

16

A SPRING

Deliberately, for fun, Molochko spread the rumour that the general had come back from town. And Shmit fell for it. He immediately began seething: I'm on my way!

He stood in front of the mirror and gloomily turned a starched collar around in his hands. He put it down on the pier-glass table and called Marusya.

"Have a look at this, please: is it clean? Can I put it on again? I haven't got another one. We don't have anything now, do we?"

Slender – even more slender than she had been – with two funereal lines at the corners of her lips, Marusya came over.

"Show me? Yes, it... yes, it'll likely still do…"

And still turning the collar around in her hand, without taking her eyes off the collar, she said quietly:

"Oh, to not be alive! Let me die… let me, Shmit!"

Yes, this is her, Marusya: a gossamer and death, a collar and not being alive…

"Die?" Shmit smiled ironically. "Dying's never difficult, but killing…"

He quickly finished dressing and went out. He walked over frosty, resonant ground and didn't feel the ground: so tautened were all the sinews inside him, like steel strings. He walked, malevolently firm, sharpened, quick.

The hatefully familiar door, covered in yellow oilcloth, the general's hatefully radiant Larka.

"His Ex'lency hasn't even thought of coming back, honest to God, may I be struck down!"

Shmit stood taut, ready to pounce, and held something in readiness in his pocket.

"If you don't believe me, Y'r 'onour, then come in, take a look for yourself…"

Larka threw the door wide open, and himself stood aside.

"If he's opening up, that means he's not here, it's true..." thought Shmit. "Do I burst in, and make a fool of myself again?"

So abruptly did Shmit turn around on the threshold that Larka even leapt back and screwed his eyes up tight.

Shmit clenched his teeth, clenched the grip of his revolver, squeezed his whole body into an angry spring. Oh, to uncoil and strike! He ran to the barracks – even he himself didn't know why.

In the barracks – emptily clean log walls. Everyone was out there, behind the powder magazine: something no one knew about was being arranged for the general's wife's name day. There was just the one barracks orderly loafing around sleepily – a grey soldier, everything about him grey: his eyes, his hair, his face – everything like soldiers' broadcloth.

Shmit ran alongside the log wall; the stripped plank beds flickered in his eyes. Something touched his epaulette – he looked up at the wall: swinging there on one eyelet was a saluting chart.

Shmit tugged at the chart:

"Wha-at's this? I'll give you..."

And so hard did his voice strike that "wha-at", so fully did he release his agonizing spring in that word, that a simple "what" must have sounded terrifying: the grey soldier staggered as if from a blow.

But Shmit was already a long way off: this grey soldier wasn't the one. Shmit was running to where they were working – to the powder magazine, where there were a lot of them.

There were only three soldiers who hadn't been sent out to work today: the orderly in the barracks, the sentry by the magazine and the painter who was painting cartridge boxes.

And it wasn't some nincompoop painting the boxes, someone who didn't even know to put on a coat of primer – painting the boxes was Private Muravey, a well-known master of his trade. And not just doing any old stuff, but even when they were putting on a play the year before last – *King Maximyan and His Unruly Son Adolf** – even for the play, then, it was Private Muravey who'd decorated everything. And he, Muravey, was the number-one expert on the accordion too: no one could play a sad love song like him. Private Muravey knew his own worth.

And there he stood, small, dark-haired, as though not even Russian – stood gratifying his soul. The job of daubing the boxes with green paint – that could wait. And for the time being he was painting a view on a box in priming paint and green: a river, absolutely to the life their little river Mamura, and above the river – white willows, and above the wil—

"A-ah!" Shmit's hand struck him from above like a thunderbolt. "Y-you're painting? You're… painting? What… were… my… orders?"

And Shmit was shouting something else – perhaps not even words, and really it's quite plain that it wasn't words – shouting and hitting Muravey, who was propped up on the ammunition box. Hitting him and wanting to hit him more and more: till there was blood, groans, rolled eyes. Just as uncontrollably as he used to want to be forever picking slim Marusya up in his arms and kissing her.

Whether out of fear or because he saw himself as a really very serious offender, Muravey didn't cry out. But this seemed to Shmit to be stubbornness. He needed to prevail, he needed… needed – Shmit was gasping – needed cries and groans.

Shmit pulled his revolver from his pocket – and only now did Muravey start yelling blue murder.

In the field behind the powder magazine they'd heard. Black figures were waving their arms about, jumping over ditches, hurrying towards them. And out in front was Andrei Ivanych: he was on duty with the soldiers today.

Shmit looked at Andrei Ivanych and wanted to say something to him, but the soldiers were already breathing close by, panting from having been running. Shmit gave up and slowly walked off.

The soldiers stood in a circle around the prone man, craning their necks, and for a long time no one had the courage to approach him. Then a big, clumsily steady fellow stepped out of the circle, grunting, and got down on all fours beside Muravey:

"Oh dear, matey, he's fixed you up good and proper, then!"

Andrei Ivanych recognized Arzhanoy. Arzhanoy lifted Muravey's head and, proficiently, as though it wasn't his first time, wound a calico kerchief around it.

"Yes," mused Andrei Ivanych, "that's Arzhanoy, the same one that killed the Chinaman. The same one..." And he became lost in thought.

17
THE LANZEPUPPES' CLUB

Absolutely everyone already knew that Shmit was running around just like a madman. And when, out of the blue, he came into the mess dining room, everyone, as if on command, fell quiet, dried up, even though they were tipsy.

"Well, what's the matter with you, gentlemen? What are you talking about?" asked Shmit, leaning on a table with a heavy grin.

Everyone was sitting down, while he was standing up: and it was as if this was the thing that was most awkward, and they were fidgety. It was too much to bear for one of them, who leapt up:

"We... a j-joke..."

"Wha-at joke?"

...What joke? As ill luck would have it, everything had slipped his mind. "What if his instinct tells him we were talking about him," he thought, "and..."

It was Captain Nechesa who came to the rescue. He picked at his purple nose and said:

"We... it's the, yes, the Armenian one – you know? Vun come along, a second come along... a tvelf come along – what is it?"

Shmit almost smiled:

"A-ah, a tvelf come along? It must be Captain Nechesa's children..."

Everyone joined in cackling with relief.

"Why, he's perfectly all right, he's even cracking jokes…" they thought. Shmit cast his sharp iron-grey eyes over them all, probed each of them individually, and said:

"Gentlemen, aren't you sick and tired of it here? Isn't it time for something a bit, sort of, stronger? Eh? Should we slip off to town, to the Lanzepuppes' Club, for instance? After all, we haven't been in almost a year or so."

Shmit looked, searching: "Will they come, or won't they? And what if they do come, and somewhere there we come across Aza… Azancheyev? What if we come across him – after all, it could…"

The group was humming and hawing.

"Now? But it's already around midnight, isn't it… It'd be crazy: struggling all night to get there, travelling… It's windy, it'll be rough…"

"Well? What about it?" Shmit lashed Andrei Ivanych with a sneer, staring at Andrei Ivanych's broad forehead.

Andrei Ivanych stepped forward and, although he didn't even have a proper idea of what the Lanzepuppes' Club was, said bullheadedly:

"I'll come."

The first step is the hardest, and then things get going. They began clamouring: me too, me too! They started bustling about, buttoned up their greatcoats and set off for the shore. The only one not to go was Nechesa.

It was so freezing cold on the water that they were all soon holding their tongues. The wind whistled and filled them with dread. They sat and dozed. Endlessly, all night long, the waves beat their heads against the boat's iron side.

At dawn they were drawing near. Slowly, disdainfully, majestically, the sun was rolling out of the water. Immediately feeling ashamed to be nodding off, they leapt up and gazed at the town on the hill, pinky-blue and yet to wake up.

They shook the Chinese carters on the jetty awake and drove in single file in five rattly carts to the very edge of town.

In answer to their ringing, the door, as in Kaschey's palace,* swung open by itself: there was no one to be seen. In a whisper, furtively, they entered a room which had been prepared, a room of unusual appearance, a very long one: a corridor, not a room. Along one wall was a narrow table, covered in bottles. And opposite, where the windows were, there was nothing: it was empty and plain.

Shmit poured himself a full tumbler of rum and drank it down; his hand was trembling slightly, his eyes narrowing and prickling.

"Well, gentlemen, lots?"

Coins were tossed. Heads came up for four of them: Shmit, Molochko, Tikhmen and Nesterov. Molochko's rosiness for some reason faded in a flash.

"My throw!" cried Shmit, and he tossed a large, cheerfully sparkling gold rouble out of the window.

The blind was down at the open window and billowing like a sail. They took up positions by the window in two pairs – to the right and to the left – drew their revolvers, stood up straight and waited. Shmit's severe, forged profile, sharp, jutting chin, closed eyes...

"But why are they..." said Andrei Ivanych, starting to raise his head: he didn't understand a thing.

He was shushed and fell quiet. Everyone had wild red eyes and a greenish cast to their faces: maybe because of the sleepless night. There were some senseless fragments of words whirling in their heads. They poured alcohol into themselves. Their hearts were gripped in intolerable, sweetly agonizing vices.

A square of sunlight was drifting upwards on the white curtain. Everyone sat just as silently. Nobody knew – had an hour passed, or two, or?...

Footsteps on the pavement below the window. A kind of identical spasm in them all – and four disorderly, scattered shots.*

Everyone leapt up, began clamouring excitedly and rushed to the window. Right by the wall, on his back, in a wadded blue jacket, lay a Chinaman: he'd started to bend down for the new gold rouble, but couldn't have had time to pick it up.

What happened next Andrei Ivanych didn't see. Whether because of the sleepless night, or an alcoholic haze, or something else, he simply passed out: as he had stood at the window, so did he sink down right there onto the floor.

He came to – and Shmit's iron-grey eyes were very close above him.

"Is it conceivable?" asked Shmit, rising from his knees and straightening up. "An officer, like a schoolgirl, can't look at blood! What I always say is: an officer should learn to kill in peacetime…"

Andrei Ivanych was rising slowly from the floor when he staggered and grabbed hold of Tikhmen.

Tikhmen took him by the arm and led him towards the exit:

"Come on, dear fellow, come on. It's too soon for you yet, just wait…"

They went out into a small, bare garden with a blackened fence and sadly exposed earth. The sun had come out in the sky still only a little while before, but its eye was already being shrouded in a deathly film of fog.

Tikhmen threw off his cap, ran a hand over his receding hairline and glanced up:

"It's vile. Everything's vile. So vile!" he said in a rasping voice. He waved a hand and again sat in silence, too lanky and frail. The rusty, rusting, yellow fog was creeping on.

"If only there were a war, maybe…" Tikhmen growled out through his nose.

"We'll be great in a war!"

Whether he'd only wanted to say this or had said it, Andrei Ivanych didn't know himself: in his head there was a pounding, things flying around headlong in tatters, things getting confused.

18
THE ALLIANCE

Lent, wet, warmth. The mud slurps underfoot – slurps so much that at any moment it'll swallow a man up.

And it does. With no strength left to back away, the sleepy man goes under and, falling asleep, prays: "Oh, let there be a war, maybe... Let there be a fire, or some hard drinking, maybe..."

The mud slurps. Wretched people wander along the spit jutting out into the ocean. Little white stripes – ships – can be traced on black in the distance. Oh, won't one of them put in here? After all, from Lent onwards they always start calling in. In February last year a whole two of them called in – put in, my sweet, oh do put in... No! Well then, maybe tomorrow?

And tomorrow arrived. Descending on them like snow, cheerful snow from out of the blue, came the Frenchmen.

Molochko and Tikhmen were sitting on the jetty at the time, reminiscing about the Lanzepuppes' Club, gazing into the distance. In the distance there was a plume of smoke, and it's ever closer, ever faster, and now here it is, fully visible: a cruiser, white and graceful, like a swan, and the French flag. Tikhmen lost his nerve and took to his heels. But Molochko stayed, started prancing, leapt for joy: he'd be first to learn everything, he'd be first to meet them, he'd be first to tell the tale!

"I'm happy to welcome you, albeit by chance, to this remote, albeit Russian... that's to say, to this Russian, albeit remote, land..."

That's the way Molochko expressed himself: he's not going to fall flat on his face in the mud – not for nothing had he had a French governess...

The French lieutenant to whom Molochko's speech was made didn't smile – he restrained himself and replied with a bow:

"Our admiral requests permission to inspect the battery and post."

"Good Lord, but I... I'll run and be back in a moment," said Molochko, dashing off.

But who was he to butt in on? Who was he to run to? There's no top brass here – the general's in town; Nechesa's been left in charge. But Nechesa can be really unintelligible if he's woken up at the wrong moment after dinner. It's a disaster, it really is!

"Captain Nechesa, Captain... Do get up, there's a French admiral here and he wants to inspect the post..."

"Khrr... pf... khrr... Who?"

"An admiral, I'm telling you, a French one!"

"The admiral can go to the d-devil – I want to sleep. Khrr... pff..."

Molochko pulled off the Chinese robe the captain had on top of him and called to Lomailov:

"Lomailov, *kvas* for the captain!"

But Lomailov's not there: Lomailov's gone out today sweeping chimneys. The *kvas* was brought by the captain's wife herself, Katyushka. The captain took a gulp and started to understand certain words:

"Fre-enchmen? What, gone mad, have they? Why?"

"Captain, make haste, for God's sake! I mean, we're in an alliance with the French... Honest to God, we're going to catch it!"

"Oh Lord, where from? What for? The soldiers – what do the soldiers look like with this work for the general! Molochko, go quickly, to the powder magazine, this second. Get them all away into the wood, the devils! Not one s-son of a bitch is to show his face!"

And now Captain Nechesa is finally standing on the jetty, his greatcoat wide open, all his regalia on his tunic. The main cog in the wheel is Molochko: he's hovering, sparkling, translating. The French admiral isn't in the first flush of youth, but he's slim and neat, as if wearing a corset. He's taken out a little book and he's being inquisitive, making notes.

"And what rations do you have for the soldiers? Right, right. And for the horses? How many companies? And how many crew per gun? Aha, right!"

The whole bunch of them went to the barracks. They'd already had time to tidy up and clean there: it was fine. But the smell there was very Russian. The Frenchmen were in a hurry to get out into the fresh air.

"Well, it only remains to take them to the powder magazine now, and that's it, thank God."

And there was already just one block left before the powder magazine, when out of Lieutenant Nesterov's house came Lomailov. He'd finished sweeping the chimneys, had swept everything very thoroughly in both the hall and the bedroom. He'd finished and was making his way home with his brush, in his rags – a shaggy, black oaf.

The admiral jerked his pince-nez up inquisitively.

"Aha... And who is that?" he asked, turning to Molochko for an answer.

Molochko, floundering, looked in supplication to Nechesa, but Nechesa was rolling his eyes in symbolic fury.

"It's... it's a Lanzepuppe,* Your Excellency!" Molochko squawked, squawking the first thing that popped into his head. He and Tikhmen had been talking about the Lanzepuppes just before, and so...

"Lan-ce-poupe? That... what does that mean?"

"It's... a lo-lo...local tribesman, Your Excellency!"

The admiral was very interested:

"Re-eally? I've never even heard of such a name before now, and I'm very interested in ethnography."

"They've only recently been discovered, Your Excellency!"

The admiral made a note in his book:

"Lan-ce-poupe... Very interesting, very. I shall give a talk to the Geographical Society. Without fail..."

Nechesa was choking with impatience to learn what had transpired and what this strange conversation had been – about Lanzepuppes. But the admiral – it was one thing on top of another – had already thrown Molochko a new curve ball:

"But... why don't I see your soldiers, not one?"

"Th-th-they're in… in the wood, Your Excellency."

"In the wood? All of them? Hm, what on earth for?"

"These Lanze-la-lanze-puppes, Your Excellency… That is, they've all been sent, our soldiers, that is, to suppress the, you know, Lanzepuppes…"

"Ah, so they're not yet a fully subjugated people, then? You have surprises at every turn here!"

"Surprises!" thought Molochko. "What surprises are there still to come from you? I'm going to get muddled up, tie myself in knots and ruin everything with my lies…" Molochko was already breaking out in a cold sweat from terror.

But these discoveries alone were enough for the admiral. He was walking around now and just nodding his head: "Good, very good, very interesting." After all, it's not every day you discover new tribes.

19

MARTYRS

And where on earth did such a blundering dullard as Captain Nechesa find the vim? It must have come from delight that everything had gone off so unexpectedly well with the Frenchmen. And Nechesa made up his mind to organize a feast fit for a king for the Frenchmen in the mess.

The Frenchmen agreed: they couldn't do otherwise – the Alliance.* And things really took off. In the officers' quarters there was the sudden smell of petrol, the orderlies dropped all their work to wind curl papers for the officers' wives, and the general's Larka delivered the invitations.

Marusya saw through the window that Larka was knocking at their gate – and she immediately grew flustered, flushed and hysterical. As clear as day there arose before her that damned evening: the ominous sunset, the seven crosses, she and Andrei Ivanych alone together, and Larka handing her the letter from the general…

"Shmit, don't let him in, Shmit, don't let him in, don't!"

Inside Shmit the spring compressed, started tormenting him, aching and begging for torment.

Shmit smiled ironically:

"You should have been unable before. So now just be able," he said, deliberately opening the door from the dining room and calling into the kitchen: "Hey, whoever's there, come in here!"

All the same, Shmit was unable to utter Larka's name. Larka ran in, coppery and radiant, handed him a card and recounted:

"So much trouble, so much trouble over these Frenchmen, it's terrible!"

Shmit forced himself – deliberately asked a lot of questions, even squeezed out a smile. And Larka suddenly ventured:

"Well then, Y'r 'onour, may I be so bold as to ask: do the French take vodka, or what? Otherwise, I mean, what are we going to do with them?"

And Shmit even burst out laughing. Burst out laughing – and he's ringing out ever higher, ringing out in the highest heights – oh, that he doesn't fall...

And Marusya's by the window with her back to Larka: she hasn't dared to leave, she's standing, and her thin little shoulders are shaking furiously. Shmit can see it, but can't stop laughing, he's ringing out ever higher, ever higher...

They're alone. She threw herself towards Shmit, onto the cold floor in front of him, and stretched out her arms:

"But Shmit, I mean, it was for you... it was for you I did *that*. For me it was horribly disgusting, you know – you do believe me, don't you?"

Shmit's smile had got cramp:

"And I'll say it for the hundredth time: that means it wasn't foul enough, not disgusting enough. That means pity for me was stronger than love for me."

And Marusya doesn't know what to do to make him... Her fingers are tightly entwined... Lord, what on earth can she do if she has love, and he has intellect, and you can't say or think of anything. But he doesn't really believe in what he's saying himself, does he? Oh, she doesn't understand a thing, not a thing! He's enchained himself, locked himself up, he isn't him, isn't Shmit...

Marusya got up from the cold floor and went away quietly into the hall. The dark corners frightened and tormented her. But not like they used to, like in her childhood: it wasn't the long-haired Bogeyman she fancied she saw, not Half-Ear – the merry madman – not The Enemy – the jumping evil spirit – it was Shmit's alien, incomprehensible face.

She lit one lamp on the table, climbed onto a chair and lit a wall lamp. But it only became even more like that evening: then, too, she'd gone around by herself and lit all the lamps.

She put them out and went into the bedroom. "All Shmit's socks have holes in them," she thought, "and for a whole month I've been forever just meaning to... Don't let yourself go, you mustn't let yourself go."

She sat down, bent over and did some darning. She wiped her eyes in annoyance: they kept on filling up, getting obscured; she couldn't see her work. It was already late, past midnight, when she finished all the darning. She pulled out a drawer and put the things away, and the candle on the chest of drawers flickered.

Shmit came in. Heavy, tall, he paced the bedroom, backwards and forwards, and the floor creaked. That same spring was beating inside, tormenting and seeking out torment. He stopped and said... no, not said – he cast a stone at Marusya:

"Get into bed – it's time."

She undressed, obedient, small. In her chemise she was just like a little child: so slim, such thin little arms. Only those two old woman's lines at the corners of her lips...

Shmit came over, breathing like an exhausted beast. Lying with her eyes closed, Marusya said:

"But Shmit, I mean... Shmit... you do love me, don't you? I mean, you want this – not just, not simply, like..."

"Love? I used to..."

Shmit caught his breath. "Marusyenka," he thought, "Marusyenka, I'm dying, you know. Marusyenka, darling, save me!" Yet out loud he said:

"You continue to assure me that you love me, though, don't you, hm! Well, that should be enough for you. Whereas I... simply want."

"No," she thought, "he's just saying that, he's pretending... It'd be awful..."

"Shmit, don't, please don't, for the love of... for the love of..."

But how could she possibly stand up to Shmit? He crushed her completely, twisted her up, compelled her by force. It was agonizing, deathly sweet to maul her, a thin, dear little child, her – so pure, so guilty, so beloved...

So humiliating, so painful was it for Marusya that her final, most desperate cry didn't burst out, but went deep down, stifled, and pierced her with fierce pain. And for a minute, for one second, she was lit up by a distant flash of lightning: for a second she understood Shmit's great malevolence, the sister of great...

But Shmit was already leaving... He went off into the drawing room to sleep there. Or maybe not to sleep – to pace around the whole night long and look out of the blue, owl-eyed windows.

Marusya lay alone in the darkness, all doubled up. The pillow grew wet from her tears, and it had to be turned over onto its other side.

"He said: you're a great woman," she thought, remembering Andrei Ivanych. "How am I great? I'm pathetic, shameful. If he'd known everything, he wouldn't have said it..."

Who knows?

20

A FEAST FIT FOR A KING

The music: five soldiers with bugles and Private Muravey on his accordion. Oh dear, so the music was a bit of a let-down, otherwise it would all have been really good. Green branches on the walls, little flags fluttering. The lamps even smoking somewhat in their zeal. The silver shining on full-dress sashes. Granny's beloved brooches and bracelets jangling on the ladies. And isn't the best thing of all the rosily radiant master of ceremonies, Molochko?

But Tikhmen was still completely sober and so looked upon everything very sceptically:

"Of course, this is all a lie," he thought. "But, yes, it glitters. And since the only truth is death, and since I'm still alive, then I have to live a lie, superficially. So the Molochkos are right and you have to be empty-headed... But in practice? Oh, I'm getting rather muddled today..."

Past Tikhmen to the musicians dashed Molochko:

"The fanfare, the fanfare! 'The Double-Headed Eagle'!* They're coming, they're coming..."

The band began blowing and screeching; the ladies stood on tiptoe. In came the Frenchmen – all tight-laced, scented, lean, graceful in every way.

At first, for a moment, Tikhmen gawped along with everyone else. Then he separated them out, pondered: the Frenchmen – and the Russians. The Russians' familiar frock coats, shiny with wear, their timid faces, the redyed dresses of the ladies...

"Yes..." he thought. "And now, if the lie turns out to be lying yet again... Well, yes: n squared, a minus times a minus is a plus... Practically, therefore... What, then? I'm getting muddled, muddled..."

"Listen, Polovets," said Tikhmen, giving Andrei Ivanych a tug, "just for now, let's go and have a drop to drink, I'm feeling a little bit wretched somehow..."

Yes, Andrei Ivanych needed a drink too. They each knocked back a shot. In the buffet, Nechesa was guzzling brandy – to keep his spirits up: after all, he was the stand-in man in charge, wasn't he; he bore responsibility.

"Shmit's very cheerful today, hm!" Nechesa mumbled through his wet moustache.

"What, is Shmit here, then?" Andrei Ivanych rushed back into the hall.

A bittersweet ache had started aching in his heart: it wasn't Shmit he was looking for, no… Frenchmen were drifting past, and in the lightest down of the waltz there was a glimpse of Molochko, sweaty and red with happiness.

"Nechesa was lying," he thought, "and why? She's not here. There's no one here…"

And suddenly – Shmit's loud laugh, ringing with iron. Andrei Ivanych rushed in that direction. Couples were whirling, spinning, jostling: it seemed impossible to get there.

Shmit and Marusya were standing with the French admiral. Shmit looked right through Andrei Ivanych – through an empty tumbler, drained completely dry.

Andrei Ivanych's eyes misted over. He quickly turned from Shmit to Marusya, took her slender little hand, held it… oh, if only it were possible never to let it go! "But why is she trembling?" he wondered. "Yes, of course – it's her hand trembling."

Andrei Ivanych had a hard time understanding French and listened intently.

"…It's a pity the general's not here," Shmit was saying. "He's the most amazing man! My wife here is a great admirer of the general's. Look at her, look at her: she can't hear his name with indifference. I'm positively jealous! One fine day she might…"

The Frenchmen were smiling, Shmit's voice was ringing and lashing. Marusya started to droop, her whole body, like a weeping birch. And she would have fallen, maybe, but Andrei Ivanych sensed it – he alone had seen – and held Marusya up by the waist.

"A waltz," he whispered, heard no reply, and bore her off in light circles. "Well away from that damned Shmit, well away…" he thought. "Oh, he's such a…"

"How he torments me… Andrei Ivanych, if you only knew! These three days and today. And the three nights before the ball…"

It seemed to Andrei Ivanych that Marusya was speaking from somewhere down below, from the depths; she'd been buried. He stole a glance: those two funereal lines by her lips – oh, those lines!

They sat down. Marusya looked at a Quinquet lamp* and didn't take her eyes off the dancing, angry tongue of flame: take them off, turn them away – and everything would be over, and the dam would burst, and there'd be a surge...

During the waltz Shmit came up close to them. Smiling – Shmit was looking at them, after all – smiling, Marusya uttered alien, wild words:

"Kill him, kill Shmit. Let him better be dead... than like this... it's beyond me..."

"Kill? Is this you?" Andrei Ivanych looked in horror, disbelieving. Yes, it's her. A gossamer and death. A waltz and kill...

Shmit was whirling around with Captain Nechesa's nicely rounded wife, whirling around, springy, sharp, and the floor creaked beneath him. He'd narrowed his eyes and was grinning.

Andrei Ivanych answered Marusya:

"Very well."

And with clenched teeth he drew her on, spun her around – oh, to be spun to death...

Here, though, heads were spinning not so much from the waltzes as from the potions that had been drunk. Once in a lifetime, with the French, and not drink to the Alliance? That would have been just rock bottom.

The French drank as well, but in a cunning sort of way: they drank, but their hearts weren't in it. And they drank mostly half-glasses too, not a good look at all. A different matter altogether were our boys: doing their best, the Russian way, their hearts on their sleeves. It was plain to see they'd been drinking: they're going around hazy, merry, dull-eyed.

And that was when Tikhmen felt his height: it's dreadfully awkward being tall. For someone small, even if they teeter, it's all right. Whereas someone tall – a bell-tower – buckles, on the very verge of crashing down, and it's a fearful sight to see.

But on the other hand, upon leaning against the wall, Tikhmen felt very steady, strong and bold. And so, as Nechesa was tottering past, Tikhmen caught him resolutely by the skirt, thinking: "No, I've had enough now, now I'm going to ask..."

"Cap-tain, tell me in all ho-onesty, well, for the love of God Himself: whose son is Petyashka? I'm dying of anguish – d'you understand, of an-guish: is Petyashka mine or not mine?…"

The captain was well pickled, but he did understand there was something amiss here and asked:

"What are you… what are you on about, brother, eh?"

"My dear fel-low, te-ell me!" Tikhmen began to cry quietly, bitterly. "You're my last hope, hm! Hm!" Tikhmen sniffled. "I asked Katyusha and she doesn't know… Lord, what am I to do-o now? My dear fellow, tell me – you know, don't you?"

Nechesa gazed obtusely at Tikhmen's nose, which was bobbing about right in front of the captain's eyes with a teardrop on its tip, quite unnaturally twisted to the side – and it made him want to grab hold and straighten it.

Drawn by a higher power, Nechesa took a firm hold of Tikhmen's nose with two fingers and started pulling it to the right and to the left. And this was such a surprise for Tikhmen that he stopped snivelling and submissively, even with a certain curiosity, followed the captain's hand.

And only when he heard cries from behind him: "Tikhmen, Tikhmen," did he realize and jerk free. All around, everyone was in stitches.

Tikhmen turned his dumbfounded gaze on them, fixed it on one – it was Molochko – and asked:

"You there, did you see? Was he… was he trying to put my nose out of joint?"

They split their sides laughing. Molochko barely got his words out:

"Well, brother, who's put whose nose out of joint, at the end of the day, that's unclear."

All around everyone gasped. Now Tikhmen needed to do something. Reluctantly, doing his duty, Tikhmen set upon the captain.

And now things took an utterly ridiculous turn: Nechesa lay belly-down on top of Tikhmen and thumped him anywhere he could. Some tried to pull the figures on the floor apart, while others tugged at those who were pulling them apart: let them finish their fight, like, don't interfere. And had it not been for Captain Nechesa's wife, God knows what the mayhem would have come to.

The captain's wife ran up, shouted and stamped her foot:

"You, blockhead, idiot! Get off at once!"

For ten years the captain had been obeying that voice: he got off instantly. Tousled, dishevelled, befuddled – they hadn't let him finish the fight – he stood and scratched his head.

The Frenchmen had gathered in a corner, marvelling, and wondering if they should leave or not. And leaving wasn't possible: the Alliance. And staying was awkward: the Russians evidently had some domestic business going on.

"Nonetheless... They're all such... Lancepoupes of a kind," said the admiral, raising his eyebrows. "What's their reason for this?"

Molochko was summoned. Molochko tried to explain:

"The reason's a son. Whose son, Your Excellency..."

"I don't understand a thing," said the admiral with a shrug of the shoulders.

21
A LIGHT IN THE DARKNESS

In the mess there was a window cut through from the hall into the corridor. Why, for what purpose, is a mystery. It's just that in all the buildings here that's what they did – and so they'd done it in the mess too. Now, though, the orderlies are enjoying every minute: they're crowded together by the window and feasting their eyes.

"Ooh, but they're a clever lot, these here Frenchmen!" exclaimed the general's Larka, radiant as a samovar. "That's no Jepanese for you, brother, not some Chinaman. The Jepanese, he ain't up to much, so..."

Larka didn't finish what he was saying: in front of the gentleman Lieutenant Tikhmen he had to stand to attention.

All crumpled, wet and covered in dust, Tikhmen had stepped into the corridor – and stopped, lost: where was he to go?

He had a think, turned left and started to climb the creaking steps into the watchtower.

Yashka Lomailov stared after him disapprovingly.

"Where's he off to now, for instance, where's he off to now? Why, what the hell does he want up there? Oh, Larka, these gentlemen of ours, they're barmy, I'm telling you! They act ba-army, act ba-army, and each in his own way... And what more do they want, you'd think: they've got heating, they've got food to eat..."

Larka snorted:

"Idiot: food to eat! It's for you, an animal, that food to eat's enough, but people who are true gentlemen, not some self-styled ones, why, they, brother, hold a dream inside them, yes..."

"Me, for instance, I'd marry Mr Tikhmen off – that'd be the thing!" Lomailov grumbled with his slow tongue. "Give him half a dozen little kids or so, and those there dreams of his, they'd be gone in a flash..."

Lomailov looked outside through a window in the direction of the Nechesas' house. "How's Kostenka getting on now?" he wondered. "Has he got to sleep without me or not?"

Darkness, cold gloom outside the window. Somewhere not very far away someone was yelling blue murder: "He-elp, he-elp!" Scratching their heads, yawning indifferently, the soldiers listened: a commonplace, customary thing.

Lieutenant Tikhmen was already standing up top now, shaky, insecure, lanky.

"Well, all right, all right, and to hell with you, and I'll go, I'll go... Pulling my nose, hm! For you it's a laughing matter, but for me..."

Tikhmen pushed the frame, and the window flew open. Down below, in the darkness, they were shouting "help" again, loudly and plaintively.

"He-elp, aha, help? And do you think *I* don't want help? Do you think *we're* not shouting? But who hears, well, who? Well, just keep on shouting and shouting."

But Tikhmen leant out all the same, put his head into the wet, black mouth of the night. From here, from the watchtower, a cheerful light could be seen in the bay: their cruiser, presumably.

This light in the utter blackness was now a kind of support for Tikhmen – it let his eyes live; it would have been impossible without it. A cheerful little bright-eyed light.

"Petyashka, my little Petyenka, Petyashka…"

And suddenly the light flickered and vanished. Maybe the cruiser had gone about, or maybe something else.

It had vanished, and insuperable darkness had fallen.

"Pe-tyashka, my little Petyashka! Nechesa is the last one… No one knows now, no one will say… Oh dear, oh dear, oh dear!"

Tikhmen shook his head ruefully and sniffled. Drunken tears started flowing, and are there any tears more bitter than drunken ones?

He laid his cheek on the window ledge: the window ledge was wet, dirty and cold. The cold on his face sobered him up a little. Tikhmen recalled a conversation he'd had with somebody:

"Anyone who has children is a dullard, an idiot, a pea-brained fish who's been hooked… That was me, me… I said it. And here I am crying over Petyashka. I'll never find out now whose he is. Oh dear, oh dear, oh dear!"

Never – thus did the lid slam down and do for drunken, bitter Tikhmen. The insuperable darkness had taken possession of him. The light had gone out.

"Petyashka-a! Petya-shen-ka-a!" Tikhmen was snivelling, choking and slowly crawling out onto the window ledge.

The window ledge is terribly dirty; Tikhmen's got his hands quite filthy. But it's a shame to wipe them on his frock coat. Well, he'll just have to do as he is.

He was crawling out more and more… oh dear, there's no end to it: after all, he's so lanky. By the time he'd crawled out and leant over the edge – by then he'd crashed down from the watchtower, headfirst into the darkness.

Maybe he'd even cried out: the orderlies heard nothing. They'd already forgotten even to think about that barmy Tikhmen: who cares about Tikhmen when here are the Frenchmen coming out. Oh, and what a fine-looking lot they are, and dead nippy too.

The Frenchmen came out in a merry throng, half-cut, slipping on the steps and thinking: "Oh, these funny Russians... Lancepoupes... But they do... they do have something about them..."

And crawling after the Frenchmen came the hosts too. If the Frenchmen were half-cut, then it was the hosts' sacred duty to have drunk themselves into a stupor: some were still walking, hugging the handrail, while others were already on all fours...

Tikhmen was found only in the morning. He was lugged over to the Nechesas': he lived with them when alive; with them, then, dead too. And he lay peacefully on a table in the hall. His face was covered with a white headscarf: it was very badly knocked about.

Katyusha, the captain's wife, sobbed violently and pushed her husband aside:

"Go a-way, go a-way! I love him, I loved him..."

"You, madam, loved everyone, out of the goodness of your heart. Calm down, stop blubbing, that'll do!"

"Just to think... I... I may be to bl-blame... Lord, truly, if I'd known whose Petyashka was! Lord, if I only knew... a-a-ah! I should have lied to him!"

Lomailov chased the eight children away from the doors: they just kept clinging on to them, they just kept poking their noses into the opening, oh, what an inquisitive lot!

"Yashka, Yashutnichek, do tell: doesn't the man hurt any more? How's that? I mean, he's had an accident, but he doesn't hurt?"

"Little idiots, he's dead, isn't he: course he doesn't hurt."

The eldest girl, Varyushka, started positively jumping for joy:

"Tsk! See? I sayed he didn't hurt. I sayed! And you didn't believe me. Tsk, see?"

It's oh so nice for her to rub her brother's nose in it.

22
THE FLEDGLING JACKDAW

It was already February, but the general was still hanging around in town, still afraid to come home. And Shmit continued to behave cruelly, completely imbued with his torment, and this could be sensed in every tiny little thing.

Well, for example, he came up with an idea for a humiliation: teaching his orderly French. This is Neprotoshnov! Why, he'd even forget all his Russian words when standing in front of Shmit, and now – French. Those rotten Frenchmen had made everything go haywire: they'd dispatched Tikhmen to the next world, and Shmit had got a thing like this into his crazy head…

Neprotoshnov, a black-whiskered, black-eyed, fine-looking fellow, but with the eyes of a fish, stands shaking in front of Shmit:

"I c-can't say, Y'r 'onour, I've f-forgotten…"

"How many times have I drummed the word into you?! Well, so how do you say 'forgotten', eh?"

Silence. Neprotoshnov's knees can be heard knocking against one another.

"We-ell?

"Joub… joubelye, Y'r 'onour …"

"Ooh… you dummy! By tomorrow you're to know it by heart. Get out!"

Neprotoshnov sits in the kitchen and goes over the damned heathen words; the millstones are knocking in his head, he gets muddled and trembles. He hears somebody's footsteps, leaps up like clockwork and stands straight as a ramrod. He doesn't even see in his terror that it's not Shmit who's come in, but the mistress, Marya Vladimirovna.

"What's wrong, Neprotoshnov, eh? Well, what's wrong, what's wrong?"

And she strokes his shorn soldier's head. Neprotoshnov wants to catch and take hold of her little hand, but doesn't have the courage, and so it remains just wanting.

"Mistress dear... Mistress dear! I mean, all of it – I mean, absolutely all of it... I'm not blind..."

Marusya went back into the dining room. Her eyes were burning with something to say. But she took just one look at Shmit – and shattered on his steel. She lowered her eyes, submissive. Forgot all the angry words.

Shmit was just sitting, not reading. He never reads now – he can't. He's sitting with a cigarette, with his eyes hooked in torment on a single point – on the cut-glass pendant of the lamp. And it's so unbelievably difficult to look at Marusya.

"Well? About Neprotoshnov, of course?" Shmit sneered.

He went right up close to Marusya.

"How I..."

And he fell silent. He just squeezed her arms painfully above the elbow: there'd be bruises there tomorrow...

There are lots of bruises blooming on Marusya's slim, child's body now – the result of Shmit's vicious caresses. Shmit is ever crueller, ever more violent with her. And it's always one and the same thing: she cries, dies, struggles in the ring of Shmit's arms. And he drinks the sweetness of her dying, her tears, his destruction. She can't save herself from Shmit, there's nowhere she can do it, and, worst of all, she doesn't want to save herself. The other day at the ball she'd said to Andrei Ivanych – the thing had simply burst out: "Kill Shmit." And now she knows no peace: what if?

Andrei Ivanych hadn't forgotten those words of Marusya's; he remembered them every evening. Every evening – one and the same circle of torment, rounded off by Shmit. If Shmit weren't tormenting Marusya – if Shmit hadn't caught him that time by the frozen window – if at the ball Shmit hadn't...

Most importantly, there wouldn't now be this thing that had already become habitual and essential: Guslyaikin wouldn't be standing in front of Andrei Ivanych every evening, wouldn't have the smirk on his blancmange mug, wouldn't be recounting...

"But Lord, I mean, I never used to be such a bad person," thought Andrei Ivanych in the night, "not so very bad... How on earth could I?"

And again: Shmit, Shmit, Shmit... "Kill," he thought. "She wasn't joking then – her eyes were dark, they weren't joking."

And then suddenly somehow, out of the blue, Andrei Ivanych decided: today. It must have been because there was sunshine, the annoyingly cheerful drip of thawing snow, smiling, pale-blue water. On such a day nothing is frightening: quite ordinarily, like a purse, Andrei Ivanych slipped his revolver into his pocket; quite ordinarily, as if he'd come visiting, he tugged on Shmit's bell.

The bolt made a clatter, and the gate was opened by Neprotoshnov. Shmit was standing in the middle of the yard, without his overcoat, for some reason with a revolver in his hands.

"A-ah, Lieu-te-nant Polovets, the mus-sician! It's b-been a while..."

Shmit hadn't moved: as he'd been standing, so he stood, heavy, tall.

"Neprotoshnov..." It suddenly came to Andrei Ivanych: "I can't in front of him," and he turned to Neprotoshnov:

"Is the mistress at home?"

Neprotoshnov got flustered and cowered under Shmit's gaze: he had to reply in French without fail, but the words, of course, were all immediately forgotten.

"Joub... joubelye," Neprotoshnov mumbled.

Shmit laughed; it rang out in iron. He shouted:

"Go, tell the mistress she has, yes, an uninvited guest..."

He held Andrei Ivanych where he was with his gaze:

"What are you looking at? Don't you like the revolver? Don't be afraid! For the time being it's only this fledgling jackdaw here I want to bump off, to stop it making a din outside the window."

Only now did Andrei Ivanych see: a young jackdaw had perched, taken cover, underneath a wheelbarrow. Its wings are lowered to the ground; it doesn't know how to fly – it can't, it's still a youngster.

There was the crack of a shot. The jackdaw set up a strained, hoarse croaking; its wing became stained with red; it hopped under the shed. Shmit contorted his mouth – it must have been a smile. He took aim once more: he needed to kill, needed to.

With quick, long strides, Andrei Ivanych ran over to the shed and stood facing Shmit, with his back to the jackdaw.

"I... I won't allow you to shoot any more. You should be ashamed! It's persecution!"

Shmit's iron-grey eyes narrowed into a blade:

"Lieutenant Polovets, if you don't get out of the way this very second, I'm going to shoot at you. It's all the same to me."

Andrei Ivanych's heart started pounding with wistful joy. "Marusya," he thought, "look, do look! It isn't for the jackdaw I'm doing this, you know..." He didn't budge.

There was a flash of light, a shot. Andrei Ivanych bent down. Felt himself in astonishment: all in one piece.

Malevolently, like a wolf, Shmit bared his teeth, and his lower jaw was shaking.

"B-bas... Well, this time I won't miss!"

Again the revolver rose. Andrei Ivanych screwed up his eyes:

"Should I run?" he wondered. "No, for God's sake, another second – and that's it..."

It had completely slipped his mind for some reason that he, too, had a revolver in his pocket, and he had, after all, come to... He stood quietly and waited.

One second, two, ten: no shot. He opened his eyes. Shmit's lower jaw was jumping so badly that he'd thrown the revolver to the ground and was squeezing his chin, holding it with both hands for all he was worth. Inside Andrei Ivanych everything started to move, shifted.

"I pity you. I'd meant to, but I won't do it..."

He took his revolver from his pocket and showed it to Shmit. And walked quickly towards the gate.

23
GOOD AND STEADY

It was still before dawn, the February day was still only breaking, and there was someone knocking on Andrei Ivanych's door. Andrei Ivanych wanted to say: "Who is it?", but didn't, and sank back into sleep. Marusya's come and said: "Do you know, I'm now no longer…" What she was "no longer", though, she doesn't finish saying. But Andrei Ivanych almost knows anyway. He's almost caught that "no longer", almost…

But the knocking on the door is ever louder, ever more annoying. There's evidently nothing for it. Andrei Ivanych needed to crawl out of the dream, needed to get up and open the door.

"Neprotoshnov, you? What is it – why are you here? What's happened?"

Neprotoshnov came over to the bed, bent down close to Andrei Ivanych and, in an utterly unsoldierly way, said:

"Y'r 'onour, the mistress told me to tell you that our master, Y'r 'onour, is threatening to kill you. So the mistress, Y'r 'onour, asked you not to do anything, for God's sake…"

"But what… what am I not to do, then?"

But Andrei Ivanych couldn't get another sensible word out of him.

"I wouldn't know, Y'r 'onour…"

"Well, and how's your mistress, Marya Vladimirovna, how's she?"

"I w-wouldn't know, Y'r 'onour…"

"…Oh, you damned blockhead, at least tell me how she is," he thought.

But Andrei Ivanych looked into Neprotoshnov's hopeless, fish-like eyes and dismissed him.

Left alone, he lay for a long time in the darkness. And suddenly leapt up, thinking:

"Good Lord! I mean, if she sent him to say that, then she… Good Lord, can it be that she really does… Me?"

Catch up with Neprotoshnov, catch up with him and give him his last silver rouble! Andrei Ivanych ran outside, onto the porch – Neprotoshnov was long gone.

But now Andrei Ivanych couldn't leave the porch. The sky is huge, the air is full of pine forest, and the sea is like the sky. It's spring. Oh, to stretch out his arms like this – and hurl himself forward, to the place where...

Andrei Ivanych was screwing up his eyes, turning his face upwards, towards the warm sunshine.

"Dying?" he thought: "All right, then... Dying's easy for us. Killing's harder, and hardest of all is living... But anything, anything, even killing – if only she wants it."

The sunshine was such that he could even create for himself this absurdity, this foolishness, that she, Marusya, that she really did... But what if? After all, such sunshine.

To see her from first thing in the morning, from daybreak... Nothing – only the very least little thing, the very lightest of touches, like that time... The snow had been falling outside the window. And that's already happiness. From the very first thing in the morning until last thing at night, everything is happiness.

Oh, to run over there now, just as he is, not dressed...

Even working with the soldiers was good today. Even Molochko seemed new.

Molochko, to be more precise, was truly radiant, and his calfishness was solemn, not as it usually was.

"I have some business with you," he said, stopping Andrei Ivanych.

"What? Come on, quick, no beating about the bush!"

"Shmit's asked me – can you imagine? – to be his second. Here's his letter."

"A-ah," thought Andrei Ivanych, "so that's it... so that's why Marusya..." Andrei Ivanych opened the envelope, skipped through the lines, swallowed them, ah, quickly!

During yesterday's... with the jackdaw... My shot in the duel...
Your turn... I shall stand stock-still, and if... I shall be very
glad, my time has come.

Andrei Ivanych read the end out loud:

"Permit me! What's this? 'Just you alone are to shoot. But if
you're not happy with that, we'll see.' Permit me, what sort of
duel is that?* Strange demands! That's not a duel, but the devil
knows what! What does he think, that, as he did, I'll... You're
the second, you have to..."

"I... I don't know anything... He just... he sent me – Shmit...
I don't know," Molochko mumbled, timidly throwing glances at
Andrei Ivanych's broad, furrowed forehead.

"Listen, you'll go right now and tell Captain Shmit that I don't
agree to such a duel. Would he be happy for us both to shoot
together? Otherwise, no duel... It's the devil knows what!"

Molochko trotted off to Shmit with his tail between his legs.
Breathlessly reported everything. Shmit was smoking. Indifferently
he flicked off the ash.

"Hm, well now, not in agreement? Although that's just what
I..."

"...No, what more does he want? Can you imagine: he yelled
at me too! What have I got to do with it? It's on your part... It's
so noble – giving up your shot, and he..."

"Noble, d-damn it!" thought Shmit, contorting and distorting
his face, then out loud:

"No-ble, y-yes... Well, here's a job for you: tomorrow you'll tell
everyone that Polovets called me... a scoundrel, that I challenged
him, and he refused. Got it?"

"Good Lord, but I... But why tomorrow?"

Shmit gave Molochko a hard stare, smirked unpleasantly and
said:

"And now, farewell."

Shmit sat alone with a stony, immobile face, smoking. His
revolver was lying on the table.

"Shall I wake Marusya?" he wondered. "Tell her? But what? That I love her, that I loved her? And the more I loved her..."

He went into the bedroom. Worn out by nocturnal crucifixions, Marusya was dead asleep. Her face was all smeared with the traces of tears, like a small child's. But those two lines by the lips...

Shmit's stoniness split asunder; deathly torment came through on his face. He knelt down, began to bend at her feet. No... He made a wry face, flapped a hand:

"She won't believe it," he thought. "It doesn't matter... she won't believe it now." And he went hurriedly into the garden.

In the garden, Neprotoshnov was pottering about by the flowerbeds: something, at least, to make his sweet mistress smile, as he'd noticed she sometimes used to stretch both arms out towards the flowers.

Neprotoshnov caught sight of Captain Shmit, flinched and stood to attention. Shmit froze, tried to grin – but his face didn't move.

"He's still afraid of me..." he thought. "Odd fellow!"

"Go away," was all he said to Neprotoshnov.

Neprotoshnov ran for his life: thank the Lord – he'd got away in one piece.

Shmit sat down on a big white rock and set his left elbow against his knee.

"No," he thought, "not like this... I need to lean against a wall... Right, now... good, steady."

He took out his revolver. "Yes, good, steady." And that same baleful spring relaxed and freed him.

24

THE WAKE

Andrei Ivanych was sitting writing a letter to Marusya. Maybe it was absurd, senseless, but it couldn't go on – he needed to shout out everything that...

He didn't notice it had already grown dark. Didn't hear Neprotoshnov come in and stop by the doorpost. God knows how long he stood there before plucking up the courage to call out:

"Y'r 'onour... Lieutenant!"

Andrei Ivanych threw his pen down angrily: that fish-eyed creature again!

"Well, what is it? Still about the same thing? He wants to kill me?"

"No, sir, Y'r 'onour... Captain Shmit himself... He's killed himself... Com-completely..."

Andrei Ivanych leapt over to Neprotoshnov, grabbed him by the shoulders, leant over – right into his eyes. His eyes were human – shedding tears.

"Yes," he thought, "Shmit's gone. But then that means Marusya's – that means, she's now..."

In the blink of an eye, he was already there, at the Shmits'. He raced through the hall – on the table lay something long and white. But that wasn't the point, not that...

Marusya was sitting alone in the cheerful, log-built dining room. The samovar was there. That was Neprotoshnov making every effort on his own initiative: if there was something amiss, how could you do without the samovar? Marusya's dear, dishevelled chestnut-haired head was lying on her arms.

"Marusya!" In one word Andrei Ivanych cried out everything that was in his letter and reached out his arms – to fly: it was all over, all the pain.

Marusya stood up. Her face was wild, wrathful.

"Out! Out! You – I can't... This is all – this is you – I know everything..."

"Me? What's me?"

"Yes, you! Why did you refuse? What would it have cost you... What would it have cost you to shoot into the air? I sent to you... Oh, you wanted, I know... you wanted... I know why you wanted. Go away, go away, I can't, I can't!"

Andrei Ivanych leapt out like a scalded cat. There by the gate he stopped. Everything had got muddled in his head.

"How's that?" he wondered. "Did she actually... after everything, after everything... love him? Forgive him? Love Shmit?"

With difficulty, slowly, he got to the depths, to the bottom – and shuddered: it was so deep.

"Shall I go back?" he wondered. "Get down on my knees, like then: a great woman..."

But from the house he heard a wild, inhuman cry. He realized: he couldn't go there. Couldn't ever again.

The general came back from town for Shmit's funeral. And he gave such a funeral oration that even he himself shed a tear – as for the others, it goes without saying.

Everyone was at the funeral, paid their respects to Shmit. The only one not there was Marusya. She'd left, hadn't she, hadn't waited: how about that? Collected up her bits and pieces and left. And that's what's called loving him, too. A fine kind of love.

She upped and left – and as things stood, Shmit would have been left with no wake. So we have to thank the general, a good-hearted man: he organized the wake at his house.

Shmit's no more in the big wide world – and now at once he's become a good man for everyone. A bit harsh he was, a bit difficult, it's true. But on the other hand...

Everyone found a good word to say for Shmit: only Andrei Ivanych was silent and sat looking down in the dumps. We-ell, the fellow must have been feeling pangs of conscience. After all, he and Shmit had had an American duel,* so they say – is it true or not? But it's always women, always women, the cause of everything... Oh dear!

"You have a drink, brother, you have a drink – it may well, you know..." said Nechesa, compassionately topping Andrei Ivanych up.

And Andrei Ivanych drank, drank obediently. Drunkenness is an affectionate father: if you've nowhere to lay your head, then drunkenness will take it, give it loving care, trick it into merriment...

And when the sozzled Molochko thrashed out 'The Mistress'* on the guitar (this at a funeral repast), Andrei Ivanych was suddenly swept away, whirled away by drunken, hopeless merriment, that same final merriment which is today the manner of making merry for Rus, driven to the end of the earth!

Andrei Ivanych leapt out into the middle, stood for a second, wiped his broad forehead – brushed something off it – and started kicking his knees up like you wouldn't believe.

"That's the way! Attaboy, you're one of us – attaboy, Andrei Ivanych!" Nechesa cried approvingly. "I told you, brother, have a drink, I told you. Attaboy, you're one of us!"

1913

The Cave

Glaciers, mammoths, wastelands. Nocturnal black cliffs, in a way resembling houses; in the cliffs – caves. And no one knows who it is that trumpets at night on the stone path between the cliffs and, in sniffing out the path, stirs up the white snowy dust: perhaps a grey-trunked mammoth; perhaps the wind; or perhaps the wind is actually the icy roaring of some most mammoth mammoth. One thing is clear: it's winter. And you have to clench your teeth really tight so they don't chatter, and you have to chop wood with a stone axe, and every night you have to move your campfire from cave to cave, ever deeper, and you have to wrap more and more shaggy animal skins around you.

Between the cliffs, where ages ago was St Petersburg, there roamed by night a grey-trunked mammoth. And wrapped in skins, in overcoats, in blankets, in rags, cave-people retreated from cave to cave. On the feast day of the Intercession, Martin Martinych and Masha boarded up the study; on the feast day of Our Lady of Kazan* they moved out of the dining room and hid away in the bedroom. There was nowhere for them to retreat any farther; here they had to withstand the siege or die.

In the St Petersburg cave-bedroom it was just as it had been not long before in Noah's Ark: diluvially jumbled clean and unclean creatures. A mahogany writing desk; books; ceramic-looking stone-age flat-cakes; Scriabin's Opus 74;* an iron; five potatoes, lovingly washed to whiteness; the nickel-plated frames of the beds; an axe; a wardrobe; firewood. And in the centre of this entire universe – the god, the short-legged, rusty-red, squat, greedy cave-god: the cast-iron stove.

The god was droning mightily. In the dark cave, a great fiery wonder. The people – Martin Martinych and Masha – reverentially, silently, gratefully stretched their arms out to it. For one hour in the cave, it's spring; thrown off for one hour were the animal skins, claws and fangs, and breaking through iced-over cerebral crust came green shoots – thoughts.

"Mart, have you forgotten that tomorrow... Well, I can see: you have forgotten!"

In October, when the leaves have already yellowed, shrivelled, drooped, there are sometimes blue-eyed days; throw your head back on such a day so as not to see the ground, and you can believe there's still joy, it's still summer. So it is with Masha: if you close your eyes and just listen to her you can believe she's the old Masha and is about to laugh, get up from the bed, give you a hug, and the knife on glass an hour ago wasn't her voice, wasn't her at all...

"Oh dear, Mart, Mart! How everything... You never used to forget. The twenty-ninth: Marya's, my angel's day..."*

The cast-iron god was still droning. There was, as ever, no light: it would come on only at ten. The rough, dark vaults of the cave were flickering. Martin Martinych – on his haunches, knotted, tighter!... even tighter! – with his head thrown back, is still looking into the October sky so as not to see the yellowed, drooping lips. But Masha:

"The thing is, Mart, what if we could light it first thing tomorrow so it would be like now all day! Eh? So how much do we have? Do we still have half a *sazhen** or so in the study?"

Masha had been unable to get to the polar study for a long, long time and didn't know that there was already... Tighter the knot, even tighter!

"Half a *sazhen*? More! I think there's..."

Suddenly – light: it's exactly ten. And without finishing, Martin Martinych screwed up his eyes and turned away: it was harder in the light than in the darkness. And in the light it could be seen clearly: his face was crumpled, clayey (many had clayey faces now – back to Adam). But Masha:

"And do you know, Mart, I'd try – maybe I'll get up... if you can light it first thing."

"Why, Masha, of course... Such a day... Why, of course – first thing."

The cave-god was dying down, shrinking away, has died away, barely crackling. Downstairs in the Obyortyshevs' they can be heard chopping the knotty wood from a barge with a stone axe – with the stone axe they're cutting Martin Martinych to pieces. A piece of Martin Martinych was smiling clayily at Masha and grinding some dried potato peelings on the coffee mill for flat-cakes – and, like a bird that had flown into the room from outside, another piece of Martin Martinych was senselessly, blindly bang-ing against the ceiling, the windowpanes, the walls: "Firewood, where – firewood, where – firewood, where?"

Martin Martinych put on his coat, belted it on the outside with a leather belt (the cave-people have a myth about this making you warmer) and made a clatter with the bucket in the corner by the wardrobe.

"Where are you going, Mart?"

"I shan't be long. Downstairs for water."

On the dark staircase, coated in ice from splashes of water, Martin Martinych stood and vacillated for a little, sighed and, clanking the bucket like shackles, went downstairs to the Obyortyshevs: they still had running water. Obyortyshev himself opened the door wearing an overcoat drawn in tight with a rope, long unshaven, his face a wasteland, overgrown with some kind of completely dust-imbued red weeds. Through the weeds – yellow stone teeth, and between the stones a momentary lizard's tail – a smile.

"Ah, Martin Martinych! What, come for water? Come in, come in, come in!"

In the narrow little box between the outer and inner doors it was impossible to turn round with the bucket – in the box was the Obyortyshevs' firewood. Clayey Martin Martinych banged his side painfully on the firewood – a deep dent in the clay. And an even deeper one in the dark corridor from the corner of a chest of drawers.

Through the dining room. In the dining room: the female Obyortyshev and three Obyortyshev young; the female hurriedly hid a bowl beneath a napkin: a man from another cave had come, and God knows – he might lash out and grab it.

In the kitchen, turning on the tap, Obyortyshev was smiling stone-toothedly:

"Well, then – how's the wife? How's the wife? How's the wife?"

"Why, Alexei Ivanych, just the same. Not well. And tomorrow's her name day, and I've got nothing to use for heating."

"Martin Martinych, use chairs, cupboards… books, too: books burn really well, really well, really well…"

"But I mean, you know: all the furniture there, nothing belongs to us, only the piano…"

"Yes, yes, yes… It's a shame, a shame!"

The bird that flew in can be heard in the kitchen whirring and rustling its wings, to the right, to the left – and suddenly, in despair, it's flung itself breast-first against the wall.

"Alexei Ivanych, I wanted… Alexei Ivanych, couldn't you let me have just five or six logs…"

Yellow stone teeth through the weeds, yellow teeth coming out of the eyes – Obyortyshev is completely covered in teeth, and the teeth are ever longer.

"Come now, Martin Martinych, come now, come now! We ourselves… You know for yourself how everything is now, you know for yourself, you know for yourself…"

Tighter the knot! Tighter, even tighter! Martin Martinych tightened himself, picked up the bucket – and through the kitchen, through the dark corridor, through the dining room. On the threshold of the dining room Obyortyshev thrust out a momentary, lizardly darting hand:

"Well, all the best… Only don't forget to slam the door shut, Martin Martinych, don't forget. Both doors, both, both – you can't get the place warm enough!"

On the dark, ice-coated landing Martin Martinych set the bucket down, turned, slammed the first door tightly shut. He listened closely and heard only the dry, osseous trembling inside him and his shaky, dotted-line breathing. In the narrow little box between the two doors he reached out a groping hand and found a log, then another, then another... No! He hurriedly bundled himself out onto the landing, pulled the door to. Now it just remained to slam the door tightly shut for the lock to click.

And now – he hasn't the strength. Hasn't the strength to slam the door on Masha's "tomorrow". And on a line marked by barely perceptible dotted breathing two Martin Martinyches began grappling to the death: the old one, with Scriabin, who knew he mustn't, and the new caveman who knew he must. The caveman, gnashing his teeth, pinned the other down and throttled him – and Martin Martinych, breaking his nails, opened the door, dipped a hand into the firewood... one log, a fourth, a fifth, inside his coat, into his belt, into the bucket – he slammed the door and was up the stairs with the huge leaps of a beast. In the middle of the staircase, on some ice-coated step, he suddenly froze, flattened himself against the wall: downstairs the door had clicked again, and Obyortyshev's dust-imbued voice:

"Who's – there? Who's there? Who's there?"

"It's me, Alexei Ivanych. I... I forgot the door... I wanted... I came back – to shut the door tight..."

"You? Hm... How could you have done that? You must be more careful, must be more careful. Everything gets stolen now, you know for yourself, you know for yourself. How could you have done that?"

The twenty-ninth. From first thing, a low, holey, cotton-wool sky, and through the holes comes an icy draught. But the cave-god has filled its belly from first thing, started droning benignly – and let there be holes there, let the tooth-covered Obyortyshev count the logs – let him, it doesn't matter: as long as there's today; "tomorrow" is incomprehensible in the cave; only when ages have passed will "tomorrow" and "the day after tomorrow" be known.

Masha got up and, swaying a little in an unseen wind, combed her hair the old way: over the ears with a centre parting. And this was like the last, withered leaf dangling on a bare tree. Out of the middle drawer of the writing desk Martin Martinych pulled papers, letters, a thermometer, some kind of blue phial (he hastily thrust it back again so that Masha didn't see) and, finally, from the farthest corner, a small black lacquered box: there, on the bottom, there was still some real – yes, yes, perfectly real – tea! They drank real tea. Throwing his head back, Martin Martinych listened to a voice so like the old one:

"Mart, do you remember: my blue room, and the piano under a cover, and on the piano the little wooden horse – the ashtray – and I was playing, and you came up behind me…"

Yes, that evening the universe had been created, and the amazing, wise face of the moon, and the nightingale trill of bells in the corridor.

"And do you remember, Mart: the window's open, the green sky, and from down below, from another world – the organ-grinder?"

Organ-grinder, wonderful organ-grinder – where are you?

"And on the embankment… D'you remember? The branches are still bare, the water rosy, and floating past is the last blue ice floe, looking like a coffin. And we just find the coffin funny because, after all, we're never going to die. D'you remember?"

Downstairs they'd started chopping with a stone axe. Suddenly they stopped, some kind of running around, shouting. And he was chopped in two: one half of Martin Martinych was seeing the deathless organ-grinder, the deathless little wooden horse, the deathless ice floe, and the other – with dotted-line breathing – was counting the logs of firewood along with Obyortyshev. Now Obyortyshev has finished counting, now he's putting on his coat, all covered in teeth he slams the door furiously and…

"Hold on, Masha, I think – I think there's someone knocking at the door."

No. No one. No one yet. He can still breathe; he can still throw his head back and listen to the voice that's so like that one, the old one.

Dusk. The twenty-ninth of October has grown old. Intent, dull, old woman's eyes – and everything shrinks, wrinkles, hunches under the intent gaze. The vaults of the ceiling are sinking down;

squashed are the armchairs, the writing desk, Martin Martinych, the beds and, on her bed, quite flat, paper Masha.

In the dusk, the house chairman,* Selikhov, came. Once he had weighed six *poods*, but by now he had half leaked away and bobbled about in the shell of his jacket like a nut in a rattle. Yet at times he still grumbled with laughter in the old way.

"Well, sir, Martin Martinych, firstly – secondly, best wishes to your spouse on her saint's day. Yes indeed, yes indeed! Obyortyshev told me..."

Martin Martinych was shot out of his armchair; he dashed, hastened – to talk, to say something...

"Some tea... right away I'll – this minute I'll... Today we have the real thing. You understand: the real thing! I've only just..."

"Tea? I'd prefer champagne, you know. Don't have any? Surely not! Gra-gra-gra! Do you know, the day before yesterday a friend and I were distilling alcohol from some Hoffmann's drops.* What a laugh! He got sloshed... 'I'm Zinoviev,'* he says, 'on your knees!' What a laugh! And from there I'm on my way home, and coming towards me on the Field of Mars is a man wearing nothing but his waistcoat, honest to God! 'What's happened to you?' I say. 'It's nothing,' he says. 'I've just had my clothes stripped off me and I'm running home to Vasilyevsky Island.'* What a laugh!"

Squashed, paper Masha was laughing on her bed. Tying the whole of himself into a tight knot, Martin Martinych was laughing louder and louder – to throw more firewood onto Selikhov so that he didn't stop, so he didn't stop, so he'd talk about something else...

Selikhov was stopping, chortling a little; he fell silent. In the shell of his jacket he bobbled to the right and to the left, stood up.

"Well, birthday girl, your hand. Bah! What, don't you know? As they have it, it's been an honour – bah.* What a laugh!"

He grumbled in the passage, in the hallway. The last second: in a moment he'll be gone, or...

The floor was swaying slightly, spinning slightly under Martin Martinych's feet. Smiling clayily, Martin Martinych was holding on to the door jamb. Selikhov was puffing, hammering his feet into enormous snow boots.

In snow boots, in a fur coat, mammoth-like, he straightened up, got his breath back, then silently took Martin Martinych by the arm, silently opened the door into the polar study, silently sat down on the sofa.

The floor in the study was an ice floe; barely audibly the ice floe gave a crack, broke away from the shore and carried Martin Martinych away, carried him away and set him spinning – and from over there, from the distant shore of the sofa, Selikhov could scarcely be heard.

"Firstly – secondly, my good sir, I ought to tell you I'd squash that Obyortyshev like a louse, honest to God... But you can understand for yourself: since he's making a formal statement, since he's saying – tomorrow I'm going to the criminal... Such a louse! I can give you one piece of advice: go and see him today, straight away, and stuff those logs of his right down his throat."

The ice floe – ever faster. Tiny, flattened, barely visible – just a splinter – Martin Martinych replied – to himself, and not about the logs – what were the logs?! – no, about something else:

"Very well. Today. Straight away."

"Well, that's excellent, that's excellent! He's such a louse, such a louse I tell you..."

It's still dark in the cave. Clayey, cold, blind, Martin Martinych ran obtusely into the diluvially jumbled objects in the cave. He gave a start: a voice like Masha's, like the old one...

"What were you talking about there with Selikhov? What? Ration cards? I've been lying here all this time, Mart, and thinking: we should pull ourselves together and go away somewhere where there's sunshine... Oh dear, what a clatter you're making! As if on purpose. I mean, you know very well – I can't bear it, I can't, I can't!"

Like a knife on glass. But anyway – it doesn't matter now. Mechanical arms and legs. They have to be raised and lowered, like a ship's booms, with chains of some kind, a winch, and one man's not enough to turn the winch: you need three. Forcing himself to pull on the chains, Martin Martinych put the kettle and a saucepan on to warm up, threw on the last of Obyortyshev's logs.

"Can you hear what I'm saying to you? Why don't you say something? Can you hear?"

This isn't Masha, of course, no, it's not her voice. Martin Martinych was moving slower and slower; his feet were getting stuck in quicksand; it was ever harder to turn the winch. Suddenly a chain tore loose from some block or other, a boom-arm crashed down, caught stupidly on the kettle, the saucepan – there was a clattering onto the floor; the cave-god hissed like a snake. And from over there, from the far shore, from the bed – an alien, piercing voice:

"You're doing it on purpose! Go away! Right now! And I don't need anyone, or anything, I don't need anything, I don't! Go away!"

The twenty-ninth of October had died, and the deathless organ-grinder had died, and the ice floes on the water, rosy in the sunset, and Masha. And it's a good thing, and it's necessary, so there should be no incredible "tomorrow", no Obyortyshev, no Selikhov, no Masha, no him, Martin Martinych, so that everything should die.

Mechanical, distant Martin Martinych was still doing something. Perhaps he was stoking up the stove again and picking the saucepan up off the floor, boiling the kettle, and perhaps Masha was saying something – he didn't hear: there were only dully aching dents in the clay made by certain words and the corners of the wardrobe, the chairs, the writing desk.

Out of the writing desk Martin Martinych was slowly pulling bundles of letters, the thermometer, sealing wax, the box with the tea and, again, letters. And finally, from somewhere, from the very bottom, the dark-blue phial.

Ten: the light came on. Naked, harsh, plain, cold – like cave life and death – electric light. And so plain, beside the iron, Opus 74, the flat-cakes – the blue phial.

The cast-iron god began droning benignly, devouring the parchment-yellow, pale-bluish-white paper of the letters. The kettle gave a gentle reminder of itself, rattling its lid. Masha turned around.

"Has the tea boiled? Mart, dear, give that to me!"

She'd seen. A second, pierced right through by the clear, naked, cruel electric light: Martin Martinych convulsed before the stove; on the letters a rosy glow, like water at sunset; and there – the blue phial.

"Mart! Do you… do you want?…"

It's quiet. Disinterestedly devouring the deathless, bitter, tender, yellow, white, pale-blue words, the cast-iron god was gently purring. And Masha, just as simply as she'd asked for tea:

"Mart, dear! Mart, give that to me!"

Martin Martinych smiled from afar:

"But Masha, you know very well, don't you: there's only enough there for one."

"Mart, there's no longer any me all the same, you know. This is no longer me, after all – I mean, all the same I'm soon going to… Mart, you can understand – Mart, have pity on me… Mart!"

Ah, that very – that very voice… And if you throw your head back…

"I deceived you, Masha: we don't have a single log in the study. And I went to see Obyortyshev, and there between the doors… I stole – do you understand? And Selikhov told me… I should take them back now – but I've burned everything – I've burned everything – everything! I'm not talking about the logs – what are the logs! – you understand, don't you?"

The cast-iron god is disinterestedly dozing off. The vaults of the cave, dying away, are quivering a little, and quivering a little are the buildings, the cliffs, the mammoths, Masha.

"Mart, if you still love me… Come on, Mart, come on, remember! Mart, dear, give it to me!"

The deathless little wooden horse, the organ-grinder, the ice floe. And this voice… Martin Martinych rose slowly from his knees. Slowly, turning the winch with difficulty, he took the blue phial from the desk and handed it to Masha.

She threw off her blanket and sat up on the bed, rosy, swift, deathless – like the water that time at sunset – grasped the phial, laughed.

"There, you see: it wasn't by accident I was lying and thinking about going away from here. Light the lamp too – that one, on the desk. That's it. Now put something else in the stove – I want there to be fire…"

Without looking, Martin Martinych raked papers of some sort out of the desk and threw them into the stove.

"Now… go and take a walk for a while. I think there's a moon there – *my* moon: do you remember? Don't forget – take your key, or else you'll slam the door, and then opening it…"

No, there was no moon there. The low, dark, blank clouds are vaults, and everything is one enormous, quiet cave. Narrow, endless passages between walls, and dark, ice-coated cliffs resembling houses, and in the cliffs – deep, crimsonly illuminated holes; there, in the holes, beside the fire – people on their haunches. A light, icy little draught blows the white dust away from under your feet, and unheard by anyone – over the white dust, over the blocks of ice, over the caves, over the people on their haunches – is the enormous, even tread of some most mammoth mammoth.

1920

Mamai*

In the evening and in the night, there are no longer houses in St Petersburg: there are six-storey stone ships. A solitary six-storey world, the ship scuds over the stone waves amidst other solitary six-storey worlds; the ship sparkles with the lights of countless cabins into the mutinous stone ocean of the streets. And, of course, they're not tenants in the cabins: they're passengers. In the manner of a ship, all are just unacquaintedly acquainted with each other; all are citizens of a six-storey republic, beset by the nocturnal ocean.

The passengers of stone ship No. 40 scudded in the evenings in that part of the St Petersburg ocean that is designated on the map by the name of Lakhtinskaya Street.* Osip, formerly the janitor, but nowadays Citizen Malafeyev, was standing by the main gangway and gazing through his spectacles out there into the darkness: occasionally, one person or another was still being washed up by the waves. Citizen Malafeyev pulled them out of the darkness, wet and covered in snow, and, by shifting his spectacles on his nose, regulated for each his level of respect: the reservoir from which the respect flowed was linked by a complex mechanism with the spectacles.

There – the spectacles are on the tip of the nose, like a strict pedagogue's: this is for Pyotr Petrovich Mamai.

"Your spouse, Pyotr Petrovich, is expecting you for dinner. Came here, she did, very upset. How is it you're so late?"

Next the spectacles are settled firmly, defensively into the saddle: him, big-nose from 25, in a motor car. It's really troublesome with big-nose: you can't call him "Mr", but "Comrade" seems awkward. How to manage so that...

"Ah, Mr-Comrade Mylnik! This weather, Mr-Comrade Mylnik... troublesome..."

And finally – the spectacles go up onto his forehead: Yelisei Yeliseyich has boarded the ship.

"Well, thank the Lord! Safe and sound? In that fur coat, aren't you afraid you'll have it stolen? Allow me, I'll brush the snow off…"

Yelisei Yeliseyich is the ship's captain: the house's authorized representative. And Yelisei Yeliseyich is one of those gloomy Atlantes that, bent over, brows furrowed in anguish, have for seventy years been carrying the cornice of the Hermitage* along Millionaya Street.

Today the cornice had clearly been even heavier than usual. Yelisei Yeliseyich was out of breath:

"Around to every apartment… Quickly… To a meeting… To the club…"

"Good Heavens! Yelisei Yeliseyich, again something… troublesome?"

But no reply is required: just look at the forehead furrowed in anguish, the shoulders weighed down by their burden. And Citizen Malafeyev, with virtuoso control of his spectacles, set off running round to the apartments. His knocking at the door to sound the alarm was like the archangel's trump:* embraces froze, quarrels were suspended like motionless puffs of cannon smoke, a spoonful of soup stopped on its way to a mouth.

The soup was being eaten by Pyotr Petrovich Mamai. Or to be more precise: he was being extremely strictly fed by his spouse. Presiding in an armchair magnificently, graciously, many-breastedly, Buddha-like, she was feeding the mundane little man with the soup she had created:

"Do hurry up, Petyenka, the soup will get cold. How many times do I have to tell you I don't like you having a book at the dinner table…"

"Oh, Alyonka – oh, I'll just be a moment – oh, just a moment… I mean, it's the sixth edition! Do you understand, Bogdanovich's *Dushenka* – the sixth edition! In 1812 under the French absolutely everything was burnt,* and everyone thought only three copies had survived... And now here's a fourth: do you understand? I found it yesterday on Zagorodny..."*

The Mamai of 1917 captured books. As a shock-headed ten-year-old boy he had studied Scripture, rejoiced in pens and been fed by his mother; as a bald forty-year-old boy he worked for an insurance company, rejoiced in books and was fed by his spouse.

A spoonful of soup – a sacrifice to the Buddha – and once again the mundane little man had frivolously forgotten about providence with the wedding ring, as he tenderly stroked and fingered every letter. "In exact accordance with the first edition... With the approval of the Censorial Committee..." Oh, how nice, how sweet is that old-fashioned long "s" on its fat little leg...*

"Petyenka, now what's going on? I'm shouting and shouting, and you're here with your book... Have you gone deaf, or something? There's someone knocking."

Pyotr Petrovich at full tilt into the hallway. In the doorway – the spectacles on the tip of the nose:

"Yelisei Yeliseyich said to come to a meeting. Quickly."

"There you are, as soon as you sit down with a book... Well, what is it now?" There are tears in the bald boy's voice.

"I couldn't say. Just to come quickly..." The door of the cabin slammed shut; the spectacles hurried on...

Things were clearly not well on the ship: perhaps they were off course; perhaps there was an unseen breach somewhere in the bilge and the terrible ocean of the streets was already threatening to gush inside. Somewhere up above, both to the left and to the right, there was alarming staccato knocking on the cabin doors; somewhere on half-dark landings there were stifled conversations in low voices, and there was the tramp of soles running quickly down the stairs – down to the mess, to the house's clubroom.

There – a plastered sky, all covered in tobacco storm clouds. Stuffy, calorific silence, a suggestion of someone whispering. Yelisei Yeliseyich rang a bell, bent over, knitted his brow – in the silence his shoulders could be heard cracking – lifted the cornice of the unseen Hermitage and brought this crashing down upon their heads:

"Gentlemen. According to reliable information – there are going to be searches* tonight."

A buzz, the clatter of chairs, people's pates going pop, beringed pinkies, carbuncles, bows, sideburns. And onto the bent Atlas from the tobacco clouds comes a torrent:

"No, allow me! We're obliged…"

"What? Paper money too?"

"Yelisei Yeliseyich, I propose that the gates…"

"In books is the safest – in books…"

Yelisei Yeliseyich, bent over, stonily withstood the torrent. And to Osip, without turning his head (perhaps it couldn't actually turn):

"Osip, who's on the night watch in the courtyard tonight?"

Amidst silence, Osip's finger slowly made its way down the schedule on the wall: the finger was moving not letters but Mamai's heavy bookcases.

"Today's M: Citizen Mamai, Citizen Malafeyev."

"Well then. Take revolvers – and in the event that there's no warrant…"

Stone ship No. 40 scudded down Lakhtinskaya Street through the storm. There was rocking, whistling and snow whipping against the sparkling windows of the cabins, and somewhere an unseen breach, and no one knows if the ship will battle through the night to the morning's jetty – or founder. In the fast-emptying mess the passengers clutched at the stonily motionless captain:

"Yelisei Yeliseyich, what if we put it in our pockets? After all, they're not going to…"

"Yelisei Yeliseyich, what if I hang it up in the lavatory as toilet paper, eh?"

The passengers scurried from cabin to cabin and inside the cabins behaved in an unusual manner: lying on the floor, they groped about under a cupboard; they peeped sacrilegiously inside Leo Tolstoy's plaster head;* they removed from her frame the grandmother who'd been smiling serenely on the wall for fifty years.

The mundane little man Mamai stood face to face with Buddha and hid his eyes from the all-seeing, awe-inspiring gaze. His arms belonged to someone else entirely, were superfluous: the docked wings of a penguin. His arms had been an encumbrance to him for forty years, and if they hadn't been an encumbrance now, maybe it would have been really easy to say what needed to be said – and that was so frightening, so unthinkable…

"I don't understand: what are you so scared about? Even your nose has gone white! What is it to us? What thousands do we have?"

God knows, if the Mamai of 1300-and-something had also had arms that belonged to someone else and just such a secret and just such a spouse, perhaps he would have acted in the same way as the Mamai of 1917: somewhere in the midst of the threatening silence a mouse began scratching in the corner – and the Mamai of 1917 rushed over there at full pelt with his eyes and, cowering in the mousehole, trembled out:

"I have… that is – we have… F-four thousand two hundred—"

"Wha-at? You-u have? Where from?"

"I've… all the time, bit by bit, I've been… I was afraid to ask every time—"

"Wha-at? You mean you've been stealing? You mean you've been deceiving me? And there was I, poor me – there was I thinking: my Petyenka… Poor me!"

"It was for books I…"

"I know those books in skirts! Shut up!"

Ten-year-old Mamai had been whipped by his mother only once in his life: when he had bent back the tap on the newly acquired samovar – the water had run out, everything had come unsoldered, the tap had drooped sadly. And now Mamai felt for the second time in his life that his head was clamped under his mother's arm, his trousers were down and…

And suddenly, with his cunning little boy's nose Mamai sensed how he could make the sadly drooping tap – the four thousand two hundred – be forgotten. In a plaintive voice:

"I'm to be on watch in the courtyard tonight until four in the morning. With a revolver. And Yelisei Yeliseyich said if they come without a warrant…"

Instantly – instead of the blazing Buddha, a many-breasted, tender-hearted mother.

"Good Lord! What, has everyone gone mad or something? This is all Yelisei Yeliseyich. You watch your step – and indeed, don't even think of—"

"No-o, I'll just have it in my pocket. Am I really capable? I wouldn't even hurt a fly…"

It was true: if Mamai got a fly in his glass, he would always pick it out carefully, blow it dry and let it go – fly away! No, that doesn't scare him. The four thousand two hundred though…

And again – Buddha:

"The things I have to put up with because of you! So where are you going to put your stolen – no, shut up, please – stolen, yes…"

Books; the galoshes in the hallway; toilet paper; the samovar chimney; the quilted lining of Mamai's fur hat; the rug with the blue knight on the bedroom wall; the half-open umbrella, still wet with snow; an envelope tossed carelessly onto the table with a stamp attached, addressed in clear handwriting to an imaginary Comrade Goldebayev… No… too dangerous… And finally, around midnight, it's decided to base everything on the subtlest psychological calculation: they'd look absolutely anywhere – but not right on the threshold, and just by the threshold there's this little loose square of parquet. With a small knife used for cutting the pages of books the square is deftly lifted. The stolen four thousand ("No, please – please shut up!") is wrapped in the greaseproof paper from some sponge cakes (it may be damp under the threshold) and the four thousand is interred beneath the little square.

The whole of ship No. 40 is like a string, on tiptoe, in a whisper. The windows sparkle feverishly into the dark ocean of streets, and on the fourth, on the first, on the second floor a curtain is drawn back, and at the sparkling window there's a dark shadow. No, it's pitch black. Anyway, there are two of them there in the courtyard, aren't there, and when it starts, they'll let it be known…

Gone two o'clock. Silence in the courtyard. Around the lamp above the gates there are white flies: without end, without number they were falling, swirling in swarms, falling, getting singed, falling down.

Below, with his spectacles on the tip of his nose, Citizen Malafeyev was philosophizing:

"I'm a mild, good-natured man – it's troublesome for me living in anger like this. Why don't I take a trip home, I think to myself, to Ostashkov. I get there, and the international situation – why, it's downright impossible: they're all at each other just like wolves. But I can't be like that: I'm a mild man…"

In the mild man's hands is a revolver with six deaths compressed in the cartridges.

"How did you manage in the Japanese war,* Osip? Kill anyone?"

"Well, in the war! In the war, of course."

"Well, and what's it like with a bayonet?"

"How can I put it… It's a bit like getting inside a watermelon: it's hard going to begin with – the rind – but then it's fine, really easy."

The watermelon sent a shiver down Mamai's spine.

"Well, I'd… Even if I myself right now was being… not for anything!"

"You wait! When it comes to the crunch, then you too…"

It's quiet. The white flies around the lamp. Suddenly from afar – the long whip of a rifle shot, and it's quiet again, the flies. Thank God: it's four o'clock, they won't be coming now, not tonight. In a moment there'll be the handover, and off home to the cabin to sleep…

On the wall in the Mamais' bedroom the blue checked knight swung his blue sword and froze: before the knight's eyes a human sacrifice was being made.

Reposing upon white linen clouds was Mrs Mamai – all-embracing, many-breasted, Buddha-like. Her appearance said: today she had completed the creation of the world and recognized that all was exceedingly good, even this little man, despite the four thousand two hundred. The little man stood doomed beside the bed, chilled to the bone, with a red nose and someone else's docked penguin-wing arms.

"Well come on now, come on…"

The blue knight screwed his eyes up: it was so clear, horribly so, that in a moment the little man was going to cross himself, stretch his arms out in front of him, and like plunging into water – plop!

Ship No. 40 scudded safely through the storm and docked at the morning's jetty. The passengers hurriedly took out business briefcases, baskets for provisions and hastened past Osip's spectacles to the shore: the ship was at the jetty only until the evening, and then – back into the ocean.

Bent over, Yelisei Yeliseyich carried the cornice of the unseen Hermitage past Osip and brought this crashing down on Osip from above:

"There's going to be a search tonight for sure. So let everyone know."

But before the night there's still a whole day to be lived. And in the strange, unfamiliar city – Petrograd* – the passengers wandered in bewilderment. It's somehow so like – and so unlike – Petersburg, from where they sailed almost a year ago now and to where they're unlikely ever to return. Strange stone-snow waves, frozen overnight: mountains and hollows. Warriors from some unknown tribe in strange rags, weapons on cords over their shoulders. The outlandish custom of going out visiting and staying the night: in the streets at night are Walter Scott's Rob Roys.* And here on Zagorodny – little drops of blood scorched in the snow… No, it's not Petersburg!

Bemused, down unfamiliar Zagorodny wandered Mamai. The penguin wings were an encumbrance; his head hung like the tap of a samovar that had come unsoldered; on his worn-down left heel is a snowy *globus hystericus** – every step is torment.

And suddenly his head jerked up, his feet started prancing twenty-five-year-oldly, on his cheeks – poppies: smiling at Mamai from a window…

"Hey, dozy, out of the way!" Sweeping unstoppably straight towards him were red-faced men with enormous bags.

Mamai leapt aside, his eyes fixed on the window, and just as soon as they had swept past, he was back to the window: smiling at him from it was...

"Yes, for the sake of this one you'll steal, you'll deceive and everything."

Smiling from the window, stretched out seductively, voluptuously, was a book from the time of Catherine the Great:* *A Descriptive Depiction of the Beauties of Sankt-Piterburkh.** And with a casual movement, with feminine cunning, the book allowed a glimpse inside – there, into the warm cleft between two supplely arched bluish marble pages.

Mamai was twenty-five-year-oldly in love. Every day he had been coming to the window on Zagorodny and silently, with his eyes, singing serenades. He hadn't slept at night – and had been deceitful with himself: as if the reason for not sleeping was a mouse working away somewhere under the floor. He had been leaving in the morning – and every morning that same little square of parquet on the threshold had pricked him with a sweet nail: interred beneath the square was Mamai's happiness, so near, so far. Now, when everything about the four thousand two hundred had been revealed – what now?

On the fourth day, with his heart squeezed in his fist like a fluttering sparrow, Mamai entered that very door on Zagorodny. Behind the counter was a grey-bearded, bushy-browed Chernomor* in whose captivity *she* dwelt, *the book*. Inside Mamai his warlike ancestor rose from the dead: Mamai advanced bravely on Chernomor.

"Ah, Mr Mamai! It's been a while, it's been a while... I've got some things set aside for you."

Squeezing the sparrow even tighter, Mamai leafed through the books, occasionally stroking them with feigned fondness, but he was living through his back: behind his back in the shop window, *she, the book*, was smiling. Having selected a yellowed 1835

Telescope,* Mamai spent a long time haggling – before giving it up as hopeless. Then, prowling around the shelves in foxy circles, he made his way to the window – and, as if by the by:

"So how much is this, then?"

Pit-a-pat – the sparrow flitted out – hold it, hold it! Chernomor raked through his beard with his fingers:

"Well now, as the first sale of the day… it'll cost you a hundred and fifty."

"Hm… maybe…" (Hurrah! Bells! Cannons!)* "Well, all right… I'll bring the money tomorrow and pick it up."

Now he had to get through the scariest part: the little square beside the threshold. Mamai spent the night roasting on coals: must, can't, can, it's unthinkable, can, can't, must…

Omniscient, gracious, fearsome – providence with the wedding ring was having tea.

"Come on, do have some, Petyenka. Whatever is the matter with you? Couldn't you sleep again?"

"No. M-mice… I don't know."

"Put the handkerchief down – stop twisting it! Really, what is all this?"

"I… I'm not twisting it…"

And now at last the glass has been drunk: not a glass, but a bottomless, hundred-and-five-gallon barrel. Buddha is in the kitchen accepting a sacrifice from the cook. Mamai is in the study alone.

Mamai gave a tick like a clock just before it strikes twelve. He took a gulp of air, listened closely and tiptoed to the writing desk: the knife for books was there. Then, in a fever, he's doubled up like a gnome on the threshold, on his bald patch there's an icy dew, he's thrust the knife under the square, dug it up and… a wail of despair!

At the wail, Buddha thundered out from the kitchen – and at her feet she saw: a little pumpkin bald patch; lower down – a doubled-up gnome with a little knife; and lower still – the finest shreds of paper.

"Four thousand – mice… There, there it is! There!"

Cruel, merciless, like the Mamai of 1300-and-something, the Mamai of 1917 rose up from all fours – and was into the corner by the door with his sword: cowering in the corner was the mouse that had shot out from under the little square. And with the sword Mamai bloodthirstily nailed his enemy. A watermelon: hard going for one second – the rind – then easy – the flesh, and stop: a little square of parquet, the end.

1920

X

The principal lines on the spectrum of this story are gold, red and lilac, for the town is full of domes, revolution and lilac bushes. The revolution and the lilac bushes are in full bloom, whence it can be concluded with some degree of reliability that the year is 1919 and the month is May.

This May morning begins with the appearance, on the corner of Pancake Street and Rosa Luxemburg Street,* of a procession – evidently a religious one: eight clerical persons well known to the entire town. Yet the clerical persons are brandishing not censers but brooms, which transfers all the action from the plane of religion to the plane of revolution: it is simply a non-labour element doing labour service for the benefit of the people. Soaring golden to the sky instead of prayers are clouds of dust, and the people on the pavements are sneezing, coughing and hurrying through the dust. It is still only a little after nine, and the church service is at ten, but today for some reason everyone has flown out early and they are buzzing like bees before swarming.

On this day (1919, 20/V), all citizens aged from eighteen to fifty, with the exception of the most unrepentant bourgeois, were in employment, and today there was evidently something unusual awaiting everyone from eighteen to fifty in every possible Disecpodep, Disecodep and Disdeppe-ed.* The main thing was that it was "something", that it was an "x", and human nature is such that it is precisely the "x"s that attract it (a point that is brilliantly exploited in algebra and stories). In this instance the "x" had its origins in the repentant deacon Indikoplev.

Deacon Indikoplev, having publicly confessed that over the course of ten years he had been deceiving the people, naturally now enjoyed the trust of both the people and the authorities. It was sometimes even the case that he would go fishing with

Comrade Sterligov from the Disexcom,* as had happened, for example, the previous evening. They had both been gazing at their floats, at the gold-red-lilac water, and chatting about chub, the leaders of the revolution, beetroot syrup, the fugitive Socialist Revolutionary* Perepechko and the sharks of imperialism. Here, bashfully taking refuge behind the palm of his hand, the deacon remarked – quite malapropos:

"Forgive me, Comrade Sterligov, but your... trousers, at the back... they're not exactly, you know, but would appear to be..."

Comrade Sterligov merely scratched the fur coat on his face:

"Never mind, they'll do till tomorrow! And tomorrow they should be giving out prodwear* to officials – a document's come from the centre. I'm telling you this confidentially though..."

Of course, on his way home, as he was returning with two ruffe, the deacon knocked on Alyoshka the telegraphist's window and told him – confidentially, of course. And Alyoshka the telegraphist, as you know, is a poet; he's already written eight pounds of poetry – it's there, in his chest. As a poet, he didn't consider it his right to keep a secret in his soul: a poet's mission is to reveal his soul to all. And by morning, everyone from eighteen to sixty knew about the prodwear.

But nobody knew what the prodwear was. The one thing that was clear to everyone was that prodwear was something that traced its lineage back to the fig leaf, i.e. something that cloaked the nakedness of Adams and embellished the nakedness of Eves. And at that time the overall area of nakedness significantly exceeded the area of fig leaves – to the extent that, for example, Alyoshka the telegraphist had for some time been going to work in long johns, transformed by means of linseed oil, soot and red lead into grey waterproof trousers with a red stripe.

It's natural, therefore, that prodwear for Alyoshka was embodied in trouser form, while for the beautiful Marfa that same thing blossomed into a pink Maytime hat, for the former deacon it was condensed into boots – and so on. In a word, prodwear is evidently something like protoplasm, the primary matter from

X

which there arose everything: both baobabs and lambs, tigers and hats, Socialist Revolutionaries and boots, proletarians and unrepentant bourgeois, and the repentant deacon Indikoplev.

If you now risk plunging into the dusty clouds on Luxemburg Street with me, then through the sneezing and coughing you will clearly hear the same thing as I do: "The deacon... With the deacon... Where's the deacon? Have you seen the deacon?" Just the deacon alone, as an experienced fisherman, was capable of reeling in this "x" hook, which had caught everyone with its bait of prodwear. But the deacon wasn't here: the deacon had to be sought now not in the red line of the spectrum, but in the lilac, Maytime, amatory one. That line runs not down Rosa Luxemburg, but down Pancake Street.

At the very end of Pancake Street, beside a house painted the most delicate lilac-pink colour, stands the repentant deacon. Now he's knocked at the gate – in a minute we shall hear Marfa's pink voice in the yard: "Kuzma Ivanych, is that you?" and the gate will open. While waiting, the deacon scrutinizes the physiognomy with a villainous moustache that is drawn on the gate with the inscription beneath: "So be it." What this means is unknown, but the deacon immediately remembers that he is clean-shaven: ever since he removed his moustache and beard after repenting, it had constantly seemed to him as though he had removed his trousers, that his nose was protruding in a perfectly indecent manner and needed to be covered up with anything that came to hand – it was sheer torment!

Covering his nose with the palm of his hand, the deacon knocks again, then again: no one. And yet Marfa is at home: the gate is locked from the inside. Which means – what then? – which means she's with someone... The deacon sets down inside him this very ellipsis depicted graphically here just now and, stumbling over it at every moment, walks towards Rosa Luxemburg.

A few minutes later, on the very same spot, beside the most delicate pink house, we can see the telegraphist and poet Alyoshka. He, too, knocks at the gate, contemplates the moustachioed physiognomy and waits. He's standing with his back to us: there's just the dark back of his head and his ears, sticking out in a somehow very proper and hospitable way like the handles of a samovar.

Suddenly the whole of Alyoshka becomes a superfluous garnish for his own right ear: only the ear is alive – it swallows the whispering, the rustling, the footsteps in the yard. The poet needs to know everything and see everything: he's dashed towards the fence, grabbed hold of the top, jumped up, torn his sleeve – and there, in the yard, by the shed, for one instant he's seen something.

It's probably not worth tearing sleeves and climbing up onto the fence after the poet: we'll find out what Alyoshka saw there sooner or later anyway. And for the time being a judgement can be made about it from his face. With gaping mouth and round eyes, Alyoshka now resembled those ruffe, mercilessly threaded on a string, which had dangled in the deacon's hand in front of Alyoshka's window the previous evening. Alyoshka stood in ruffe mode for exactly as long as was required for him to find a rhyme for what he had seen (note: the rhyme was the words "go, wretch, go"). Then he broke loose from the string onto which his fate had been threaded and darted onto Rosa Luxemburg.

Being prepared there now was the calamity of a collision. A collision in a certain human point of two antagonistic lines of the spectrum – the red and the gold, the revolutionary and the domical.

That human point was the deacon. He was dressed in maroon trousers and a Tolstoy shirt* made from a ceremonial cassock – and could be seen from a distance, like a blaze or a banner. Just as soon as he appeared, crimson in the clouds of dust, the whole of Rosa Luxemburg Street turned to him as to a magnet – cleaving to him were dozens of questions, hands, eyes. The deacon was in an invisible pulpit and to each one from the pulpit he gave out: "Yes, prodwear... Yes, yes, a document from the centre."

But one of the people (a bass) blurted out:

"What document's that? Tell us another one!"

"That is, how do you mean – 'tell us another one'?"

"Just that... it's quite straightforward."

"You don't believe me? Well, look – well, here's a holy cross for you, all right?" and, to hold his ground on high, in the pulpit, the repentant deacon, forgetting about his repentance, did, indeed, cross himself. Then he suddenly turned crimson – the reflex of the other line of the spectrum – and (invisibly) came crashing down.

The calamity came about because gazing fixedly at the deacon from the neighbouring cloud of dust was a bent rollie set in a furry face: Sterligov from the Disexcom. And, of course, he had seen the deacon crossing himself.

Agonizingly, the deacon sensed his naked nose, covered it up with one hand and pressed the other to his heart.

"Comrade Sterligov… Comrade Sterligov, forgive me, for Christ's sake…" and, turning even more crimson, he froze.

Sterligov took the cigarette from his mouth and went to say something, but said nothing – and that was more frightening still: he just looked at the deacon in silence and walked off. The deacon, like a sleepwalker, still pressing his hand to his heart, followed him.

Another five or ten lines, and the deacon might well have thought of what he should say and would have been saved, but at precisely that moment out from around a corner came Alyoshka. He bounded up to Sterligov and, instead of the requisite word, he blurted out the rhyme:

"Go, wretch, go! That is, I… I'd like to have a word with you…"

And he fell silent, looking around, shifting from one foot to the other – his waterproof trousers were giving the occasional little rumble, like the bulls' bladders on which youngsters learn to swim.

"Well? On what matter?"

"It's… a confidential matter," whispered Alyoshka. Floating in the dusty waves all around were dozens of ears – the whisper was heard, and it carried on running, like a flame along a line of gunpowder. Alyoshka's confidential matter, the mysterious prodwear, the deacon's calamity – it was too much now, there were thousands of volts flying around in the air, a discharge was required.

And the discharge took place: it started pouring with rain. Everyone from eighteen to fifty fled into doorways and gateways, whence they gazed at the continuous, swishing glass-bead curtain. Never mind, let it pour – the rain is equally essential for both the republic's grain and the subsequent events of this story: it'll be easier for pursuers on the trail in the dusk to search for a certain "x" running away from them on ground that's damp.

* * *

All who have seen the deacon, if only just now, on Rosa Luxemburg Street, know he is a hefty man. And so I may be risking unpleasantness in the event of a chance meeting with him in another short story or tale – but I consider it my duty nonetheless to unmask him fully here.

Having repented and shaved his head, deacon Indikoplev published a bull to his former flock in the Disexcom's *Izvestiya*.* Set in bold cicero, the bull was pasted up on fences, and from it everyone learnt that the deacon had repented after hearing a touring Muscovite's lecture on Marxism. It's true that the lecture made a great impression generally – to the extent that the club's next address, on astronomy, was announced thus: 'The Planet Marx and its Inhabitants'. But I know for certain: the thing that occasioned upheaval in the deacon and compelled him to repent was not Marxism but Marfism.

The progenitor of this non-class teaching, who has until now been shown only a little between the lines, was going down to the river early one morning to bathe. She undressed, hung her frock on a willow branch, dipped the toes of her right foot into the water from a rock – how was the water today? – splashed once, twice. Beneath a bush a *sazhen* to the left sat the (at that time not yet repentant) naked deacon Indikoplev, hauling up a trap net which had been set in the night for crayfish. With the accustomed ear of a fisherman the deacon heard the splashing:

"Wow, that must be a big one biting!" He took one look... and was done for.

Marfa wiggled her shoulders (the water was a little cold) and started laying her plait around her head like a chaplet – her hair was ripe, rich, light brown, and she as a whole was rich and ripe. Ah, if only the deacon had been able to draw like Kustodiev!* – her, against the dark greenery of the leaves, with a hand raised to her head, in her teeth a hairpin, her teeth pearly, pale bluish, a green enamel cross on a black cord between her breasts...

The deacon couldn't get up and leave at once on account of his nakedness; as for getting dressed – his underwear was just shameful. Against his will he had to endure it all right through to the end – until Marfa had had a good swim, emerged from the water (that alone: the way the drops rolled off her tips!), dressed – without haste. The deacon endured, but that was the day from which he became a confirmed Marfist.

In essence, Marfism was much closer to the Gospels than to Marxism... Thus, for example, there is no doubt that the commandment Marfa considered fundamental was "love thy neighbour". For her neighbour she was always ready, in accordance with the Gospels, to take the shirt off her own back. "Oh, you poor dear thing, whatever am I to do with you? Well, come here to me, sweetheart – come on now!" That's what she said to the Socialist Revolutionary Perepechko ("poor dear, doing time in prison!"), what she said to Khaskin from the Bolshevik cell ("poor dear, a neck just like a little chick's!"), what she said to Alyoshka the telegraphist ("poor dear, always sitting writing!"), what she said to...

And it was at this point that there came to light in the deacon that accursed legacy of capitalism, the proprietary instinct. And the deacon said:

"I want you to be mine – and no one else's! If I... well, like this... well, I don't know how to... d'you understand?"

"Oh, you poor dear! I do understand, I do! But whatever am I to do with them when they're begging in Christ's name? I'm not made of stone, you know – I feel sorry for them!"

This was on a quiet revolutionary evening, on the bench in Marfa's garden. A machine gun was chattering away gently somewhere, calling to the female of the species. On the other side of the wall in the shed the cow was sighing bitterly – and in the garden the deacon was sighing more bitterly still. So it would have continued, had fate not brought into play the colour red with which all the upheavals in history are stained.

On one occasion, instead of bread citizens were each given a can of red lead mixed with linseed oil. The deacon spent all day lumbering about barefooted over iron, painting the roof the colour of bronze. And when it got dark, the deacon's wife (the neighbours had long been whispering to her about the deacon by then) stole by way of backyards into Marfa's garden. In her hands was a bundle, and in the bundle was something round: perhaps a bomb, perhaps a severed head, or perhaps a pot of something. Ten minutes later the deacon's wife climbed out of the garden, wiped her hands on some burdock (were they bloodstained?) and went back home. Then – as always: the stars, the machine gun, the cow sighing in the shed, the deacon on the bench in the garden. He sighed once, then a second time, and then swore:

"D-damn it all! It stinks of paint here too – you can't get away from it anywhere, over the day today it's soaked right the way through me!"

But fortunately, pinned to Marfa's bosom was a sprig of lilac. Dear Comrades, are you familiar with this superstructure on the most delicate foundation – in accordance with the teachings of Marfism? If you are, you'll understand that the deacon soon forgot about the paint and everything else in the world.

It's not surprising that in the morning the deacon barely managed to open his eyes in time for mass. Get dressed quick – he grabbed his trousers... Holy Lady! – not trousers, but nothing less than the evidence of a crime: everything was smeared with red. The seat of the grey inner cassock was all red, and the skirts were all red... The bench in the garden yesterday had been painted – no wonder there'd been that smell!

The deacon rushed to the cupboard to put on a different pair of trousers that weren't a visual diagram of his sin, but the cupboard was empty: the deacon's wife had hidden everything away.

"No, you Grishka, you Rasputin,* you, you go as you are!" cried the deacon's wife. "Go, go, for all good people to see! No-o, I'm not going to give, go!"

And so off he went – as did once the prophet Elisha* – with a flock of cackling small boys behind him.

No one has ever yet succeeded in giving a proper description of a sandstorm, an earthquake, childbirth or a hangover. And it's impossible to describe what was going on inside the deacon as he was serving that mass. One thing is important: by the end of the mass the deacon had come to appreciate the gains of the revolution and, in particular, the fact that the revolution had demolished the prison of bourgeois marriage.

Next day, the deacon took his ceremonial cassock to a tailor. And two days later, in a maroon Tolstoy shirt, clean-shaven, shamefacedly covering with a hand the nose which had shamelessly sprung out, he turned up at Marfa's to tell her that because of her he had decided to condemn his soul to perdition, renounce everything, divorce his wife and marry her, Marfa.

"You poor dear! Well, come here, come here to me… But why is it your eyes are so funny?"

"Never mind my eyes! All this is enough to make my brains go skew-whiff."

The deacon's brains *were* going skew-whiff: as in the seminary, he sat learning texts – now from Marx – by rote, and every evening went to classes with a study group. But concealed beneath the deacon's Marxism was the purest Marfism: after my impartial testimony that should be clear for the verdict of history. And then, citizen judges of history, was it not before your eyes that this supposedly repentant minister of religion just crossed himself in public? It was seen by the whole of Rosa Luxemburg, including the esteemed Comrade Sterligov from the Disexcom – isn't that enough?

The whole of Rosa Luxemburg was now a theatre auditorium: the glass-beaded curtains of rain have been drawn back, the audience is filling the gateway boxes, hundreds of eyes are glued to the stage. The stage is two Constructivist platforms in the style of Meyerhold:* two covered doorways at the entrances to Perelygin's haberdashery shop (the entrances are, of course, boarded up: the year is 1919). The action unfolds on both platforms simultaneously: to the right are Sterligov and Alyoshka the telegraphist; to the left are the Marfist deacon and Marfa.

Alyoshka is as pale as Pierrot* – only his protruding ears have been reddened with make-up. With difficulty (the audience can see it) Alyoshka finally pronounces some word – Sterligov's cigarette falls to the ground; he grabs the holster of his revolver. He then raises both hands to Alyoshka's head, as if to take it by the handles, like a samovar, and lift it from its shoulders. The head remains on the shoulders, but Sterligov undoubtedly says something like: "Well, if you're lying, your head will be a weight off your shoulders!" And both characters walk off the stage, or, rather, run: Sterligov is hauling Alyoshka somewhere backstage by his sleeve.

On the left-hand platform is an evidently amatory dialogue. The deacon begins it sparingly, without gestures – and it can only be seen that something in the pocket of his Tolstoy shirt is thrashing about and jumping, as if there were a cat sewn up inside it: this is the deacon's fiercely clenched fist. It can be guaranteed that he is asking Marfa: "Why didn't you open the gate to me this morning? Who was with you? No, tell me, who? D'you hear?" Marfa raises her eyebrows, pouts her lips – in the same way as when people are saying "coochy-coochy-coo" to a baby. This no longer works on the deacon – his brains have evidently gone askew, and in a moment the cat will be jumping out of his pocket. But the audience in the boxes restrains him – he can only be seen to say (the approximate text): "Well, all right – you wait!" and to walk off with the firm intention (the cat in his pocket turns to stone) to hide in Marfa's garden that evening and lie in wait for his rival.

The performance is over. Marfa remains alone on the stage and takes her leave of the audience. The audience is still not breaking up – the rain has started coming down harder, and the only ones who choose to get soaked to the skin are those who by the will of fate are entwined in the principal narrative strand – such as, for example, Sterligov and Alyoshka the telegraphist.

Wet, they were now already entering an establishment which in that year bore a name much more expressive of its duty to check up on people than now.* A pockmarked soldier indifferently skewered Alyoshka's pass on his bayonet, where a dozen other Alyoshkas were already quivering, transformed into scraps of paper. Then an endless corridor, fleeting, almost transparent faces of some sort, made of human gelatine. And at a desk in front of the door of an office a young lady of that special breed – secretaries (in the canine universe the secretaries are undoubtedly lapdogs).

Coming through the fur on his face – or out of agitation – Sterligov's voice is muffled:

"Is Papalagi in?"

The lapdog darted into the office, slipped back out and wagged her tail at Sterligov:

"Do go in."

And a second later Alyoshka the telegraphist was already standing before Comrade Papalagi himself. On the desk beside him is a plate of the most ordinary millet porridge, and, astonishingly, he is eating it in the most ordinary way, like everybody else. But Papalagi's moustache is huge, black, pointed, Greek – or some other kind of moustache...

"Well, Citizen – what's your name? Aha! – talk. Well?"

Alyoshka's knees were shaking so much that he himself could hear his waterproof trousers fizzing like bubbles. Stammering, with full stops and semi-colons after every word, Alyoshka reported that this morning in Citizeness Marfa Izhboldina's yard he had seen the Socialist Revolutionary Perepechko, which Socialist Revolutionary had evidently spent the night on the hay mattress in the shed.

"So much the better: he's asking us for trouble, and if you mess with the bull, you get the horns." (Indeed, his pointed moustache was like a pair of horns.) "So much the better, so much the better..." Papalagi rang a bell and a gelatine face appeared in the doorway.

"Here's what – this evening on Pancake Street... Later, though. For the moment, go. You can go too." (This is now to Alyoshka, and Alyoshka fizzes waterproofedly out of the office.)

Silence. Millet porridge. The horns are aimed at Sterligov.

"Damn it! D'you understand: my men are declaring they should be given prodwear... What on earth possessed them up there in Moscow to think of it! Listen, Sterligov: have you anything left there in the shops to requisition and give out to them?"

Sterligov rummages around in his fur, staring at the millet porridge.

"Hm... There's just Perelygin who maybe might have something..."

"Well, if it's Perelygin, then so be it. But make the arrangements quickly to have it brought here. The moment's such that, you understand... That son of a bitch Perepechko..."

Porridge. Silence. The silk of rain outside the open window. The scent of lilac penetrating even here without a pass. In the boxes of the gateways on Rosa Luxemburg Street the audience is still awaiting a dry interval, even if only a short one.

But instead of an interval – the performance unexpectedly resumes: onto one of the stage platforms enter three policemen (actors with non-speaking parts) and a man in a fluffy white jacket made from a bathing sheet. The people in the boxes recognized him at once and began fretting in a whisper:

"Syusin! Syusin from the Disfoocom!* Syusin!"

A faint motion of the great Syusin's hand, the snap of the boards being torn off the doors and the policemen are already hauling some kind of cardboard boxes out of the shop and piling them up on what was once the mayor's wagonette.

The rain immediately stopped – the way a naughty boy stops bawling when he notices no one is looking at him any more. Gleaming in the sun on the wagonette was a black oilcloth, still wet. Sparrows were crying something to the people from a roof. The people from eighteen to fifty were crying at the stage:

"Hey, comrades! What's that you've got there?"

The policemen, who had been given no words by the author, were silent. Syusin paused and, half turning, casually tossed out – the way people toss away a match after lighting up:

"Prodwear."

And Syusin's match immediately set the whole of Rosa Luxemburg from eighteen to fifty alight:

"Prodwear? Where's it going? Who to? Aha, so that's how it is, and we get damn all? Citizens, workers, stop them! Citizens!"

Syusin leapt up onto the wagonette, followed by the policemen. One of them began whipping the horse as though it were a class enemy – or maybe even without the "as though": the horse used to belong to a merchant. The grey class enemy set off at full tilt, carrying away the secret of the prodwear.

Half an hour later the telephone was ringing in Papalagi's office about there being unrest on the matter of prodwear. Everyone from eighteen to fifty to get an additional coupon. And matches were issued – one box between three. The people from eighteen to fifty started buzzing even more, like bees; a swarm of events could be sensed in the air, and all that remained unknown for the moment was where they would settle, where they would suspend themselves in a tangled, dark, winged ball.

* * *

The repentant deacon Indikoplev was renting a room now. Domesticity, his lady wife, the kiddies, spondulicks, the divan – all those solid "d"s the deacon had left behind, and now he was living amidst a maelstrom of "r"s:* photographs of Marx and Marfa, a rough mattress, scraps of provisions, revolutionary tracts, cigarette butts. When the deacon returned here in the dusk and buried his naked nose in his grubby pillow, all the "r"s started whirling around; the mattress rocked and, along with the deacon, sailed away from real-life shores.

Straight away his arms, legs, digits were somewhere a hundred *versts* away and at the same time right there beside him, like the rings representing towns on a map. The deacon slipped out of himself by some spiral and came to a halt in a corner from where everything could be seen. And it was absolutely clear that there, where the deacon's naked, shaved nose was – there was Moscow, nestled in the sour feathers of the pillow. So as not to suffocate he needed to raise a hand, to work Moscow free of the feathers, but domesticity, his lady wife, the kiddies, the divan pressed him down – it's the end! He'd cross himself, but can't: the deacon can see from his corner that he's wearing not a cassock, but a maroon Tolstoy shirt, and on the wall is a furry Marx, who looks like Sterligov...

Because of Sterligov, as if pricked by a knitting needle somewhere in the stomach, the recumbent hundred-*verst*-away deacon and the tiny deacon in the corner merged into one, and this one leapt up and opened the window. The bell was being rung at the cemetery for the night service; around the corner there were some soldiers singing the 'Internationale'* – and it wasn't possible for all this to be happening together; he needed to disentangle things quickly, to hunt out Sterligov quickly and explain to him that, honest to God – there is no God, but there is... but there is... what, well, there is what, what?

The deacon gave up in despair and ran off to the Disexcom. There they said that Sterligov was probably upstairs in the club. The deacon climbed the stairs, opened a door upholstered in tattered oilcloth and went in.

In the huge hall – a hundred *versts* away, in its depths – there was a paraffin lamp twinkling in the smoke. A little old woman at a piano was playing a *valse mignonne** and five policemen were dancing the *valse mignonne* backwards, bumping into one another and roaring with laughter. A ballet and drama studio class for policemen was taking place, and there was the heavy smell of a train's hospital car.

The deacon shouted:

"Is Comrade Sterligov here?"

The *valse mignonne* froze; the old woman took out a handkerchief and was either blowing her nose or crying. The deacon covered his naked nose with the palm of his hand and said, as he looked at somebody's cheerful teeth, hanging independently in the smoke with a cigarette:

"I'm to explain to Comrade Sterligov that God... I'm here on an urgent matter: can it be done now? Find out."

"All right..." and, dancing the *valse mignonne* backwards, the policeman disappeared into a dark corner.

A short 3/8 rest, filled with a mixture of the bell and the 'Internationale' (the window is open). When the 3/8 was over, the deacon heard through the smoke from the distance a hundred *versts* away:

"It can't. He said to detain you. Sit here for the moment." The deacon sat down obediently. The old woman let out a final sniffle and began playing, and the policemen started drifting backwards in the smoke. And only then, across the *versts*, did that word come home to the deacon – "detain". Detain! He was done for: they'd shortly be coming with guns and taking him away... On the way to his boots his heart stopped in his legs; his legs became an independent, logically thinking entity, in a second decided everything, quietly picked the deacon up – and to the music, moving backwards like everyone else, he walked towards the door. There he took in as much hospital air as he could – then it was headlong down the stairs, into the street, and off he ran.

Like in a train – telegraph poles, the black squares of windows, tiny pins of light, a samovar on a table. And suddenly somewhere an oblique bright light, heads, shoulders, noses cut out of the darkness, a crowd. There was nowhere farther to go, and to go back was impossible. The deacon squeezed himself into the brick heel post of some gates, closed his eyes tight and waited: they'd be coming shortly.

And someone did indeed come up and shout right in the deacon's ear:

"Given away!"

Who had given him away didn't matter: he needed to run. The deacon gave a jerk and opened his eyes.

Before him was Alyoshka the telegraphist. With his arms stretched out, in his cupped hands he was holding – tightly, like a bird which was about to fly away – a piece of black bread.

"Being given away," he cried, "in lieu of prodwear! I was the last to get some, there's no more left."

Lengthily, like the cow in the shed, the deacon breathed everything out... And immediately realized he was hungry, he had eaten nothing since morning, there was porridge in the cupboard at home, he needed to go home! But Alyoshka grabbed him by the sleeve:

"Look, look, look! Look, will you!"

In the oblique light from a window, on some steps stood Syusin in his fluffy white jacket with pockmarked Puzyryov alongside him – the one who had been missing for two years in German captivity. Puzyryov was poking two fingers at Syusin, like a fork at a cucumber.

"Is that what you're saying – there's no more bread? Well, if that's so, then the question is: what was I, for example, posted as missing for? Citizens, hit him!"

Everything in the oblique white strip lurched over. Syusin fell, a dense, shifting swarm set upon him, and very clear for a second was Syusin's hand with a key clenched in it...

Here there are a few deleted lines – or maybe the deacon really couldn't remember how he found himself in his room, orchestrated to "r", eating cold porridge. When he'd had something to eat, he wanted to cover the saucepan with a tract by Trotsky,* but changed his mind: he knew he would never be coming back here now, because the story's finale was bound to be tragic. And, seizing for that finale the iron chopper he used to chop kindling for the samovar, the deacon went out to meet the inevitable.

Beside the house the lilac was hanging down over the fence – now it was black, iron. Sitting close together on logs beneath the lilac were two people, and showing white in the darkness were a stocking and a bare knee – they were kissing smackingly, revolutionarily. As a result, it was as if a switch had at once been turned on in the deacon, lighting a room where (inside the deacon) it was

Marfa kissing someone. Everything else went out, and now the deacon could remember only one thing: he must go there quickly, to Marfa's house, and lie in wait for him.

There, on Pancake Street, there was one window lit, and on the white curtain a shadow was shifting – it had just raised its hands to its head: she must have got undressed and was laying her plait around her head like a chaplet, like that time at the river. The deacon was burnt, as though he had drunk a glass of pure alcohol. He began stealing on tiptoe right up to the window to lift the curtain – but behind him someone sneezed. The deacon flinched and turned – and beside Marfa's gate he saw him. It was impossible to make out his face – all that could be seen was that his collar was raised, and pulled down over his eyes was a dapper boater, like a white bowl.

With trembling fingers, the deacon groped in his pocket – far off, a hundred *versts* away – for the chopper. Then: no, let him climb into the garden, let him! And he walked past the lit window, past Perelygin's ruined house. At that point he looked back: the boater was turning the corner where, in the side street, the garden gate was. Marfa's window went out: so she was expecting him…

The deacon delayed a little – the way that the bombs, spinning around, always delay exploding in Leo Tolstoy.* He pulled out the chopper, wiped it for some reason with his skirt and, slipping over the fence into the garden through the wet, lashing lilac, flew like a bomb towards the bench to finish off at a single stroke both him and this story.

We've been covered in calluses for a long time now and don't hear killing going on. Nobody heard the deacon scream as he took a swing with the chopper: everyone from eighteen to fifty was busy with peaceful revolutionary things – they were preparing herring rissoles, herring stew, herring pudding for dinner. Somewhere, with a key clenched in his fist, lay white Syusin. There was the scent of lilac from the window. Comrade Papalagi was interrogating five men arrested next to the bread shop and enquiring over the telephone how the business on Pancake Street had ended.

But on Pancake Street it hadn't ended, as the bomb continued to spin more furiously still: the deacon had found no one on the bench – and, ragged, wet, blazing, he had slipped back out onto Pancake Street. On the corner he paused, spinning around, and saw: white in the lilac Maytime ink, floating quickly straight towards him was a boater.

The room dedicated to Marfism instantly went out (inside the deacon) – another flared up, where there were Marx, Sterligov and other fearsome furry people. And furry Sterligov-Marx had sent the boater to detain the deacon – this had now lit up in the darkness perfectly clearly. Run – wherever your feet will carry you!

The deacon – the huge one – was dashing down Pancake Street and could see his swinging arms. But it wasn't him: he himself, tiny, the size of a pinhead, was standing in the middle of the road and watching the other one running. And suddenly there was a prick of fear in his stomach: he had noticed that the deacon – the huge one – was running, doing the *valse mignonne* backwards, as the policemen had been then... why yes, there he was now, going backwards right past the grimy walls of the Perelygin house. He needed to stop and figure out what was going on – the deacon dived into a bare hole in the wall without doors and, breathing loudly, sat down.

There was a strong smell – as in all empty houses that year. From above, through a black quadrangle the stars gazed indifferently down on Russia, like foreigners. Audible all at the same time were rapid breathing, the third bell at the cemetery, gunshots. And, of course, it's unthinkable that one person could hear all this at once and see the stars and smell the stench. It follows that the deacon is not alone, but...

Flat, flopping footsteps beyond the wall. Slowly, pulling himself open joint by joint, like a folding yardstick, the deacon half rose, looked out through the hole in the wall – and gasped: the one in the boater had bifurcated and was now already double, in two identical boaters, had squatted down and, lighting matches, was examining the deacon's tracks on the damp ground. To bear any more was impossible: the deacon cried out and, jumping over beams of some kind, stoves, bricks, he flung himself through Perelygin's house. From behind came the sounds of *him* tumbling and swearing with two voices – he'd stumbled – and falling behind.

Through empty side streets, stuffed with black cotton wool, the deacon ran as far as the cemetery – it began immediately beyond Pancake Street. There he hid by the fence where the cemetery went down into a gully and where the dead were buried en bloc that year. Salty, caustic drops from his forehead were getting in his eyes – the deacon wiped himself and sat down on a gravestone. A red, breathless moon came out and the deacon saw a marble plaque with gold lettering: *Doctor I.I. Phenomenov. Surgery hours 10–2.* This plaque used to hang on the doctor's door, but when the doctor had moved to the cemetery, the plaque had been screwed to the gravestone. The deacon understood very well: there was something wrong with his head, he ought to have a talk with a doctor – he decided to wait until the start of Phenomenov's surgery hours.

But he didn't need to wait: above the cemetery fence *he* appeared again, the one in the white boater. And he was multiplying at a horrifying speed: he was no longer doubled, but quintupled – in five boaters. The deacon realized that this was the end, there was nowhere to go, and yelled: "I surrender! I surrender!"

When the apprehended man was brought before him, Papalagi turned the green lampshade to illuminate him and asked:

"Name?"

"Indikoplev," replied the deacon.

"Ah, Indi-ko-plev! Right then! Ancestry, parents?"

Somewhere far off, a hundred *versts* away, the deacon knew: his parent couldn't be an archpriest. The deacon shielded his naked nose with the palm of his hand and said uncertainly through his palm:

"I had no... no parents."

Papalagi levelled his terrifying black moustache – like horns – at him:

"Stop playing the fool! Confess!"

The deacon was transfixed. Everything was known already, then – in that case it didn't matter.

"I confess," he said. "I crossed myself. Even though I'd renounced it, I crossed myself in public, I confess."

Papalagi turned to someone in the corner:

"What's he doing – trying to play the madman? All right, let him try!" Papalagi pressed a button.

And then *he* came in – the unclear gelatine face, the raised collar, the boater. The deacon turned pale and, backing away, started muttering:

"It's him… five hats – it's them… Please don't. For Christ's sake… that is – no, for no one's sake!"

Papalagi looked at the hat, shifted his moustache angrily. Then he pointed at the apprehended Socialist Revolutionary who was pretending to be mad:

"Take him away to cell 10 – and get yourselves back here to me at once!"

When the deacon had been taken away and all five men in the dapper boaters had then lined up in the office, Papalagi shouted:

"What's this masquerade, what are these hats, what's this non-sense? Whose idea was this?"

The one who was standing closest took his hands out of his pockets, took off the boater and turned it in his hands.

"You see, Comrade Papalagi, it's… it's according to orders, the prodwear that's been given out to us, then, to wear."

"Take them off now! Well, did you hear me?"

And five prodwears obediently lay down in a pile on the desk.

Thus ended the myth of the prodwear. And apparently the story has ended too, because there are no more "x"s left, and apart from that, vice has now been punished. And the moral (every story must have a moral) is perfectly clear: ministers of religion are not to be trusted, even when they're supposedly repentant.

1926

Flood

The world lay around Vasilyevsky Island like a distant sea: there was war there, then revolution. But in Trofim Ivanovich's boiler room the boiler kept on humming in just the same way; the manometer kept on showing the same nine atmospheres. Only the coal had changed: it had been from Cardiff, now it was from Donetsk. The latter was crumbly – the black dust got everywhere and there was nothing that could wash it off. And it was as if this same black dust had imperceptibly enveloped all the buildings too. Basically, outwardly, nothing had changed. They lived as before, the two of them, without children. Sofya, although she was already nearly forty, was still just as light and taut in body as a bird; her lips, seemingly forever compressed for everyone, would open up to Trofim Ivanovich in the night as before – and all the same, something was not quite right. What was "not quite right" was not yet clear, had not yet solidified in words. It was expressed in words for the first time only later, in the autumn, and Sofya remembered it: it was on a Saturday, during the night; it was windy and the water in the Neva was rising.*

During the day, the gauge tube on Trofim Ivanych's boiler had fractured, and he had had to go and get a spare from the store-house at the machine shop. It was already a long time since Trofim Ivanych had last been in the shop. When he went in, it seemed to him he was in the wrong place. Previously, everything here had been moving, ringing, buzzing, singing – as if the wind had been playing with the steel leaves in a steel forest. Now it was autumn in the forest, belt drives were flapping idly, there were only three or four lathes sleepily turning, and there was some kind of washer shrieking monotonously. Trofim Ivanych had an unpleasant feeling, as you sometimes do if you stand over an empty pit, dug for some unknown purpose. He made haste to go back to his boiler room.

Towards evening he returned home – he still had the unpleasant feeling. He had dinner and lay down to rest. When he got up, everything was already over and done with, forgotten – and it was simply as if he had had some sort of dream or lost a key, and what sort of dream, the key to what, he was quite unable to remember. He remembered only in the night.

All night the wind from the seashore was beating straight against the window, the panes of glass were ringing, the water in the Neva was rising. And as though connected to the Neva by underground veins, his blood was rising. Sofya was awake. Trofim Ivanych found her knees with his hand in the darkness, and they were together for a long time. And again, it wasn't quite right, there was some sort of pit.

He lay, and the glass tinkled monotonously in the wind. Suddenly the washer, the machine shop, the idly flapping belt came to mind... "That's the thing," said Trofim Ivanovich out loud.

"What?" asked Sofya.

"You don't have babies, that's what."

And Sofya realized it too: yes, that was the thing. And she realized: if there was no child, Trofim Ivanych would go away out of her, would imperceptibly flow out of her completely, drop by drop, like water from the cracked, dried-out barrel. The barrel stood in the lobby outside the door. Trofim Ivanych had long been meaning to re-nail the hoops on it, but never had the time.

In the night – when it was probably already nearly morning – the door opened, banged hard against the barrel, and Sofya ran out into the street. She knew this was the end, that she couldn't go back now. Sobbing loudly, violently, she ran to the Smolensk Field,* and there, in the darkness, there was someone lighting matches. She stumbled and fell, with her hands going straight into something wet. It got light, and she saw that her hands were covered in blood.

"What are you shouting for?" Trofim Ivanych asked her.

Sofya woke up. There was indeed blood, but it was her usual woman's blood.

Before, these had simply been days when walking had been uncomfortable and her legs had been cold and grubby. Now it was as if every month she was on trial and awaiting sentence. Whenever her time was approaching, she couldn't sleep, she was afraid, wanted it to come quickly: but what if this time it didn't – what if it turned out she was… But nothing turned out – inside was a pit, empty. Several times she noticed that when, embarrassed, she called to Trofim Ivanych in a whisper in the night for him to turn towards her, he pretended to be asleep. And when Sofya dreamt once again that she was alone in the darkness, running to the Smolensk Field, she shouted out loud, and in the morning her lips were pressed even tighter together.

During the day, the sun floated unceasingly in birds' circles above the earth. The earth lay bare. At twilight the whole of the Smolensk Field gave off steam like a heated horse. On one particular day in April the walls became very thin – the youngsters in the yard could be heard distinctly shouting: "Catch her! Catch her!" Sofya knew that "her" meant the carpenter's girl, Ganka; the carpenter lived above them, and he lay sick, probably with typhus.

Sofya went downstairs into the yard. Rushing straight towards her with her head thrown back was Ganka, and after her – four of the neighbours' boys. When Ganka saw Sofya she said something to the boys behind her as she ran and walked up sedately to Sofya alone. Heat was coming off Ganka, her breathing was rapid, and her upper lip with its little black mole could be seen moving. "How old is she? Twelve, thirteen?" wondered Sofya. That was exactly how long Sofya had been married. Ganka could have been her daughter. But she was someone else's, she had been stolen from her, from Sofya…

Suddenly something tightened in her stomach, rose up towards her heart, and what Ganka smelt of and that slightly moving lip of hers with the black mole became hateful to Sofya.

"A lady doctor's come to see Papa – he's unconscious," said Ganka. Sofya saw how Ganka's lips had begun to tremble, how she had bent over and must have been swallowing her tears. And at once Sofya was pained by shame and pity. She took Ganka's head and pressed it against her. Ganka gave a sob, tore herself away and ran into a dark corner of the courtyard; the boys darted after her.

With pain lodged somewhere like the tip of a broken needle, Sofya went into the carpenter's apartment. To the right of the door, at the washstand, the doctor was washing her hands. She was buxom and snub-nosed, and wore a pince-nez.

"Well, how is he?" asked Sofya.

"He'll hang on until tomorrow," the doctor said cheerfully. "And then you and I will have some extra work to do."

"Work... What work?"

"What work? There'll be one person fewer – it'll be for us to have some extra children. How many do you have?" The button at the doctor's bosom was undone and she tried to do it up, but the button and its hole wouldn't meet – she laughed.

"I... don't have any," Sofya said, but not at once – it was hard for her to part her lips.

Next day, the carpenter died. He was a widower and he had no one. Some women neighbours came and stood by the doors talking in whispers, then one, her head hidden under a warm shawl, said: "Well then, my dearies, are we just going to stand here?" and started taking the shawl off, holding the pin in her teeth. Ganka sat on her bed in silence, doubled up, her legs thin and pathetic, her feet bare. On her lap lay an untouched piece of black bread.

Sofya went downstairs to her apartment – she needed to do something for dinner, as Trofim Ivanych would be back soon. When she had prepared everything and begun laying the table, there was already the evening sky, precarious, and it was punctured by a solitary, melancholy star. Upstairs the door was being slammed: the neighbours must have already finished everything up there and were going home, while Ganka was still sitting on the bed just the same with the piece of bread on her lap.

Trofim Ivanych came home. He stood beside the table, broad and short-legged, as though his legs were embedded ankle-deep in the ground.

"The carpenter's dead, you know," said Sofya.

"Ah-ah, dead?" Trofim Ivanych questioned absent-mindedly at once; he was taking bread out of a bag, and bread was more unaccustomed and uncommon than death. Bending over, he started cutting careful slices, and at this point, as if for the first time in all these years, Sofya saw his burnt, ravaged face, his Gypsy head with its abundant sprinkling of grey hairs, like salt. "No, there aren't going to be any children, there aren't!" cried Sofya's heart despairingly in a rush. And when Trofim Ivanych took a piece of bread in his hands, Sofya instantly found herself upstairs: Ganka was sitting there alone on the bed; she had the bread lying on her lap, and looking in at the window was the spring star, sharp as the tip of a needle. The grey hairs, Ganka, the bread, the solitary star in the empty sky – all of it – merged into a single whole, incomprehensibly interlinked, and to her own surprise Sofya said: "Trofim Ivanych, let's take the carpenter's Ganka in, let's have her in place of…" She couldn't go on. Trofim Ivanych gave her a surprised look, then through the coal dust the words went into him, inside, and he began to smile – slowly, just as slowly as he had untied the bag with the bread. When he had completely untied the smile, his teeth started gleaming, his face became new and he said: "Well done, Sofya! Bring her here – there's enough bread for three."

That night, Ganka was already sleeping in their kitchen. As she lay, Sofya listened to her fidgeting about there on the bench and the way she then began breathing evenly. Sofya thought: "Everything will be fine now" – and fell asleep.

2

The youngsters in the courtyard played in a completely new way now: they played "Kolchak".* One "Kolchak" would hide, the others would hunt him out and then, with the beating of a drum and singing, they would shoot him dead with sticks. The real Kolchak had been shot as well; nobody ate horsemeat any more now; sugar, galoshes and flour were on sale in the shops. The boiler at the factory was still fired with that same Donetsk coal, but Trofim Ivanych shaved his beard now and the coal dust washed off easily. He had been beardless many years ago, before his wedding, and now it was as if he had gone back to those years – sometimes he even laughed like before, and his teeth were white like the keys on an accordion.

This would be on Sundays, when he stayed at home and Ganka was at home. She was close to leaving school now. Trofim Ivanych made her read the newspaper out loud. Ganka read quickly and chirpily, but garbled all the new words in her own way: "mollybization", "Sense Directorate".

"What, what?" Trofim Ivanych asked her to say it again, his laughter simmering.

"Sense Directorate," Ganka repeated calmly. Then she recounted how some new man had visited their school the previous day and had started explaining that there were bodies on earth and bodies in the sky as well.

"What bodies?" said Trofim Ivanych, now barely containing himself.

"Why, what bodies? Here!" Ganka's finger prodded her breast which was becoming more pointed beneath her dress. Trofim Ivanych could now take no more, and laughter ripped out of his nose and mouth like steam from the safety valves of a boiler bursting under pressure.

Sofya sat to one side by herself; the Science Directorate, heavenly bodies, Ganka with the newspaper – for her, all of it was equally incomprehensible and remote. Ganka talked and laughed only with Trofim Ivanych, and if she and Sofya remained alone together she was silent, stoked the stove, did the washing-up, talked to the cat. Only at times would she slowly, intently approach Sofya with her green eyes, evidently thinking something about her, but what? Cats look that same way, staring into faces, thinking their own thoughts – and all of a sudden their green eyes and their incomprehensible, alien, feline thinking start giving you the creeps. Sofya would throw on a warm jacket and a thick shawl and go out somewhere – to the shop, to church, simply into the darkness of Maly Avenue* – anything to avoid being left alone with Ganka. She would walk past as yet unfrozen black ditches, past fences of roofing iron, feeling wintry, empty. On Maly, opposite the church, there stood a similarly empty house with corroded windows. Sofya knew: no one would ever live in it again now; never would cheerful children's voices be heard in it.

She walked towards this house in the evening once in December. As always, she was hurrying to pass it by quickly, without looking. For a brief moment, out of the corner of one eye, the way birds see, she caught sight of a light in an empty window. She stopped: it's not possible! She went back, peeped into the hole of a window. Inside, amidst broken pieces of brick, there was a bonfire burning, and around it sat four ragamuffin boys. One, facing Sofya – black-eyed, probably a Gypsy – was dancing up and down with a silver cross bouncing on his bare chest and his teeth gleaming.

The empty house had come alive. In some way the Gypsy boy resembled Trofim Ivanych. Sofya suddenly felt that she, too, was still alive, and that everything might yet change.

Agitated, she went into the church opposite. She hadn't been here since 1918, when Trofim Ivanych, along with the other men from the factory, had been leaving for the front. It was still the same small, moss-grown, grey-haired priest officiating. The singing made her begin to feel warm – the ice was melting, a sort of winter was passing, up ahead in the darkness candles were being lit.

When she returned home, Sofya wanted to tell Trofim Ivanych about everything, but what exactly was that everything? She herself no longer knew now, and she only said one thing: that she'd been to church. Trofim Ivanych burst out laughing:

"You go to the old church. You might at least go to the Living Church people* – their God sort of has a Party card, after all." He gave Ganka a wink. With one eye screwed up, without a beard, his face was mischievous, like the Gypsy boy's, an awful lot of teeth, cheerful and greedy. Ganka sat rosy, hiding her eyes, and only from under her brows, greenishly, did she look at Sofya a little askance.

From that day on Sofya was often at the church, until one day a new Living Church priest appeared in time for mass with a crowd of his folk.

The Living Church man was a red-haired beanpole in a short cassock, like a soldier in disguise. The little old grey priest cried: "I won't allow it, I won't allow it!" and grabbed hold of him; the two of them rolled onto the church porch and above the crowd there were glimpses of men's fists, like banners. Sofya left and never went back there again. She began travelling to the Okhta,* where Fyodor, a cobbler with a yellow bald patch, preached "The Third Testament".*

Spring that year was late – on Whit Monday the trees were still only just beginning to come into leaf, the buds on them were trembling with a tremor imperceptible to the eye and bursting open. The evening was precarious, light; swallows were whizzing about. Fyodor the cobbler gave a sermon about the imminent Last Judgement. Large drops of sweat rolled over his yellow bald patch, his wild blue eyes gleamed so – it was impossible to tear yourself away from them. "Not from the sky, no! But from here, from here, look, from here!" Trembling all over, the cobbler struck himself on the chest, tore the white shirt that covered it, and his crumpled yellow body appeared. He clutched at his chest to tear it apart like his shirt – he could barely breathe; he cried out in a despairing final voice and flopped onto the floor in a fit of falling sickness. Two women stayed by him, and everyone else quickly dispersed, leaving the meeting unfinished.

Feeling all strained, like the buds on the trees, because of the cobbler's wild eyes, Sofya returned home. There was no key on the outside, and the door was locked. Sofya realized Trofim Ivanych and Ganka had gone out somewhere for a walk and would probably be home only around eleven – she herself had told them not to expect her before eleven. Should she go upstairs and sit there until they got back?

Living upstairs now were Pelageya and her husband, a cabman. Through the open window she could be heard saying: "Goo-goo-goo-kins. That's it, that's it!" to her child. She couldn't – she didn't have the strength to go up there now and look at her and at the child. Sofya sat on the wooden steps. The sun was still high; the sky was gleaming like the cobbler's eyes. Suddenly from somewhere came the smell of hot black bread. Sofya remembered: the catch on the kitchen window was broken and Ganka had probably forgotten to tie the window shut – she was always forgetting. So you could open it from the outside and climb in.

Sofya went around. And, indeed, the window wasn't tied shut; Sofya opened it easily and climbed into the kitchen. She thought: there's no telling who might get in this way – or maybe had already done so? There seemed to be some sort of rustling in the next room. Sofya stopped. It was quiet; there was just the clock ticking on the wall, and inside Sofya, and everywhere. Without knowing why, Sofya set off on tiptoe. Her dress caught on the ironing board leaning against the door and the board crashed to the floor. At once there came the slapping of bare feet in the main room. Sofya gave a soft gasp and backed up towards the window to slip out, to call for help...

But she had no time to do anything; in the doorway appeared Ganka, bare-footed, in nothing but a crumpled pink chemise. Ganka was dumbfounded, opened wide round eyes and mouth at Sofya. Then she shrank, the whole of her, like a cat when a hand is raised against it, cried out: "Trofim Ivanych!" and darted back into the room.

Sofya picked up the ironing board, put it back in place and sat down. She had nothing, neither arms nor legs – only her heart, and that, turning somersaults like a bird, was falling, falling, falling.

Then at once in came Trofim Ivanych. He was dressed – he evidently hadn't undressed. He came to a standstill in the middle of the kitchen, large-headed, broad, with short legs – as though he were embedded knee-deep in the ground.

"How... how is it you're back early today?" said Trofim Ivanych, surprising himself: why had he said that? How could he have said that?

Sofya hadn't heard. Her lips were twitching – the skin on milk twitches like that when it's setting: "What is this, what is this, what is this?" Sofya pronounced with difficulty, not looking at Trofim Ivanych. Trofim Ivanych shrivelled, all of him, huddled up in some sort of corner inside himself and stood like that in silence for a minute. Then he uprooted his legs from the ground and went off into the main room. In there, Ganka was already tapping around in her ankle boots, dressed.

Everything in the world was continuing as before and life had to go on. Sofya got things ready for dinner. Ganka, as always, handed out the plates. When she brought the bread, Trofim Ivanych turned and caught it with his head and the bread fell into his lap. Ganka burst out laughing. Sofya looked at her, the eyes of the two of them met, and for a moment they gazed intently at one another in a manner quite new, compared to before. Sofya felt something rising roundly, slowly, from below, from her stomach, then ever hotter, quicker and higher, and she started breathing rapidly. It was impossible to look at Ganka's light-brown fringe and the black mole on her lip any more – she needed to shout out straight away, like Fyodor the cobbler, or do something. Sofya lowered her eyes. Ganka grinned.

After dinner, Sofya washed the plates; Ganka stood with a towel and dried them. This was endless. This was, perhaps, the most difficult thing in the whole evening. Then Ganka went off to bed in her place in the kitchen. Sofya started making up the bed – everything inside was burning; she was shaken. Trofim Ivanych turned away and said to her: "Make up a bed for me on the bench by the window." Sofya did so. In the night, when she had stopped tossing and turning, she heard Trofim Ivanych get up and go into the kitchen to Ganka.

3

On Sofya's windowsill stood an upturned glass jar; in some unknown way, a fly had got inside the jar. There was nowhere for it to go, but it crawled around all day nonetheless. The sun made for indifferent, slow, dull heat inside the jar, and there was the same heat all over Vasilyevsky Island. Nonetheless, Sofya walked around all day and did things. Storm clouds would often gather in the afternoon, growing heavier, as if at any moment the green glass overhead would crack, and torrential rain would finally burst out and pour down. But the clouds would inaudibly creep away and by night-time the glass had become ever thicker, stuffier, duller. Nobody heard the different ways the three of them breathed in the night: one buried in a pillow so as to hear nothing, two through clenched teeth, greedily, hotly, like a boiler burner.

In the morning, Trofim Ivanych went off to the factory. Ganka had already left school and she stayed alone with Sofya. She was very remote from Sofya: Sofya now saw and heard Ganka, Trofim Ivanych and everything around her from somewhere far away. From there she spoke to Ganka without parting her lips: sweep the kitchen, rinse the millet, chop some kindling. Ganka swept, rinsed, chopped. Sofya heard the blows of the axe, knew that it was her, Ganka, but it was very remote, wasn't visible.

Ganka always chopped the kindling squatting down with her round knees spread wide apart. On one occasion, for some unknown reason, it so happened that Sofya saw those knees and the light-brown, slightly curled fringe on her forehead. There was a sudden knocking in her temples; she hurriedly turned away and, without looking, said to Ganka:

"I'll do it myself... Go outside." With a flick of her fringe, Ganka ran off cheerfully and returned home only towards dinnertime, just before Trofim Ivanych arrived.

She started going out first thing every day. Pelageya upstairs said to Sofya once: "Your Ganka keeps running off to the empty house with some boys. You should keep an eye on that girl, or she'll end up running into trouble."

Sofya thought: "I must tell Trofim Ivanych about this…" But when Trofim Ivanych came home, she did not feel she could pronounce the name Ganka out loud. She said nothing to Trofim Ivanych.

Thus, glassily, tearlessly, its dry storm clouds oppressive, the whole of the summer went by, and the autumn carried on just as dry. One blue and unseasonably warm morning, the wind began blowing in from the sea. Through the closed window Sofya heard a pudgy, wadded gunshot, then soon another and a third* – the water in the Neva must have been rising. Sofya was alone; neither Ganka nor Trofim Ivanych was there. Again the cannon knocked softly on the window, the panes of glass rang in the wind. Pelageya came running from upstairs, out of breath, spreading, all undone, and cried to Sofya: "What are you doing? Are you out of your mind, sitting here? The Neva's overflowed – it's about to flood everything."

Sofya ran out after her into the courtyard. Straight away, whistling, the wind wrapped the whole of her up tight, as if in a cloth. She heard doors being banged somewhere, a woman's voice shouting: "The chicks, gather up the chicks, quickly!" Overhead, a big bird of some kind was blown rapidly sideways by the wind, its wings spread wide. Sofya suddenly began to feel relieved, as though this was precisely what she needed – a wind like this, so that everything would be swamped, swept away, flooded. She turned to meet it, her lips opened; the wind burst in and started singing in her mouth – her teeth felt cold and good.

Together with Pelageya, Sofya quickly carried her bedding, clothing, food and chairs upstairs. The kitchen was already empty – only in one corner there stood a small chest with a painted floral decoration.

"What about that?" asked Pelageya.

"That's… hers," Sofya replied.

"Whose – hers? Ganka's, you mean? Why are you leaving it, then?" Pelageya picked the chest up and, with her stomach sticking out to support it, lugged it upstairs.

Upstairs, at about two o'clock a window pane was smashed by the wind. Pelageya ran over to stop it up with a pillow, but suddenly howled at the top of her voice: "We're done for... Lord, we're done for!" and caught her child up in her arms. Sofya glanced out of the window and saw: there, where the street had been, there was now rushing green water, rippled by the wind; turning slowly, someone's table was floating along, and on it sat a white cat with ginger patches, and its mouth was open – it must have been miaowing. Without calling her by her name, Sofya thought of Ganka, and her heart began pounding.

Pelageya stoked the stove. She dashed back and forth from the stove to the child to the window where Sofya was standing. In the building opposite, on the ground floor, a small ventilating casement was open; you could see it being rocked to and fro by the water now. The water was continuing to rise, carrying logs, planks, hay; then there was a glimpse of something round that appeared to be a head: "Maybe my Andrei and your Trofim Ivanych..." Pelageya didn't finish; her tears were rolling – undone, wide open, simple. Sofya was surprised at herself: how could she – it was even as though she had forgotten about Trofim Ivanych and was thinking all the time about the one thing – about her, about Ganka.

At once they both – Pelageya and Sofya too – heard voices somewhere in the courtyard. They ran into the kitchen, to the windows. There was a boat moving across the courtyard, pushing some firewood aside, and in it stood two men of some sort and a hatless Trofim Ivanych. Over a quilted sleeveless jacket he was wearing a blue smock, wrapped tight around him on one side by the wind and billowing on the other, and it seemed as if he was broken down the middle of his body. The other two asked him something; the boat turned around the corner of the building and the firewood, colliding, followed it.

Wet to the waist, Trofim Ivanych ran into the kitchen; water was pouring off him, but he didn't seem to notice. "Where... where is she?" he asked Sofya.

"She went out first thing," said Sofya.

Pelageya understood who was being asked about too. "I've been telling Sofya for ages... Now she's enjoying the fruits, floating about somewhere."

Trofim Ivanych turned away towards the wall and started running a finger over it. He stood like that for a long time – water was pouring off him; he didn't feel it.

Towards evening, when the water had already receded, Pelageya's husband came home. Under the pendant lamp his strong, ripe bald patch gleamed; he recounted how a gentleman with a briefcase had swum overarm into the entrance to his building and how ladies had been running, lifting their skirts up higher and higher.

"And are there a lot drowned?" asked Sofya.

"An awful lot. Fousands!" said the cabman, closing his eyes.

Trofim Ivanych stood up. "I'll be going," he said.

But he didn't go anywhere: the door opened, and in the doorway stood Ganka. Her dress was stuck to her breast, to her knees, she was all grimy, but her eyes were gleaming. Trofim Ivanych started smiling, unpleasantly, slowly, with his teeth alone. He went up to Ganka, grabbed her by the arm and led her into the kitchen, shutting the door tight behind him. He could be heard saying something to Ganka under his breath and starting to beat her. Ganka was sobbing. Then she spent a long time splashing water about and came back into the room cheerful, flicking the fringe on her forehead.

Pelageya put her to bed behind a partition in the pantry and made up a bed on a bench in the kitchen for Trofim Ivanych and Sofya. They were left alone together. Trofim Ivanych put out the lamp. The window turned pale; the moon trembled in a thin chemise of clouds. Sofya, showing up white, undressed, then Trofim Ivanych.

As she lay, Sofya thought of only one thing: that he shouldn't notice her trembling. She lay stretched out as if covered all over with a crust of the thinnest ice: sometimes the branches of trees are in such fragile icy coverings in the early morning in autumn, and if they are stirred just a little by the wind – everything crumbles to dust.

Trofim Ivanych didn't stir, he couldn't be heard. But Sofya knew he was awake: he always smacked his lips in his sleep, like little children when they are suckling. And she knew why he was awake: here he could no longer go to Ganka. Sofya closed her eyes, compressed her lips and the whole of herself – so as not to think about anything.

Suddenly, as if he had decided something, Trofim Ivanych turned quickly to Sofya. All the blood inside her stopped in full flow, her legs froze, she waited. The moon, wrapped up in a blanket, trembled outside the window for one minute, two. Trofim Ivanych raised his head a little, looked out of the window, then carefully, trying not to touch Sofya, turned his back on her again.

When he finally began breathing evenly and started smacking his lips in his sleep, as children do, Sofya opened her eyes. She quietly leant over Trofim Ivanych, leant very close, so that she could see one long black hair hanging down from his eyebrow right into his eye. He moved his lips. Sofya looked, and she could no longer remember anything about him; she just felt sorry for him. She reached out a hand – and immediately jerked it back again; she wanted to stroke him, like a child, but she could not, she dared not...

It was like this every night for the entire three weeks while the lower apartment was drying out. Every morning before the factory Trofim Ivanych would go down there for half an hour and put something right. One day he came back again cheerful, joking with Pelageya, but Sofya saw him running his eyes over Ganka: Ganka was bent over, sweeping the room. As he was leaving, Trofim Ivanych said to Sofya: "Well, move downstairs, it's time – everything's ready." And then to Ganka: "Heat the stoves up good and proper, don't spare the firewood, to make sure it's warm by this evening."

Sofya understood: not by this evening, but by tonight. She didn't say anything, didn't raise her eyes, only her lips twitched a little, like the skin on milk when it's setting.

4

Pelageya's husband, the cabman, was driving out only after noon that day; before then, together with Sofya and Ganka, he quickly lugged everything downstairs. "Well then, what should it be: congratulations on moving into your *old* home, perhaps?" he said to Sofya.

Quickly, in a few sweeps, like a big bird, Sofya's eyes flew all around the room. Everything had become as before: the chairs, the dull mirror, the wall clock, the bed where Sofya would again be alone in the night-time. The way things had been upstairs seemed to her happiness: there in the night she had heard his breathing; he hadn't been with *her*, with the other one, he had been no one's, but now – today, this very day...

Ganka wasn't there – she had gone out for firewood. Sofya stood with her forehead pressed against the window. The glass was ringing from time to time, the wind was howling, grey, urban, low stone clouds were flying – as though those same stifling storm clouds that had not once all summer been burst by a thunderstorm had come back again. Sofya felt the storm clouds were not beyond the window but in her herself, inside; they had already been piling up stonily one on top of another for months on end – and for them not to suffocate her now she needed to smash something to smithereens, or to run away from here, or to cry out in the sort of voice the cobbler had that time about the Last Judgement.

Sofya heard: Ganka came in, shook the firewood out of the sack onto the floor, then began laying it in the stove. The window shuddered, as if a heart had struck it from the outside. It was a cannon – the water was again being driven by the wind and was straining the Neva's blue sinews. Sofya remained standing the same way, not looking round so as not to catch sight of Ganka.

Suddenly Ganka began softly singing through her nose – this had never happened before. Sofya looked round. She saw: having dropped the axe, Ganka was squatting down and chopping up sticks with a knife; her round knees, spread wide, were jumping under her dress, and the fringe on her forehead was jumping. Sofya tried to look away from her but couldn't. Slowly, with difficulty, like a barge being hauled towards the shore against the current with a cable – the cable is quivering and going to break at any moment – Sofya went over to Ganka. The work had got Ganka all flushed. Sofya was overwhelmed by the hot, sweetish smell of her sweat – she must have smelt just like this in the night.

And as soon as Sofya had breathed this smell in, something from below, from her stomach, rose in her, gushed through her heart, flooded the whole of her. She wanted to grab hold of something, but she was borne away, as the firewood and the cat on the table had been borne away that time down the street. Without thinking, caught up by a wave, she picked the axe up from the floor, not knowing why herself. Once more an enormous cannon heart struck the window. Sofya's eyes saw she was holding the axe in her hand. "Lord, Lord, what on earth am I doing?" one Sofya cried despairingly inside, while another at the same second struck Ganka on the temple, on the fringe, with the butt of the axe.

Ganka did not even shout anything out, only banged her head against her knees, then softly toppled over from her haunches onto her side. Sofya quickly, rapaciously struck her on the head several times more with the blade, and blood gushed onto the iron sheet in front of the stove. And it was as if the blood had come out of *her*, out of Sofya, some sort of abscess had finally burst inside her and it was pouring out of it, dripping, and with every drop she was feeling ever easier. She let the axe fall, took a deep, free breath – she had never breathed before, only just now for the first time had she taken a gulp of air. Neither fear, nor shame – there was nothing, only a kind of novelty, lightness throughout her whole body, like after a lengthy fever.

Thereafter it was as if Sofya's hands were thinking and doing everything required independently of her, while she herself, somewhat removed, relaxed blissfully, and only occasionally did her eyes open, did she begin to see, did she look at everything in surprise.

Ganka's shoes, brown dress, chemise, doused in paraffin, were already burning in the stove, and she herself, all naked, pink, steamy, lay face down on the floor, and over her, unhurriedly, confidently, there crawled a fly. Sofya saw the fly and brushed it off. Sofya's other person's hands easily, calmly chopped the body in two – otherwise there was no way it could be taken away. Sofya at this time was thinking that the potatoes Ganka hadn't finished peeling were still on the bench in the kitchen and needed to be boiled for dinner. She went into the kitchen, dropped the latch to lock the door and lit the stove there.

When she went back into the main room, she saw that the new, grey, marbled oilcloth had been pulled out of the chest of draw-ers and was lying on the floor, torn in two. Sofya wondered: who was it that had torn it? Why? But at once she remembered, spread the oilcloth out on the bottom of a sack and put half of the pink body inside. That same fly kept settling on her hands, sticking to them. Once, Sofya got a very close look at it: its legs were slender, as if of black cotton thread. Then the fly and everything else disappeared and there was only one thing: someone banging on the kitchen door.

Sofya went over to the threshold on tiptoe and waited. They banged again, harder and harder. Sofya watched the latch shaking from the blows – and didn't watch, even, but felt: the latch was now a part of her herself, like her eyes, her heart, her feet, which had instantly gone cold. A seemingly familiar voice shouted on the other side of the door: "Sofya" – she remained silent; someone's footsteps were going down, had begun stamping down the steps. Then Sofya started breathing and looked out of the window. It was Pelageya; the wind was whipping her dress tightly around her from behind and she seemed to be walking with her knees bent.

Again, for a long time there were only Sofya's hands, and she herself wasn't there. Suddenly she saw that she was standing on the edge of a ditch; the water in the ditch was lilac, glassy from the sunset, and the whole world, the sky, the madly rapid clouds had been thrown away into it, into the ditch, and on Sofya's back was a heavy sack, and there was something under her coat that her hand was holding on to – Sofya couldn't understand what.

But the hand remembered it was a spade, and everything became simple once more. She crossed the ditch, independent of herself, with her eyes alone, looked around: nobody; she was alone on the Smolensk Field, and it was quickly getting dark. She dug a pit and tipped everything that was in the sack into it.

When it was already quite dark, she brought a full sack once again, filled in the pit and went home. Under her feet was uneven, bulging black earth; the wind was whipping her legs with cold, stiff towels. Sofya was stumbling. She fell, thrust her hand into something wet and went on afterwards like that, with a wet hand, afraid to wipe it. Far away, probably on the seashore, a little light was coming on and going out, or perhaps it was just nearby – someone lighting a cigarette in the wind.

At home, Sofya quickly washed the floor, washed herself in a pan in the kitchen and put on all clean things, like after confession before a holiday. The firewood that Ganka had lit had burnt down long before, but the last little blue sparks were still darting over the coals. Sofya threw in the sack, the oilcloth, all the rubbish that still remained. The fire flared up brightly, everything burned away, and now the room was completely clean. And in just the same way, all the rubbish in Sofya had burnt away – she too had become clean and quiet inside.

She sat down on a bench. All the knots inside her immediately slackened, came loose; she suddenly felt she was tired in a way she had never once been in all her life. She laid her head on her arms on the table and that same second fell asleep, fully, happily, all of her.

5

The pendulum on the wall flew to and fro like a bird in a cage that senses a feline eye fixed upon it. Sofya was asleep. This went on for maybe an hour, maybe only from one swing of the pendulum to the next. When she raised her head, before her, his legs embedded in the ground, stood Trofim Ivanych.

He felt constricted; he unbuttoned the collar of his shirt. "Where is she?" he said, bending down towards Sofya. There was the smell of wine, there was taut, intense heat coming from his body. "Where's Ganka?" he asked again.

"Yes, where is she now?" Sofya wondered and answered out loud: "I don't know."

"Aha... You don't know?" said Trofim Ivanych slowly, wryly; Sofya saw his eyes very close by – they were bared, like teeth. He had never beaten her, but now it appeared he was about to hit her. Yet he only looked at Sofya, then turned away – if he had hit her, perhaps she would have felt relieved.

They sat down to dinner. Sofya was alone; she felt Trofim Ivanych couldn't see her, it wasn't her he saw. He swallowed a mouthful of cabbage soup and paused, squeezing his spoon tightly in his fist. Suddenly he began breathing loudly and banged his fist on the table, and cabbage was tossed out of the spoon into his lap. He picked it up and didn't know what to do with it – the tablecloth was clean; comically, perplexed, he held the cabbage in his hand and was like the little Gypsy Sofya had seen that time in the empty house. Pity made her feel warm and she moved her own already empty plate over towards Trofim Ivanych. Without looking, he dropped the cabbage onto it and stood up.

When he came back, he had a bottle of Madeira in his hand. Sofya realized it had been bought for *her*; her heart immediately froze, and again she was sitting alone. Trofim Ivanych poured and drank.

After dinner he silently moved the lamp closer to him and picked up the newspaper, but Sofya could see he was reading one and the same line over and over again. She saw the newspaper quiver: the floorboards in the lobby had creaked... No: it wasn't someone for them, it was for upstairs. It grew quiet again – only the pendulum on the wall flew to and fro, like a bird. Upstairs, they could be heard moving something heavy around – they must have already been going to bed up there.

There was still no Ganka. Trofim Ivanych walked past Sofya to the coat rack, put on his hat, stood for a while, then tore it off as though he wanted to tear his head off, too, along with the hat, so as not to think any more, and he lay down on a bench with his face to the wall.

"Wait, let me make up the bed," said Sofya.

He got up, looked, and his eyes went through Sofya like a draught.

She made the bed, went over to the door to lock it by putting the latch down, had already reached out her hand – and paused: what if Trofim Ivanych asks how she knows Ganka won't be coming back? She shouldn't have, but Sofya looked round all the same. She saw Trofim Ivanych was watching her, watching her hand, outstretched and not daring to touch the latch. "What? What have you stopped for?" he asked, and gave an uneven half-grin.

"He knows everything…" thought Sofya; the pendulum in front of her swung once and froze. Trofim Ivanych was growing red in the face; slowly and silently, he pushed the table back and something fell – it was in Sofya, inside. Right now, this minute, he was going to say everything…

Onerously dragging his legs out of the ground, he moved towards Sofya; a blue vein on his forehead had swollen like the Neva. "Well? What's the matter with you?" he cried: everything in the room paused. "Lock it! Let her spend the night wherever she wants with whoever she wants, on the street, in the gutter, with the dogs! Lock it, d'you hear?"

"What… what?" said Sofya, still in disbelief.

"Do it!" snapped Trofim Ivanych, turning around. Sofya dropped the latch.

She was still trembling under the blanket for a long time before she finally got warm and came to believe that Trofim Ivanych couldn't know, didn't know. The clock above her hammered loudly on the wall with its beak. Trofim Ivanych began tossing and turning on his bench and breathing greedily through clenched teeth. Sofya heard this as though he were talking about everything loudly, out loud, in words. She saw the hateful white curls on the forehead – and at that same second, they disappeared. Sofya remembered they weren't there and never would be again. "Thank God…" she said to herself and immediately thought better of it: "What do I mean, thank God? Oh Lord!"

Trofim Ivanych began tossing and turning again. It occurred to Sofya that he wasn't here either, was he, and never would be, that she was always to live alone now, in a draught, and in that case, what was the point of everything that had happened today? With difficulty, by stages, she started taking in air: with her breathing, as if with a rope, she was raising some kind of stone from the depths. At the very highest point the stone broke away. Sofya felt she could breathe. She sighed and started descending slowly into sleep, as into deep, warm water.

When she was already at the bottom, she heard bare feet slapping on the floor. She shuddered and at once came up to the surface. There, the floor was creaking now – Trofim Ivanych was gingerly going somewhere. This was how he had gone into the kitchen to Ganka in the night, and Sofya had always rolled herself into a ball so as not to breathe, not to cry out, and she did the same now. She realized: he was drawn there – maybe he was going to clutch and squeeze her pillow there, or was simply going to stand there, in front of Ganka's empty bed…

The floorboards creaked, then stopped. Trofim Ivanych had come to a halt. Sofya half opened her eyes: showing up white, Trofim Ivanych stood halfway between his bench and the bed where she was lying. And suddenly it dawned on Sofya that he was on his way not into the kitchen, but to her – to her! Heat washed all over her, her teeth began chattering, she shut her eyes tight.

"Sofya…" Trofim Ivanych said softly, and then even softer: "Sofya." She recognized it – that same, special, night-time voice – her heart had broken away from a branch and, turning over unevenly, was falling down like a bird. Without thinking, rather in some other way – with her painfully clenched knees, with the folds of her body – Sofya had the idea that it would be simpler, easier for him if she didn't respond, and she lay without breathing, in silence.

Trofim Ivanych bent down to her; she heard his breathing close by – he must have been looking at her. It was only a second, but Sofya was afraid she would be unable to endure it and she cried out inaudibly: "Oh Lord! Oh Lord!" Up above, a thousand *versts* away, where the storm clouds were now sweeping frantically by, Pelageya laughed, just audibly. A hot, dry hand touched Sofya's legs; she slowly opened up her lips; all of her opened up for her husband, to the depths – for the first time in her life. He squeezed her so, it was as if he wanted to take out on Sofya all his insatiable rancour towards *her*, the other one. Sofya heard him grinding his teeth, Pelageya laughing again in a whisper up above – and then she remembered nothing more.

6

In the morning there was a frost; the windows were of sugar candy; a blue-yellow spot of light crept over the white wall. Sofya went out into the courtyard. Everything had quietened down during the night – the morning was calm, limpid; smoke, vertical and pink, was going towards the sky.

Pelageya was in the courtyard. She said to Sofya: "Your Ganka's run away, eh? Why would you feed them, that sort?"

Sofya looked at her with light, direct eyes, made from this morning, and tried to recall the events of the day before – and couldn't: it was all very far away, and most likely none of it had happened. Pelageya recounted how Trofim Ivanych had popped in to see them before the factory and asked if they had seen Ganka. Sofya laughed to herself.

"What's that about?" asked Pelageya in surprise.

"Nothing…" said Sofya; she was looking at the vertical, pink smoke – there had been the same smoke in the village from which Trofim Ivanych had taken her. They were probably cutting cabbages there now, the stalks a bit cold, white, crisp. It seemed to her it had all been only yesterday and she herself was the same as she had been when she was eating the cabbage stalks.

On returning from the factory, Trofim Ivanych asked only: "Well? Not here?"

Sofya already knew what he was asking about and she said calmly: "Not here."

Trofim Ivanych had dinner and went out somewhere. He got back late, dark – he must have been searching, asking everyone, everywhere. He came to Sofya again in the night – just as silently, rancorously, insatiably as the day before.

Next day, Trofim Ivanych notified the police about Ganka. Sofya, Pelageya and her husband, the neighbours were summoned to the station. At the desk sat some young fellow in a cap; on his nose was a serious, frameless pince-nez, but his face was that of a chicken, freckled, and underneath the papers on the desk lay some black rusks. Everyone told him the same thing: that they had seen Ganka gadding about with some lads, and not lads from the port area, but strangers from the Petersburg Side.* Pelageya remembered Ganka once saying she was fed up with things here, that she was going to leave. The fellow in the cap made notes. Sofya looked at his freckled face, the pince-nez, the rusks, and began to feel sorry for him.

As they were walking back home from the station, Sofya asked Trofim Ivanych to buy a new axe: the old one must have been stolen, or maybe it had just been mislaid somewhere – but it was nowhere to be found. Sofya didn't think of Ganka any more. Trofim Ivanych didn't say a word about her either. Only sometimes did he sit, gazing endlessly at one and the same line in the newspaper, and Sofya knew what he was silent about. Just as silently did he raise his coal-black Gypsy eyes to her, drifting miserably, silently beyond her with his eyes, and she would start to feel frightened that he might say something awkward, but he said nothing.

The days were all just as clear and crisp, only they were getting ever shorter, as if at any time, if not today, then tomorrow, they would flare up for the last time, like the stub of a candle – then darkness, the end of everything. But tomorrow would come, and still there was no end. And all the same there was something untoward going on with Sofya. She didn't sleep one night, a second and a third, she had dark bags under her eyes, which sank in somewhere. In the same way the snow darkens, sinks, falls in, in spring, and suddenly beneath it is the earth – but the spring was still far off.

In the evening, Sofya was pouring paraffin into a lamp from a tin can with a spout. Trofim Ivanych cried out to her: "Look, look at what you're doing: it's overflowing!" Only then did Sofya see that the lamp was already full, and the paraffin must have been spilling onto the table for quite some time.

"Overflowing…" Sofya repeated in confusion – her always compressed lips were open, as in the night; she looked at Trofim Ivanych and it seemed to him she wanted to say something else.

"Well, what?" he asked. Sofya turned away. "Something… about her… about Ganka?" She heard the voice squeezed out between white Gypsy teeth. She didn't reply.

As she was serving dinner, she dropped a dish of porridge onto the floor. Trofim Ivanych raised his head, saw her eyes – new somehow, sunken, like the snow – and he found it unpleasant to look at her: this wasn't her. "What is the matter with you, Sofya?" And again she said nothing.

In the night he came to her – he hadn't been with her once after those two nights. When she heard that same night-time voice of his: "Sofya, tell me, I know you need to tell," she couldn't endure it, it was overflowing, tears gushed. They were warm – Trofim Ivanych felt them on his cheek and took fright: "What is it, what? It's all the same – say it!"

Then Sofya said: "I'm… going to have a baby…" It was in the darkness – it couldn't be seen. Trofim Ivanych drew a dry, hot hand across her face to see it as well; his fingers were trembling, and with them he could feel that Sofya's lips were open wide and smiling.

He just said to her: "So-of-ka!" He hadn't called her that for a long time now, about ten years. She laughed fully, blissfully.

"But when was it?" asked Trofim Ivanych.

It had happened on one of those two nights, immediately after Ganka had gone missing. "Do you remember too – Pelageya upstairs... and I had the idea even then that, like Pelageya, I too was going to have... No, that's not true: I didn't think anything at the time, that's me now... But even now I don't believe it... no, I do!" She was getting muddled; her tears were flowing easily, like melted streams over the earth. Trofim Ivanych laid a hand on her stomach and cautiously, timidly drew the hand up from bottom to top. The stomach was round – it was the earth. In the earth, deep down, visible to no one, lay Ganka, and in the earth, visible to no one, the white rootlets of seeds were burrowing. This was in the night, then again came the day and the evening.

In the evening Trofim Ivanych brought a bottle of Madeira to have with dinner. Sofya had seen just such a bottle once before: he would have done better to bring something different now. Sofya didn't even think this – it was as if she had simply read it with her eyes alone and it hadn't got inside: her whole body was smiling, it was full to overflowing, nothing more could have got in there. The only thing was, she was frightened that the days were getting ever shorter, they would burn down completely at any time, and then – the end, and she needed to hurry: she still needed to have time to say or do something before the end.

One day, Trofim Ivanych returned home later than usual. He stopped on the threshold, broad, his legs firmly embedded in the ground, and there was coal dust on his face. He said to Sofya: "Well, I was called in again!"

Sofya immediately realized where and why, and the pendulum inside her stopped and missed one, two, three beats. She sat down. "Well?" she asked Trofim Ivanych.

"Well, then: they said the case was closed – they haven't found her. She's gone off somewhere with her fancy man – well, to hell with her! As long as she doesn't turn up again..."

Sofya's heart came to life: not the end yet.

And at once there began to throb, there came to life inside her, a little lower, seemingly one more, a second heart. She gasped out loud, clutched at her stomach.

"What is it?" said Trofim Ivanych, running over.

"It's… moving…" Sofya barely managed to say.

Trofim Ivanych shook his head, grabbed Sofya and picked her up – she was as light as a bird.

"Let me go," she said.

He set her down on the floor; his teeth were white, like the keys on an accordion, and he laughed with all the keys at once. This must have been the first time after Ganka, and he himself realized it too. He said to Sofya: "Well, Sofka, remember this – if she turns up now, I'll…"

There was a knock at the door, both turned quickly. Sofya heard Trofim Ivanych thinking almost out loud: "Ganka," and the same thing came briefly into Sofya's head. She knew it couldn't be so, yet there it was all the same.

"Shall I open the door?" asked Trofim Ivanych.

"Yes, open it," replied Sofya in a completely natural voice.

Trofim Ivanych opened the door and in came Pelageya – loud, spreading, all undone. "What's the matter with you – white like that?" she said to Sofya. "You need to be eating more now, woman." Pelageya had given birth twice before and she started talking about it with Sofya; Sofya's whole body began smiling again and she forgot about Ganka.

In the night, when she was already sinking right down into the depths, falling asleep, suddenly, for some unknown reason, Ganka came briefly into her head again, as though she were lying somewhere in these nocturnal depths. Sofya gave a start and opened her eyes; there were light patches splashing on the ceiling. She heard the wind banging outside the window, the glass ringing – it had been the same that day too. She started trying to remember how it had all happened, but she couldn't remember anything and lay like this for a long time. Then, as if apropos of nothing at all, independently, she saw a piece of marbled oilcloth on the floor and a fly crawling over a pink back. The fly's legs were clearly visible – slender, of black cotton thread. "Who, who was it that did it? Her – this very her – me... Here's Trofim Ivanych beside me, and I'm going to have a baby – and is this me?" All the hairs on her head came alive; she took Trofim Ivanych by the shoulder and started shaking him: it was essential that he should say at once that it hadn't happened, that she wasn't the one who had done it.

"Who... who is it? Is that you, Sofka?" Trofim Ivanych could barely unglue his eyes.

"It's not me, not me, not me!" Sofya cried, then stopped: she realized that she could say nothing, nothing more, she mustn't, and she never would – because... "Oh Lord... If only I could have the baby soon!" she said loudly.

Trofim Ivanych laughed: "Silly woman! There's time enough!" And he soon started smacking his lips again in his sleep.

Sofya didn't sleep. She stopped sleeping in the night-time. And in fact there were almost no nights; heaving outside the window all the time was heavy, bright water, and the summer flies buzzed incessantly.

7

In the morning, as he was leaving for the factory, Trofim Ivanych recounted how the day before they had had an oiler get caught on a flywheel and spun around for a long time, and when they had got him off, he had felt his head, asked: "Where's my hat?" and died.

The inner window had already been taken out; Sofya was wiping the glass with a cloth and thinking about the oiler, about death, and it seemed to her it would be really simple – like the sun going down, and it's dark, and then it's day again. She got up onto a bench to wipe the top – and now she was caught up by a flywheel; she dropped the cloth, started shouting. Pelageya came running at her cry, Sofya could still remember that, but there was nothing more, everything was spinning, everything was rushing by, she was shouting. Once, she for some reason heard very clearly the distant ringing of a tram, the voices of youngsters in the courtyard. Then everything stopped in full flow, the stillness was like a pond – and Sofya could feel the blood pouring, pouring out of her. It must have been the same with the oiler when they had got him off the flywheel.

"Well, this is the end," said Pelageya.

It wasn't the end, but Sofya knew there were only minutes now until the end, everything had to be done quickly, quickly... "Quickly!" she said.

"Quickly what?" asked Pelageya's voice.

"The little girl... show me."

"And how do you know it's a girl?" asked Pelageya in surprise, and she showed the live red morsel that had been torn out of Sofya: the tiny toes on the feet drawn up to the stomach were stirring; Sofya looked and looked. "Come on, here, here, take her," said Pelageya, and, laying the child on the bed next to Sofya, she herself went off into the kitchen.

Sofya undid her clothes and put the child to her breast. She knew that this was supposed to be done only on the following day, but waiting wasn't possible, everything had to be done quickly, quickly. Choking, awkwardly, blindly, the child began to suck. Sofya could feel warm tears, warm milk, warm blood flowing out of her; the whole of her had opened up and was overflowing with juices; she lay warm, blissful, moist, resting, like the earth – for the sake of this one minute she had lived her whole life: everything had been for the sake of this.

"I'm going to pop upstairs – do you need anything else?" asked Pelageya. Sofya only moved her lips, but Pelageya understood that she didn't need anything more now.

Then Sofya seemed to doze – it was very hot under the blanket. She heard the ringing of trams; the youngsters in the courtyard shouted: "Catch her!" – it was all very far away, through a thick blanket.

"Who's 'her'?" Sofya wondered and opened her eyes. Far away, as if on another shore, Trofim Ivanych was lighting a lamp – heavy rain was falling; the rain made it dark; the lamp was tiny, like a

pin. Sofya saw teeth, as white as keys – Trofim Ivanych must have
been smiling and saying something to her, but she didn't have
time to understand what – she was being drawn into the depths.

All the time through her sleep Sofya could sense the lamp: tiny,
like a pin, it was now already somewhere inside, in her stomach.
Trofim Ivanych said in his night-time voice:

"Oh my… my own Sofka!"

The lamp began burning so – Sofya called Pelageya. Pelageya was
sitting dozing by the bed, and she jerked her head up like a horse.

"The… lamp…" Sofya uttered with difficulty – her tongue was
like a mitten.

"Shall I put it out?" she asked, dashing towards the lamp. Then
Sofya woke up completely and told Pelageya there was a burning
in her stomach, right at the bottom.

At dawn Trofim Ivanych ran to fetch the doctor. Sofya recognized her: that same one, buxom, wearing a pince-nez, who
had been at the carpenter's that time before the end. The doctor
examined Sofya. "Right… good… very good… Does it hurt here?
Right, right…" Then she turned cheerfully, snub-nosed, to Trofim
Ivanych: "Well, she needs to get to hospital quickly."

Trofim Ivanych's teeth went out, and with a coal-veined hand
he grabbed the headboard of Sofya's bed. "What's the matter
with her?" he asked.

"I don't know yet. It's likely to be childbed fever," the doctor
said cheerfully and went into the kitchen to wash her hands.

They lifted Sofya onto a stretcher and started turning it towards
the door. Past her went everything she had lived with: the window,
the wall clock, the stove – as if a steamship was casting off and
everything familiar on the shore was drifting away. The pendulum
on the wall swung in one direction, in the other – and was no longer
to be seen. It seemed to Sofya there was something else that had
to be done here in this room one last time. When the door of the
ambulance had already opened, Sofya remembered what, swiftly
undid her clothes and took out her breast, but no one understood
what she wanted, and the stretcher-bearers laughed.

For some time there was nothing. Then the lamp appeared again, and now it was up above, below the white ceiling. Sofya saw white walls, white women in beds. Just nearby a fly was crawling over the white – it had slender legs of black cotton thread. Sofya cried out and, waving it away, started sliding down off the bed onto the floor.

"Where to now? Where to now? Lie still!" said a nurse, picking Sofya up. The fly was no longer there; Sofya closed her eyes peacefully.

In came Ganka – with a sack full of firewood. She squatted down, spreading her knees wide, looked round at Sofya, grinning, and gave the white fringe on her forehead a flick. Sofya's heart began pounding – she struck her with an axe and opened her eyes. A snub-nosed face wearing a pince-nez was bent down towards her, thick lips were saying quickly: "Right, right…" The pince-nez was gleaming. Sofya closed her eyes tight. Straight away in came Ganka with the firewood and squatted down. Sofya struck her with an axe again and again; shaking her head, the doctor said: "Right, right…" Ganka banged her head on her knees; Sofya struck her once more.

"Right, right… Good," said the doctor. "Is her husband here? Call him quickly."

"Quickly! Quickly!" cried Sofya; she realized this was the end, that she was dying and needed to make every effort to hurry. The nurse ran off, slamming the door. Somewhere very nearby a cannon boomed; the wind beat furiously at the window.

"Flood?" asked Sofya, opening her eyes wide.

"In a moment, in a moment… Lie still," said the doctor.

The cannon was booming, the wind was droning in her ears, the water was rising ever higher – at any moment it would surge and carry everything away – it had to be done quickly, quickly… The familiar pain of the day before tore her in half; Sofya spread her legs. "I must have the baby… have the baby quickly!" She seized the doctor by the sleeve.

"Calm down, calm down. You've already had the baby – who else do you want?" Sofya knew who, but she couldn't pronounce her name; the water was rising ever higher – it had to be done quickly…

Ganka was squatting down beside the stove with her head buried, and Trofim Ivanych went over to her and shielded her.

"It wasn't me – not me – not me!" Sofya tried to say – that's how it had already been once. She remembered that night and immediately realized what she needed to do; her head became completely white, clear. She jerked up, got onto her knees on the bed and cried to Trofim Ivanych: "It was me, me! She was lighting the stove – I struck her with the axe—"

"She's lost her mind… she doesn't know—" Trofim Ivanych began.

"Shut up!" cried Sofya; he fell silent, and huge waves gushed out of her and swamped him, everyone; everything instantly went quiet – there were only eyes. "I – killed her," said Sofya, painfully, firmly. "I struck her with the axe. She was living with us, she was living with him, I killed her and wanted to have—"

"She's lost her b-b-bi… lost her b-b-bind…" Trofim Ivanych's lips were shaking – he couldn't articulate.

Sofya grew afraid she wouldn't be believed; she gathered all that still remained inside her, made every effort to remember and said: "No, I know. Afterwards I threw the axe under the stove – it's there now…"

Everything all around was white; it was very quiet, like in winter. Trofim Ivanych was silent. Sofya realized she had been believed. Slowly, like a bird, she sank onto the bed. Now everything was good, blissful – she was finished, all of her had spilt out.

The first to come to his senses was Trofim Ivanych. He darted towards Sofya, grabbed at her bedhead to keep hold, to not let go. "She's dead!" he cried.

Women were jumping out of beds, running over, stretching their heads out. "Go away, go away! Go back to bed!" said the nurse, waving them away, but they didn't.

The doctor lifted Sofya's hand, held it for a moment, then said cheerfully: "She's asleep."

In the evening, the white became slightly greenish, like calm water, and outside the windows the sky was the same. The buxom doctor was standing beside Sofya's bed again; next to her was Trofim Ivanych and also some young, clean-shaven man with a scar on his cheek – the scar made it seem he was in pain all the time, but he was smiling nonetheless.

The doctor took out a trumpet and listened to her heart. Sofya's heart was beating evenly, gently, and her breathing was the same. "Right, right…" For a second the doctor became thoughtful. "She's going to pull through, you know, honest to God, she's going to pull through!" She put on her pince-nez and her eyes became like those of children when they're looking at a fire.

"Well then – let's begin!" said the clean-shaven young man, taking out a piece of paper – he was in pain, but he smiled with his scar.

"No, you can't – do let her sleep," said the doctor. "You'll have to come back tomorrow, dear Comrade."

"Very well. It's all the same to me."

"Well, it's certainly all the same to her – do whatever you want with her now!" The doctor's pince-nez was gleaming; the young man, smiling through his pain, left the room.

The doctor still stood looking at the woman. She was sleeping, breathing evenly, quietly, blissfully, and her lips were wide open.

1929

Notes

p. 3, *Streltsy*: The name given to the area of the town where at one time the members of the army corps of the same name – meaning "archers" or "gunmen" – would have lived.

p. 4, *verst*: A Russian unit of length equivalent to just over one kilometre.

p. 4, *Empress Alexandra's Day*: The reference here is unclear as the feast day of Alexandra of Rome (d. 303) is 21st or 23rd April according to the Julian Calendar, or Old Style, or 4th or 6th May according to the Gregorian Calendar, or New Style (the switch from the old calendar to the new was made in Russia on 14th February 1918, which followed immediately after 31st January).

p. 8, *hegumen*: The title of the head of a monastery in the Orthodox Church.

p. 8, *promenage*: The priest means a promenade, i.e. a walk.

p. 10, *kvas*: A fermented, low-alcohol drink made from rye flour or bread with malt.

p. 13, *Martin Zadek*: A book of predictions purported to be by this author (1664–1769) was published in Basel in 1770. The same pseudonym was used by S.I. Komisarov in 1800 to publish a popular Russian fortune-telling book which included a section on the interpretation of dreams.

p. 17, *Along you, street… walk*: The first half of a four-line popular song or *chastushka*, which continues: "Here with you, my lovely girl I sit / One final time and talk."

p. 18, *Provincial Secretary*: A modest rank in the Russian Civil Service, the twelfth of fourteen in Peter the Great's Table of Ranks (1722).

p. 24, *Elijah's Day*: The feast day in honour of the Old Testament prophet is on 20th July (Old Style, 2nd August New Style). In the Slav folk tradition Elijah is associated with thunder, lightning, rain and the harvest, and his day is marked by baking, but doing no other physical work.

p. 26, *for the sick and the suffering*: The words come from a petition from the Great Litany of the Russian Orthodox Church.

p. 28, *Hyena*: Chebotarikha garbles the word Gehenna (also Hinnom, Gehinnom), a valley near Jerusalem associated with divine punishment – the destination of the wicked, and thus, for simple folk, hell.

p. 32, *O gladsome light*: A very early hymn used in the Russian Orthodox vespers service.

p. 32, *On the mountain... people*: A variant on part of a vulgar popular folk ditty or *chastushka*.

p. 33, *Brokar Pot*: Henri Brocard (1837–1900) was born in Paris but moved to Russia in 1861, where he Russified his name and became a hugely successful manufacturer of soap, perfume and cosmetics.

p. 34, *Feodor Romanov... Filaret*: Fyodor Nikitich Romanov (1553?–1633) was the father of the first Romanov tsar. Exiled in 1600 and forced to become a monk, he took the name Filaret and subsequently, in 1619, became the Moscow Patriarch.

p. 35, *that Tikhon of yours, of Zadonsk*: Tikhon (1724–83) was Bishop of Voronezh and Eletsk; canonized for his lofty spiritual values, his feast day is marked on both 19th July (Old Style, 1st August New Style), and, as here, on 13th August (Old Style, 26th August New Style).

p. 37, *re-enlisted men*: Those who voluntarily elected to extend their military service.

p. 37, *Tyapka, the Brigand... Coachman*: Since such cheap, popular editions were not held in libraries it is uncertain whether these titles actually existed or were invented by Zamyatin. But Tyapka was a historical figure who ended his life of crime as a monk in Lebedyan's Trinity Monastery, so the first two titles at least can clearly be linked with the criminality described in the story.

p. 52, *Kitezh-grad*: A legendary city believed to have sunk beneath the waters of Lake Svetloyar when threatened by a Mongol army.

p. 53, *a minister's been bumped off*: This may be a reference to the assassination in Kiev of Russian Prime Minister and Minister of the Interior Pyotr Arkadyevich Stolypin (1862–1911).

p. 53, *Piter*: The popular abbreviation for St Petersburg.

p. 60, *Rus*: A name for medieval Russia used to refer to the country in later times when suggesting a traditional or old-fashioned milieu.

p. 60, *Cannon cigarette*: A popular brand from the factory of Alexander Fyodorovich Miller, founded in 1849.

p. 60, *Narzan*: Sparkling mineral water.

p. 63, *Maremyana the aged nun*: The identity of the original Maremyana (otherwise Mariamne), whose name became associated in this popular saying – often ironically – with soft-heartedness, is unknown.

p. 63, *Kronberg beer*: A beer from the Bavaria of Eletsk brewery, owned by the family of Karl Kronberg.

p. 71, *Hofmann*: Jozef Kazimierz Hofmann (1876–1957), a Polish pianist, was a child prodigy who enjoyed great success as a touring performer across Europe and America.

p. 71, *Chopin's funeral march*: The third movement of the second piano sonata (Opus 35, No. 2) of 1837 by Polish composer Frédéric Chopin (1810–49).

p. 72, *my life's competition*: The tongue-tied orderly presumably means "companion".

p. 74, *Mayne Reids*: Thomas Mayne Reid (1818–83) was an American author of popular adventure novels which were particularly widely read in Russia.

p. 74, *changshan*: A traditional Chinese long shirt or tunic.

p. 75, *we eat not... live to*: The actual quotation, ascribed originally to Socrates (470–399 BC), is from Act III, Sc. 5 of

The Miser (*L'Avare*, 1668) by Molière (real name Jean-Baptiste Poquelin, 1622–73): "We must eat to live, and not live to eat".

p. 75, *potatoes à la lyonnaise*: Lyonnaise potatoes are a simple dish of fried potatoes with fried onions.

p. 75, *Raphael*: The great master painter and architect of the High Renaissance, Raphael (1483–1520).

p. 78, *Schopenhauer or some... Kant*: The two German philosophers Arthur Schopenhauer (1788–1860) and Immanuel Kant (1724–1804).

p. 79, *such a princess... pea*: 'The Princess and the Pea' (1835) by Hans Christian Andersen (1805–75) features a princess whose aristocratic authenticity is confirmed by her sensitivity to the pea placed deep beneath a huge pile of mattresses and eiderdowns.

p. 80, *The Book of Needs*: The Slavonic version of this Orthodox tome contains the sacraments and other sacred rites as well as short prayers for various needs, a Church calendar and a list of Christian names.

p. 83, *some incomprehensible Lanzepuppes' Club*: This club existed in Vladivostok between 1873 and 1887, apparently founded by, among others, one Dr Leopold, a military or naval doctor of German origin; the club members met in the Tupishev hotel on the outskirts of town. Its membership quickly became exclusively male, and its activities revolved around drinking and outraging the rest of the populace. The meaning of the club's name is obscure – "incomprehensible" – with German words for "lance", "spring", "shaking", "puppet" and "pupa" all suggested as possibly relevant to its origin.

p. 92, *three-line bullet*: Bullets for the three-line rifle M1891, also known as Mosin's rifle after its designer, Sergei Ivanovich Mosin (1849–1902). In production from 1892, Mosin's rifle was standard issue in the Russian army.

p. 93, *attendez*: "Wait" (French). The word was very commonly used in Russia in card games.

p. 95, *Naval sloop veers uprun*: This is a meaningless phrase (in which the last word is nonsense), which can be used to identify one chosen pair of cards, unknown to the person performing the trick, from twenty cards comprised of ten pairs: each pair of identical letters in the phrase corresponds to a pair of cards, e.g. n = two queens, and if the ten pairs of cards are laid out in four rows of five in accordance with the ten pairs of letters making up the four words of the phrase, the chosen cards can be identified simply by ascertaining in which row or rows the pair can be found: any answer will be unique to one pair of letters in the phrase, and hence to one pair of cards.

p. 97, *There was a... hog*: A never-ending folk song used by children as a counting rhyme.

p. 99, *Grieg's sonata*: The piano sonata in E minor, Opus 7 (1865, revised 1887) by Norwegian composer Edvard Grieg (1843–1907).

p. 104, *the substance that... turkey*: The reference is to the phrase, rhyming in Russian, "fate is a turkey and life is a kopek", roughly meaning "fate's batty and life's tatty".

p. 105, *to play "coachmen"*: A children's game in which two players must join points on a sheet of paper without crossing a line already drawn.

p. 107, *O Soldier Boys... Lads*: A traditional Russian military song expressing commitment to service.

p. 108, *right-flank man*: The man who determines the position of the others in his rank and thus someone to be relied upon to set an example.

p. 110, *oh, you animal... least*: A line from a children's folk song.

p. 120, *The Field and Homeland*: Two richly illustrated publications. *The Field* (1869–1918) was a popular weekly magazine with literary, historical and popular scientific content; *Homeland* (1879–1917) was originally a monthly magazine, and from 1883 a weekly newspaper, with a literary, social and political orientation.

p. 120, *Alexander III*: Born in 1845, Russia's penultimate emperor reigned from 1881 until his death in 1894.

p. 121, *'The Little Oak Tree'... contractor*: 'The Little Oak Tree' was a revolutionary song which often incorporated additional improvisations by workers aimed at their local bosses. The text was composed by Vasily Ivanovich Bogdanov (1837–86) and published in 1865, then reworked in the 1880s by Alexander Alexandrovich Olkhin (1839–97).

p. 127, *Felicitas the Holy Martyr*: The mother of seven martyred sons who then accepted martyrdom herself, Felicitas of Rome (101–65) is celebrated in the Russian Orthodox tradition on 25th January (Old Style, 7th February New Style).

p. 129, *in her own voice... a dog's:* Zamyatin recalls such an incident from his own childhood in his autobiographical sketch of 1929.

p. 130, *The School of Health... Book*: The former work, subtitled *A Book of Home Medicine*, by Pyotr Vasilyevich Andreyevsky (1848–90) was the first book of its kind in Russian and went through numerous editions from the 1870s onwards. *The Home Veterinary Book*, the equivalent veterinary work, was first published in 1873 by German Frantsevich Undrits.

p. 130, *brother Pushkin*: Alexander Sergeyevich Pushkin (1799–1837) is considered Russia's greatest writer. The use of his name here is perhaps indicative of Tikhmen's local reputation as an intellectual and Nechesa's limited knowledge of things literary.

p. 133, *King Maximyan and... Adolf*: A popular folk drama which was to be found in numerous versions in nineteenth-century Russia.

p. 137, *Kaschey's palace*: Kaschey the Deathless is the villain of a number of Russian folk tales.

p. 137, *four disorderly, scattered shots*: This incident may have been suggested to Zamyatin by accounts of the Club's founder, Dr Leopold, having dropped a silver coin outside its meeting-place, betting it would not be picked up over the course of some hours and thus proving the honesty of the locals; when a woman was seen to threaten his bet by taking the coin, he allegedly scared her off by firing a shot at her.

p. 141, *it's a Lanzepuppe*: Zamyatin may have been inspired here by an account of poorly uniformed soldiers in a remote post in the Far East being hidden in undergrowth during an inspection by local dignitaries; upon springing up at the command "Attention!", they were seen by the visitors and identified by their horrified commander as members of the local tribe of Lanzepuppes.

p. 142, *The Alliance*: The Franco-Russian Alliance referred to was formed by a series of agreements between 1891 and 1894 and lasted until 1917.

p. 146, *'The Double-Headed Eagle'*: This may be the military march 'Under the Two-Headed Eagle' of 1893 by the Austrian composer Josef Franz Wagner (1856–1908).

p. 148, *a Quinquet lamp*: The oil lamp dating from 1780 designed by, and in the anglophone world named after, the Swiss scientist François-Pierre-Amédée Argand (1750–1803) was adapted in 1783 by French pharmacist Antoine Quinquet (1745–1803), and it is his name it bears in both France and Russia.

p. 160, *what sort of duel is that?*: This is a reversal of the duel in Pushkin's story of 1830, 'The Shot', in which it is the man who has been shot at, but has not returned fire, who insists on the duel's subsequent completion.

p. 163, *an American duel*: A Russian term which describes a situation that amounts to forced suicide. Perhaps to avoid punishment in view of the ban on duelling, antagonists would draw lots to decide on a winner, and the loser would be required to take his own life. Involvement in such a "duel" was punishable after 1903 by hard labour.

p. 163, *'The Mistress'*: A Russian dance, and the music to which it is performed, both of which are marked by their high tempo and often wild vivacity.

p. 165, *the Intercession... Kazan*: The Feast of the Intercession is celebrated on 1st October (Old Style, 14th October New

Style), and that of Our Lady of Kazan on 22nd October (Old Style, 4th November New Style).

p. 165, *Scriabin's Opus 74*: Five preludes by Alexander Nikolayevich Scriabin (1872–1915) date from 1914 and were the composer's final work.

p. 166, *Marya's, my angel's day*: The Blessed Maria of Mesopotamia (d. 371) was the niece of St Avramios the Recluse who repented of a life of sin when chastised by her uncle. Her feast day is 29th October (Old Style, 11th November New Style).

p. 166, *sazhen*: A Russian unit of length equivalent to 2.13 metres or 7 feet.

p. 171, *the house chairman*: The chairman of the House Committee, which dealt with the many problems arising for the numerous inhabitants of an apartment building's residences in the post-revolutionary years.

p. 171, *Hoffmann's drops*: Compound spirit of ether, one part diethyl ether in three parts alcohol. Named after Friedrich Hoffmann (1660–1742), the German physician and chemist who first introduced its use as a drug.

p. 171, *Zinoviev*: Grigory Yevseyevich Zinoviev, pseudonym of Ovsei-Gershon Aronovich Radomyslsky (1883–1936), an Old Bolshevik, leader of the Communist International (Comintern, the Third International) between 1919 and 1926. He was responsible for the defence of Petrograd when it was under threat from White forces in 1919.

p. 171, *the Field of Mars... Vasilyevsky Island*: The huge imperial parade ground just south of the Neva River in the heart of the city acquired its name, the Field of Mars, in 1805. In 1917 it was chosen as the site for a mass grave and monument commemorating those who had died in that year's two revolutions. In 1918 it was officially renamed Victims of the Revolution Square. Vasilyevsky Island is the westernmost island immediately to the north of the Neva, also in the centre of the old city.

p. 171, *it's been an honour – bah*: The ironic use of the initial letters of the words of a formal, deferential phrase from the pre-revolutionary period, "been an honour", was particularly widespread in the 1920s.

p. 177, *Mamai*: Mamai (1325?–80?) was a Mongol commander of the Golden Horde; a highly influential kingmaker, he was finally defeated in battle at Kulikovo Field by Moscow's Dmitry Donskoy in 1380.

p. 177, *Lakhtinskaya Street*: The street is situated in the Petrograd Side district of the city to the north of the River Neva but does not extend as far as No. 40.

p. 178, *carrying the cornice… Hermitage*: The New Hermitage was opened to the public as part of the Hermitage museum complex on 5th February 1852. Its entrance on Millionaya Street is marked by a raised portico incorporating ten 5-metre-tall Atlantes of grey granite who ostensibly support the weight of the architrave. They were carved in 1846 in the workshop of the sculptor Alexander Ivanovich Terebenyov (1815–59).

p. 178, *like the archangel's trump*: In the Christian tradition, the Archangel Gabriel sounds a horn to signal the onset of Judgement Day.

p. 178, *Bogdanovich's Dushenka… burnt*: By far the best and best-known work by Ippolit Fyodorovich Bogdanovich (1743/4–1803) is *Dushenka*, a narrative poem based on *The Loves of Psyche and Cupidon* (1669) by Jean de La Fontaine (1621–95), itself based on parts of the second-century *The Golden Ass* of Apuleius. Its first edition was published in 1783, and the sixth edition came out in Moscow in 1811. Almost all copies of this edition were lost, presumably in the infamous fire that marked the conclusion of the occupation of the Russian capital by the forces of Napoleon Bonaparte in September and October 1812.

p. 179, *on Zagorodny*: The strength of Mamai's bibliophilia is underlined by his haunting of a bookshop in the south of the city on Zagorodny Avenue, a considerable distance from his home.

p. 179, *old-fashioned long "s"... leg*: Mamai is captivated by an element of the archaic typeface used in the book, which is redolent of the past of imperial Russia.

p. 180, *searches*: In the terrible conditions prevailing in the city during the Civil War, the Bolshevik authorities carried out regular systematic searches for secreted valuables and money which, if found, would be confiscated.

p. 180, *peeped sacrilegiously... head*: This refers to a bust of Lev (Leo) Nikolayevich Tolstoy (1828–1910), the great literary figure and thinker. In 1908 Lenin wrote a pamphlet about Tolstoy as "the mirror of the Russian Revolution", marking the eightieth anniversary of the writer's birth and focusing on his political and social views, which were frequently unacceptable to the Tsarist regime. The approval he thus enjoyed after the Bolshevik Revolution may explain the use of the adverb here.

p. 183, *the Japanese war*: The Russo-Japanese conflict of 1904–5.

p. 184, *Petrograd*: The city of St Petersburg was officially known as Petrograd from 1914 until 1924.

p. 184, *Walter Scott's Rob Roys*: Sir Walter Scott (1771–1832), Scottish novelist and historian, has always been very popular with Russian readers. *Rob Roy* (1817) is a novel set in the period of the Jacobite rebellion of 1715 and reveals much about the harsh social conditions of Scotland at the time. The eponymous hero is a fictionalized version of the less romantic, real-life outlawed robber Robert Roy MacGregor (1671–1734).

p. 184, *globus hystericus*: Globus is the sensation of a lump in the throat. In 1707 John Purcell (1674–1730?) coined this term, attributing the condition to "hysteric fits".

p. 185, *the time of Catherine the Great*: The Empress Catherine II (1729–96) ruled Russia from 1762 until her death.

p. 185, *A Descriptive Depiction... Sankt-Piterburkh*: No publication details of such a work have been found; the title, including the original Dutch-inspired name of the city, regularly used by its founder, Peter the Great (1672–1725), again contrasts the St Petersburg of the past with the post-revolutionary Petrograd depicted in the story.

p. 185, *Chernomor*: The villain of Pushkin's narrative poem *Ruslan and Lyudmila* (1820), an evil wizard who kidnaps the heroine and holds her captive.

p. 186, *Telescope*: One of the leading progressive journals of its day, published in Moscow between 1831 and 1836 by Nikolai Ivanovich Nadezhdin (1804–56).

p. 186, *Bells! Cannons!*: Perhaps an allusion to the celebratory bells and cannons of the '1812 Overture' (1880) by Pyotr Ilyich Tchaikovsky (1840–93).

p. 189, *Pancake Street and Rosa Luxemburg Street*: Rosa Luxemburg, born Rozalia Luksemburg in 1871 in Poland, became a naturalized German in 1897 and was a member of a series of left-wing political parties. In January 1919 she was co-leader of the new Communist Party of Germany. Despite her criticism of Lenin's Bolsheviks, her execution that same month saw a surge in her prestige in Russia, leading to, for example, streets being renamed in her honour. The comic contrast of the modern, politically inspired street name and the mundanely traditional Pancake Street reflects the story's theme of the clash of the old and new in the provincial Russia of the immediate post-revolutionary years.

p. 189, *Disecpodep, Disecodep and Disdeppe-ed*: The period following the Bolshevik Revolution saw a proliferation in administrative bodies, such as the District Department of People's Education, which rejoiced in sometimes impenetrable acronyms.

p. 190, *Disexcom*: District Executive Committee.

p. 190, *Socialist Revolutionary*: The Socialist Revolutionary Party was founded in 1902 under the leadership of Viktor Mikhailovich Chernov (1873–1952), building on the positions of the nineteenth-century Populists. Many in the movement were bitterly opposed to Bolshevik rule.

p. 190, *prodwear*: Another of the abbreviations of the post-revolutionary years, the decoding of which is at the heart of the narrative. The Russian term *prozodezhda*, production wear, was used widely by leading artists and designers of the period as they produced designs for clothing suitable in all kinds of work settings, from the factory to the theatre.

p. 192, *Tolstoy shirt*: A long, loose men's shirt worn with a belt, of a type favoured most famously by Leo Tolstoy.

p. 194, *Izvestiya*: Literally "news", the word formed part of the title of many newspapers in the Soviet era, most famously that of the official government organ.

p. 195, *Kustodiev*: Boris Mikhailovich Kustodiev (1878–1927) was a painter whose images of provincial Russian life often included the figures of nubile young women, e.g. *The Beauty* of 1915. Zamyatin loved his images of "old Russia" and collaborated with him on productions of his play *The Flea* in both Moscow and Leningrad.

p. 197, *you Grishka, you Rasputin*: Grigory Yefimovich Rasputin (1869–1916) is as well known in the popular imagination for his libido as for his influence over the imperial family, founded on his ability to ease the heir to the throne's suffering from his haemophilia.

p. 197, *as did once… Elisha*: A reference to the Old Testament prophet being taunted by a group of "boys" (though some argue that the translation should be "young men") from Bethel – see 2 Kings, 2:23.

p. 198, *Constructivist platforms… Meyerhold*: The reference is to Vsevolod Emilyevich Meyerhold (1874–1940), innovative and experimental actor, director and producer. He revived the tradition of *commedia dell'arte* in Russian theatre, and his application of scenic Constructivism involved sets utilizing such features as ramps, catwalks and individual small stages, often on multiple levels.

p. 198, *Pierrot*: The sad, white-faced clown, unlucky in love, from the *commedia dell'arte*.

p. 199, *a name much… now*: Zamyatin plays with the name of the Cheka, the Bolshevik secret police organization founded in 1917. The abbreviation stood for Extraordinary Commission, itself an abbreviation of the organization's full name, the All-Russian Extraordinary Commission for Combating Counter-Revolution and Sabotage under the Council of People's Commissars of the RSFSR. In 1922 its name was changed to GPU, the State Political Directorate, and from the following year until 1934 it was known as OGPU, the Joint State Political Directorate.

p. 200, *Disfoocom*: District Food Committee.

p. 201, *all those solid… "r"s*: In 'Instrumentation', lecture notes from 1937, Zamyatin explains his belief that the sounds of letters have associations with moods, emotions, etc.: "Every sound of a human word, every letter in itself arouses in a person certain impressions, sound images… every sound has its own quality… R speaks clearly to me of something sonorous, bright, red, blistering, rapid… D and T of something stifling, leaden… stale…" (all the exemplar words contain one of the relevant letters).

p. 202, *the 'Internationale'*: The international socialist anthem dating from 1871, words by Frenchman Eugène Poltier (1816–87), music by Belgian Pierre de Geyter (1848–1932). From 1918 it became the anthem of Bolshevik Russia and the Soviet Union, with its words adapted from the original Russian version of 1902 by Arkady Yakovlevich Kots (1872–1943) to recognize the achievements of the October Revolution.

p. 202, *valse mignonne*: "Delicate waltz" (French). The best known, perhaps being played here, is Opus 104 (1896) by Charles-Camille Saint-Saëns (1835–1921).

p. 204, *Trotsky*: Lev Davidovich Bronshtein (1879–1940), better known by his revolutionary pseudonym, Leon Trotsky, was leader of the Red Army in 1919, but by 1926 had been ousted from the Politburo, and exile beckoned.

p. 205, *bombs, spinning around… Tolstoy*: An example comes in *War and Peace* (1869), Book 10, Chapter 36.

p. 209, *the water in... rising*: Built on marshy ground and islands at the mouth of the Neva, St Petersburg had been subject to flooding ever since its foundation in 1703. The worst floods were in 1724, 1824 – the background to Pushkin's narrative poem *The Bronze Horseman* – and 1924.

p. 210, *the Smolensk Field*: A sizeable area of open land at this time, to the west of the built-up part of Vasilyevsky Island and adjoining the Smolensk Cemetery.

p. 213, *"Kolchak"*: Alexander Vasilyevich Kolchak (1874–1920), admiral and leader of the White movement from 1918, was betrayed, handed over to the Bolsheviks and executed in February 1920.

p. 215, *Maly Avenue*: The northernmost of the three main east–west thoroughfares of Vasilyevsky Island.

p. 215, *the Living Church people*: With support from the political authorities, the Living Church organization arose in May 1922 under the leadership of Vladimir Dmitrievich Krasnitsky (1881–1936), becoming part of a more general schismatic movement working for the renewal of the established Orthodox Church. Its aims, among others, were to remove Patriarch Tikhon for anti-Soviet activity, abolish the monastic orders, modernize Church services and democratize Church governance.

p. 216, *the Okhta*: A tributary of the Neva which gave its name to the surrounding area in the far east of the city, the end farthest away from Vasilyevsky Island.

p. 216, *"The Third Testament"*: The concept of a Third Testament in addition to the Old and New Testaments of the traditional Bible goes back as far as the twelfth-century Gioacchino da Fiore (1132–1202).

p. 220, *a pudgy, wadded... third*: When there was a threat of imminent flooding, guns would be fired in the St Peter and Paul Fortress to warn the city's population of the danger.

p. 232, *the Petersburg Side*: The area had been known officially as the Petrograd Side since the renaming of the city in 1914.

EVERGREENS SERIES

Beautifully produced classics, affordably priced

Alma Classics is committed to making available a wide range of literature from around the globe. Most of the titles are enriched by an extensive critical apparatus, notes and extra reading material, as well as a selection of photographs. The texts are based on the most authoritative editions and edited using a fresh, accessible editorial approach. With an emphasis on production, editorial and typographical values, Alma Classics aspires to revitalize the whole experience of reading classics.

For our complete list and latest offers visit

almabooks.com/evergreens

ALMA CLASSICS

ALMA CLASSICS aims to publish mainstream and lesser-known European classics in an innovative and striking way, while employing the highest editorial and production standards. By way of a unique approach the range offers much more, both visually and textually, than readers have come to expect from contemporary classics publishing.

LATEST TITLES PUBLISHED BY ALMA CLASSICS

www.almaclassics.com